The Voices Here

Leo Stills' Divine Adventure

Jay T.R.

<u>Opening</u>

"To hell with you!" The mile-high, glass walls vibrated as the voice of the Mighty One resounded throughout the chamber, with all those surrounding the throne awestruck at His majesty and power.

"Your Excellence – please, I have to object on behalf of my client. This evidence has not been…"

"Enough," the Great Judge sighed, almost whispering. The audience's attention was fixed upon that magnificent glow, staring up out of respect and anticipation at the perfect justice about to be exacted upon this one, finite soul.

He continued, "The words came forth from his own lips. What further necessity survives to analyze or weight any additional testimony."

The crowd was stunned at the severity but appreciated the undeniable and simple truth uttered by their Lord. As the Judge paused to let the gravity of the moment sink in, He consulted the Eternal One, in Whose image He was perfectly begotten. In so doing, He seemed to retreat into the sun, though still unmoved from His seat on the bench. His radiance was inexplicable, and no created eye could withstand that gaze. Moments passed by, what seemed like eternity to the recently judged.

Returning from that Beatific union, He continued, "This man denies Me. He denies My reign supreme and refuses to bow, even as he looks his Maker face to Face. His arrogance clouds his wisdom, and he has cut off any possibility of redemption because he relies not on Me, but on his own intellect. For him, what he knows is everything. Foolish creation that fills Me with pity and, if not for My complete understanding of the entire manner of being, would drown Me in despair at the lost opportunity. Another of infinite potential, lost to the hubris of the created mind. How can any creation, human or spirit, understand all? Though, perhaps in that temporary life in which all creation finds itself before entering the eternal paradise to which all things are originally destined … perhaps then, he did not understand. But now!"

His righteous fury was mounting, in part because of the insolence of this lost soul, but also due to the knowledge of all the souls that will be lost to this same thinking; an unfortunate result of free will… a weight no created thing could shoulder.

Free will - that ultimate good, the prime necessity of the greatest of things, Love. Without the free choice to hate, love is nothing more than a façade. The very thing that allows us to choose our own hell, is necessary in order to develop true love shared in communion with another. For no greater thing can be conceived than love: willing true good for the other, freely given, totally understood.

The Eternally-Created, the Perfect Image of Proper Existence Itself, the Rightful Judge - after arousing His emotions for the benefit of those listening, calmed Himself down as He continued softly, "But now, He looks into My face, the One through Whom and for Whom *all* things were made… and he understands.

"Free choice isn't free unless it is not only purely his decision, but he must also perfectly understand his past, present, and potential future. He now knows what his past means – the mistakes he made, the people he hurt. He comprehends the fragile condition of his present and the eternal weight riding on this one moment.

"On top of all of that, he is fully aware of his choices today. I do not send him to hell; that dark, cold, rotting place, devoid of Life. I do not choose his damnation. I simply judge. He chooses this hell. He chooses his torment. He has decided to follow the initial anarchist's rebuke of my sovereign rule. That is his right. He would choose to be a slave to himself rather than a child of Mine."

Turning to the gentleman before Him, He saw the man full of pride… full of certainty. The Righteous One softened His face, lowered His voice and, without saying anything that the audience could hear, He spoke directly into his soul – the soul He created uniquely for him, and to whom He destined its eternal fate – saying, "I will not beg for your obedience, though I do wish it. Is it so bad, being a child to a loving father? Who are you, that you would demand reign over Being Itself! I am He that has always been and will always be… the Perfect Incarnation of Proper Being – there is no other before, nor will there be one after. I ask again, for your benefit, that you reconsider - who are you to challenge Me?"

The crowd didn't dare to speak, yet some faint murmurs could be heard throughout the auditorium, as they all watched the now silent interaction, paralyzed by fascination.

"I, Who created not only what you see within time and space, but the very foundation of existence upon which that reality rests. If I were to fill you with the knowledge and power needed to even just see those underpinnings, it would utterly destroy the vessel in which a fragment of Myself, your soul, has been housed. That power you could not hope to contain, let alone understand. Why then, do you stand there before me, fully erect, as an indignant child might stand against an abusive father - which I am not. I am He that knows all, sees all, creates all and sustains all. I want only the best for you. But! You do not get to sit in My seat, given to Me by My Father. Were I to simply cease thinking about you, even for just a moment of what you call time, you would be erased from existence. Yet, I do not. It is My will that keeps you here; keeps you alive. I care for you greatly, I think of you constantly – and I long for a loving relationship with you, as with all of My creations."

Then speaking aloud again for the crowd to hear, our Judge asked the final question, "So, my friend, your eternal consequence rests in your hands. What is your decision?"

<u>Story 1</u>

"To hell with it!" Leo mumbled to himself, grabbing another miniature raspberry Danish that he had packed for his long day at work. "Maybe just one more. I can always get extra for tomorrow."

Leo Stills is a pretty average guy; six feet tall and a standard build. He didn't follow the skinny-jeans trend that some people seemed to think was fashionable these days. Leo aimed for the classic look and tried to stay away from the latest-and-greatest trends currently being adopted by the masses. He liked the idea of being different.

Now, don't get the wrong idea. Leo is extraordinarily special in his own way. He hears voices in his head, but no… you don't need to call any mental health experts on his behalf. He hears the voices we all perceive – some people call them thoughts. However, it seems to Leo as if these voices are autonomous entities, completely separate from him, that all have their own goals and desires. That they are hoping to utilize our physical bodies in order to carry out their intangible objectives.

That might sound crazy, but have you ever considered where your thoughts come from? We don't know, but they come from somewhere. Better yet, maybe they come from someone who is somewhere; or perhaps many different someones that are all battling for airtime in the news network that we call our minds.

These thoughts bubble up from some dark, mysterious place, way out there in the void beyond space and time. We don't choose our thoughts, our interests or what motivates us. We can guide them, certainly. We can accept and feed certain feelings or opinions when they arrive in our consciousness, allowing them to grow and develop a stronghold in our cognitive capacity. We can reject and starve certain views and judgements that we don't want, causing their hold on us to weaken and die over time. We can choose to eat the chocolate ice cream instead of the vanilla. However, one thing is certain: we do not choose to like chocolate more than vanilla. That just happens. If someone asked you why you like chocolate ice cream more, would you even have a coherent answer?

Now, Leo hears these voices just like everyone else, but he is unusual in one regard. Perhaps as any of us might be able to do eventually given the appropriate self-discipline and grace, Leo has developed an ability to hear and understand these voices better than most anyone. He hears them loud and clear and is getting better and better at picking out the good and loving voice – the one that would guide him on the straight and narrow path towards victory.

He learned long ago to follow the hopeful, loving, optimistic voice in his head and had always found great success in doing so. He also figured out how to better block and reject those negative, pessimistic, hateful voices that attempted to cloud his judgement and to lead the revolt against any semblance of morality. The key to discerning effectively between the two, was being truthful in everything; with others, and perhaps more importantly, with himself. Because, if you can't trust you, who can you trust?

Be careful!

"HEY! Watch it, ugh," a snarky, red-headed woman screeched at a scrawny, quivering man in a gray raincoat.

Leo watched the far-too-often occurrence with some amusement. Two people on their cell phones looking down at their screens and crashing into each other as they both walked around a particularly busy corner at the Belmont train station. It was another overcast day in October. Leo loved the coolness of the refreshing rain misting around the lush, green foliage that pervaded his resident state. So, he was actually in pretty high spirits today and optimistic about how things were shaping up… but it was still too early in the day to commit to a particular stance.

Jeeze. Take it easy, Red. She must be having a bad day…

Leo pitied the hostile woman as he tried to come up with a justification for such a confrontational response.

"God bless… at least I'm not angry enough about life to be that rude. Too early in the morning to get that excited about anything," Leo mumbled to himself as he continued on his way, trying to find a good spot to wait for the train.

"Morning, Mr. Stills," a daring young girl semi-shouted at Leo as she skipped along, smiling unabashedly.

Leo nodded ever so slightly in acknowledgement and kept moving forward on his journey. For such a young man, Leo seemed to know most of the people in his neighborhood – or, better yet, they knew of him. Leo strode along, finally getting to his platform where he waited aimlessly for the next train to arrive.

The trains ran every couple of minutes, so he wasn't bothered by the fact that the previous train pulled away seconds before he arrived at his gate.

I… was… so… close! It's all good, all good.

Without a second thought, he devoured the last three Danish pastries and threw the cardboard box into the recycle bin.

He said to himself, "I can never remember what Sera told me about recycling plastic and cardboard items that are soiled by food. Whatever… someone along the way will sort it out."

He reminded himself to go with the flow and trust in the fundamental nature of reality – specifically that, when he made choices that he believed were morally good, the best possible reality will come into existence. He supposed that, as co-creators of the universe that we see unfolding around us constantly, we shared in the divine ability to confront the infinite potentiality of the future. We use our free will in the present moment to choose which potential reality will become the next actual present. If we do this morally, the best possible reality will be the one that unfolds before us. This was his version of faith in God. He trusted in God's plan, even though he didn't understand it at all sometimes, because he wasn't quite arrogant enough to pretend to know everything about everything in the universe.

"Mr. Stills. Good morning, sir," a tall man said softly, approaching Leo's side.

Without saying a word, Leo handed him a fragrant bundle of goods wrapped neatly in a brown paper bag and accepted a $100 bill in exchange.

After that business was concluded, Leo retreated into the recesses of his mind as he patiently waited and let the morning wake up around him.

He was a fairly relaxed father of one beautiful boy, and the long-time boyfriend to one smoking hot girl of his dreams, Sera - though, she would blush if he ever dared to say that to her so directly. He recently started his third year as a corporate attorney and had several fledgling businesses he has been trying to start on the side ever since his second semester at college years ago.

Well, by the time I am looking to retire, Social Security will be no more and most companies these days don't offer pension plans. All that means is I gotta take my retirement into my own hands.

He had developed a straightforward and relatively realistic retirement plan; one that did not rely on someone else to take care of him in his old age.

My son is going to play professional sports and he will buy me a house… easy. Haha! Sera hates that joke every time I tell it. I don't like to count on other people. It is difficult for me to humble myself that way, and I am generally effective enough to get things done on my own.

That being said, he did have a lifelong business partner, his oldest brother, Rome.

I couldn't, and probably wouldn't, get all or any of these side businesses going without Rome.

Leo and Rome, who was a broker of all things for sale, created their first Limited Liability Company back in 2036. They were constantly starting new ideas, and throwing out endless lines into the business world, hoping that someday one of those ventures would propel them into the upper echelon of wealth and well-being for their families.

Since Rome was a young child, he wanted to become an astronaut. As time progressed, he narrowed his sights and was waiting for his opportunity to join the colony America had finally set up on Mars twelve years back. Just over a decade ago, we blasted 300 volunteers on the Mars Homemaker VII Rocket for a one-way trip with the hope of making a new life. Given the various risk factors that face humanity's presence on Earth, including meteors or nuclear weapons wiping out the entire species – it made sense to not put all our eggs in the one basket we have called our home planet for the last few millennia.

Leo and Rome definitely did not share this vision. You couldn't pay Leo to go to Mars on even a vacation. Nonetheless, today, only a short time after the initial launch, Mars now houses over 500,000 adventurous people and the economy there is growing at an exponential rate.

But I digress. Most people in Leo's generation had an absolutely solid, and horrifying, retirement plan: work forever.

One of the reasons Leo and Rome got along so well, was their shared values. Temperamentally, they were complete opposites, but they had a common vision of their highest objective: grind constantly, never give up, sleep when they are dead - all so they can retire early and spend their glory years cultivating a loving and safe environment for each of their families. So, despite the personality differences, they were able to work together to achieve that ideal regardless of what specific qualms they had in carrying out their mission.

Leo worked about 50 hours a week as an attorney and spent another 15-20 hours a week maintaining and trying to grow his side hustles. Like all future lawyers, the question of which field to select while he was in law school was crucial. The debate between low-paid public defender of the unjustly prosecuted and highly-paid, industry workhorse was not long held. He went with the lucrative field of corporate law specializing in real estate.

Leo was from the Bible Belt, where large families are the norm. So, now that he worked way out on the coast of this young, vibrant America – he experienced a much different set of ideals in the community in which he currently resided. Most of his neighbors liked expensive cars they couldn't really afford, having pets instead of kids and spending the rest of their savings on lavish vacations multiple times each year.

I don't take too many vacations myself. I got too much to do. Plus, I feel better when I'm working anyway.

"Except on Mondays, that is," Leo laughed, now talking to himself.

Is it normal for people to talk to themselves? Well, either way – I do. It helps me straighten my thoughts out… to detach myself from what my body is doing… to step back and listen to the words I say and the things I do, as if I am watching and judging someone else. At times, I wonder who is saying some of the nonsense that comes out of my mouth.

"Haha!" Leo couldn't help but grin at the conversation going on in his head.

The train finally arrived, and Leo was happy to get on board and warm up a bit. He was heading for the doors as they opened a few feet away when he saw the loud woman that he earlier named Red. She was dashing straight in without any regard for the other people that were already waiting ahead of her.

She must be thinking that everyone will just yield to her, or she simply isn't afraid of a collision.

Trip her!!!!

Leo heard these instructions coming from deep within his subconscious.

"Pardon me, ma'am," Leo said to Red, as he mumbled back to the evil voice in his head, "Whoa, whoa, whoa. Quiet down in there."

I have the weirdest thoughts sometimes, I swear.

Against his bitter judgement, Leo slowed down and allowed Red to board the train first. After all, he still believed in chivalry and, frankly, human decency even in the face of someone who apparently had none.

As the train was barely half full this early in the morning, Leo muttered sarcastically, "I hope I can find a seat on this crowded train. Better sit down fast before someone else takes the last one."

He was unable to help himself from giving Red that fun little verbal poke, wondering how self-aware she was of her own unsavoriness.

At this point, the train was speeding along, rocking back and forth melodically as Leo sat there with his eyes closed streaming music on his phone. About 45 minutes into the ride, he stood up from his seat and prepared for the upcoming exit. The doors opened and he departed the train. Without thinking, he headed toward his favorite breakfast cart on First Street. They make an incredible egg sandwich, with crispy bacon and tons of cheese.

I'm a firm believer in starting the day out eating a butter sandwich, with a little eggs, bacon and cheese mixed in. You need a good, solid meal to carry you through until lunch time.

He approached the cart at the same time as a young, husky fellow.

"Go ahead," Leo smiled politely, inviting the man to join the line before him.

With two headphones plugged securely into the round orb perched atop his shoulders and music playing so loud the rest of the line around him could tap their feet to the beat, the gentleman grunted back in acknowledgement.

That's what constitutes manners these days.

Technology was supposed to connect us, but instead, has made it easier to insulate ourselves from each other. The result being a sense of loneliness and a lack of community, all while we pack ourselves tighter and tighter together in these growing cities. The effects being distance, coldness and death of the soul.

The food cart's owner, Phinny, saw Leo in line and she began making Leo's breakfast sandwich in advance. Leo tended to get the same thing every time he ordered from one of his local food spots.

I find the one item on the menu that I like best and stick with it. Why would I ever choose the second best? I'm always tempted to say, "my usual please," but that just seems so presumptuous… haha.

While Leo was still four people from the front of the line – Phinny put his steaming hot sandwich on the pickup counter and nodded to Leo. "Order up!" she shouted.

Watch. This guy in front of me isn't going to be happy about that.

"Hey! What gives!" blurted an unwittingly careless tourist standing next to his wife, as he watched Leo exit the middle of the line and head to pick up his fresh sandwich. The man continued, "My wife and I have been…,"

"Yo!" a local homeless man breathed silently as he lurched from the corner of the street a few feet away, reaching out and grabbing the tourist's arm. Clutching the visitor's soggy trench coat, the homeless man continued, "Quiet down man, if you know what's good for ya. Let that man right there go ahead."

Without even a glance in their direction, Leo forgave the ignorance of the couple that was visiting his neighborhood. He tipped his cap to Phinny, appreciating the reciprocity that follows in any sustainable business relationship. Leo threw a $20 bill in the tip jar, covering the $8.50 sandwich and then some.

A little (kindness) goes a long way. It is easy to see the utility in acting morally. By creating a mutually beneficial relationship, we both win. God will never be outdone in generosity, as they say. Who is the 'they' that said all this smart stuff? Even though I could basically buy an extra couple sandwiches each week if I didn't tip so much – it's a good interpersonal investment. I tip her, because she deserves it… a good, hard-working, honest

American. By doing so, I get exceptional service – and she generally adds extra ingredients to my sandwich anyway.

"Always a pleasure, Phinny."

"Keep making it a great day, Leo!"

Leo continued on his way. He passed by the newly opened coffee stand on the corner of First Street and High Avenue.

"Mr. Stills, how's it going today?" inquired a group of teenagers as they approached.

"Johnny boy," Leo said almost smiling, while pulling out a larger brown bag this time and exchanging it promptly for $750… more than he was planning on making that day at his actual job.

Turning back to his previous business, Leo peered into the new coffee shop, checked their prices and evaluated the length and quality of their customer line. Washington was only the fifth state to legalize the distribution and consumption of coffee products. This legal shop had been packed since it opened, as legal licenses to grow and distribute coffee were incredibly rare, with only a handful of well-connected and powerful people able to obtain one. Coffee has been widely used for centuries across the globe, but for as long as Leo could remember in his short couple decades of life, it had been an illegal substance in America.

The governmental agencies cited the dangers all the time, especially towards the youth. People would have three or four coffees each day – at work, school, everywhere they could sneak in a cup of joe without being noticed and judged accordingly. There were some people, who could afford it, that you would never see without a warm flask tucked inside their sweaters.

I wonder how this will go. Coffee is only decriminalized in these five states… it is still an illegal substance at the federal level… and they aren't shy about targeting their political enemies. When they need leverage, they have it on stand-by. The fed's 'official' policy is basically to let the states run things and they promise not to mess with you if you follow state law. However, some of the fed's more recent and well-known arrests have sparked controversy… with its agenda being carried out in a very ambiguous manner. The stories told about why some particular people were arrested seem unbelievable – but what can ya do.

Leo finally arrived at the ticket booth in his office lobby. His company offered discounted tickets for public transportation in an attempt to promote sustainable modes. An older gentleman, Robert, stood behind the counter and smiled as he watched Leo approach. Leo handed him a $20 bill and received his proper $7.50 in change, which Leo tucked away in the pocket of his business slacks.

The two had become friends of a sort. Leo empathized with the elderly man's loneliness and Leo felt that it was his duty to engage him as a fellow human being. Humans, more than any monetary gift, need to feel useful in order to keep their faith in humanity. As such, Leo went out of his way to take care of Robert as he could. Leo would occasionally bring him food on Christmas and Thanksgiving, and sometimes interesting treats he found at small street shops on his way to work.

"How's the day, Robert?" Leo asked.

Hunched over the counter, Robert cracked a warm grin and while smiling through his missing teeth he said, "Every day is good, sir – some are better."

Leo appreciated his wisdom and responded, "I like that saying, Robert. Mind if I steal that for use at a later date?"

Elated at the idea of adding value to someone's life, Robert darn-near yelled, "You betcha! Here's your change."

Leo took the $7.50 and shoved it in his breast pocket. "Take care, Robert."

Leo walked over to the elevator and pressed the UP button on the shiny gold elevator bank. There were eight elevators, four on each side. He appreciated the building in which he worked. The architecture was beautiful, and it was located near a very peaceful park that he too rarely was able to enjoy. This building was not like all the other modern construction, devoid of any transcendence in its design. These days, you can literally feel the secularism in the contemporary, box-like and lifeless structures of the 21st century.

The elevator dinged rather quickly, signaling its arrival on the lobby floor.

Love the fast elevators here…

A horde of people exited one of the elevator carts, all of which were constantly crowded. Much unlike the smaller town of Belmont where he lived, the big city here was bustling with activity and business nonstop.

I don't even think there is an elevator anywhere in my city back home. Maybe the Town Hall building has one?

Leo then joined the crowd boarding the elevator cart, and when it was his turn, pressed the button marked '42'.

I don't like being up on the top floor. We are fifty years overdue for the next major earthquake here and I can't imagine it will be fun if it happens while I am up there.

As he found a nice open spot along the right edge of the cart, he put his hands in his pockets and leaned against the railing.

"Wait… what," he mumbled, digging into the pocket of the low-cost, high-value business slacks that he found on clearance at the local second-hand store. These pants were almost his size, but not quite and Leo could swear one leg was longer than the other.

"Oh, great." Leo felt some loose bills and a 50-cent piece in his pocket. He patted his breast pocket and felt the same. "Robert… I swear," Leo cursed the old man's forgetfulness, realizing that Robert had given him the correct change… twice. "Well, I may as well keep it. That's capitalism for you – finders' keepers, losers' weepers."

What! You know that doesn't belong to you. Head back down and return it. Robert is going to be worried about that. You realize he will have to cover any shortfall in the register out of his own pocket. $7.50 might not seem like a lot to you, but that might mean him having to skip dinner one night this week. You're going to make an eternal decision that damages your soul for a couple bucks?

"Fine, fine… I will return it when I pass back through the lobby on my way home today," Leo begrudgingly compromised with himself.

If I don't forget.

"I won't forget!" Leo snapped back at the thought.

The golden elevator door opened on the top floor, he exited and walked to the cubicle he shared with his co-workers, Steven and Conner. Lazily not wanting to correct the situation right now, he took a pen out and wrote a note on the back of his hand: ROBERT'S CHANGE.

At the end of his shift, Leo took the elevator down to the lobby, and looked for Robert, who had apparently gone home early for the day.

I did my best though! Try again tomorrow. Should have done it right away, you bum.

As he exited the large glass doors, trimmed in gold metal, he felt the comfortable and all-too-familiar drops of rain begin to dampen his dark hair.

"Ahhhh," he sighed, breathing in the fresh, cool air – feeling good after a hard day's work.

He decided to spend a quiet night at home, taking the night off from work. He got home, cracked a beer, and turned on the grill. He threw a couple ribeye steaks on the sizzling barbeque a short while later, and he ate dinner alone. He had a couple more drinks throughout the night and fell asleep on the couch watching reruns of his favorite sitcom.

As he slept, his consciousness popped into a recurring dream, or better yet, nightmare, that had been plaguing his nights, leaving them dark and sleepless. He was never sure what to make of it because they seemed so bizarre and yet terrifyingly real at the same time.

Suddenly, he found himself running through a dark, damp forest as a torrential rain poured down from the heavens. He was unfamiliar with the actual place but had been here many times before in his dreams. He was running, endlessly – though unsure from what. Panting, he paused and bent over with both hands on his knees. He was hardly able to keep going, but he just needed a moment to breathe. Then, a crackling noise came from behind him – perhaps the sound of branches breaking beneath something's feet. Whatever it was, it was coming this way… fast – and Leo knew it would never give up until it had him. Relentlessly, the figure pursued Leo in his dreams. No matter how far or how fast Leo ran, it was inescapable. Not daring to wait any longer, Leo took off in a mad sprint again with the only benefit being the coolness he felt on his forehead as perspiration mixed with the wind. Clearly unsustainable for much longer, as his muscles began to seize and his chest started to cramp from the rapid breathing, he saw a grove of mossy trees fallen over crisscrossed, forming a nice little bunker to hide behind. Leo dashed towards it and burrowed his way into the overgrowth of the forest, certain he was not seen doing so by the pursuer. The cool breeze from the wind now gone, he was hotter than hell, burning up from the inside and ready to pass out from exhaustion. It felt like he had been running for hours. He heard the familiar torment of the dead tree branches crackling on the forest floor nearby as the predator tracked its prey. Leo held his breath. The sound kept going on passed the treed bunker, off into the distance until Leo heard it no more. Leo gasped a sigh of relief. Could it be over now? That monster, who never ceased to find Leo's weaknesses, apparently moved on and spared him. As Leo was trying to catch his breath, leaning against the back of the mossy sanctuary, the unyielding hunter doubled back and suddenly ripped apart the bunker in a splintery explosion.

Too scared to turn around and face it and with his heart about to fail, Leo screamed, "NO!!!"

At that, Leo shot up in his bed – sweating, panting, and sleepless once again. He went through the motions of lying back down, but he simply stared at the ceiling of his room as he awaited the sweet comfort of the coming dawn.

<u>Story 2</u>

Leo was a decorated soldier in the U.S. army. He was honorably discharged after two overseas tours, receiving both the Medal of Honor and the Distinguished Service Cross. He never could understand how he was supposed to consider himself a hero for killing a bunch of people, just because they weren't Americans.

We are all brothers and sisters in the metaphysical sense – children of God, as some might say, though Leo probably wouldn't. He was still haunted by those nightmares; the faces of those lives he destroyed. The only way he ever got any sleep most nights, was downing a few of the government-provided 'feel-good' pills. These Paradise Pills at least turned his mind off for a few hours.

Almost a decade ago, biotechnology companies made a revolutionary and life-changing breakthrough in medicine. They created a synthetic medication that, once ingested, cured you of any physical ailment. We literally erased disease and physical pain from the lives of anyone who desired to escape reality enough to take this pill.

One pill could last almost all day for most people. Not only would it cure your sickness, it also clouded your consciousness, causing you to only focus on the current moment. The effect was actually quite delightful, as it didn't allow for any emotional suffering either.

We no longer had to constantly and forever bear the tremendous burden that is a knowledge of our mortality and a foreknowledge of our eventual death. So many times, when Leo was plagued by anxiety in the middle of the night for one reason or another, he took a Paradise Pill and promptly drifted off into a pleasant slumber without a care in the world.

This allowed him to fall asleep for about four hours a night, before the faces of his victims, though supposedly killed honorably in the name of war, crept back into his psyche and started tearing at his skin while he dreamt.

He shot up in bed this morning, dripping with a cold sweat. Unable to get back to sleep, or perhaps unwilling to try for fear the faces might come back, he rotated in bed, sat up, and put his clammy feet on the cold, creaky, wooden floorboards of his old home.

There was a bottle of whiskey there for extra fire power, just in case a rough night got out of hand and hindered his sleep, which it all-too-often did.

"Might as well get to work," he sighed, "Better to keep busy anyway."

He poured a small glass of cheap whiskey, put on his robe and walked down the stairs to his home office so he could wake up slowly.

As he sat down in his black leather chair, he took a few sips from his glass, started a roaring inferno in the faded red brick fireplace and turned on the morning news to hear this: "… and, following up on our U.S.A. debt tracker today, the national debt has now reached $84.6 Trillion. Man, hope we get a handle on this soon."

Leo sighed at his country's depressing financial state of affairs.

The news continued, "With that, we are going to kick it over to Jackie. Don't forget to tune into the 2048 abortion rally, where we will see who can perform the most abortions in under thirty minutes, from the 1st trimester all the way to the 4th!"

Decades ago, we legalized abortions, which was controversial to say the least. However, once society accepted the fact that we weren't really killing human beings in the womb, just human tissue, a Roman Colosseum-type sport gradually emerged and finally became a mainstream, annual spectacle for all to enjoy.

Destruction of humans, by humans. The ultimate betrayal – the ultimate revenge on God.

The news continued without a hitch, "Hello everyone, Jackie Nicks here on this beautiful morning – the fourth day of February 2048. We come to you with a live update. Over the past 20 years, we have adopted some amazingly generous policies that had good intentions but unfortunately, catastrophic results. Keep in mind, we were never able to get enough support from the other side of the aisle to implement the programs the way we really wanted to. Compounding upon our dire domestic financial straits - Braxton, the dictatorship that utilizes the forced slave labor of its own citizens, is now going on over a decade as the sole superpower of the world, primarily accomplished through their weaponization of artificial intelligence."

Leo moaned as the news chugged along, "Braxton called our debt due in 2033 and we couldn't pay, forcing us to go into default. Since our most recent recession, our homeland has regressed back to the times of the wild, wild west due to massive governmental spending cuts on essential functions. This resulted in the termination of a dangerously high percentage of firemen, police officers and other emergency personnel. Technology also took a giant leap backward when our deficit got out of control and we were forced to divert funds from defense and technology sectors to cover our budget shortfall. When we increased taxes, it hit more than the richest of our country in the end. Instead of investing in more business and hiring more people, profits were seized through government taxes and squandered, hampering growth for years. There was a mass exodus of businesses leaving America, to relocate their headquarters to another, more business-friendly country. Then, things really hit the fan when our government introduced tariffs to prevent U.S. companies from headquartering overseas. Well, then they just left America altogether and headed for less regulated pastures. America was already hurting when companies left, because so many of us lost our jobs. However, it got even worse when foreign companies stopped shipping their products here and all the domestic product became exorbitantly expensive. Mass homelessness ensued, because no one had jobs to pay their mortgages or rent - and the little money they did have was spent on $18-per-gallon gasoline and $3,500 for a bottom-of-the-line microwave. So, reminder that a policy with good intentions, doesn't mean you will get the outcome you want…"

Nothing new there. Our country has gone downhill for decades. The news is always so depressing. Hmmm, Rome should be finishing up that job at the pier today. Another day, another dollar. Should be pretty standard… nothing we haven't done before.

Rome, his oldest brother, was carrying out a routine operation with just two trusted members of their humble crew. In the dead of night, they would sneak down to the dock after paying for a tip from the local skipper and proceed to commandeer some of the coffee containers. The ships' captains were paid well by Leo's crew and the local coast guard and border patrol stationed at the docks were also on the family's payroll.

Leo's team paid for the location of the shipments, for the captains to leave the containers unattended, and the law enforcement personnel to look the other way.

Clockwork.

Small crimes like these weren't even prosecuted anymore. This sort of petty corruption was a lot more common than you might think these days – and Leo was the disputed king of this game throughout all the Belmont area.

Just then, Leo heard a knock at his door.

"Come in!" he hollered, not worried about who it might be.

He listened to the front door open and close. Seconds later, Rome peaked his head into Leo's home office.

"Can I come in?" Rome almost whispered.

"Come on, come on. How'd it go? Want a drink?"

Without hesitation, Rome nodded, "Three fingers, no ice. We might have a problem."

We…

Funny the terminology Rome used. After all, the whole family relied heavily on Leo's advice and intellect.

Happy to be doing something other than sitting and thinking, Leo walked over to the liquor cabinet and poured a healthy amount of his better whiskey into his best glass. As he handed the glass to Rome, Leo let out a heavy sigh. He wasn't lamenting because of the potential problem that Rome just announced; it was something heavier still… life.

"Tell me," Leo ordered passively as he sat back down in his chair and motioned for Rome to do the same.

"Well, we went down to Dock 5 today, according to the plan we discussed at the last family meeting," Rome muttered staring at the floor.

He took a sip and looked back up at Leo.

Confused at Rome's hesitation, Leo urged, "… and…?"

"And… I thought the plan was for only two containers?" Rome continued to be coy, somewhat afraid Leo would disapprove of the split-second decision he had to make in the field earlier that morning.

"Rome, you know the plan. Eli knows the plan. Phil knows the plan. Michelle knows the plan. I… know… the freaking plan. What happened!? What are you saying?" Leo urged, losing patience.

Rome just blurted it out, "Well, there was three damn containers, bro!"

"Hmmm. Did we take all three?" Leo asked, somewhat intrigued.

Even though it could end up being trouble, there is something about how interesting life can be when mother nature throws you a curveball.

At this point losing a bit of his anxiety, Rome said "Well, of course we did. I only had seconds to call an audible and our protection was about to expire, so… regardless, I mean, of course we took all three."

Leo chuckled.

Rome sighed.

Leo continued, "… but everything went smoothly? You took all three containers to our warehouse, no problems?"

Pleased this hadn't upset Leo so far, Rome continued, "Yes, everything else went according to plan."

"So, what's the problem, brother?"

"Well, the first two containers were the standard, salmon-colored containers we always pull…"

"Salmon-colored," Leo interrupted, finishing his drink and setting it down on his oak end-table. "What the hell are you talking about. Haha! You mean orange? When did you grow…" Leo stopped, smiling from ear to ear at this point, "… anyway, continue please."

"Like I was saying, the first two containers were… orange… like normal. The third container though, was black and had several barcodes… heavily padlocked," Rome reported.

"Hmmm, that is very unusual for a small-town Belmont shipment. Black generally means government orders. What was inside?" Leo asked.

"We didn't have time to open the third container while we were at the dock," Rome cryptically responded, pausing to measure Leo's face.

Leo grunted, frustrated.

Rome continued, "But, when we got back to our warehouse, we opened it up. I'm not sure what exactly was inside. It was nothing I've ever seen before. It looked like… I don't know… metal hover boards???"

"What the hell are you talking about… hover boards?"

"Look! I don't know what was inside. I've never seen anything like it before," Rome pleaded.

"I'll check it out. Don't tell anyone about the third shipment. Get to the office, open up shop for the day. Michelle will be there soon, and I don't want her to be alone," Leo ordered. "When our lovely sister gets in, tell her to meet me at 9:00 a.m. near the south dock on Western Street. She called me last night saying there was something she needed to discuss, but I didn't have time."

"Will do, brother." Rome got up, nodded to Leo and left.

Leo just stared into the roaring fire from his armchair and continued to watch the wood burn a little longer. Thinking about nothing but the flames, he was at peace, even if only momentarily.

A while later after a shower and a shave, Leo headed down to the south dock to meet his sister.

Michelle was the oldest sibling in their family, and a senior member of their crew. She kept all the boys in line, as they would readily admit. When Leo arrived, he felt the cool breeze from the water and saw Michelle sitting on a bench reading the morning's paper.

"What did you do!?" she shot up as soon as she saw him, pointing at the front page.

The headline read:

DIRECTOR OF THE FBI TO SEND SENIOR SPECIAL AGENT TO BELMONT – MUST RECOVER STOLEN GOV'T CARGO.

She paused, waiting for a response.

Leo simply nodded and allowed her to continue.

Frustrated, she said, "I've been trying to get ahold of you the last couple days. I got a tip that the government had a shipment coming through our ports, and it was not to be touched. My source didn't tell me exactly when or where, but I wanted to make sure you knew not to tamper with anything outside the ordinary. Now, someone's taken it," she began. Looking worried, she asked, "It wasn't us, was it?"

Hm. Should I tell her? It will only worry her. Ehhh, it'd be nice to have her on board. She's not going to like this.

"Ya… it was. Our boys picked it up last night, somewhat by accident. It must be a big deal, if the feds are already dispatching a team to recover it. I'm going to figure out what was in the boxes, and we can go from there," Leo concluded, articulating a position he thought was very reasonable.

"What are you talking about!? Are you crazy in the head, bro? We don't need this kind of heat growing around us. We have a simple business model, and it doesn't include pissing off the federal government!"

Michelle stared at Leo in disbelief, amazed at how he could consider doing anything other than returning the stolen loot.

She continued, "Whatever is in there, the feds want it back, and they want it bad. My contact says it is some kind of cutting-edge technology that they don't want our foreign enemies getting their dirty hands on."

Always thinking about the current situation and ten steps ahead, Leo seemed to be staring off into the distance.

Refocusing his gaze on his sister now, he half-heartedly agreed, "Okay, I will figure it out."

"Figure it out, Lee?!? Take that container and torch it in the middle of Main Street so the coppers will find it. Maybe then they will call off the dogs."

"Michelle!" he shouted, beginning to embody his sister's agitation. "Enough. Goodness gracious. I got it. Please, get back to the office and make sure things are up and running. We can't afford any late orders. Our cash flow has been incredibly tight lately."

Frustrated, and unappeased by his lack of confirmation, she stormed off. Left to sit on the bench by himself, Leo finished reading the paper, unbothered by the continuous pitter-patter of the misting rain falling on the now-soggy pages.

A short while later, Leo headed to the office himself. Along the way, he did some reconnaissance on the legal coffee stands he passed by - noting the size of their lines, the prices on their boards, and the murmurs of the customers that were so willing to wait in line for their daily dose. As he walked in the door of the Stills family office building named the Bravo Tower, he went past the bullpen and marched up the stairs. He saw that Rome was discussing with one of the team members about how to improve their discretion while out making deliveries.

Rome looked up to see Leo and yelled, "Hey!"

Seemingly unaware, Leo did not respond.

"Bro!" Rome tried again, shouting all the way across the bustling first floor.

Leo turned his head towards Rome and motioned for Rome to follow him upstairs to their private offices. The leaders of the family all had their own offices upstairs, except the youngest brother, Sammy, who was still just a kid at this point. Sammy followed Leo around like a puppy whenever he could but was officially assigned to work under and report directly to Elijah, the second youngest.

Michelle is the oldest, then Roman who is just two years older than me. Phil is next, then Elijah. Then Sammy - the baby of the family. I think there is a part of all of us that wants Sammy to stay pure. He is so smart, so hard-working… he could do anything. It frustrates him at times, that we don't include him as much in the darker sides of our business, but he is only fifteen years old and has his whole future ahead of him. We've spent our whole lives protecting him since mom left us.

"Morning, bro. How'd it go with Michelle?" Rome asked, jogging up the stairs behind Leo.

Leo hung up his wet raincoat on the rack, then turned and leaned against the rugged oak desk. Silently, he raised his eyes ever so slightly, inviting Rome to continue by saying whatever it was he really wanted to say.

"So… what is this I hear about us fixing the real estate auctions down on Barber Street?"

Man, word travels fast. Can't anyone keep a secret these days? Don't tell him anything! What? No, we should tell him everything!

"We?" Leo mumbled the question to himself, wondering how many entities were battling for airtime within his head.

He had long since given up on the notion that he was the only one living in his brain and, thus, was resigned to sharing space along with the other tenants who also apparently had interests in the decisions he enacted through the use of his free will.

Turning back to the conversation at hand, he addressed Rome, "It's still tentative. You know we've been looking for ways to expand our business, especially since coffee was legalized. Plus, all we did was leak some information about some of the housing packages that are being auctioned off, letting a few of the prospective buyers in the neighborhood know which bundles are full of junk so they can adjust their underwriting."

Unconvinced, Rome continued, "Did you get Hansel's approval?"

Libby Hansel ran the auctions in Belmont, and she most certainly had a vested interest in how each auction turned out as part of the larger picture. She personally owned several coffee shops that have benefited from her ability to get prime distribution and warehouse locations for a 'fair' price.

Rome wasn't buying the story Leo was selling, "She definitely wouldn't appreciate you meddling with her business, and we do not want someone so powerful even knowing we exist, let alone being unhappy with our performance."

He's right. Hansel is dangerous. Wait. What? We are dangerous too… we aren't scared of Hansel! Good business would still seek to steer clear of her altogether.

These thoughts poured through Leo's mind, as Rome went on, escalating his voice in a mix of anxiety and excitement as he went, "What if we lose this bet anyway? We are looking to start buying some good properties ourselves, and this will drive the prices way up on the quality housing bundles! Lowering the price on the bad bundles doesn't help, because we don't want to buy the bad bundles!"

Leo countered his exasperated brother, frustrated at having to explain himself, "Our sources are being paid well to influence a couple auctions, and no one else knows about it. It won't be good for them or their families if our little secret becomes public. And you're right about the pricing. This auction, we will pass on the worthless bundles, and the prices will be higher for the quality ones. We will overpay for what we do buy, and we might not buy anything at all. The same will happen with the next auction. We will lose that battle again, but…we will win the war here, brother. Our competitors will use up most of their allotted purchasing power as they see the year coming to an end. They will begin to trust the data we leak, as they are repeatedly rewarded for taking the easy way out by relying on our inside information. Two days before New Year's Eve, three auctions from now, the largest sale in over a year is set to take place. Hansel has yet to release this date and location to the public, so any other interested parties will already be underprepared. Only the most aggressive buyers will even attempt to do their due diligence in the short timeframe between that announcement and the auction date. With the Stills Corporation being local, we have an advantage over the national corporations, who will leave a large enough piece of the pie untouched for us. This time, we strike. We will put out the same information again, the same information that had been proving true and oh-so-profitable for our competitors during the last few auctions. When we leak details to them about two of the super bundles on

East Hill that make up 85% of this auction being worthless, they won't even bother coming all the way out to the auction site just to spend what little purchasing power they have left in this year's investment fund. Except this time, we add a layer. We will 'let it slip' again that those two housing bundles on East Hill are practically condemnable. This is the motherload, Roman. Yes, it is a little risky, but when this works out, it will be exactly the foundation that we need to become a respectable player in this town. We might hurt a bit in the short run by giving our competitors some small wins here and there. But! The bigger picture, bro! We will buy more homes in those two bundles on East Hill than our rivals will have purchased in the last nine months, and we will get them for pennies… PENNIES on the dollar!" Leo sighed.

It seemed so obvious to him.

Rome was less hesitant at this point, but he still disagreed with the specific avenue of expansion and worried about Hansel's certain retaliation. They had long discussed during their regular family meetings that with the legalization of coffee becoming more popular, the family needed to diversify into other means of production.

Messing with Hansel certainly wasn't a business strategy they would normally pursue, but when the opportunity arose shortly after the most recent family meeting, Leo saw it as a sign… and he wasn't one to ignore the path that presented itself. Plus, they were getting quite desperate for growth.

Rome went on, "Well, I think it is too risky and it's outside our wheelhouse. We don't know these auctions enough to trust them, and certainly not enough to control them. We just have so many lines in the water and it feels like we are spreading ourselves too thin."

"It has been noted, Rome," Leo assured, beginning to look away and contemplate what he considered to be more pressing matters.

"I want it up for vote at the next family meeting," Rome continued quietly, his face full of conviction, though staring down at the hard-beaten wooden floorboards.

"Done. How's the day starting off?"

"Well, routes 291-327 have had a couple no-shows in the Waterstead housing community, but other than that – shipments are tracking nicely. Payments are all being received on time now. I think our last *demonstration* was effective. People would rather skip their rent payment than be late on any amount owed to our gang," Rome chuckled proudly.

"… owed to our company," Leo corrected his elder sibling.

Leo smiled, though maybe not for the same reasons as Rome. It had been a tough go of it for a while there. The percentage of people in their neighborhood who were 'not able' to make the payments for their coffee orders in a timely manner was rapidly on the rise. That is, it *was* on the rise until the Stills family was forced to make a rather gruesome example of several delinquent accounts that still walk around town with a limp to this day. The economy wasn't what it used to be, and everyone here lived paycheck to paycheck, but there were still only a few things more important to the citizens of Belmont than food, shelter and their coffee.

People need their coffee. With the governmental policies recently pushed by the majority party in Congress, people no longer owned homes. Instead, the only economical thing to do was rent. Homes are mostly owned by several large corporations, which in turn rent it out to almost 85% of eligible Americans. So much power. The 15% of Americans that still own houses have either had them for generations and were smart enough not to sell them for a small premium to one of the major Real Estate Corporations (REC's) — or, and for the most part, are the owners of the REC's themselves. It's a shame too, really, because a few decades back, real estate was one of the last major avenues that people could use to move up a socio-economic class here in America. But, long ago, people traded away their freedom for comfort. They outsourced all decision making to the government, and now they have more apparent equality, but their lives are controlled by the rich like never before.

His thoughts continued:

These days, people don't donate to charity, they just pay taxes and assume the government does all that. However, this numbs the joy of giving and the appreciation one would feel receiving help from their neighbors. Admittedly, the success that comes from the grace of God is inseparable from the duty to share it, but there is something wrong about that same compulsion being written into the law of man and taken out of hard-working American's pockets. There is a difference between right and wrong, and what the government should regulate so inefficiently by use of force.

"I am late for work," Leo concluded.

The two brothers shook hands and Leo walked out into the rain. His smile quickly turned to chagrin, as he recalled the sad moment when Sera found out about this last *demonstration* and finally understood the type of business Leo was running. She decided then and there to take their young son far away from the dangers this lifestyle posed and the monster who was in charge of it all.

Leo still hasn't been able to contact them.

<u>Story 3</u>

Leo arrived at his corporate office building just after 10:45 a.m.

"I've got a little less than three hours before the company's mandatory diversity training," Leo sighed, looking at his rusty silver watch that was attached to a worn-out, black leather band.

Every so often, his company required everyone to attend training sessions to address any privilege they had in society.

"Unconscious bias, they call it. Obviously. We all have biases. We all discriminate… every day, in every decision. Every decision to turn left is a discrimination against the choice to turn right. Discrimination isn't inherently bad – and if it is based on merit, it is actually a good thing."

Forget this. I should just skip it. They can't make me do this. Ugh. But I need a job. Better to go along to get along – not worth fighting the heavy current of this social justice movement. It's too strong at this point. I would drown. This training might make some people feel good, but it constantly brings race and gender to the forefront of every conversation, blaming each and every disagreement on these unchangeable characteristics. Frankly it's exhausting.

Leo turned off that conversation in his mind, and put his head down, working furiously to counteract the effect of taking a three-hour chunk out of his workday for the training session that was coming up.

It's time.

He felt a desire nudge him to check his watch again and he saw that it was already 1:25 p.m.

"I've got a few minutes before that misery begins," he mumbled.

Procrastinating as long as he could, Leo reluctantly got up from his cubicle a couple minutes after 1:30 p.m. He followed the lagging crowd of his coworkers over to the main conference room. He was the last one to arrive, but people were still clamoring away casually. The training session's organizer, Gregory Sr., noticed Leo moseying in.

He saw Leo's head immediately switch back to staring down at the floor quickly after the two men made eye contact for a brief moment in time. Leo was obviously not excited to be at this event.

Brilliantly, Gregory picked up on this and decided to make an example of Leo, saying, "All right, guys. Whoops. Guys and girls. People. People, thank you for coming. Heh Heh – I just displayed unconsciously some of my bias there. I know not everyone identifies with male or female, and some of you find being constrained by those labels offensive – so, I apologize."

Leo looked around in amazement.

Gregory went further, "I think it is critical that we use real life examples with the people you work with every day."

Pointing to Leo – who was nestled ever so nicely into the back of the room on the far side and had just started a fun little daydream – Gregory said, "Excuse me. Looks like you forgot your nametag, uhhhhhh…"

Now, Leo wasn't quite paying attention at all, so Gregory had to repeat himself. "Excuse me, what's your name?"

Guided by the snickers, Leo looked around to find that Gregory was talking to him.

One of Leo's department mates nudged him, chuckling quietly, "I think he's talking to you, Leo!"

Gregory, at this point having walked over that way, heard this and said, "Leo is it? Ahh, great. Would you come on up here to the front of the room. I want to get you your nametag, so you get credit for attending this session during your next employee review. I'm sure you want to move ahead in this company like the rest of your ambitious colleagues. Also, as part of paying your dues, as it were, I think you'd be the perfect candidate to lead us off today."

Not one to normally follow instruction, Leo was instinctively hesitant – but he could really use a good raise this year. He knew how the game was played, and even if you don't believe in this stuff, you have to go through the motions if you don't want to be ostracized. Still, he was a bit surprised by the invitation, as there were over 200 people to choose from in the large conference room.

What a joke. This isn't right. I shouldn't do it. But I have to do it, or I won't get a good raise and I won't get my promotion. I need that extra money until the Stills Corporation gets firmly off the ground. The family company is doing quite well right now, but there is a lot of uncertainty when running an underground business. Ugh. I have no choice.

Begrudgingly, Leo moaned his way out of the stiff, plastic chair he was in, and slowly made his way up to the front of the room. Clearly, it didn't pay to stand out from the herd.

Gregory handed Leo his nametag and continued, "Perfect. All right, Leo. As you clearly don't fit into many of the oppressed and marginalized groups of today's society, why don't you start off with a quick explanation and example of how your privilege oppresses the various minority groups here today."

Dumbfounded by that train of thought, Leo began to recite the 2048 version of the national anthem, where he declared that any good things he attained by working hard, were actually the result of a corrupt social structure that inherently favored him, in part, for not being bald while at the same time oppressing others. He then apologized for the genetic code with which he was born that determined what we use to rudimentarily interpret as biological sex before we became a more sophisticated society.

A short while later, the meeting ended. Leo went back to his desk, drained – and finished up the rest of his day, working without eating a lunch. The environment here was numbing.

Leo left his downtown office building in a hurry that day and hustled toward the train station so he could get back to Belmont. As Leo stood there on the platform waiting for his train, thoughts ran wild in his head.

I don't think I can stomach doing that training ever again. My employee review is scheduled for next week. That should go well, especially after today's performance. I'm just going to stop thinking about it for now, because it makes me simply not want to try anymore. Any effort I exude, and any benefits that come to me as a result – are criticized as simply furthering the tyrannical and unfair, oppressive social structure that more and more Americans have been systematically dismantling for decades. I don't want to end up like most people who rebel against these extremists though; jobless and then eating out of the trash cans on the sidewalks. The policies put in place over the last few decades have bankrupted most of America. Stay strong. It will get better. I have to start standing up for what

I believe in, whatever the cost. I can get through this. Sir, we have an emergency!

"What was that?" Leo was bewildered at that last statement, which sounded like a secretary storming into her boss' office. He mumbled, "That didn't sound like any voice I've ever heard before."

The Henneson case has been moved up and we need to get over there now. Fine, pack my things and I will finish with this last… Sir! Your mic is on! I think your human can hear you! What? Oh, shoot!

Then, all the sudden… silence. Leo heard nothing but silence.

"I must be losing my mind. The stress is killing me."

Unable to muster the energy to address what must have been a schizophrenic episode unlike anything he'd ever experienced, he kept on his way when he was soon approached by a stranger in a black raincoat. Leo quickly turned his attention to what could be a local rival or enemy.

The stranger asked, "I hear you can help me out with something. How much for a half?"

Charge him extra for being a stranger. He won't be a repeat customer and he looks like a schmuck. What a dumb shirt. He probably doesn't know the fair price of this anyways. We can get one over on him.

Still distracted from the last conversation in his head, Leo thoughtlessly pulled out a brown paper bundle from his backpack and handed it to the man, saying, "$825."

The stranger smiled, grabbed the bundle and instead of handing Leo the money, he slapped some cuffs on Leo's wrist and asked if he could give Leo a ride in the back of a warm police vehicle.

"Damn it all to hell," Leo mumbled as he slogged on behind who apparently was an undercover sheriff and, without a fight, climbed out of the rain and into the back of a squad car.

Hmmm, what did he mean when he said 'I hear you can help me'… who did he hear that from? Got to call Rome. It will be okay. We will beat this. We have a couple friends in the Belmont police department. But maybe we should just take our lumps and learn from this. You know, change our ways? We keep going deeper and deeper down the rabbit hole.

"Ya, maybe you're right," Leo replied to himself.

A short while later, Rome made a phone call to some of their friends in blue that were on the Stills' Corporation payroll and Leo was home before dinner got cold.

<u>Story 4</u>

Months went by and the search for the fed's stolen cargo was heating up. Federal agents had been seen going door to door in the Belmont community, asking about the missing shipment and offering a hefty reward for any tips leading to its whereabouts.

Michelle walked into Leo's office, hoping to confirm he executed the plan they discussed previously.

"So?" she began.

Leo, a bit confused, maybe intentionally so, put on a puzzled face, raised a single eyebrow and slanted his head like a newborn puppy.

Unamused, Michelle continued, "Did you dump the problem like we agreed so that we can get back to our normal course of business?"

Leo, who had been waffling before on whether they should dump it or not, said matter-of-factly without breaking his gaze, "If the feds want it this bad, it must be worth a lot to them. It's simply bad business to throw away something so valuable. It only makes sense to get a fair price for it."

Now incensed at his temerity, Michelle yelled back as she stormed out of the room, "This should have been a family decision!"

Shaking that off, Leo was surprised by a loud noise downstairs in the lobby of their family office. Without getting out of his leather chair, he peered over the edge of his office window to see what was going on. To his surprise, he saw Eli stumbling in the front door with Sammy's help.

As Eli struggled to find the nearest chair before collapsing to the ground, Rome handed him a glass of whiskey.

Leo was coming down the stairs as Eli took a big gulp and gathered his breath. Leo saw that Eli had two black eyes, bruises everywhere and seemed to be covered in blood.

Leo asked, "What happened?"

"The cops picked me up over on 2nd Street, by Pinky's Doughnut Shop. They were asking about a stolen shipment. Obviously, I didn't tell them anything about our operations and man they beat the hell out of me. To make it stop, I finally said I would cooperate any way I could."

Rome did not know that Leo had already discussed the stolen shipment with Michelle. He looked worriedly at Leo, who nodded back in an effort to reassure his older brother. Leo then turned around to find Michelle glaring at him. He quickly avoided that gaze and started pacing around the lobby floor.

Leo asked, "The cops, Eli? They should know better. We have an agreement."

After taking another large sip of the cheap whiskey, Eli finally sighed and settled back into the chair a little bit, letting out a small moan from the pain.

"They weren't local dogs, that's for sure. Maybe undercover. Their uniform was not Belmont PD."

Leo could literally feel Michelle's stare burning holes in the back of his freshly pressed, white shirt.

Eli continued, "The questions they were asking made it sound like some covert weapon they were scared might get out or stolen by the Braxton forces."

The People's Militia of Braxton was another growing force found popping up across the globe. Braxton is a country located overseas, but they have networks sewn throughout North America and countless sovereign states around the world where they seek occupations like police officers, teachers, politicians and businessmen. Here in Belmont, they have a small syndicate aimed at creating chaos and stealing our intellectual property so they can copy and produce cheap replicas using the slave labor of the dictatorship's citizens.

The militia is likely the fed's prime suspect for the theft of the shipment that contained the new cutting-edge technology. It would be easy for us to frame them for the stolen shipment. We are tiny compared to both of those two organizations, and we really have no political motives here. We just want to be left alone to make our money, but with so much pressure being placed on the other two organizations' crews, we will need to be tactful here. That being said, haha, we do have the shipment. Attention from the feds is definitely bad for business.

Eli went on, "The coppers said they would overlook our *alleged* coffee distribution business, if we gave them whatever information we had and kept our ears to the ground for any new useful tidbits that might come our way. These guys meant business, obviously," he paused, dabbing some of the blood from his still-open wounds. "I know we aren't snitches, but it should be good for business since it probably means taking down one of our rivals. So, I said we would help. Plus, they know about our company already, so we don't really have a choice unless we want to go up against the criminal-devouring machine that is our government. When I told the police that it wasn't our crew that stole their stuff, they asked me about the Braxton militia and then about SOPA."

Leo wondered how to best spin this.

SOPA represented a fast-growing portion of Americans who were supporting the extreme changes of recent decades. They are Socialism's Official Party of America. Unimaginable at first, that the third most official party to join the Democrats and Republicans on the political stage would be SOPA, but here we are in 2048… it's happening.

Phil chimed in, "It wasn't SOPA. I've been talking with someone that's involved in their efforts and she was just venting to me the other day how much negative spotlight this has drawn from certain authorities."

"She?" Eli inquired skeptically. Continuing rather irately, he asked Phil, "Jane? Again, bro?"

A little less vocally now, Phil replied with a soft sigh, "Yes, Eli… I am talking about Jane. I thought it was important for the family to hear."

"What is important, Philly boy, is that our family doesn't associate with those crackpots! Psh. Morally reprehensible it is - and everyone in this room knows all too well about morally reprehensible behavior! Being connected to SOPA has been nothing but bad for our family and it definitely put a target on our businesses! How can you…"

"Enough," Leo sighed, silencing the two quarrelling brothers, this obviously not being the first time they've had this rather taxing conversation. "Who Phil talks with shall remain untouched for now. Let's figure out a solution here."

"But, Leo…" Eli returned, "…the feds not only asked about SOPA and any coordination or support our crew may have provided in the heist, they interrogated me specifically about Jane! I told them it was nonsense, but apparently Phil is making me a liar."

"Okay, Okay. I'm going to the Coffee Spot," Leo said, ending the conversation there.

He needed some time to come up with a plan.

"I'll come with you," Rome said, and Eli silently followed his older two brothers to the local coffee watering hole at which their family regularly liked to unwind.

They had a private room in the back corner, with a large sliding window that could open when they wanted to enjoy the shows of local performers. As the three brothers arrived at the run down, but still bustling, coffee shop – the owner nodded at them from behind the bar and the three boys seated themselves in the backroom suite. Small talk then ensued; friendly banter back and forth that, to any outsider, would seem like a full-fledged fight.

The owner of the small shop knocked on the door. After waiting for a silent invitation, the owner placed a full bottle of whiskey in the center of the old round table. Not missing a beat, Leo beckoned for Rome to tip the man and the owner exited just as silently as he entered.

Most of the patrons here came for the legal coffee these days, but the Stills family didn't partake in coffee consumption – they only engaged in its distribution. However, a shining new face, wearing a clean apron wrapped around a flattering black skirt, came back to drop off the boys' whiskey glasses. She apparently was unconcerned about interrupting the men's conversation.

"Lee, you can't argue with the facts," Rome said, continuing their lively discussion as he grabbed an empty glass to begin their next informal meeting session.

Leo wasn't listening, but instead was somewhat irritated by the young women's brazen disregard for the unspoken respect the family normally received in this and every other local establishment.

"I didn't know we hired any new help," Leo stated, just as she was headed back out the door of the family's suite.

After continuing along her way another few steps, she swung back around when she realized he must be talking to her. After all, she was the one and only employee here.

"We?" she replied smiling, again painfully unaware of the local politics in Belmont.

However, though playfully intended, her question went unanswered as she looked away from Leo's straight-faced demeanor towards the other two men in the room who were intentionally busying themselves by pouring some whiskey in their clean glasses.

Clearing her throat, she choked out, "My name is April. I, uhhh, just started here yesterday."

With little acknowledgement, Leo turned back and resumed the conversation he was previously having with his brothers before he was interrupted, albeit perhaps somewhat delightfully. Unsure of how to proceed, April backed out slowly and then went to wipe down some of the dirty tables in the front room.

A short while later, Leo walked up to the bar and said aloud to either, or both, the owner and April, "Whiskey, please."

The owner quickly leaned over and whispered to April, "Whatever he wants is on the house... every time, no limit. When he asks for something, get him a full bottle and keep the chit chat to a minimum. 'Yes, sir' and 'No, sir' and 'It's on the house'. That's about all we need to say to him, though I'm not sure when saying 'no' would be appropriate or wise."

She quickly grabbed a new bottle of whiskey from the counter, walked it over to the bar, cracked open the seal and reclosed the lid.

She slid the bottle across and as he went to hand her payment, she recited, "It's on the house," and promptly disengaged to get back to work.

Without skipping a beat, Leo placed a $50 bill on the bar and walked back to the family's suite.

A few hours later, the shop was winding down; getting ready to close up for the night. April grabbed a warm washcloth to wipe down the tables. She was straightening some chairs when Leo and the boys noisily got ready to leave.

As they departed, Eli got into an impromptu conversation with the shop owner causing Rome and Leo to wait near the front door discussing private business quietly amongst themselves. Just then, the owner of the bakery next door came by to chat with the Coffee Spot owner about some problems she'd been dealing with regarding drunks loitering in the dark, shadowy alley between the Coffee Spot and her bakery.

The Stills family frequently picked up breakfast pastries from her bakery, one of the best in town. The bakery owner, not wanting to disrupt Eli's conversation with the coffee shop owner, decided to introduce herself to the new hire.

"Hi there, missy," she said to April. "I don't believe we've had the pleasure of meetin'. How are ya, sweetie? I'm Mama Anita."

"Miss Anita, so nice to meet you. My name is April. I just started here. Haha, trying to get the hang of how things work around these parts."

"Well, I'm just certain you're doing a fantastical job. If you need anything, feel free to stop on by, honey. I'm just next door at Bagels B' Gone. I'm sure you would love our dessert scones, though you don't look like you have too much of a sweet tooth, darlin'. We need to put a little meat on those bones!"

April blushed and Mama Anita continued without taking a breath, "If you need anything done around here in Belmont – now, I don't want to misspeak - but Mr. Stills here would be the man to help ya."

Having overheard, Rome and Leo briefly nodded a formal greeting to Miss Anita.

Anita went on gesturing towards Leo, "April, have you met Mr. Stills here?" Clearly having an angle that's better left unsaid, Anita kept rattling on, "He is intelligent, brutal, sweet and, here in Belmont, all things are possible for him."

April took the opportunity to learn more, "We've met, in a way. So, Mr. Stills – what line of work are you in?"

Leo didn't answer.

However, Rome, clearly having had a touch too much to drink, blurted out, "We were stationed along the African coast years ago when it looked like World War III was going to breakout. The local towns were dominated by the coffee cartels and tons of soldiers were smuggling coffee back on military flights."

What the hell is he doing?

Unhappy with the extra attention and flabbergasted at his brother's extreme carelessness, Leo patted Rome on the shoulder and walked out the front door without saying a word.

Taking his cue, Rome hollered, "Eli! Let's get to gettin'."

Eli obliged and the three went on their way.

After the Stills boys were long gone, April finished her shift and went out to the payphone located in front of the Coffee Spot. She dropped in two quarters, took out a card with her handler's phone number on it and began to dial. She turned around, leaning her back against the cold, rusty booth and looked around to see if anyone was watching.

After hearing the other line pick up, she said, "Sir?"

A man answered on the other end of the line, "April, tell me you know where it is."

Story 5

After Leo left the Coffee Spot around 2:00 a.m. on Saturday morning, Sammy called his phone from the office. "Leo, we got a problem."

Here we go again. Another problem to solve. I don't mind helping everybody, but there is always someone in the family who is unhappy with how I choose to solve any problem.

"What's up, Sam Man?"

"Axel went crazy again. He almost beat one of the boys from the O'Connor Clan to death in a night club earlier tonight. They aren't happy and want retribution. Out of respect, and in an effort to avoid a war, they reached out to our office."

Forget O'Connor – that old windbag. They aren't really a threat anymore but could still be a nuisance. Let's be diplomatic. Or we could rule with an iron fist. Make another example of them. The last example cost me my wife and kid.

"Terrible. I will take care of it," Leo replied. "Tell O'Connor to send a couple boys down to Marx Circle in 45 minutes. They can witness. Where is Axel?" Leo said, checking off items one-by-one to clean up this chaos.

Sammy replied, "Axel came straight to the family office. He's in the other room sleeping off that last bottle of vodka and icing his bloody hands."

Without skipping a beat, Leo ordered, "Have him meet me at 6th and Main. I will be there in forty minutes."

Leo arrived at 6th and Main thirty minutes later and Axel was nowhere to be found. To pass the time, Leo grabbed a cigar from his coat, brutishly bit off the end and lit it up. He stood in the rain, puffing his cigar for a few minutes when he saw a large figure turn the corner a couple blocks down.

As the intimidating shadow approached, Leo heard, "Hey, boss. Sorry about that O'Connor brat. He was really disrespecting me and my girl. You know we can't tolerate that behavior towards our crew."

"This isn't the first time we've had a problem like this, Ax…" Leo retorted, ignoring the rationalization his employee just spit out of his noisy mouth. "… and it's always you."

"But, boss…"

"This can't stand, Ax. The O'Connor Clan wants blood and they ain't wrong. It's either your head or a battle in the streets. The kid you beat to a pulp was the main enforcer's son. The boy is fifteen years old and hasn't even been initiated yet. He was off limits and whether you were explicitly out of line or not, something has to happen here. War is bad for business."

Silence.

Leo continued, "Let's go. Follow me."

They walked down the hill from the corner towards Marx Circle. As they made their last turn, they almost ran into a few members of the O'Connor Clan sitting on a bench along the sidewalk.

A still-drunken Axel turned to Leo and blurted out, "What gives, boss! You can't do this to me. I won't mess up again. That kid had it coming. He was…" Axel's voice trailed off as he saw Leo shaking his head.

Leo explained, "I've arranged for you to get picked up by some of our friends in blue that we have on our payroll. You will be treated well, but you have to be taken in. That's the least we can do at this point. These fellas are here to witness the arrest."

"Sorry, sir. Yes, sir. I appreciate the leniency and your generosity. I didn't mean to cause the family any trouble."

At that, they walked past the two gentlemen perched on the deteriorating city bench. Leo's mind wandered far off as they meandered along hearing only the pitter-patter of the rain hitting the cold sidewalk on a dark, windy night in Belmont.

After that was wrapped up and Leo saw the two O'Connor boys nod in approval, signaling the end of their beef - Leo headed back home.

As he walked through the cold, lonely streets, a homeless man came up to Leo begging for spare change. Leo dug in his pocket and pulled out the first bill that came loose from his wallet.

He handed the man the $100 bill and, unsure exactly why, said, "God bless."

Another eventful day in Belmont.

<u>Story 6</u>

The sun began to rise on a beautiful Sunday morning in the Belmont neighborhood as Leo and Rome drove down to the water's edge to attend an upscale real estate auction.

Rome said, "Check it out, Leo; looks like an undercover behind us. Don't they know better than to hassle us? Why aren't they following instructions?"

Ever since the incident with Axel and the O'Connor Clan, Leo decided to increase the amount he paid the local Belmont Police Department for protection and insulation from legal penalties.

"They *are* following instructions," Leo replied calmly, not bothering to either turn around and investigate or explain to Rome any further, and Rome didn't need any additional clarification.

The whole Stills Corporation, and the entire Stills family, relied on Leo. They trusted him implicitly. Counting the crew's foot soldiers, the Stills currently employed over eighty people working for and within the family network. Leo and the Stills family achieved status and power within the local Belmont community by lining the poor people's pockets with a small portion of their ill-gotten gains. Leo gave them a voice just loud enough to feel like they had some amount of control in their lives and for that, the community loved him. A love, though, that was perhaps born mostly out of need and fear.

The brothers arrived at the auction a little early so they could discuss some of the properties with their contact from one of the local crime families, the Harold Boys. These were a scrappy crew, not very organized and not very big. Eli led the way for his brothers as they walked across the grassy hill towards the sign-in area.

One of the Harold Boys came over and yelled, "Yo, Eli! My man. What's going on!"

Rome snickered.

Eli replied, "Well, now. If it isn't Jackson Harold… Mr. HB. Sure do appreciate you meeting us here. What do we got today and how does it work?"

Jackson said, "We got some bee-ee-a-utiful units up for auction today. They are a bit pricey, but I think the value…"

Eli and Jackson walked off a ways to discuss, their conversation trailing off from earshot as they went.

Leo and Rome kept walking down to the pier, not saying much as they went. As they passed by the remaining bunch of HB's, one of the HB soldiers made a comment in their direction that was inaudible to the Stills brothers, but the semi-stifled laughter that followed certainly was not.

"Is there a problem here?" Rome asked, as he diverted from the sidewalk and walked straight up to the raucous group.

One of the HB's scoffed dismissively, "Watch where you're walking, pal. You don't want any trouble here. Just keep it movin'."

Now if you weren't yet aware, the Stills family didn't take kindly to disrespect – and especially not in their own neighborhood. They weren't used to having to swallow that bitter pill. Most people understood how things worked around here and the HB's were no exception to that rule. This HB young gun might not fully grasp the situation, but definitely felt confident having Leo and Rome outnumbered three to one.

Ever since the government decided the constitution was an outdated document, the powers-that-be repealed the second amendment and confiscated darn near every single gun in America, almost causing another civil war. So, there weren't many, if any, guns left on the streets. That didn't stop evil people from being evil. Nowadays, crimes simply ended up being more gruesome beatings and violent knife attacks.

Clearly comfortable with these odds, Rome directed his gaze towards the vocal HB member and inched closer with clenched fists.

Not wanting to disrupt the business of the day and having a cleaner way of dealing with things, Leo said, "Roman, I'm sure his boss doesn't know or appreciate what nonsense this knucklehead is spewing out here on the streets while representing their crew. Everyone in this stretch of the woods knows the pecking order and the HB's are hardly even worth a response."

Then, addressing the strapping young HB that was clearly looking forward to a scuffle with the legendary Stills brothers, Leo said, "Have Jackson tell his father that Leo Stills says 'Hello.'"

We should have destroyed them. Why would we let that go!? It's better to just let sleeping dogs lie. No sense getting beat up here. They have us outnumbered. Humble yourself and move on. We could take 'em. We have nothing to prove to them. If you know it, you don't say it. If you say it, you don't know it.

Without waiting for a response, Leo fearlessly turned his back on the unruly group of HB's and walked towards the pier. Disappointed there would be no bloodshed today, Rome spit on the ground and then turned to follow his brother.

Waiting until he and Leo made it down to the waterfront, Rome questioned Leo's decision privately, "Bro, those insects don't get to insult us like that. What you thinking? Our family has pride and if we let them walk on us, it will turn into a bigger problem."

"I will handle it. Their disrespect will not go unpunished. I hate that damned family."

A short while later, Eli came back and reported, "Got it, guys. We are ready to go."

Leo said, "Good. Let's get the hell out of here."

As they walked back to their car, Rome kept a hopeful eye on the HB crowd, still rather optimistic they might do something stupid.

Laughing somewhat, Eli asked Leo, "What was the commotion earlier with the HB's? Were you guys playing nice with the other kids?"

Leo said nothing.

Rome shook his head, as if to tell Eli to drop it.

Leo ordered, "Get in the car. I'll be right back."

He then walked over to the undercover BPD car that was tailing them earlier on the way here. He said a few words and, after a nod of his head, walked back to the car. He got in the front passenger seat as Rome turned over the engine, readying them to leave.

"Wait," Leo said, almost whispering, a slight grin forming.

After a couple moments passed, Eli and Rome grew confused, still waiting for something to happen. As they looked around, they saw two coppers walk from behind the family car with batons drawn. They marched up the grassy hill obviously on a mission.

The Stills brothers watched as the two boys-in-blue walked up to the HB group and were met with extreme animus. Some yelling ensued, but the rule of law was no doubt respected these days. The HB's, as loud as they are, were not silly enough to lay their hands on a cop.

Son of the gang's leader and the HB's general, Jackson Harold, was in the front of the group talking to the cops, but the officers were pointing their batons at the troublemaker that disrespected Rome. As the coppers went to arrest the young man, he put up a fight and both he and Jackson ended up taking batons to the head.

Jackson was knocked out cold and left there on the grass for the rest of the HB's to deal with. The troublemaker was promptly hauled off in handcuffs and as he was being dragged down the grassy hill, Rome pulled out of the parking lot. Eli excitedly sprung up from the backseat with a smile and honked the horn twice as Leo rolled down his tinted window and waved.

A short while later, Leo and the boys were relaxing at their office when Phil came busting through the front door.

"Leo!" Phil yelled, out of breath from running. "Guys!?" he tried again.

The family quickly gathered downstairs around Phil.

Phil continued hysterically, "I was hanging out with Jane down at the SOPA house on Broadway. The feds busted in and raided the shop looking for the stolen government shipment. A couple local cops we have on the payroll were coordinating with the feds and they let Jane and me slip out. I put Jane on a train to New Havers and I came straight here."

"Are you all right, Phil?" Leo asked defensively. "Did they hurt you?"

"No, no, I'm fine. What are we going to do, though?"

"There's nothing to do right now, Phil. Jane knew what she was getting herself into when she became a part of that movement. We can't solve the SOPA's problems. There will never be lasting peace between SOPA and the official United States government."

Just then, Michelle came storming through the front doors and yelled, "The feds just hit three of our warehouses, including the one on West Street where I was working this morning. They didn't knock, they just busted in with warrants. About twenty feds and some of the local coppers. They weren't interested in our coffee, though they did confiscate everything. I think we know what they were looking for."

Leo sighed, "This day just keeps getting better. Get back to work everyone."

Leo needed some time to think, but Michelle pulled him aside and said to him privately, "Give the shipment back. Hell, do you know how much money we lost today when they took all of our inventory? Plus, they obviously now know where at least three of our stash houses are located. What if they found the stolen shipment in our possession! We would be going away for a long time – maybe for life. The FBI Special Agent from the paper, Nathan Long, showed up at the raid today personally and treated me *very* roughly. I think his career hinges upon him retrieving this shipment, Leo, and he means business. This is getting serious."

"You think I don't know that, sis!? Look… what we lost today will be pittance next to what the shipment is worth to the government, but I agree we will give it back… eventually. However, it is bad business to negotiate from a position of weakness. We will have to regain leverage. Just last week, the FBI Director was the suspect in an assault case with a young lady over in New Havers. They did a good job of suppressing that story and with the help of the media, it was only discussed briefly for a couple days and there has been silence ever since. Let's track her down and get her to tell her side of the story, considering they likely paid her off."

Michelle nodded reluctantly, "Yes, sir."

Shortly after Michelle coordinated for the 'alleged' victim to get an interview from the National News Network (NNN) – the station was almost immediately contacted and ordered to retract the story. At the same time, Michelle called the number on Agent Long's business card that she received during the raid and arranged a lunch at a local restaurant for the Special Agent to meet with Leo.

Leo arrived at the steakhouse a short while later and Special Agent Long was already there with some of his team, who were clearly sitting at nearby tables for protection.

Leo walked in, alone and unarmed.

The hostess smiled, "Good afternoon, Mr. Stills."

Leo nodded and then joined the Special Agent at the table.

It was a beautiful place setting with a white tablecloth and candles lit in the middle of the freshly picked wreath centerpiece. The waitress came up to the table and offered them some menus.

Being a local and having been here many times, Leo waved her off and replied simply, "Two Prime Ribeyes cooked to 132 degrees. I will have a whiskey and the Agent, here, will have water - I assume - because he is on the clock. Thank you, ma'am."

The Special Agent didn't object, but instead just stared intently at Leo.

The two generals sat there completely quiet for several minutes with an odd tension in the room. After Leo's whiskey was brought out, he sipped that for another few minutes in silence before the steaks arrived.

After taking a bite, the Agent asked, "So, I was told you wanted to speak with me, perhaps regarding some stolen goods."

"What was stolen?" Leo asked coyly, as he enjoyed watching the Special Agent squirm in his seat.

Agent Long replied, "I'm not at liberty to say specifically, but something very important to our government and we will be as heavy handed as necessary to ensure its safe return."

Leo smiled, "How can I help you if I don't know what it is that we are talking about?"

The Special Agent began to object again, when Leo stated plainly, "We have your drones."

Agent Long's jaw dropped for only a moment. Caught off guard and unsure of what to say, he just pressed his lips together again. Leo calmly took a bite of his steak, sipped on his whiskey and then returned his gaze to the Special Agent – certain that his words had sunken in at this point.

Leo continued, "I assume you caught that young lady's interview on NNN last night. Your boss must not have been happy. The head of the FBI caught up in such an embarrassing scandal regarding quite a young victim on top of that. His wife couldn't have been too pleased either."

"Director Monroe is innocent. He just doesn't appreciate these lies being promulgated."

Leo came back quickly, "Do you know she wasn't the only victim? There were two even younger girls that we can introduce to the American public anytime we need."

"What do you want, Mr. Stills?"

"I don't appreciate how my employees were treated during the recent raids and the searches themselves are obviously problematic for me. We have no affiliation with SOPA or the militia. We are humble businessmen in this small-town Belmont neighborhood trying to thrive by helping the locals survive. My company poses no national security threat."

"*Company…*" the Special Agent scoffed before regaining his composure, "… anyways, understood."

Leo continued, "I hear you served overseas in Braxton for three years and made great progress in stifling their theft of our intellectual property and weaponized technology… like these drones, for example. That accomplishment single-handedly saved your controversial and, until then, somewhat disappointing career, did it not?"

"What do you want, Mr. Stills?" the Special Agent continued, losing patience.

"Very simple proposition for you, Agent Long. So, you should have no issues understanding my position," Leo said as he finished off his expensive steak, though the Special Agent's plate was hardly touched. "Leave my company and my family alone, and I will return the drones to you," Leo said with a shrug.

"You're nothing but a common criminal; a two-bit thug. Why would I allow you to continue your illegal activities when I already have so much of your operation mapped out?" the Special Agent shot back. "It makes me sick to sit at the same table with the likes of you."

Ignoring the disrespect as if he didn't hear the Special Agent's previous condescension at all, Leo quietly continued, "Illegal? What we do is legal, it's just not totally legal, if you know what I'm sayin'. Plus, if we continue to be inconvenienced, not only will we reveal the two other victims abused by FBI Director Monroe, but we will also send these drones first-class mail to the Braxton militia. That might undo the big landmark success you had there over the past few years, would it not?"

Choking down his repulsion, Agent Long agreed, "You have a deal."

Leo finished off his glass of whiskey, and smiled at the FBI Agent, "I knew you would be reasonable."

In no way out of kindness, the Special Agent procedurally began to pay for the meal, in accordance with policy guidelines when interviewing a witness.

Leo replied, "Let's not waste the taxpayers' money now, Agent. Plus, the bill has already taken care of – it's on my company. I hope you enjoy your time in our quaint town."

With that, Leo got up from the table, thanked the hostess on his way out, and headed back to Bravo Tower. After Leo had left, the Special Agent made a call.

When the other line picked up, he started, "April, it's not the militia that took the drones. The Stills' family is in possession of them, but we don't know where they are holding them. I need you to do whatever it takes to find out the location."

April began to object, "They are very secretive and incredibly dangerous, sir. Everyone around here fears them, especially Leo. It seems he…"

She was cut off by Agent Long, who was surprised at her conclusion. "Leo?" he asked.

"What about him?" she responded.

"We were under the impression that Roman or Michelle Stills was the head of the family. They are the oldest after all."

April responded, "They all have their notable qualities, but Leo is definitely the boss. Roman is ruthless. Eli is loyal to a fault and ambitious as hell. Michelle has tact – but Leo is the intellect, the final decision maker."

"We need you to get to know him. Gain his trust. Find me those drones."

"But, sir…"

"April, do this and you will get that corner office you've always wanted on the top floor. Either way, there is going to be no more discussion about it."

"Yes, sir."

Meanwhile, Leo asked Michelle to set up another meeting with Jane, who was the focus of Phil's romance and affection. The other day, Phil came to Michelle in confidence and told her that he and Jane were now pregnant.

Michelle met Jane in one of the backrooms on the lobby floor of Bravo Tower. They were talking next to a roaring fire, sitting in two burgundy leather chairs. When Leo walked up, Michelle promptly excused herself, not quite knowing what Leo was up to.

"Hello, Ms. Jane," Leo said greeting her.

The two had never been particularly cordial and Jane knew Leo was not terribly fond of her involvement in SOPA or the problems it caused for Phil and the rest of the family.

"Mr. Stills," she replied plainly, nodding her head.

"I hear congratulations are in order," Leo continued as he replaced Michelle in one of the leather chairs by the fire.

Jane was shocked. She didn't realize Phil told the rest of the family their big news, which, of course, he did not.

Jane wasn't sure what to say, so she said nothing.

Leo went on, "When is the little gift from God due to be born?"

She gathered herself a bit - knowing this to be a dangerous conversation, as all talks with Mr. Stills were – and said, "I'm seven weeks along."

"Are you wanting to keep it? In today's day and age, it's almost an expectation that women have an abortion so they can get back to work. Women Power and all that jazz."

Silence.

Leo said, "Let me cut to the chase. There is $1,000,000 in this suitcase. It's yours… to take care of the baby."

"But Phil said…" Jane began.

However, Leo continued on, speaking over her as if she wasn't even in the room, "… and to leave Belmont for good."

After only several heartbeats, Jane said, "You can't be serious," really asking a question more than making a statement.

"Your involvement in our family has always caused trouble because of your association with SOPA. The baby will only make things worse. Plus, Belmont is not a safe place for SOPA members anymore, especially pregnant ones. To make the decision easier, the family will also give you $200,000 each year to make sure you and the baby want for nothing. It's the least we could do."

At that, Jane's face changed. Without speaking a word, she stood up and grabbed the large duffle bag suitcase, which was almost too heavy for her to carry. Leo sighed in relief; happy the situation didn't have to get any more complicated.

Phil will just think she ran away, and we won't even have to explain. The circumstances were obviously too much for her to handle. He will be heartbroken, though. For the good of the family, sometimes tough decisions have to be made. People often don't understand what it takes to keep everything running. For the good of the family.

Enjoying the silence, Leo closed his eyes and leaned back in his plush chair, inhaling the aroma of fine cowhide. He loved when things worked as they should.

Life always seemed to work out for Leo in the end, even though his business wasn't always exactly lawful. Although he wasn't particularly devout and overtly religious, he did his best to speak what he thought to be true with the noble intention of taking care of his loved ones. He had what some might call faith, in that, after operating according to that truth, he accepted whatever result followed as if that is what should happen. He believed the best outcome was always the one that came after you do whatever you truly believe to be right. He gave up long ago trying to control the world. After all, it was hard enough for him to just govern himself.

I don't know why I'm so successful. I'm not a good person. I'm actually quite rotten at times. But I have hope. There is always hope - I guess.

His thoughts were interrupted by the roar of the fire crackling after a loud thud.

"Go to hell," she said indignantly.

The sound of her high heels speeding rapidly across the wood floor resounded deep into what some people might call their soul – though Leo wasn't sure he had one.

He waited for a couple minutes, until the silence returned, and he was alone again, before he opened his eyes. He poured himself a whiskey, leaned forward towards the fire to light his cigar and simply sat there watching the most expensive suitcase in the world burn, traded for something as simple as love.

Who would pay $27.50 for a movie ticket when you can watch a show like this?

<u>Story 7</u>

Bright and early the next morning, Leo was sitting in his office at Bravo Tower when he heard a knock on the door. He was the first one into the office that morning, so he got up and walked down the wobbly, wooden stairs.

Who would be here this early that doesn't already have a key?

Leo opened the creaky, wooden front door and to his surprise, found no one. It wasn't infrequent that the company got uninvited guests, but this was odd. As he looked around, he saw a note stabbed into the wooden floorboards of the front porch. He took out the knife and carried the note inside.

It didn't take long to read, as the note only said:

HB

Investigating further, he saw his name carved into the wooden handle of the knife.

Well, there is only so many ways to take that message.

He walked back to his office and placed the death threat on his old, worn-out desk.

Just another day in paradise, I guess.

As Leo stared at the knife and stoically pondered the meaning of life, Phil busted through the door.

Leo asked, "You don't know how to knock?!"

"YOU HAD NO RIGHT!" Phil screamed, while in the process of catapulting himself over the desk and tackling Leo.

"Phil! Stop!"

"No! You went too far this time. You don't always know what's best for everyone!"

Still tussling and punching, Leo finally got his enraged little brother into a headlock and waited a few seconds for him to calm down.

"Get off me! Get... off!"

They pushed back from each other, sitting on the creaky floorboards.

Panting, Leo tried to rationalize why he felt forced to do what he did, "Philly, what's the problem? She didn't take the money. Now you know she really loves you. Ha, she must really love you to turn down a retirement package like that."

He must literally feel like a million bucks right now. Haha, get it? Not the time for jokes…

Phil simply said, "I'm done," and walked out the door.

The family hasn't heard from him since, but a few days later they did receive congratulations from various townsfolk regarding the news of Phil and Jane's engagement.

Later on - Leo, Rome and Eli headed to the Coffee Spot to relax for the night. It was about 7:45 p.m., a cool night filled the air and a light breeze swept through the streets. As they walked down the cozy roads of Belmont, Leo looked around and actually saw the city he lived in for the first time in a long time.

Most of the time, I'm just walking through the streets to get somewhere else. We forget about the beauty that surrounds us constantly. On occasion, we see its splendor for what it really is — the way a child views something new for the first time. Even with all the turmoil, it is an amazing time in which we live. Just don't ask me to live on Mars. I'll go down with the Earthly ship before that happens. Ha… Captain Leo. Still, Mars has a booming real estate industry and we might be able to make some money there one day.

As Leo's mind wandered and the other two were engaged in a friendly but spirited argument, the three boys didn't notice the pack of men closing in behind them.

Just as strangers' raucous voices entered Leo's consciousness, three more men came out from the side alley in front of the Stills and stood directly blocking Leo's path. It wasn't often, especially in this neighborhood, that people would get in the Stills' way.

"You have my attention," the Stills boss said to the crowd that was now around him.

"Ms. Hansel would like to see you."

"I wonder why," was all Leo said.

The three brothers followed the mob down the wet sidewalk as the sun set on another beautiful night in Belmont. As they continued, Leo saw a white limousine parked alongside a fire lane.

Well, that's unsafe.

As they approached, the back window rolled down. Leo nodded to Rome and Eli, who took up positions between Leo and Hansel's henchmen. Leo looked around, then bent over and leaned on the window. As Leo was never one to speak first, especially when someone else called the meeting, he simply looked Ms. Hansel in the eyes and waited.

"Mr. Stills. I hope you are having as bad a day as I am."

How pleasant — ha, but not sure what else I expected. Wonder how much she knows about us fixing those auctions.

"The Harold Boys told me about my last few auctions being fixed," Ms. Hansel blurted out, looking for any telling reaction on Leo's face. Leo was silent and stone-faced, so she continued, "I'm sure you know nothing about that?"

Leo waited a second and finally responded, saying, "I don't know what you think I could know."

Hansel continued, "Funny. The HB's said it was you. They seemed certain."

"That doesn't surprise me. I'm not sure if you've heard about our recent beef with their crew."

I still haven't said a lie yet. Deceit is the same as lying. Stop being a girl scout.

"The whole town is aware of that, Mr. Stills."

"Call me, Leo."

"So, Mr. Stills, I lost a lot of money in the last few months because someone has been fixing my auctions. When the HB's told me that it was you, I looked into it a bit more and do you know what I noticed?"

Silence.

"I noticed that you made a rather large purchase at our New Year's Eve auction. Much larger than you normally transact."

Silence.

"A whopping 1,000 homes, I believe."

"1,238 – yes."

"Well, when I saw that, Mr. Stills, I must admit – I was certain it was you. So, I ordered your stash house on Rain Court be seized and be brought under the control of my company, which is happening as we speak. Are you saying I should give it back to you?"

She's not buying it.

"Keep it. That shop is my smallest one and the old building was falling apart. Consider it my initial contribution to our joint venture."

"Joint venture?" Hansel asked, somewhat intrigued. "Whatsoever could you be thinking?"

Her demeanor changed quickly, and she took on a much softer tone. This was not uncommon when Leo dealt with people. They liked him for some reason.

The Stills family was a relatively large player in Belmont, but they were not *the* big fish by any stretch. On the other hand, Hansel was one of the most influential people in Belmont, as well as a few other nearby cities. She wasn't as loved by the people in Belmont, not as connected to them – but powerful with people higher up and she managed a much bigger organization overall.

Happy not to have his proposal followed by the window rolling up in his face, Leo went on, "We can help each other. The information we've collected reflects that the HB's cost you over 14% of your profit from these cash real estate auctions. They mug your potential customers on the way in, making them less likely to come back and they steal the money that was going to be used to pay for the homes. Don't you also pay them 10% of gross profits for security services on top of that?"

Silence.

Leo continued, "We can put a stop to that. All we would ask is half the savings from the reduced HB theft itself, and we would secure your events for only 5% of profits. The HB's are nothing but a pest – insignificant, yet annoying. You and I together can be a force in this town."

Careful how close we get to Hansel. Shouldn't trust her as far as we can throw her designer handbag.

She reached her gloved hand out the window and Leo met hers with his own. He bent down and kissed her hand softly. With that, the deal was made.

Leo straightened up and nodded again to his brothers. As they continued the walk to their original destination, Leo peered back and watched the window of the limousine roll up. He saw the crowd of men getting into several SUV's that were also parked illegally. Seemingly unaware of the previous encounter that would have most people's hearts racing, Rome and Eli picked up their argument right where they left off.

The boys arrived at the Coffee Spot a short while later and Eli said, "I'll get us some whiskey."

Leo stopped him, saying, "I will get it. Finish your conversation with Rome."

So, the other two brothers headed to the family's back room and Leo walked up to the bar.

When April saw Leo approaching, she stopped helping another customer, saying to him, "Excuse me, I'll be right back."

As she walked up to Leo, she had a smile on from ear to ear. "Three shots of Tequila, right?"

"Of course," came the curt reply.

Contrary to her remark, she pulled a bottle of their finest whiskey off the shelf and handed Leo three stacked glasses.

Hmmm… we are on the same page. She just thinks she's funny. Glad I didn't have to fire her.

"It's on the house, Mr. Stills," April went on according to script, happy to do something nice for the mysterious and powerful man standing before her. Still not smiling, Leo put down more than enough money on the bar to pay for the bottle and give a generous tip.

She asked him, "I thought you didn't have to pay for your whiskey, sir?"

Leo simply said, "I don't.

He smiled, tipped his cap to the lady, took his bounty to the backroom and the boys didn't come out the rest of the night.

<u>Story 8</u>

After the Stills brothers left the Coffee Spot for the night around 1:30 in the morning, April was cleaning up around the bar with only a handful of patrons remaining. She heard two men in particular being noisy, talking about the Braxton militia's presence here in Belmont. It wasn't very common to hear that topic discussed aloud so freely, as the United States government didn't take kindly to foreign militia on American soil. As she wiped down the row of tables by the far window, she heard these two men, clearly drunk, slurring Leo's name.

"Man, Stills gots it coming. I hear that boy done got his hands full with that government shipment. My guy says, 100% Stills took that container from down off the pier."

"Dude, no way. He wouldn't be breathin'. How you know that? Who told you that?"

"Look, I'm telling you, 100%… my source is reliable. Plus, even if it ain't true, all we gotta do is put a little pressure on Stills and he'll pay us just to go away. Bad publicity and all."

At this point, April had noticeably stopped wiping the tables and was keenly listening.

"Hey, Cutie!" one of the militia men shouted in April's direction causing her to jump out of her skin in surprise. "Another pitcher…" *hiccup* "…over here."

April disgustedly replied, "Last call was over an hour ago. Plus, it looks like you've had enough anyway."

Astonished at her brazenness, the militiaman replied, "What did you just say to me, little girl? You better watch…"

"Easy, big fella," said his comrade, chugging the rest of his own glass. "Let's head out."

"Hmmph," was all the first guy replied.

Both men got up, threw some bills and loose change onto the table and walked out the front door. A short while later, April closed up the Coffee Spot and locked the front door as the bottom of her long dress rested in a puddle.

"Oh, no!" she exclaimed, feeling the cold moisture against her warm ankle. "My favorite dress…" she muttered to herself as she began walking home.

She was shaking the water off her dress when she felt someone's presence behind her, and then let out a sharp gasp when she heard a muffled voice say, "Hey, Cutie…"

She instantly whirled around, only to be dragged into the nearby alley, which was concealed in the shadows, hardly lit by the moon that was hidden behind the clouds.

WHACK! Came the heavy hand of the drunk Braxton militiaman, his punch to her chin almost knocking her unconscious. She felt the icy rain hitting her cheeks, as he pulled her by the hair into a dark spot, midway down the backstreet.

She could hardly scream because of the yanking and pulling, and at the same time struggled not to pass out from the extreme pain. The man thrust her against the brick wall, grabbed the bottom of her dress and jerked it up. As he clumsily loosened his belt, he held the bottom of her flowery blue dress high in the air exposing her legs.

April gathered her strength and made the all-or-nothing decision to stop struggling for just a moment in an effort to wiggle free. She stopped fighting, lunged sideways and then hit the ground like a rock, letting out a loud moan. Her attacker fell forward at the unexpected cessation in resistance and hit his head against the jagged bricks; if only that was enough time for her to get back up and run away.

He turned back to finish the job, blood now leaking from above his left eye and then… bang!

In his drunken stupor, he didn't notice her thigh-high lace garter, which held a small, government-issued pistol. His eyes opened wide, shocked and after what seemed like an eternity to April, he fell like a sack of sweet potatoes to the cold, hard pavement.

Panting, April looked at the gun, then at the body of the man now wearing his pants at his ankles.

"Oh, my God, please help me," she cried out in breaths.

She saw a police officer's shield on the man's belt.

"I've got to get out of here," she said as she slowly made her way to the end of the alley in her soaking wet dress.

She did her best to pull her tattered sweater back up to cover her cold shoulders. When she got back to the entrance of the alley, she quickly glanced around both ways and, seeing no one, left the area in a hurry… not quite sure yet of her final destination.

Knock. Knock. Knock. Knock. Knock. Knock.

Though he was happy to awaken from his latest nightmare, Leo struggled to open his eyes.

Who in the hell is stupid enough to knock on my door like that in the middle of the night? If I just wait long enough, they'll go away. Someone could need my help though. I can help them in the morning. Get up, lazy bum!

Bang. Bang. Bang. Bang!

The quiet knocking quickly turned to panicked thumping.

"I'm up. I'm up," Leo complained to himself, putting on his robe and slippers before he went down the stairs to see what all the commotion was about.

He opened the door and physically had to stop his jaw from dropping in confusion.

"I don't know why I came to you… I just didn't know where else to go," April cried.

"Come in," he ordered.

She walked through the doorway as Leo took a step out on the porch, looking around. He closed the door and turned to find her standing there in a wet dress, completely covered in dirt.

Her ripped clothes weren't the only clue. She stood there, staring off into the distance, obviously reliving something traumatic somewhere else in her mind.

"This way," Leo continued, softer than his normal demeanor.

As his hand touched the small of her back in an attempt to guide or maybe comfort her, she gasped loudly and pulled away. He stepped back to give her some space and he walked in front of her to his library.

He motioned for her to sit in one of the old, leather chairs and she complied. He tossed her a blanket and started a roaring fire. He poured two glasses of whiskey, handed her one and sat down in the adjacent chair.

"What happened to you," Leo inquired after a moment or two.

"I'm sorry for coming here. I didn't know where else to go," was all she was able to say.

He let the whiskey kick in and the fire begin to dry her wet dress before asking again.

Staring into space, playing it back in her mind, she recounted the awful tale, "I was walking home from work at the shop and something awful happened."

Trying to lighten the mood, Leo half joked, "A pretty girl like you really shouldn't be walking home alone so late at night."

"This man hit me, dragged me into an alley and tried to force himself on me. I was barely able to get away before he was successful."

"Who was it? I will take care of it," Leo replied, puffing up a bit and now fully appreciating her disheveled state for the first time since she arrived.

"You can't help me."

Almost chuckling at the thought, Leo said, "Do you know who I am? This doesn't get to happen in my city. I take care of people here and they take care of me. Just tell me who it was and…"

"You can't help me…" she said again, and before Leo got too frustrated, she quickly continued, "… because I shot him. He's dead."

"Hmm." Leo thought for a moment, not sure why he was so relieved that nothing more happened to her.

Surprised at his lack of reaction to that news and touched at his offer to rescue her… April sat silently and took small sips from her glass waiting for him to lead the conversation forward. She didn't know what to make of Leo at this point. At first, she thought he was a no-good thug. Now, it seemed like there might be a miniscule amount of feelings underneath that incredibly hard exterior after all.

Leo spoke next, "You are now fired from the Coffee Spot, effective immediately."

Not really thinking, April instinctively replied, "You can't fire me. You're not the boss."

"I don't *technically* own it, you're right – but I can fire you. Either way, you quit then. Call it what you want."

No longer arguing that point and appreciating his chivalrous intentions, she asked, "What about the dead body? He's just lying there in the alley bleeding."

"As scum should be," was all Leo had to say about that.

"Perhaps, but won't the police trace it back to me. It got very physical. I lost pieces of clothing and my blood has to be all over the bricks from being dragged and hit. Plus, he was a copper and it was right outside my workplace."

She decided to leave out the part that he was also a member of the Braxton militia faction here in Belmont.

"I have friends in blue places… this case will not see the light of day." Leo continued, "You will sleep here tonight…" As he said this, he saw her eyebrows skeptically rising, and he continued, "… I will make the guest bed for you. Tomorrow, you will start your new job."

"Thank you," she said.

Exhausted, she forgot to ask what her new job was. She just stared into his green eyes, seeing the kindness and warmth that lay millimeters beneath the stone exterior. Likewise, he couldn't help but admire her angelic features shimmering amidst the flames of the crackling fire.

After they finished their whiskey together in silence, he walked her to the guest suite. When they arrived at the door, they stood close and looked at each other.

Aren't you going to invite me in? Ha, classic movie line. Shouldn't be joking about things right now. Focus.

Overwhelmed with emotion, April leaned towards him, not knowing why exactly. Leo resisted the temptation, stepped back, opened the door and said, "Good night, Ms. April. Let me know if you need anything."

What are you doing, man? What about Sera? What about Sera? Sera has been gone a long time. She's not coming back. It's time to move on. Besides, even when Sera was here, she was only your girlfriend. You never even got married. Now, she moved away and stole your kid from you. You haven't heard from her in years. You don't owe her anything. There is still hope.

Leo departed and made his way back to his own room, shaking the racings thoughts out of his clouded head. He had no nightmares that night.

Bright and early the next morning, Leo woke up to the smell of bacon. He didn't often cook at home. In fact, he didn't even really know where the pans were. Michelle often brought food over for him when he wasn't eating out at restaurants. He walked downstairs, surprised to see April there wearing one of his shirts, which was so big it looked like a dress on her.

I forgot she spent the night. Sera always did the cooking. Forget about Sera!

"Goooood morning! I hope you don't mind. My dress was terribly dirty, and my sweater was ripped. Would you like some bacon and eggs?" April asked, smiling up at Leo.

"Sure. Do we have orange juice?" He asked as he sat down at the head of his kitchen table.

She poured him a glass of orange juice and brought over a big plate of bacon with a side of eggs.

"Sure. You're welcome," she said somewhat stiffly, a little offended at his lack of manners.

He was still sleepy, but noticing her scowl, he quickly replied, "Thank you, thank you. I'm not used to having visitors. Good morning."

Now content with his domesticated compliance, she continued, "Thank you for last night. You never told me what my new job was."

"Just call me, boss," Leo said without skipping a beat.

"Boss?" she asked, not necessarily complaining, while she handed him the morning paper.

"I have been needing a personal assistant for a while now. You will help me with anything and everything. That is, if you want the job."

He continued eating while he began reading the newspaper, still not seeing any reason to look up at her. She was excited by the idea. Then she remembered that it will also be a great opportunity to get more information on the location of the drones. Right.

"So," she asked. "What's first?"

"Go get ready for the day. There is a shower in the guestroom bathroom. I'll have a new dress sent here by the time you get out. We have a trade show to get to in the next couple hours, so don't be too long. We have to make one stop along the way at the docks to let my friends use my boat for the afternoon. Please call the security booth at the pier there and let them know to expect us later this morning."

April acquiesced and Leo just couldn't help himself glancing at her as his oversized shirt wafted around her figure ever so slightly while she walked away. When April got out of the shower, she saw on the bed a hairbrush, various perfumes, and six of the same exact dress in different sizes. Flattered that most of them were too small, she put on the one that fit best.

After she brushed her hair and finished getting ready as quickly as she could in a home not-her-own, she walked out to see Leo sitting in a chair quietly by the front door, doing nothing but waiting.

"Finally," he said somewhat jokingly, and they went out together.

They got to the docks and Leo said, "Wait here. I won't be long."

April watched Leo go meet up with three men and you could see police officer shields on their belts and holsters on their waists. They talked briefly. Leo pointed at their truck and then at his boat. After they shook hands, he came back to the car and Leo and April were off to the show. The two of them arrived for the event located at a huge warehouse in Luxentine, just a few miles outside Belmont. They began to look around and familiarize themselves with the environment. As they perused the various selections and brands, they were approached by Ms. Hansel, who was accompanied by several men in black suits.

Hansel introduced herself to April, "I don't believe we've had the pleasure of being introduced, sweetheart," she said, peering over at Leo in a fun, teasing way.

Leo responded, "This is my assistant, April. April, the lovely Ms. Hansel."

The two females smiled and nodded at each other according to common social etiquette.

Leo went on, "Ms. Hansel, appreciate us getting the chance to meet you here today."

Almost as if she didn't hear, Ms. Hansel replied, "You look just dashing, Mr. Stills. It is my pleasure indeed. I'm interested in hearing what you have to say."

Leo said, "Show me what you got."

"This way, please," she said, turning and smiling back at Leo.

Given her power and status in these parts, Ms. Hansel definitely had no need to use such politeness. She wasn't really asking, even when she said 'please.' Hansel led Leo to a large display booth in the corner of the warehouse, the biggest booth on site. April followed quietly behind the pair.

"Go ahead and look around," Hansel said, inviting Leo to take stock of the inventory she was displaying for him.

Hope she means the coffee.

"It's very nice," Leo said, examining the weights and packaging quality. "I can't help but notice more than half of these have an HB supply label. That's the Harold Boys, yes? Do you currently use them as a primary distribution source?"

I already know she buys from them. Let's see how honest she is. If even half truthful, we may be able to get what we came here for, after all. Just don't rush it.

She said, "We do. What of it?"

Leo went on, not wanting to show too much of his hand too soon, "I'd love for the Stills Corporation to help you with that, instead."

"We are happy with their service so far. What is in it for me?" she asked nonchalantly, pretending to be studying some of her products.

She is ready. Tell her what they are doing to her coffee.

"I'm quite sure you are paying for a higher-grade quality than you are actually getting. Do you think the HB's dishonesty stops at their theft and assault incidents at your real estate auctions?"

Silence.

He said, "Let's just see. Don't take my word for it. Hand me one of your packages."

Hansel gave Leo one from the top of the nearest pile and he quickly cut it open. He smashed a couple raw beans up into a powder on the table and put them into a vial containing a clear liquid. Instantly, the liquid turned a very, very light shade of green.

"Uh-huh," Leo said, "Just what I thought."

"What?"

"Easy. The darker the green, the more potent the bean. It is likely the HB's repackaged their low-quality product in this high-quality wrapping in an effort to get one over on you. Here, also take note of the beans' aroma," Leo invited.

While she bent over to smell the freshly crushed beans that the Harold Boys had been providing, Leo pulled out a package of his own product. He took out some beans and crushed them on the table a foot or so away from the first pile. After inhaling the smell of her product, Hansel was still pleased with the beans' quality.

"Now, try mine," Leo invited, holding his coffee out for her.

"Wow, the aroma is totally different," she admitted. "What you have to offer is much more intense and, quite frankly, appealing… definitely something I'd like to wake up with in the morning."

Hope she means the coffee. Don't rush your offer yet.

Pushing slightly further, Leo continued, "Besides getting and ensuring you the highest available quality merchandise on the market, I will do it for 5% less than what you were paying the HB's in exchange for this faux product. Higher quality, less cost."

As he was saying this, he put some of his beans in a different vial and the color instantly turned to a very dark, forest green.

"I'm impressed. My real estate auctions *have* been running smoothly since we switched from the HB's service to your company. It seems to only make sense that we further that integration. I'd love to get closer with your business."

Uhhh. This chick talks crazy.

Hansel continued, "What is in it for you though, besides the pleasure of my company and a few extra sales dollars?"

Leo coyly replied, "Now that you mention it, there is one thing you could do for me."

"Yessss?" she asked.

Hit her with it. She's ready.

"Well… a legal license to grow and distribute coffee beans and coffee products. If you can make that happen for me," Leo said smartly, playing at her pride, "Win-Win," he finished.

She obviously could make that happen. After we hinted that she might not be able to obtain a license though, her pride will probably make her more inclined to prove it.

Hansel pondered, "Well, I suppose it's hard to argue with you there. You are clearly just the expert I need for my business and as long as you intend to stay out of my way, I don't see any harm in legitimizing your operations as well. I will do what I can, but I don't foresee any problems. You will likely have it by the end of today."

She leaned forward, seemingly as if to kiss Leo goodbye on the cheek – to which, Leo stuck out his hand and shook hers softly.

"Until then," Leo said, backing away slowly and checking to make sure April was still following.

Speaking for the first time, April asked, "What's next, boss?"

Hmmm, I like when she says that.

"I've got to get to my day job. You head home and get changed or freshen up or something. Whatever you need. I know you haven't been home in a day or so at this point. Then, head into the family office and call me the minute the official state license arrives as Ms. Hansel promised. I'm excited for that news. That should take a lot of heat off our backs and reduce the number of bribes we need to pay the coppers."

"Yes, sir."

Leo headed to the train station to go into work. He was not terribly excited about it. He'd been looking for the opportunity to quit for a long time and getting this legal coffee license might just be the kicker that makes the dream possible.

There is still a long way to go before I can stop working as an employee. Doesn't happen overnight. Need to come up with a plan to slowly but surely build up a more stable base in the legal coffee industry before we can stop the day job. First things first when we do get that license, though - we need to select a prime spot for our first legal location.

Leo woke up from his wandering daydreams when he opened the door to the lobby of his corporate office.

He passed by Robert at the front counter and greeted him with a smile, "Beautiful day, eh, Robert?"

Happy to be engaged by someone during his otherwise mostly monotonous day staring at monitors, Robert replied, "It sure is, Leo."

The people here didn't know Leo's background, or fear him like the Belmont townsfolk who were living a couple hours away had grown to do. The people of Belmont knew the real Mr. Stills.

It is tough living a lie.

Leo continued on to the golden elevators, admiring one of the new art pieces hanging on the wall. Well, admiring might be the wrong word. After all, it was just a painting of a wooden box in an empty room.

Nothing else? Just a box sitting on the floor. 'Artists' these days… jeeze. My son could paint that picture. New rule: it doesn't count as art if my kid could do it.

"What an amazing and creatively genius work, isn't it?" a stranger asked Leo as the two waited for the elevator to arrive at the lobby floor.

Breathtaking. Hahahaha

"It sure is," Leo replied.

Come on, elevator, come on. Hurry up. Get here now please!

Just as that thought crossed his mind, the elevator arrived - none too soon for Leo, who was pleased when this stranger pressed the button for the 3rd floor. Leo continued riding the elevator up to his office's floor, got out and headed to his cubicle. He was the first one of his cubemates in today, which always pleased him. He wasn't really a talkative person.

Leo logged onto his computer and checked his calendar for the day.

Ohhhh, noooooooooooooooooooo. Not this. I feel like we just did one of those.

Once again, it was time for his unconscious bias training – mandatory for all people of his particular background, and only his. Everyone else just sat and watched – at least those coworkers who actually wanted to go and witness these events. Their attendance was optional and only the best of the best people with the topnotch character enjoyed sitting there watching people like Leo squirm.

"Damn it," Leo muttered, as he got up and made his way to the large conference room where the calendar indicated today's meeting would be held.

Coincidentally, this session had the same leader that made Leo go first last time.

He must have requested my session. There are tons of leaders. The chances of him getting my session twice in a row is miniscule.

Confirming his fear, the leader, who wasn't fond of Leo after the last teeth-pulling session, greeted him by name, "Well, Mr. Leo – welcome! So glad you chose to make time for this educational session today."

Is that what they really think this is, education?

"Uh, huh," Leo said, not breaking stride, heading for the back corner.

He's not going to let you off the hook today. A tyrant loves when they feel resistance – they will keep pushing that point further and further… actually hoping to break you. Stay strong. If you speak the truth, what comes will be what's best.

"I know, I know," Leo mumbled to himself.

The leader of the session began, "Welcome everyone. Great to have you all here today. Reminder: my name is Greg."

Wonder how much someone actually pays him to do this job. What a joke.

Greg continued, "Today, we are going to start in small groups. The victims and the oppressed, you know who you are. I want you to find one of the privileged few, one of the oppressors - and we all know *they* know who *they* are – and just form a circle around them. Nice. All right. Good. Keep it up. Who doesn't have a privileged oppressor? Over here, Cindy – go over there. Great. Great. I think we are ready. All right, privileged people, you know the drill, share what you've come up with since last session… stories of how you are benefited and how you've personally witnessed discrimination. This is real people! After thirty minutes of this, we are going to take a short break and then our favorite speaker from last time is going to come up again to share with the whole class how he's become less of an oppressor since our last session. Leo, thank you in advance."

What!! Me? Is he serious? No way. I'm not doing it again. There are thirty other people here that could do it. Screw this guy. If I don't do it, though, it's going to go on my record. I would never get another promotion. This is bull. I can't believe this.

Leo continued stressing about it silently, as he tried to convince himself to sell his soul to the tyrannical devil that currently controlled the ideology of the U.S. Government.

As discussed, after the initial session, they took a break and Leo went to the bathroom to splash water on his face.

Let's just get through it. All we have to do is say what they want to hear.

After waiting as long as he could, trying to calm down – he exited the bathroom, preparing himself to face the mob of judgement that awaited him back in the conference room.

At that moment, he felt his phone vibrate and saw his family's office number coming through.

"Hello?" he answered without masking his irritation.

A female's voice came through the other end, "Sir, April here. It arrived."

"What are you talking about?"

She replied, "Sorry. The license promised by Ms. Hansel was just hand delivered via courier, signed by the director of the state board himself. Check your picture messages. They say this license normally takes over two years to get fully approved and issued. How was Ms. Hansel able to get one for us in a matter of hours?"

"Thank you," Leo said.

He hung up and continued on towards the conference center.

He walked back in the room and the schmuck-of-a-leader said, "Leo, great! Are you ready?"

Leo nodded and went straight to the front of the room. He pulled out the notes of all the evil things he had done to be an oppressor and some other times when he stuck up for the oppressed as payment for his privilege.

He began reading, "To all of my fellow co-workers: I am sorry for my privilege of not going bald like 90% of Americans have since our atmosphere has been polluted and destroyed over time. I recognize that I don't have to work as hard as you to still get the same or even more benefit than you. You are a victim and I am not…"

Deeeep breath. He was sweating now and felt like he might vomit any second.

Something about this doesn't agree with my soul. This isn't right. We are all victims of life. We all have something we are suffering through. Amazing that so many 'victims' of this oppressive society forget how harsh the real world is when you don't have a community on which to rely. Let's pretend we take away the structures provided to all Americans by our government and various social systems. Let's just pretend there is no oppressive structure – no structure at all. What are you left with? Without this cooperative structure that we created to better work together, we would all be left to fend for ourselves in the wild, like our ancestors. Men would hunt, women would take care of the caves. Our new system, this supposedly oppressive hierarchy, is what allows us to work together as best as we possibly can. It's not perfect by any stretch of the imagination, certainly – and some people definitely have it worse than others – but, without us doing our best to work together, we would all be fighting Mother Nature alone and that would be downright brutal for all of us.

Leo paused and pulled out his phone. He checked his picture message from April, staring at the freshly printed and signed license.

"You know what, I can't do this. This is crazy. Do you guys understand what's going on here. This is exactly the type of life the King was trying to avoid. Yet, once again, we've let the pendulum swing too far the other way, from one form of unjust discrimination to another. This is not a moral system and I can't take it anymore. If I continue with this charade, this lie – then I've abdicated my duty to the community and the broader society as a whole, because the integrity of the society rests on the character of the individual. Societies crumble not because societies sin, but due to the conglomeration of a society of individual sinners. I can no longer participate in this corruption of the state, which stems from the dishonesty of the individual and ends with the corruption of the world. As individuals allow such pathology to spread when they *know* it to be corrupt and immoral, that is precisely how societies become corrupt and immoral – one sin at a time, from one individual at a time. Sure, our society will continue floating along for a short while, until we finally realize that we've eroded the very foundation upon which we once so comfortably rested our laurels. Then, we will fall off the self-created cliff into the dark ages and lose our place in the world to a country that better recognizes the divinity and worth of the individual. I can no longer allow these cretans to lord over me because I don't have the backbone to stand up for my principles. That makes me a slave to your ideologies. You can't force your corrupt opinions on me anymore and I can no longer say what I know to be a lie. I accept what consequences come from speaking what I believe to be true. We are all victims, but we are victims of life. Life is hard and we all suffer together. The point is for us to work together… together, to form a better tomorrow out of the endless potential contained within the future that we confront constantly. But you know what else too often goes unsaid these days? We are all beneficiaries as well – of such a great system of laws and amazing fellow citizens and neighbors. Anyone living in America today is blessed when compared to most of human existence. A lower-class family today lives better than a king did 200 years ago because we worked together over time. If I allow myself to continue to be a slave, that by itself creates tyrants – and tyrants keep pushing and pushing and pushing, until you push back. That's what a tyrant is – it can't help itself. Its nature is to keep pushing along all fronts until it hits a wall of morality and integrity. I'm no angel, but I'm also not even close to the devil you want me to describe myself as. You all, who sit here, self-righteously judging others, can go to hell. This company can go to hell, if it isn't already there."

And with that mic-drop, Leo walked out of the now-silent conference room. He headed straight for his desk, grabbed the few personal mementos he kept there and walked to the elevator with a small box.

On the way out of the lobby, he dug in his pocket and handed Robert $7.50.

Surprised, Robert asked, "What's this for, Leo?"

"I owe you," was all Leo replied.

He kept walking right out the front door and never looked back. He headed toward the train station, completely content with simply feeling the cool, refreshing rain drops trickle on his face.

Whoa. What a blur. I'm not sure what came over me. It's like I was possessed. This is the same thing that happened to that guy on the news the other day. Before he had a chance to be found innocent or guilty by the courts after receiving due process – he was instantly condemned by the court of public opinion within a matter of hours on social media, without even getting to tell his side of the story. Screw it, though. This country is corrupt – and when they play dirty, we play even dirtier. Due process is dead. People are crazy. Why should I to continue to placate people that continuously spit in my face and hate me, while at the same time they ask me for something out of my pocket. What's the point? It's no use. If this is good, I'm done trying to be good. Whatever this is, it just isn't worth it.

When Leo arrived back at Bravo Tower, he filled in Rome and Eli, saying, "We are going to double down now on coffee. We can use the legal license as a shield; a cover to hide our other illegitimate ways. Now, we can funnel our illegal income through that legal entity."

Leo's rant was interrupted when Sammy burst through the front door out of breath and yelling, "Guys! The Harold Boy's hit our warehouse on Nexxum Ave. They took everything." Sammy paused, awaiting orders from Leo. "Did you hear me?! Should I get the boys ready to respond?"

Leo ordered his ambitious baby brother, "Sammy, calm down. We will handle this. What were you doing down there anyway? Get back to work sorting this year's files. Thank you for letting us know. Rome, Eli – the HB's are retaliating from all their lost business. April, bring me the license. Guys, this is what we've been waiting for. This license makes our operations legal and it crippled the HB's even further because it now put us in a position to replace them as Hansel's coffee bean supplier. This is our chance. Let me figure out how we will respond to the HB's disturbance. Nobody do anything for now."

His crew nodded in agreement, extremely surprised and pleased at Leo's ability to obtain a legal coffee license.

Eli came up to Leo, saying, "Hey, bro. Can I have a minute?"

"Sure, what's going on Elijah?"

"Ever since my wife died last year, I haven't been able to keep up. I've been getting deeper and deeper in a whole with my kids and with work. I can't maintain as it is. I don't know what to do."

"I'm always here for you," Leo reassured him. "I'll figure something out."

A few days later, Leo called Eli into his office and a pretty, young girl was sitting across from Leo's desk.

"Sit down, Eli," Leo invited. "Eli, this is Justine Harold."

Eli interrupted, "Harold, as in... the Harold Boys?"

Leo continued, "Yes, she is Jackson's sister. Look, she's been struggling to maintain a job lately, ever since she lost her family in the plane accident. She knows how to be a mother…"

"Whoa! Leo… all due respect, you can't marry me off. This is 2048! Arranged marriages don't exist. I can't…"

"Eli! You nutjob. She's not here to become your wife. She needs work nannying. You need a caretaker for your children, and both the Stills and the HB's need to come to some sort of peace treaty. The continuous conflict is bad for business. No one expects anyone to get married – but, hey, you're both single… nothing's off limits. Heh, Heh. No? Not funny? Anyway - so, what do you say, Eli? She's already agreed, and I've worked it out with their boss. We need this."

We need this more than ever if we are going to knock off Hansel. Hansel could crush either us or the HB's separately, so I'm glad Jackson Harold's father agreed to work together to take down Hansel whenever the opportunity presents itself.

Eli looked at Justine and said, "Uhhhh, nice to meet you. Sorry, I'm just a little caught off guard. Hmmm. Well, why don't you come with me and I'll show you around?"

Justine stood up from her chair, curtsied to Leo, and walked out with Eli who was saying, "I guess we can start by meeting the kids. Then I can show you around the house. There is a room for you to sleep there where you can have your privacy."

Leo leaned back in his chair as the two lovebirds trailed off down the stairs.

What a crazy life. Finally, though – the company is growing in numbers, strength and resources. We have less enemies and more power than ever. We can't really trust any of our new allies though, especially if they turn out to be half as dangerous as me.

As he sat there contemplating the surrealness of life, he got a call from a blocked number.

"Hello?" he answered.

There was a pause on the other end of the line, then a male voice said defeatedly, "Leo? Is that you? It's good to hear you, bro."

Surprised, Leo shot up in his chair asking, "Philly?! How are you? Is everything okay? You've been missed around here."

News of Phil and Jane's marriage had found its way back to Leo. He wasn't thrilled to say the least, but he did miss his brother and hadn't heard from him in quite a while.

Phil went on, "Well, we didn't tell you guys everything, but when Jane was pregnant..."

Leo cut him off, "*Was* pregnant?"

Phil explained, "She just gave birth yesterday at the Northolk Hospital. Fifteen minutes after our baby boy was born, they arrested her. She spent the night handcuffed to the bed, Lee. They are planning to take her away as soon as tomorrow. I wanted to tell you, I'm taking my son and leaving. I can't do this anymore. It's all too much. My son deserves better. I hope you understand."

"Phil, is that really necessary? Why don't you come in and we can talk about it? That's what family is for…"

Phil simply repeated, "I just wanted to tell you so you wouldn't worry."

Before Leo could finish his sentence, "But Philly, I *am* worrie…" a click was all Leo heard and the line went dead.

Leo sat back for a moment before standing up, walking down the stairs of the family office, locking the doors and heading home. When he got there, he was plagued by another terrible dream.

One of his nighttime movies popped on in his dormant mind sometime during the quiet night, where he found himself walking along the street with the rain trickling from overhead. It was damp, cold and empty. Not empty in the sense that there were no people around, because there were plenty – but it felt empty, nonetheless. People walked by, though he never really paid attention to their faces. Not sure where he was or where he was going, Leo walked on and on, alone. Unsure why, he felt someone's eyes burning a hole in the back of his head. He turned around and saw two guys walking behind him. They were engaged with each other in a lively conversation. Nothing special about them and Leo didn't think much of it at first. After all, the streets were fairly crowded with townsfolk. As Leo walked, it seemed like there was a lot of people sitting around carousing, loitering – like one of those parties or raves you might see on TV, depraved of morality… a simple and total enjoyment of the pleasure derived from the flesh. Nothing particularly sinister, but a feeling of Godlessness pervaded the scene. It was late at night, so the lack of children or families present was not too weird but still disconcerting. Leo kept on, observing everything as he went. He noticed his shoe was untied, so he knelt on the cold sidewalk to retie the laces. He could feel his knee getting wet as the water soaked through his jeans. He got back up and continued to his destination, wherever that was. He still wasn't sure what journey his subconscious was taking him on tonight. However, he realized that the two men who were once following relatively close behind, didn't pass by him… even though Leo stopped for quite a while to retie his shoelaces. They must have stopped too for some reason. The thought just rubbed Leo the wrong way. When he glanced around and looked at them this time, they were staring directly back at him. The two men had a seemingly creepy smile on, but that could just be Leo's jitters from walking around the cold streets alone late at night. Leo kept on, minding his own business and crisscrossing the street every now and again to avoid the attention of the endless string of various partygoing groups sitting on every fifth doorstep. He did not see any benefit to engaging with any of them. At this point, he had been walking for what felt like fifteen minutes and had traveled down quite a few blocks. He made several more turns and was now heading down a steep hill. Turning around, the two gentlemen were still behind him. Leo muttered, "No way they would still be behind me after so long, unless they are going to the same place as me… and I don't even know where I'm going!" Leo's thoughts confused him more, but something just felt wrong. So, he jogged a bit, a kind of very fast walk with a spring in his step, not wanting to necessarily draw attention to himself by committing to a full sprint. Leo got a ways down the hill and rounded a bend that circumscribed a graveyard, which also contained people drinking and having too good of a time for that particular venue. Leo turned around and, to his relief, couldn't see the two men anymore; but he could hear them off in the distance. When he turned back around to continue walking, Rome was suddenly next to him. "Hey, bro" Rome said, not noticing anything abnormal from his perspective. "Rome? What's going on." Rome didn't say anything, and they just walked for a little bit, until Leo saw the two guys coming his way again from the top of the hill. All the sudden, Rome yelled, "RUN!" Leo and Rome ran and ran, but the two guys were always close behind them. Leo and Rome cornered themselves in an alley that was blocked by a fence which had to be standing over twelve feet high. Without hesitation, Leo put his hands out to help Rome over the fence. Rome put his foot on Leo's hands and jumped at the same time that Leo pushed him up. Easily, Rome grabbed the top of the fence, hopped over and was gone from sight. As Leo got some running room, planning to jump up and climb over the fence on his own, he noticed he was holding several random items. All the sudden, Leo saw himself holding a stack of $20 bills in one hand and a can of soda in the other. The men were quickly gaining on Leo at this point, now sprinting at full speed towards him. Frantically, Leo tried to put the money and the pop can in his jean pockets, but no matter how much he pushed, they wouldn't fit in. He kept trying harder and harder to shove the items into his pockets, while glancing back and forth – watching the two men get closer and closer. After a few seconds of trying, he gave up and attempted to climb the fence while maintaining his grip on the items that would certainly be the cause of his downfall. He jumped and jumped, gripping the steel bars, trying to climb with what little leverage he could muster while his hands were full, when all the sudden he finally felt the two men slam into him at full speed and begin to drag him off the fence.

"Jesus, no!" Leo screamed, covered in sweat, as he awoke from that little slice of hell.

Why didn't I drop that stuff so I could get over the fence and save myself… let go of the part in order to save the whole. What are these dreams supposed to even mean? Wow. I guess this day is going to start a little earlier than usual.

He went downstairs, started a fire and poured himself a whiskey while he watched the wood burn.

<u>Story 9</u>

As the sun rose in the bustling town of Belmont, Leo and Rome were on their way to breakfast at the Coffee Spot where they had a meeting scheduled with their friends in blue. When they arrived, the two friendly coppers were already seated and chatting over coffee.

As they saw Leo walk in, they stood up and said, "Morning, Mr. Stills."

Leo nodded back in reply and motioned for Rome to sit down as he took his own seat.

The conversation started out with friendly discussions of recent news and various sports games. These fellows shared an avid interest in professional basketball. They were arguing about why their home team lost the game yesterday on a last-second shot when Leo couldn't help but overhear two loudmouths talking about the murder of a fellow Braxton militia member that occurred the other day in the alley just outside.

Supposedly only April and I know about that. This kind of talk can't continue.

Leo interrupted the informal basketball conversation with a quiet cough. He looked intently at the two coppers, saying nothing, and simply motioned at the militia men. The officers understood, immediately got up and arrested the two men on the spot.

"What did we do?" they argued while resisting the arrest.

The cops just dragged them out, saying, "We'll discuss it down at the station."

No, they won't. Those boys won't see the light of day again. My friends needed a few more collars this month anyway. I wonder what they will do to them exactly. Ehhh, not my problem.

Leo and Rome finished up what turned out to be a very pleasant breakfast. They headed back to the family company's place of business and each went to their respective offices within Bravo Tower.

Leo called April in and said, "Shut the door."

Without question, she obeyed and proceeded to sit down across from Leo.

He continued, "Two militiamen were at the Coffee Spot this morning asking about the murder of one of their partners."

As soon as Leo said the word 'militia' – April subconsciously rose from her seat. By the time he finished his sentence, she was basically hovering over him, soaking in every word. She has had nightmares of that incident ever since and is constantly tormented by anxiety while awake.

Frantically, she began to ask, "But…"

Leo talked over her, saying, "Don't worry about it. I took care of them too. You are safe. I won't let anything happen to you."

At that, she leaned over without thinking and hugged him, which Leo didn't exactly not enjoy.

It's been so long since I've felt a woman's touch. I miss Sera. It's time to get over Sera, dude. She's not coming back. How long are you going to torture yourself? Move on. April is wonderful and she seems to like you a lot. You deserve it. Ask her to go on a date with you. Tell her you like her. Something. Anything!

After the hug lasted a few seconds too long, Leo patted her on the back twice and pushed away a little bit, signaling it was time to release him. As April was letting go, she kissed him on the cheek. It was a warm kiss - not like the one you give your grandma on her 75th birthday.

Embarrassed now, April said, "Uhh, thank you. Excuse me. Sorry," and with that, she left her boss' office.

I like seeing her smile. You fool. Should have asked her out. It's fine. There's no rush. We'll see what happens.

Unbeknownst to Leo, April then scheduled a meeting with her handler, FBI Special Agent Nathan Long. They met in the Belmont park that was next to the town square. April showed up wearing a big hat and dark sunglasses. The Special Agent was dressed as usual in his black suit.

"April, so good to see you," Agent Long said with genuine excitement, getting up from the park bench as he folded his newspaper and set it down on the table.

He leaned in for a hug, but she moved away, saying, "Nathan, I've got bad news. I am quitting the bureau."

"What are you talking about, April? You're one of the very best we got."

"I have already made up my mind. You can't talk me out of it," she said.

"Well, if you are sure about that, then I must say I'm somewhat relieved. You know, I think you are great and working together – well, you working for me, has always made the possibility of you and I, of us…"

April quickly interrupted that awkward, stuttering train of thought by saying, "But before I go, I need to talk to you about the Stills family."

Blushing now with embarrassment from the implicit rejection, Special Agent Long too tried to pretend he didn't just attempt to court April and said, "Great. Do you know where he's keeping the drones. I want to crush that arrogant prick."

Unabashed and already anticipating that sentiment, April replied, "Yes, I think I do know where he's keeping them."

"Where? I will send a team there straightaway. This is great news. You will get a medal for this."

"Before I tell you, I need you to promise you won't go after the Stills family."

"What? What are you talking about? You're protecting those rats? Is this why you're quitting on me? So, it is true? I hear you're working for Leo Stills now. I assumed that was just so you could get close to him. Apparently, you've gotten too close."

Brushing off the whirlwind of hate, she pushed on, "I need your word, Nathan."

"Pssh. Wow. Well, you know I'd do anything for you. You have my word."

"I am pretty sure he's keeping the drones on their family boat in the harbor."

"The Stills own a boat?"

"Yes, Zone 2, Pier 13 or maybe 14… I couldn't really see. Thank you – and goodbye. I wish you the best and I appreciate everything you've done for me."

Meanwhile, across town – Eli and Sammy headed to the prison where Jane was held on account of her being an active member in SOPA. They bribed a few of the friendly guards and Jane was promptly allowed to escape. This actually wasn't terribly uncommon these days, with most of the prisons being understaffed due to budget constraints. The boys also sent word of the plan to Phil but weren't sure it had reached him until they saw him standing across the highway from the jail. Jane crossed the street to meet up with her husband while Eli and Sammy went back to the office.

Leo and Rome were on their way to the next Hansel real estate auction, which was taking place on the courthouse steps, when Leo got a text from Phil indicating he wanted to come by and say 'thanks' for helping get Jane out of prison. Leo quickly responded saying he'd be back to the office in an hour or so.

For a long time now, Leo has had his eye on taking over the legal operations that Hansel was running.

Eat or be eaten out here, man. That's the fastest way for our family business to grow. I'm made for more than what I currently am. I want the whole town of Belmont in my pocket.

Using their newfound common ground, Leo struck a deal with the head of the HB's to take over Hansel's operations.

The plan was simple. They were heading to the real estate auction, where they were supposed to provide security for Hansel; mostly protection against the HB's. Instead, Leo instructed his coppers to all take a break at 1:15 p.m. exactly, for twenty minutes. This was just at the end of the auction, so all of the cash payments would have been received and stored in the auctioneers' safes.

The HB's would then hit the auction, confiscating a crippling amount of proceeds and disgracing the reputation of Hansel all over town as a legitimate businessman. Unfortunately, Leo got a phone call from Ms. Hansel just as they were arriving at the auction.

He quickly answered, "Ms. Hansel. How nice to hear from you. We are just getting to your auction to make sure everything goes well."

"Shut your damned, lying mouth, boy. I don't think you understand quite who you are trying to screw over. I run this town and I have eyes and ears everywhere. You thought you could mess with me and keep breathing?! I'm at your office right now with your pretty assistant. You should hurry back so she stays that way."

Click – and the line went dead.

"Rome, we got to go," Leo said hurriedly.

"Should we cancel everything?"

"No, we will continue as planned. Today's the day – come hell or high water."

The brothers rushed back to their office and came busting through the front door, knives in hand. Hansel's men greeted them, also carrying their weapons. Hansel's guards escorted them to the back office, where Hansel was waving a handsome silver pistol back and forth at April, Phil and Michelle.

Where the hell did she get a gun? I want it. Tired of fighting with knives and bats… it's so uncivilized.

"Hansel – what's going on here!" Leo demanded, rather unhappy to be having this conversation on his home turf.

"You tell me, sport. I hear you were planning to knock off my auction today. That's one of the biggest auctions of the year. It would ruin me. You wouldn't want that, would ya? Tell me it isn't true, and I'll go kill the person who, I guess you would say, lied to me," Hansel sneered, as she kept waving that gun around at Leo and his family.

We have no choice. Lie.

"Hansel, you know I would never be so stupid as to try anything like that against someone as strong as you."

"Liar! Shut up! What to do, what to do? How many people in your family do I have to kill in order to teach you a lesson? Maybe your sweet, little girlfriend here too," Hansel fumed, pacing around the room.

Not quite sure what to say, Leo looked at his family and tried to let them know silently that it would be all right.

Just then, Michelle jumped up, got in the middle of both sides and screamed, "Stop! Stop. Look. Let's talk this out. No one needs to get hurt here today."

Not accepting that for a moment, Leo ordered her to sit down.

Disregarding his command, Michelle went on, "No one's going to get hurt today." Now looking directly at Hansel, Michelle continued, "Listen close, lady. If you want to hurt Leo, you're going to have to shoot me first… 'cause I ain't moving!"

She's going to kill her. She's going to kill everyone if we let her. We have to do something.

The world seemed to stop spinning for what felt like eternity. Everyone looking around at everyone else. No one even flinching. Statues.

Then, Hansel started chuckling, "I don't know who you think you are, Leo. You should really get to know your business partners better before getting in bed with them. I don't let things go."

With that, she raised her pistol at Leo, the bullet from which would first have to travel through Michelle who was still standing between the two crime bosses. At the same time, Hansel's henchmen attacked. Just before the first bullet was fired, Leo lunged and tackled Michelle out of the way with a loud groan.

At the same time, Rome stabbed two of Hansel's henchmen before he was tackled by the third mercenary. Leo and Michelle crashed onto a round table, which immediately broke apart, splintering everywhere.

They were barely hitting the floor as a second bullet rang out and then a feminine scream, "AHHHHHHH!!"

Michelle? April?!

The bullets stopped. Rome and the last remaining hired hand were still wrestling on the floor and it looked like Rome was coming out on top.

Everyone looked around, wondering why Hansel didn't unload the whole clip and kill them all.

As they searched the room with their eyes, Hansel slowly fell to her knees and only then was Sammy made visible standing behind her. Lifeless, Hansel fell to the floor and only then was Sammy's knife made visible, sticking out from the middle of Hansel's back.

Sammy, no!

Without hesitating, Leo picked up Hansel's gun and shot her last mercenary dead just before the guy got another punch in on Rome. Barely able to catch his breath, Leo looked around to make sure everyone was okay. To his dismay, he saw Phil laying there. Unmoving.

Phil's throat was the first one cut by Hansel's men just before the bullets started flying.

Leo screamed, "Phil! Rome take him to the hospital! Phil, stay with us, bro!"

Rome picked up the limp body of his younger brother and ran the ten blocks to the closest urgency care center in a dead sprint. Leo walked over to Sammy, who was in shock, and put his arm around him. April rushed over to see if Leo was okay and, without thinking, she threw her arms around him.

As she nuzzled her head into his shoulder, she whispered in his ear between gasping breaths, "Are you okay, Leo? Oh my gosh. I love you. I'm so scared."

Leo didn't stop her, and they all sat there for a few minutes, soaking up what just happened. Leo, the first to move, made a call to coordinate getting these bodies dumped in the river.

As the weeks progressed, the town was shocked by the sudden disappearance of Hansel who was such a prominent businessman in Belmont because she ran all the real estate auctions and owned multiple coffee shops. However, the town inevitably needed someone to fill the void.

It just so happened that the Stills family was in prime position to take over the auctioneering function, as well as to purchase all Hansel's coffee warehouses, products and retail shops at a steal of a deal.

Within the course of several weeks, the Stills Corporation became the largest and most powerful business in Belmont.

But at what cost?

<u>Story 10</u>

Dressed in all black on this dark day, the Stills family mourned the loss of their brother, Phil. Burying a younger sibling never seems quite right.

As they sat there by the fresh grave – they prayed, coming together in a way that only tragedy can provide, "Our Father, Who art in Heaven, Hallowed be Thy name, Thy kingdom come, Thy will be done, on Earth as it is in Heaven…"

"Leo!" someone shouted from behind.

Leo paused and said quietly, "Everyone, please continue."

The family all looked up momentarily from their grief to see Sam talking hurriedly into Leo's ear before they put their heads back down and continued their prayer for the repose of Phil's soul.

Sam said to Leo, "Our home base was broken into. Looks like the Braxton militia. For some reason they think we have the stolen government drones."

Leo responded calmly, "Let's finish here. Then we will deal with that. Thank you for letting me know, but it will have to wait."

A few hours later, Leo took Rome and a couple guys from the crew over to the local militia's stronghold. There was a dark warehouse on the corner of 8th and Creston Street, tucked back out of the way from foot traffic.

Leo walked in without an invitation and said to the first scruffy guy he found, "Who's in charge here?"

The shabby man, without putting down his glass of vodka, simply nodded back to a loud table filled with people all wearing what almost seemed to be a uniform. Everyone in that warehouse was wearing blue denim everything.

Leo walked up to the table, where he was greeted with a smile by the lone woman there, "Mr. Stills. Welcome. To what do we owe this unexpected honor?"

Without a smile, Leo replied coldly, "You have my attention. What do you want?"

The feminine figure stood up and tapped the man to her right, saying, "Luka, come. Mr. Stills, please – this way. We have much business to discuss."

Leo ordered Rome and his men to stay behind, and he followed the two militiamen into a private room.

"Please sit," she invited Leo, "I am Rimmy, and this is Luka. We have had our eye on you for some time now."

Rimmy was quite an attractive young woman, with long straight black hair that almost reached her waist. Luka was quite the opposite, his face scarred from a lifetime of battle.

"A lot of people can say the same," was all Leo cared to say, losing interest and patience. "I wish I could say the pleasure was all mine, but I'm not here because I received a friendly invitation. Our office was ransacked. You wouldn't know anything about that would you?"

"Heavens, no. I'm sure it was not done on behalf of the People's Militia. Goodness," Rimmy carried on, feigning a bit too much concern. "Buuuuut, I'm sure glad you happened to stop by our humble abode."

Real convenient. We know it was them. No sense belaboring the point, though. Let's see what we can get out of them from here. Look at this dump. What did we get ourselves into dealing with these schmucks?

"Why is that?" Leo asked, pushing the conversation along.

Luka jumped in, "You need to do something for us. Something that requires a local touch and seeing as how you are the unofficial leader of this lovely town, we thought you'd be the perfect man for the assignment."

Silence.

As Leo stared back at Rimmy blankly, waiting for the other shoe to drop, Luka raised his voice a bit, saying, "SOPA is causing a lot of problems and drawing too much attention from the feds. We need you to get rid of their local Belmont director."

"Get rid of?" Leo asked sheepishly.

"Exterminate. You know we don't have to ask, right? We could make you."

They are right. They could shoot me right now and I'm sure no one would ever find me.

Still talking to Rimmy as if they were the only two in the room, Leo asked, "Your organization is quite powerful. You fellas can't handle a simple task like that?"

Losing his patience at Leo's disrespect, Luka shouted, "Let me get rid of this guy," asking Rimmy's permission to blow Leo away right then and there.

However, Rimmy smiled at Leo's boldness and, ignoring Luka, said back to Leo softly, "Mr. Stills, we don't like to get our hands dirty unless we have to.

Your company, on the other hand, seems to deal better with that sort of lowlife activity. Now, I've been asked to obtain you specifically for this job because of your experience and your influence in this town. Our cause needs this done, and we need it done quietly – but we can't seem to get a reliable location on their director. You know the people of Belmont and you can use that knowledge to our advantage."

As she said this, she stood up and started circling behind Leo's chair like a cat in heat. "I like you, Mr. Stills. You are very smart. It is too bad you don't put that intelligence to better use and instead you choose to waste it on all your silly, little schemes. You could join an honorable cause like our own. You could be so much more than the gutter rat that you are."

At this point, after sliding a name and address into Leo's front pocket, she let her hand linger, dragging along his broad shoulders. "We need this. I need this. Won't you help a damsel in distress?"

Silence.

If I do this for them, there's no going back. It's definitely a slippery slope. If we choose to go down this rabbit hole, there is no telling when we will be able to come back out of the dark abyss for air. But what choice do I have. No - this is the easy way, but there's got to be a better way forward.

Rimmy, went on, "I would do anything for my cause and my people."
Silence.
"Anything…" she smiled innocently, leaning in and putting her feminine figure on full display.

A true wolf in sheep's clothing. This chick is crazy. I just don't have the leverage. I'll have to get that back somehow. Can't believe I'm going to get in bed with them.

Leo finally acquiesced, leaning back, resigned to his fate.
He said, "Fine. Consider it done by the end of the week. You'll see it in the news," and, standing up abruptly, he finished, "I'll let you know when you can give me something I really want."

At that, he walked out of the backroom and, nodding for Rome to follow, they all left quietly.

They arrived back at the family headquarters and found the rest of the crew waiting there. Leo had called for a family meeting to discuss some other pressing business. After giving brief direction on how Rome would be handling the unfortunate SOPA Belmont director *assignment*, he went on to propose the expansion of the family business.

"Guys, we've come a long way these past years from some lower-class schlubs. We are now the most respected and powerful family in Belmont. We earned that. SOPA and the Braxton militia are powerful, but we aren't direct competitors. SOPA wants to drastically change American politics and actually has a good chance of doing so. Braxton is a terrorist country that wants to destroy America as a whole but will likely never succeed even in part. We just want our little slice of the money pie. We can all peacefully coexist as long as we each stay in our own lane. We even have somewhat of an inroad with each of them, so that, absent any particular problems, everyone involved wants business to keep running smoothly. As much of a menace as Jane has always been and as sickening as it is to help the Braxton terrorists take out the SOPA director – these are sacrifices we must make."

Looking around, he saw only heads nodding in agreement. "Now, we are in a very safe spot. Our affairs are in complete order and our relationships have never been more secure. As such, I've decided it is time we expand beyond the Belmont neighborhoods into another large market. Considering how big of a decision this is, I wanted to hear your feedback."

Doesn't mean I'm going to listen to your feedback, but good to hear it, nonetheless.

Knowing his place as second in command, Rome began with the obvious question that the others waited for him to ask, "That's all well and good, brother. What did you have in mind? What market exactly?"

Leo said, "Rome, Eli – I have my eyes set on San Mikel, California. There is a crime family there that has just been weakened by an internal feud for power. San Mikel is the biggest coffee distribution center on the West Coast because it is right on the U.S. border with Mexico. As such, it is in a great position to smuggle over stolen shipments of coffee products at rock bottom prices... and it's now ripe for the taking."

"So was the forbidden fruit at Eden," Rome half joked.

A couple stifled chuckles were heard, but quickly faded. Everyone understood, in some sense, the dangers something like this endeavor would entail. The decision was not to be taken lightly.

Rome went on, "Seriously, though, Lee – we finally have a good thing going. We have nothing to worry about. The heat from the feds just died down. Like you said, our relationships with SOPA and the Brax crazies are quiet. Why risk it? We ain't hurtin' right now. It's good enough isn't it?"

"Good enough?!" Leo semi-shouted back at his older brother, everyone else in the room unconsciously holding their breath. "Since when have we measured decisions by 'good enough,' Roman?"

In a way, he's right though. It is incredibly risky, and we have it so good right now. But it's human nature to expand and to push forward. We aren't meant to sit still complacently, surrounded by complete order. Every now and again we need a little spice, some excitement in our lives. That is true – but that is also what led to Adam and Eve losing paradise.

Relaxing a bit, Leo said, "I mean, I hear you, bro. I understand. But we weren't made for 'good enough.' We were made for greatness. We have the foundation and the legitimacy now to really expand. After three generations of the Sanchez family leadership, they have become unstable and weak. We can take them out once and for all, and we would become a coastal powerhouse overnight. We…"

Leo was cut off mid-rant by an irate Michelle, "THE SANCHEZ FAMILY!?!?! MATEO SANCHEZ?? Have you lost your damn mind? They are one of the most dangerous organized crime syndicates in the country and definitely bigger than anyone we've faced yet!"

Fuming, she paced wildly around the room, throwing her hands in the air out of frustration.

Leo calmly explained, "I agree the risk is absurdly large, but the reward is equally appealing. If we pull it off, there will be no stopping us. If we fail, we can always retreat to Belmont. This is our stronghold. No mafia in the world could get to us in Belmont where we are insulated by the support of the local people for miles around. What's life without a little risk?"

Though hesitant to speak at a family meeting, April jumped in here, saying, "She's right, Leo. What's life without a little risk? It's life. It's living. What you're talking about is almost certainly death."

The informal vote had begun. Michelle clearly voted 'No' and even though April didn't get to cast an official vote, her sentiment mirrored Michelle's. Rome and Eli had been silent, however. Sammy didn't yet get a vote, as the baby of the family is often not taken too seriously.

Finally, Eli broke the silence by jumping on board, "I'm in, Leo. Let's do it."

Rome quickly agreed, "Hell, why not? Let's go for it."

Glad the vote landed in his favor so he wouldn't have to override their desires, Leo said, "It's decided then. Rome will be handling some business here this week. Eli, you take however many guys you need. Sanchez has a main stronghold called Hot Cups. That's their most popular and lucrative coffee shop. I want you to disrupt their business and let their patrons know about the arrival of the Stills Corporation to the San Mikel coffee scene. Word will spread like wildfire, and then the war begins."

At this point, Michelle and April had already begun storming out of the office, chattering rapidly to each other as they went.

Just before she left, Michelle shouted over her shoulder, "Leo, you and I should attend as well," and left without awaiting a response.

Bright and early the next morning, Leo, April, Michelle, Eli, and six other members of their crew got in a couple cars to head towards the airport. When they got there, April went to the ticketing kiosk and printed out everyone's boarding passes.

April had also scheduled a cart to take them to the terminal where they would board their private flight. Thank God, the Stills family no longer had to fly on those commercial airline tin cans. Instead, they avoided the lines and the security checkpoints and hopped on a used private jet that the company recently purchased. A short three hours later, they arrived in the incredibly warm city of San Mikel, California.

After grabbing a quick supper at a local diner, Leo, April and Michelle followed Eli and the guys to the Hot Cups shop a few blocks away just as the sun was setting.

Let's get this over with and get out of this hell hole. It's so hot here… and it smells funny.

Leo, April and Michelle waited out on the sidewalk, sitting on a dilapidated wooden bench across the street. Leo lit up a cigar and waited for the commotion to begin. Michelle sat there, nervously silent. April didn't know quite what to expect, as this sort of business was relatively new to her, though she was always fully supportive of Leo at the end of the day.

Seconds after Eli and the boys entered the Hot Cups shop, clanging and banging and shouting was heard. It seemed to last a long time, but in reality, it was only the excitement, or rather anxiety, that made those few moments feel like an eternity. Eli and the crew came sauntering out of the shop and, spotting Leo across the street, they went over to report on how their introduction landed with the locals.

Eli spoke first, "That went well. I think we made ourselves known, loud and clear. We smashed the place up a bit. When a couple of the Sanchez boyos came up to stop us, we tossed them over the bar. Right before we left, we introduced the Stills family and let everyone know that the Stills Corporation was the new sheriff in town."

Leo clapped softly, "Good work, bro. Everyone okay? Good. Eli, follow April. She will take you and the boys to the hotel. April, what time is our flight tomorrow morning?"

"7:00 a.m."

Leo nodded, "So, get some rest boys. Don't be up too late and don't draw any attention. Michelle and I have some business to discuss. Obviously, drinks are on the company… so have fun. You did well tonight. We'll see you in the morning."

At that, Leo and Michelle started walking down the gloomy sidewalks on that humid evening in San Mikel.

Eli responded, "You got it, Leo. Let's hit it boys. After you," he said to April.

Leo turned around for just a moment and watched April lead the pack. At the same time, April had spun around and silently mouthed 'good night' back to Leo.

Michelle kicked off the conversation, "So, what's up with you lately – you all right? You seem distracted; worn out almost. Are you depressed or somethin'?"

Silence.

She continued, "You know you don't have to do everything alone. You have us, your family. Plus, I've seen the way you look at April."

At that, Leo shot her a cutting glance before Michelle carefully continued, "I'm just saying! She'd obviously do anything for you. She already helps you organize your whole life. The way you two interact and depend on each other, it's already like a marriage. Well, without the bedroom activity, I suppose."

Silence.

She continued with a gasp and a gossipy smile, "Right?! You guys haven't… ya know…?"

Fed up at this point, Leo playfully said, "Just like women to gossip about relationships. Can we move on? We have real matters to discu…"

At that moment – far away from home and any backup, mistakenly thought to be protected by anonymity – Leo was tackled down to the ground by two men. Three more guys grabbed Michelle's arms and she was led into a dark alley, while Leo was beaten and dragged behind.

They shouted, "Who the hell are you? We saw you leaving our shop after your dogs tore it up! Do you know who you are messing with, ese!? This is Sanchez's turf!"

As they yelled, the men kicked and punched Leo endlessly, his blood leaking to the ground from countless injuries. As Leo struggled to breathe through his broken ribs, the mob turned their attention to the strikingly attractive Michelle, "Look at this pretty bird. I think we all know what a good girl like this really wants out here in the mean streets, don't we boys?"

"Hell yeah!"

"That's right!"

After a few smacks to her face and hits to her stomach, Michelle lost her ability to fight them off. The men were about to start their devilish deed when bullets rang out. Barely able to see through his swollen eyes, Leo groaned and turned his head just in time to see two of his attackers drop like sacks of flour to the dusty pavement and the rest of the men running off.

Leo passed out, bleeding internally, but not before hearing, "Pick 'em up. Clean 'em up and ship 'em off to Saint George's. You're lucky the director thinks you might be of some further use in the future, Mr. Stills."

<u>Story 11</u>

A few hours later, Leo cracked opened his swollen eyes with a loud groan as he heard footsteps enter his room. The clock said 5:42 a.m., and the room was bright and sterile. All of the sudden, Leo felt every single one of his injuries.

He couldn't make out the man that stood in front of him, but asked, "Where is Michelle? Is she okay?"

"She's fine, Mr. Stills. You, on the other hand, are not."

"Where is she? Who are you?" Leo grunted.

"I'm your guardian angel apparently. Your sister has been put on a flight home with a couple scrapes and bruises, nothing permanent. We've been keeping an eye on you for some time, even after we got what we wanted from you off your family boat. You're welcome for saving your life, by the way. There will come a time for you to return the favor."

"We'll see about that."

"Mr. Stills, I own you… and I'm losing patience. We know your crew carried out a hit on the SOPA director of Belmont. We have all the evidence we need to lock you up and throw away the key. You will spend 23 hours a day in an 8' x 4' prison cell with no windows. The only hour outside of that cell will be split between a cold shower and outdoor time spent inside a 5' x 5' cage. You will be properly treated like the animal you are."

"What do you want, Agent Long?" Leo asked.

"How's my girl, April, doing for you?" the FBI Agent poked.

What does that mean – 'his girl'?

"What do you want, Agent Long?" Leo asked, now losing *his* patience.

"I just want to remind you, that you still work for me. Whenever I need you, you better get to gettin' – you understand me, son?"

Silence.

"Good boy. Enjoy the rest of your stay. I'll be back soon. They say you are going to be discharged in a couple days. We'll go over your assignments then. Rest up for now, while you can."

With that, the FBI Agent, who Leo had hoped was out of the picture for good, left the shining white hospital room that smelled intensely of cleaning supplies.

As soon as he left, Leo used all his strength to sit up in bed, moaning as he felt a couple stitches reach their splitting point. He looked around and used the phone on the bedside table.

Without hesitation, he called Rome, "Bro, I need you to charter me a flight to Seattle."

Rome answered, "No problem. How did the event go at the Sanchez shop?"

Leo groaned back angrily out of pain, "Rome, I don't have time for this right now. I'm at this God-forsaken hospital in San Diego. Have April schedule the flight for one hour from now and tell your contact in Seattle to pick me up from the airport. Make sure Michelle and Eli make it back okay."

"Leo, are you okay!? You sound like hell…" and all Rome heard after that was the line going dead.

Leo gathered all his might, tucked the hospital gown into his pants and threw a long raincoat on top of everything. He grabbed his hat to cover the stitches on his head and shadow the giant bruise that was his face. He took a deep breath and poked his head out of the door to make sure there were no feds sitting on his location.

I'm sure Agent Long assumes I wouldn't be able to even move for a while. I can't be here when he gets back though.

With that, he quietly walked down the bright hallway, following the red EXIT signs until he smelled fresh air. April had carried out her instructions perfectly. Before he even had time to stress about what to do next, he was happily surprised. Though she was not asked to, April had a car waiting outside the hospital to take Leo to the airport. The driver was holding a sign that read: "Mr. Stills."

Amazing girl.

He was taken through the airport to the private terminal and after tipping the staff, he boarded the flight to Seattle. As soon as his head hit the back of the seat, he reclined and fell asleep, waking up to the feel of the plane's wheels touching down on the runway. He looked outside at the overcast drizzle coming down… normal for the Pacific Northwest.

It's good to be home.

As he exited the terminal – Leo looked around and saw a short, stalky man walking up to him who said, "Mr. Stills? You can call me, Mick. Roman hit me up. He said you needed a ride somewhere. What exactly can I do for you?"

Leo quietly said, "Rubenfield. You know him?"

Mick exclaimed, "I only know of one: Mr. Sal Rubenfield – but you can't mean him, right? He's a dangerous man. Loan shark. Mobster. Vast resources and extensive underground connections. Bad, bad man. No morals that one. Would sell his mother's soul to the highest bidder. Plus, he changes the terms of deals he makes faster than the wind changes direction out across a large expanse of the blue ocean, so long as it puts more bread in his sheets and more fat on his cheeks."

"Stop talking and take me to him," Leo ordered, annoyed at the man's strange dialogue.

"What do you mean? Now? Alone? Don't you have some backup to take with you?"

Another voice came up from behind, "He's not alone."

Leo's heart dropped when he saw April walking up to them in her designer travel clothes.

"Where are we going?" she asked Leo.

"*We…* are not going anywhere. *You…* are going home. *I…* am going someplace that would not be suitable for the likes of you."

Frustrated by his lack of excitement to see her and clearly not understanding the circumstances, she shot back, "Like hell I am. I didn't drag my butt all the way here just to go back home. I'm coming with you. I go everywhere with you. It's my job." Then, noticing his injuries finally, she shouted, "Wait, are you okay? What happened to you?! We have to get you to a hospital!"

"Stop. This isn't a vacation, April! I don't want to see anything bad happen to you. I've had enough heartache for one week. Why can't you just do what you're told?"

"Oh, I didn't think you had a heart – and I don't just do what I'm told, because I'm not a damned dog – and because I'm with you, until the end," she said, ending that statement a little softer than she began.

"You can't help me with this one. You being there would simply be dangerous for you and of no benefit to me."

"Oh, if it was a benefit to you, you'd put me in danger?" she said in a snarky tone, trying to deflect the conversation.

Ignoring that comment, he said, "Fine. But you are staying in the car."

"Yes, sir."

Now she listens. Jeeze.

The three of them got into Mick's car and took a 30-minute drive out of the city. They arrived at a rural estate, with a gated driveway.

They pulled up to the gate and a voice came out of the intercom: "What do you want?"

Mick replied, "Is Mr. Rubenfield here."

The intercom replied, "Who's asking?

Mick answered, "Leo Stills of Belmont."

The intercom was silent for a moment and then the gates swung wide open, like a predator inviting in its prey.

Leo addressed his compatriots in the car, "I'm going to walk in. I don't even want you guys to enter this compound. Rubenfield is old school. When you meet with him, you sign a deal, or you sign a death sentence. If I don't come out in exactly fifteen minutes, go home and never look back."

You wouldn't be able to find my body anyway.

At that, April gasped and squeezed Leo's hand. She finally understood the gravity of this situation. Leo gently squeezed her hand in return and then pulled his hand out from hers even though she didn't want to let go.

As he got out of the car, she finally mustered up the ability to whisper, "Leo, please no. It's not worth it."

Ignoring the emotion, he got out of the backseat and hobbled down the long, gravel driveway where he was quickly escorted into the mansion by four men dressed in all black robes carrying rather large weapons.

Man, everyone I'm dealing with these days has a gun. Jealous much.

"And their guns are a lot bigger than the little pistol that I picked up off Hansel," he muttered to himself, as he tapped the small handgun that he now carried with him in his coat pocket everywhere.

After traveling through the large house for a couple minutes, they finally got down to the basement where Rubenfield was sitting behind a large desk counting stacks of $100 bills and wrapping them in rubber bands.

Rubenfield looked up, with a twisted smile and shouted, "Mr. Stills! How kind of you to grace me with your presence. I don't recall inviting you, however."

Leo responded firmly, "Please, call me Leo."

The two bosses shook hands while Rubenfield inquired, "What can I do for you, Leo?"

Leo replied, "I have a business proposition for you."

Rubenfield sheepishly deflected, "For me? Are you interested in the Payday Loan business or something? I have over 100 shops sprinkled up and down the West coast, but I'm not really looking for a business partner right now. I know of your prominence in Belmont, so I assume you're not here asking me for a job. But this is the big city, slick. It's not little ole Belmont. Are you sure you're not just lost?"

At that, Rubenfield pulled out a large machete and started sharpening it for no sane reason. One of Rubenfield's men came into the room and whispered in his ear. As Rubenfield listened, another senior crew member, a rather strong and brawny fellow, said to the first crew member, "Yo, Jimmy! Mr. Rubenfield was not to be disturbed. You should have knocked."

Rubenfield sprang up out of his seat, walked over and backhanded the big oaf that was admonishing Jimmy.

Rubenfield whispered with a psychotic intensity, "I'm right here, Jude! You think I can't speak for myself! What Jimmy had to say was obviously important." Turning back to Leo, now wearing a smile from ear to ear, Rubenfield hissed, "Though, heh-heh, this is more interesting than important."

Turning back to Jimmy, he ordered, "Bring it in to the Wilson room over there." To Leo now, his tone did a 180-degree turn, and very quietly he said, "Leo, I apologize for my crew's disrespect towards our meeting, speaking out of turn. Unacceptable, if you ask me. They sometimes get me a little hot under the collar. I'm sure you can relate."

Man, this guy is crazy. Need to get back on track before he loses patience and enjoys this meeting breaking down into chaos.

Leo refocused the meeting, "No problem. As I was saying, I have a proposition for you, though it doesn't have anything to do with the payday loans you use as a legal front for your real operations." Leo paused for a moment, then went on, "I know you have had your eye on expanding your legal lending division for a long time now."

"Uh-huh…"

"Well, as I'm sure you know by this point, ever since Hansel… disappeared… The Stills Corporation has taken over all of the real estate auctions within 50 miles of Belmont. If I introduced you to the people in that product chain and allowed your loans at my functions, your legal lending business could see a 25% increase within one year, easy and completely clean."

Now intrigued, Rubenfield replied, "Well that would obviously make me very happy, but what's in it for you."

Glad things were moving in the right direction, Leo said, "I am also sure you are familiar with Mateo Sanchez's work down in southern California. I want you to help me take over his distribution channels, get rid of him altogether. He's a bit bigger than me, and you for that matter - but together, you and I would have no problem exterminating him."

Keeping a poker face when he heard the name Sanchez, Rubenfield still pushed back a little, "Why wouldn't I just team up with Sanchez myself… cut out the middleman?"

Damn it. I need to get…

Leo's thoughts were interrupted by a weird smirk on Rubenfield's bearded face.

Rubenfield said, "Ahhh, here it is. Does this belong to you, Leo? We caught it trying to climb through the front gate."

Confused, Leo turned around, only to see April being dragged out of sight through the hallway and into the adjoining room.

!!!!!

Quickly, he said, "Yes, she came here with me. She is no problem. Just a bad listener. I'll get her out of your hair as soon as we finish up with the men's business here."

"That's not exactly what I asked you, Mr. Stills. Is she yours? Look, let's cut to the chase. I could go either way on this deal with you and Sanchez. Though you are correct in my desire to increase my legitimate lending portfolio, I really dislike the thought of expanding further south. I hate it down there."

Now, leaning in close to Leo, Rubenfield whispered in his ear, "That said, I know she came with you, but would you mind if she went home with me? She is just the cherry on top that would make you a clear winner over Sanchez in my book. She is quite stunning and really looks so pure."

I have no choice. If I refuse now, we will both be killed and dropped into a tank of acid. You always have a choice. You can't agree to that. She's not an animal that can be traded. He will do what he wants, regardless of what I say.

Leo whispered back, "You may have one date. What happens is of no concern to me. I will be back in exactly four hours. We have a plane to catch. So, we have a deal on Sanchez?"

With that, Leo stood up and extended his hand, which Rubenfield grabbed onto with his dirty, crusty paw-of-a-hand, in agreement on their mutual expansion.

While Rubenfield went to take a shower in preparation for his new date, Leo proceeded to exit the compound.

When he got back, he found Mick sweating in the car, "I told her to stay in the vehicle, Mr. Stills! She wouldn't listen. Forgive me! She said she was worried about you and that we had to do something! I thought it better to follow your orders."

"Enough," Leo said with obvious concern on his face. "She is in good hands. Pull around the corner. We have to wait a few hours and then she'll be back."

So, they sat, and they sat. Fifteen minutes… Thirty minutes… one hour down, three more hours to go.

Wow. What depths, huh? They will be almost done with dinner at this point, then dessert. Then… oh, what do I care. Not my responsibility. She can take care of herself. She can do what she wants. Maybe she wants him. How am I to know? Not my concern. I had no choice.

Abruptly, Leo blurted out, "I'll be back. Turn the car on and be ready to go in a hurry."

He got out of the car, walked to the front gate and pressed the intercom, "It's Leo Stills. I have some information about his date that Rubenfield would like to know before he gets too deep into it."

The intercom came back after a few heartbeats, "He's... busy. He said he did not want to be disturbed for any reason."

"If you don't pass this information along before he enjoys himself too much, he will kill you for holding it back. It's pertinent to his current meeting."

Buzzzzzzzzzzzz

Why couldn't she listen? Going to die if this doesn't work. What's the plan? Wouldn't you like to know.

The gate unlocked and he was met by four armed guards on the other side. They escorted him in. Leo followed them through the estate to a different part of the compound than was used to conduct their previous business. One of Rubenfield's men approached the door, hesitated, and then knocked.

Silence.

The man knocked again. This time, a few moments later, Rubenfield swung the door open, banging it against the wall. He was standing there in a red silk robe sporting a flowery pattern and holding a nearly empty glass of champagne. "WHAT IS IT!?"

Seeing Leo, Rubenfield toned it down a bit, awaiting the explanation for this rude interruption.

Leo said, "May I come in? You'll want to hear this."

Extending Leo one inch of wiggle room to explain why he shouldn't be shot in the face and disposed of, Rubenfield responded, "This better be good."

Uhhh, yeah. It better be.

Leo walked into the gigantic bedroom suite and saw April there on the couch with a full glass of champagne sitting untouched on the table in front of her. They locked eyes and she was obviously scared yet gladdened that her knight in shining armor was here to rescue her. Leo could almost tell from her facial expression that she was thinking, 'Leo won't let anything bad happen to me, right?'

He walked past her without much of a visible acknowledgement at all. This didn't bother her. She trusted him. He walked over to Rubenfield's bar, which was just outside of the living room where April was sitting. Growing annoyed, Rubenfield followed. Leo proceeded to pour himself some whiskey out of the smallest, crystal decanter, obviously the most expensive liquor on the bar.

Once they were out of April's earshot, Leo explained his intrusion, "Look Rubemeister, she's no good for you. She has a terrible habit of shooting men dead that try to force themselves on her – five men by my count, using a nifty pistol she keeps on her thigh. Guessing you haven't seen that yet."

Hoping he hasn't seen that yet.

Leo continued, "Plus, even though I'm sure she would have consented for a stud like you, she's actually not a *she*… she's really a *he*. Society these days, eh? Am I right or am I right?"

Leo was not sure Rubenfield was buying it, especially because Rubenfield was probably very much primed to go at this point and certainly didn't want it to be true.

Leo doubled down on his bluff, "Craziest part is, visibly, you can't tell. She looks fine. Pure as the driven snow. I was going to let it happen because you would never find out. Buuuuut, seeing as how we are in business together now – didn't feel right to do that to you. I want you to know you can trust me. Guess my conscience got the best of me. Anyway, I'll take her back to the local pound where I found her. I'm sure you have plenty of other women you could call for tonight's entertainment."

Really trying to sell the nonchalance, Leo shot back the rest of the finest whiskey he'd ever tasted…

I've got to have April order some of this liquid gold if we make it back. That's really a nice drink. Focus. Stop overtalking to Rubenfield and get this over with.

… and walking back over to April, as if Rubenfield had already agreed, Leo said "Let's go." Then Leo muttered, "Always getting me into trouble."

Rubenfield quickly reclaimed his dignity, "Appreciate that, Leo. Yes, uh, I agree." To April, Rubenfield explained, "Our date is going to have to be postponed, Miss April. I've, uhhh, got urgent business. My men will show you two out."

Without a word, Leo and April made their way back to the car and enjoyed a long, silent ride back to the airport. Not knowing that Leo originally dealt her into the twisted agreement to begin with, April only saw him as her savior and had never been more smitten with Mr. Leo Stills of Belmont.

The past few months, Leo had been working on setting up a retirement plan for his family using all the now-excessive amounts of illicit revenue being generated. Even with their new and improved legal operations up and running, those were not near strong enough to cover up all the dirty money generated by their original, illegal coffee enterprise. Now having control over the San Mikel distribution channel, it was just too profitable to source their product illegally and then turn around and sell it at the overly regulated, artificially inflated legal prices.

Plus, we already have the illegal channels set up. It would be more work to take them down and forge legitimate relationships throughout the entire product chain. More work, for less money. Haha. Bizarre. Not as bizarre as these conversations I have in my head. Things are good though. Even in this recession of an economy with record levels of foreclosures, the coffee sales are still strong. People need their coffee.

Anyway, Leo had then decided to funnel his dirty money through the cash real estate auctions and come out on the other side with completely legitimate paperwork for his newly acquired properties.

After weeks of trying to track down Jane and her child, he found them and invited them both to come back to Belmont, saying there was something he needed to discuss with her. When Jane arrived, she was not only skeptical, but quite brash.

When she saw him standing on the sidewalk, skipping the customary social greeting, she got right down to business, saying, "Why are we meeting out here. It's freezing."

Smiling regardless and winking at his nephew, Leo said, "Well then, let's get inside. I'd like to show you something in private."

He motioned for her to go up the stairs to the front door of a brand-new townhome. They were right on the main strip in Belmont and homes here weren't cheap.

Jane replied, "I don't think that's a good idea. Why can't you tell me what you have to say here… in public… with people around?"

It's not that she had a specific reason not to trust Leo's intentions, but she just didn't.

Ignoring the warranted skepticism, as he did with most people, Leo simply walked up the front steps and opened the crimson front door. Noticing the very stylish exterior of the three-story home, Jane slowly followed at a distance. Leo walked down the hall and into the main living area. Jane immediately noticed that the home was barren, not a single piece of furniture in sight.

In a snarky voice, she asked, "Can I have the number of your design company. Love what you've done with the place."

Leo pushed on, "Haha. This isn't my house. It's yours. It's for you and my nephew."

"What? What are you talking about? I could never afford the monthly payment on something like this?"

"There is no monthly payment. Paid in full, and an escrow account set up to cover property taxes and insurance for life. All you have to do is make it a good home for this growing young man here. Let me know if you need help furnishing anything."

"What's the catch? What do you want from me?"

"It's what Phil would have wanted. Take care of yourself. You are family now. Come to me if you need anything."

With that, Leo set the keys on the counter and walked out the front door as Jane recovered from the surprise.

Leo walked out into the fresh air of a beautiful Belmont morning rush. The sidewalks were hustling and bustling, and the nice thing was – Leo was not in a hurry to get anywhere, for once. He was simply walking, with no purpose in mind and no destination charted… enjoying another God-given day.

Disturbing that tranquility, he heard someone shout, "Leo?! Is that you, man? Leo Stills?"

Leo wheeled around, not accustomed to a friendly interaction resulting from unscheduled meetings. He saw a man walking towards him in a fancy suit and another more rugged gentleman following behind him. Though the first man looked vaguely familiar, Leo moved his hand onto his pistol. He was ready for anything.

"Can I help you?" Leo curtly replied.

Blast this guy. Looks like a mad man. What's he want with you? He just happens to run into you on the street? We don't know him. Who's his friend? This isn't good.

All that he got back was an ignorantly enthusiastic response, "It is you, my man! It's me… Seth."

Silence.

Seth went on, "Your cousin, pinhead! My mother, your mother… it's been, what, eight years?"

Recalling a distant cousin by that name from his past a long time ago, Leo took his hand off his gun, but only physically. He was still skeptical of such an interaction and was caught off guard when Seth didn't stop approaching, going straight for the hug.

Seth went on, "Ha! Hah! Great to see ya, pal. How ya been?"

Leo replied, "Good, good, man. Who's your friend?"

"This is my right-hand man, Donny. You need anything, and I mean anything – Donny's your man. He's not afraid to get his hand dirty, if you know what I mean, Ha! Speaking of getting your hands dirty, I heard a couple stories about you that I'm sure can't all be true. Right? Anyway, I'm a partner at TWA now."

Seeing that Leo wasn't impressed and thinking Leo must not know what that meant, Seth said, "Only the biggest professional basketball agency firm in the country?"

I've always dreamed of owning a basketball team. Maybe one day. Still don't trust this guy. Michelle always loved him though.

Leo replied, ending the conversation, "Glad to hear things are well. Keep doing good work. See you around."

Or not.

"Definitely, man. I'll tell the family you say hello."

"Okay. Take care."

The agent within Seth came roaring out at the last minute, "Hey, I know you are doing big things, and though I'm not sure what is rumor or real yet, maybe some shady things too…"

Seeing Leo's face turn on a dime, he quickly continued, "… and hey, I got nothing against nothing. Just saying, I'd love to help you establish your footprint… your legal footprint, I mean. I'm also an attorney, so I could help you structure a real business. Here's my card. Reach out to me when it works for you."

Too convenient. He can't be trusted.

Although Leo had a law degree as well, he preferred to leave the mundane business activities to the professionals so he could stick to being the boss.

Leo accepted the card and then bid his long-lost cousin farewell, "You take care."

As Leo rounded the next street corner, he threw the business card in the first trash can he could find.

Whoops… should that have gone in the recycle?

After heading home for a rare afternoon nap, he woke up hungry. He went downstairs and cooked himself breakfast food for a late dinner. He then decided to make an impromptu trip to the office and get some work done even though it was well into the evening. He didn't quite have anything better to do. When he got to the office, it was just before 8:00 p.m. He was surprised when opening the front door to find Rome and a yet-to-be-introduced female acquaintance looking pretty chummy. The shocking part was, they were drinking coffee.

I thought we didn't use our own supply, Rome. It's supposed to be just for the customers.

Rome shot up, "Leo! Hey, bro. What you doin' here?"

Feeling the palpable discomfort in the room, Leo replied, "Just stopping by to grab something from my office." Looking at the girl, Leo said, "I don't believe we've been introduced."

Silence.

Looking back at Rome, he asked, "Should we be?"

Flustered now, Rome said, "Yeah, yeah. Ha, of course! This is Mary Anne. Mary Anne, this is my brother, Leo."

She spoke, "Pleased to meet you, Mr. Stills."

Though they hadn't met, everyone in Belmont knew the Stills family, and the stories about Leo in particular.

Leo beckoned to Rome, "Can I talk to you for a minute."

Rome excused himself from his date and followed Leo to the side room.

Leo went on, "What's up with the coffee? You drinking that stuff now, bro?"

Anticipating this question, Rome readily answered, "You know how it goes, Leo. Just a little bit here and there. Ya know? Nothing like the problems I had when we were stationed in Africa. Mostly been doing it with Mary Anne. She likes it. Plus, ya know, we are so busy lately – just taking a little bit of it to keep up with everything that we got going on, is all. It's not a problem. Trust me."

Unconvinced, Leo still replied, "Good to hear. Let me know if you ever need anything. I'm always worrying about you guys. Want the best for everyone. You and Mary Anne have a good night, bro. Love you."

"Sounds good, Leo. Thank you. Night!"

With that, Leo walked back out the front door of Bravo Tower that was now being used as a private date room.

As Leo walked down the street towards the Coffee Spot, he passed by a stranger who greeted him, "Evening, Mr. Stills."

Leo tipped his cap and, saying nothing, walked on alone.

<u>Story 12</u>

A few days later, Leo heard a knock at the front door of his home. He went to answer it and was not totally surprised to find his cousin Seth at his doorstep. Seth is an agent, a salesman – and he saw dollar signs when he looked at Leo.

"Come on in," Leo invited him, leading Seth to the den, which was directly adjacent to the front entryway.

Don't want this guy snooping all around my house. Still can't trust him.

"Please, sit. What can I do for you?"

Seth replied, "I want to talk business. I think you and I can help each other. I don't know everything you get into whilst in the shadows, but I do know you are making an impressive run at becoming a legitimate businessman here in Belmont… and perhaps all along the west coast?"

No way he knows about San Mikel… does he?

Not getting a response from Leo, Seth went on, "Anyway, I realize change can be tough and slow. I think I have a way to speed things up, and actually make it more profitable to be an honest businessman here. Are you open to the idea? I think we can make it work. What's not to love? Win-Win. The people of Belmont love you because you take care of them like no one before. You have helped shape this community for the better, more than most anyone else can say in the recent history of our town. You give them a voice. I want to help move you from the shadows into the light."

"You're not offended by the shadows? Because they aren't likely to ever disappear completely," Leo said.

"I've not got a weak stomach, Leo. Though I do find it more suitable to keep my hands clean."

"Tell me more. You got five minutes. Do you want a drink?" Leo asked, as he poured himself a glass of Irish whiskey.

"It's 10:00 o'clock in the mornin'," Seth responded skeptically, turning down the offer.

Leo shrugged, sitting down in the leather chair across from his cousin and raising his eyebrows as a silent invitation for Seth to continue with his proposition. After Leo let five minutes turn into fifteen, Leo excused himself and invited Seth to leave.

The two shook hands and Leo said, "3:00 p.m. today. Here's the address," as he handed Seth the address for Bravo Tower.

At just before noon, Leo arrived at the family office, headquarters for The Stills Corporation. Leo walked up the stairs into his private office to find April sitting in an armchair, scribbling furiously.

"Good morning," he said startling her.

"Leo, we got a busy day today. The family meeting starts at 2:30 p.m., and your 1:00 o'clock is here early. They are waiting in the conference room downstairs. Should I have them come up?"

Leo pondered and then said, "No, I will go down to them."

April took a moment to ask, "How are you doing?"

Puzzled somewhat by the introspective question, Leo said, "I'm good. Are you okay?"

April sighed, "Yes, thank you."

Not wanting to go into that sigh any further, Leo walked downstairs to his meeting straight away. When he got down to the conference room, he saw the Belmont Police Sergeant and what looked like a rookie copper sitting beside him.

The Sergeant had been on Leo's payroll a long time, maybe one of the first officers Leo ever hired. Leo was sure he helped put at least two of the Sergeant's kids through private school.

As soon as Leo opened the conference room door, the two officers stood up, fighting the instinctive urge to salute.

The Sergeant said, "Morning, Mr. Stills. Apologies for being early. Appreciate you taking the time to meet with us."

Leo nodded silently and sat down at the head of the long, oak conference table.

Knowing the drill, the Sergeant went on without wasting time, "So, the department is short a few arrests this quarter… and by a few, I mean a lot. We are 12% below our quota."

Silence.

"We were wondering if you could help out by tipping us off to any… suspicious activities that you or your company might know about… for whatever reason. Help me out. If I don't meet quota again this month, I might be looking at early retirement – and you and I go back a ways. Not to mention, I help…"

"Enough said, Sergeant," Leo quieted down the nervous policeman. "Sammy!" Leo yelled over his shoulder, calling in his youngest brother.

Sammy poked his head in, saying, "What's up, Leo?"

"Come, sit. These officers will tell you what they need. Fill them in on any... rumors... you might have heard about regarding some local activity here."

Turning back to the officers, Leo said, "Sam will take care of you and get you the details you want. If you need anything else, please feel free to reach out to my office again. If that is all, I will be on my way."

With that, Leo got up and excused himself so the real details could be exchanged.

The officers stood and the Sergeant said, "It's been a pleasure, sir."

Leo nodded and walked out. He made his way upstairs to review some financial reports until the family meeting was scheduled to begin a little while later.

At 2:30 p.m., April came and knocked on Leo's door, "Are you ready, boss? Family meeting is prepared to start whenever you get there."

"Coming," he said without looking up.

She responded, "We still on for tonight?"

Pausing to make eye contact, Leo said, "I'll see you then."

A few minutes later, another family meeting had begun. After some of the more mundane items were checked off the list, Leo took the floor. "Guys, as you know – we have been taking various steps to get our operations on the up and up. We have been largely successful thus far, but we still rely heavily on subsidization from our less-than-transparent activities."

Everyone nodded in agreement.

He continued, "As such, I would like to introduce the newest member of the Stills Corporation family, someone who is actually already family, our cousin Seth McMallin. Seth, come here."

Seth, who had been waiting in the small conference room, walked into the front lobby of Bravo Tower where all the family meetings were held.

"Seth will be heading up and driving home the up and coming, completely clean side of our business operations. He is a lawyer by background and currently a major agent for the professional basketball league. Seth needs to know nothing other than what he needs to know. Understood?"

Despite some faint murmurs, everyone nodded in agreement.

Leo continued, "The less he knows about the skeletons in the closet, the better for him and for the rest of us. Is that clear?"

Rome spoke up, "Leo, if I may? I'd like…"

Leo cut him off, "I know, Rome. You and I can touch base later. Michelle, you too. I know you have lots to say."

Michelle rolled her eyes but didn't deny it.

Leo wrapped up the meeting by saying, "Good, now that the introduction is out of the way, unless there is any other business not related to our newest division of the Stills Corporation, the meeting is adjourned. April, please put Seth in the West facing office upstairs."

Until now, only Leo, Rome, Michelle and Eli had offices upstairs and April sat at a small desk outside Leo's office. So, Seth going straight upstairs made a few of the others a bit envious.

Leo's ears unintentionally perked up as he heard the ever-enthusiastic Seth following April to his new office, saying, "Well aren't you a pretty little thing, girly. I'm Seth. How about after I get settled in, you show me your favorite dinner spot?"

Glancing back in Leo's direction, April said emphatically, "Uhhh, no. I'm unavailable. Right this way to your new office."

Leo exited the premises, not outwardly acknowledging what he just heard.

Later that night, Leo awoke to a phone call. Groggily, he opened his eyes only to find one of the local coppers that was on the company payroll daring to bother him at such a wretched hour.

This can't be good. They know better than to call about something trivial at this time of night. If it wasn't urgent, they'd make an appointment.

"Hello?" Leo answered.

"Uhhh, Mr. Stills. Yeah, it's, uh, Lieutenant Sharpe. We got a problem here."

"What is it?"

"Uhhh, it's your brother, Roman Stills, sir. We clocked him going 74 miles per hour in a 40 zone. Before we could get him pulled over, uhhh, he hit somebody crossing at the intersection as he blew through a red light… didn't even try to brake. He says he didn't see her and that she jumped in front of him."

"I'll be right there. Is Rome hurt? What's the address?"

"We are on 1st and Main. Rome is fine, sir… but this young lady passed away moments ago. We tested your brother and it came back positive for excessive amounts of caffeine and other coffee-related products – as well exorbitant levels of the Paradise Pill. That combination in this high of a dose could have killed Roman and it likely made him pass out while driving. He should be charged with Driving Under the Influence and probably felony counts of Vehicular Homicide or Second-Degree Murder."

Leo's face went pale.

What the hell, Rome! God, help us please.

"Lieutenant, put him in the back of a squad car and do not take him anywhere else. Contain the scene and get rid of the body."

"Yes, sir."

Leo went on, "I'll be there in five minutes."

"Yes, sir."

A few minutes later, Leo arrived on scene wearing a large, black overcoat to deflect the misting rain whipping around in the fierce wind. He walked past Rome sitting in the back of a squad car. Rome watched his brother converse with a couple officers, who only nodded in agreement as Leo spoke.

Leo pointed back at his older sibling, and one of the officers came over to let Rome out of the car.

Leo simply said, "Let's go, bro."

Rome followed without a word.

A few minutes later, they got back to Leo's house and walked to the library. Leo poured Rome a full glass of whiskey and handed it to his dazed brother. Rome, still shaken up, took a few sips, his mind far off.

He asked, "What did I do, Leo?"

Leo waited a moment, "Don't worry about that, man. I took care of everything. You're going to be okay."

"The girl, though… she's dead, isn't she?" Rome asked, still visibly shaking.

Leo reassured his brother, "I took care of it, Rome. Nothing will happen to you. What were you doing?"

Rome confessed, obviously jittery and talking very quickly, "Mary Anne and I were trying some different coffee products… ended up being several hours before I realized how late it was. I started getting a headache, so I took a couple of the Paradise Pills to even out. I dropped her off and when I was headed home… well, I don't even remember after that," he sighed, slumping down into his chair.

Out of love, Leo said, "Roman, you have to cut this stuff out. I won't keep enabling you. If you can't get yourself together, I'm going to have to bench you. Tell me what you need from me to get yourself better."

Rome replied quickly, "Leo, I will turn it around. I will do better than this. I *am* better than this. I got it under control… from now on."

Leo said, "I hope so. Meet me tomorrow at the Coffee Spot, 9:00 a.m."

"You got it, bro."

I feel like Rome's got no real sense of meaning in his life. Mankind was created to work. We have to work hard and contribute, or we lose our way… we got lost. When we get too comfortable, we end up drowning in our constant focus for sensory pleasures, instead of engaging in meaningful work that can give us a sense of worth and dignity. We were not meant just to consume, consume, consume. Without enough positive meaning derived from us taking on challenging responsibilities, we will be overwhelmed by the predictable suffering and the inescapable tragedy of this world. It's time I made something happen for Rome. He's been sliding down hill for a while and I can't let it go anymore.

"Good night, Rome dog."

Bright and early the next day, Leo was waiting for Rome at their local hangout. Rome walked to the backroom to find Leo already nursing a glass of whiskey and enjoying a fine cigar. It was not yet 8:45 a.m.

"Morning, dude," Leo said, motioning for Rome to sit down.

Leo began pouring Rome a glass of whiskey, when Rome waved him off, saying, "I'm cool, bro. Not now."

Hmmm, good.

Rome asked, "Did you want to talk about something or just check on me?"

Leo smiled, "Rome, it's a beautiful day outside. Wouldn't you agree? There is plenty to be thankful for – but our lives have gotten a bit more automated. As we have grown our company, the hands-on work you and I used to do ourselves is now being done by others."

Rome nodded silently.

Leo continued, "I think we need a new challenge. Maybe something fun and rewarding at the same time. I know you've always wanted your own bar and grill, so… I bought you one."

Rome looked puzzled, "What do you mean?"

Leo said, "Don't you just love this place? We've been coming here for years now. It feels like a second home." Smiling, Leo went on, "So, I bought it. It's yours."

"The Coffee Spot? For real?"

Leo chuckled, "Yes. There is no grill, so you'd have to figure out how to get that added, but there is plenty of unused space on the east wall over there. Now that this place is part of the Still's family of companies, it needs to turn a solid profit. Think you could handle it?"

"I think so. I mean, yes. Of course, I can. I didn't know it was for sale. How did you make that happen? Thank you, Leo man. I love it!" Rome's excitement was building as he started to envision the future of his own restaurant.

Leo responded nonchalantly, "You're welcome, Rome. I paid a fair price for it. The owner couldn't refuse."

Wouldn't dare refuse.

Leo went on happily, "So, next time I come in for a drink, you'll have to serve it to me."

Rome acknowledged without hesitation, "Deal. Love you, Leo."

"You too, bro. I gotta hit the bricks. I have an auction to attend and you have a business to run. Get this ship turned around," Leo said, not just talking about fixing up the restaurant.

Good luck, Rome.

And so, Leo continued to launder the corporation's dirty money into clean real estate owned directly by his family members, building up quite an empire on top of the many thousands of rental units that the company itself owned throughout Belmont.

Leo went on to meet up with Seth so they could head out for today's real estate auction. Of course, when Seth showed up, Donny was right behind him, as always. Their destination was the neighboring city of Himp. Because they were a little out of their element, Seth recommended a local broker friend that knew the area very well.

When they arrived, Seth walked up to a nice-looking woman wearing a slim red dress.

He said in the way all salesmen say, "Charlotte! Great to see you again. How's the family? Good, good. Charlotte, I'd like you to meet Leo Stills. Leo, Ms. Charlotte Smith-Jones, the very best broker in all of Himp."

Smiling, Charlotte retorted, "You're too kind, as always, Seth. Mr. Stills, it's a pleasure. I hear you would like to do a fair amount of business today."

Leo smiled and shook her hand, saying, "The pleasure is mine, I'm sure."

Covering up blushing cheeks, she quickly diverted from the charm, and began her spiel, "There are a lot of units today and the competition is fierce. You can see, there is standing room only remaining – but, I have reserved a few seats in the front row."

As she led the boys forward, Leo stopped them, saying, "I'd rather we stand in the back."

Without waiting for confirmation from the others, he made his way through the crowd and stood back row center. The others followed him.

"Whatever you want," Charlotte whispered to herself.

After a very successful auction where they picked up hundreds of new units, mostly studio apartments, the boys began to wrap it up.

Charlotte said to Seth, "You know where to send my commission check. Let me know if you ever need anything else." Turning to Leo, she smirked, "I've enjoyed your company today, Mr. Stills. Feel free to call me anytime you want anything. Day or night, I always answer for my best clients."

Anything? Day or night? Focus, Leo, focus! Always getting distracted. These women out here are going to be the death of me.

Leo concluded their business by saying with a polite smile, "Of course. Take care, Ms. Charlotte."

<u>Story 13</u>

Weeks went by, when late one night, Leo was leisurely spending some time in his home library, appreciating a smooth cigar. He was listening to some funky jazz music on an old record player when he heard a tapping at his door.

Hmm – it's after 10:00 p.m. Who could that be?

Making sure he had his pistol on him, he opened the front door to find Luka and Rimmy from the local faction of the Braxton militia forces.

Not appreciating the unannounced visit, Leo said, "What do you want?"

Rimmy smiled, "Is that any way to greet old friends? Goodness. Won't you invite us in? It's just so dreadfully chilly out here."

Sighing, Leo opened the door and moved back, gesturing them in, "You have five minutes."

After the two uninvited guests entered, Leo turned to follow, shutting the door behind him with his foot as he went.

Instead of hearing the door click shut, he heard the bumping sound of a hard shoe blocking the door from closing – followed by a familiar, yet dreaded voice saying, "Mr. Stills. Congratulations on your legal coffee license. You have built quite the legitimate enterprise on such a rotten, unlawful foundation."

After tightening his grip on the handle of his pistol, Leo spun around to find Agent Long walking through his front door.

What is he doing here? With them? An American FBI agent working with the Braxton militia. That's treason. How much does he know and who's working for who here? Stay calm. We have more questions than answers at this point.

The Special Agent went on, "I missed you at the hospital. I was hoping we could touch base before you checked out, but glad to see you recovered so well."

While saying this, the Special Agent used his walking cane to nudge Leo right on the sensitive ribs that were broken weeks ago and were still incredibly tender.

Wincing invisibly, Leo said through gritted teeth, "Right this way," making sure the front door was shut and locked this time. As Leo was the last to enter the library, he found his seat while he said to Rimmy, "Ha! Pretty ironic, you must admit."

"What is?"

"You're working for the very government you wish to take down. You think you're furthering your mission more than the feds are furthering theirs?"

Agent Long cut in, "Play nice, kids. I am told that you did good work on your last assignment, Mr. Stills. As such, we have another one for you. Only this guy will be a little trickier to track down."

Here we go, the slippery slope. One murder wasn't enough. I'm not turning into a government hitman. This stops here.

Leo shot back, "I don't work for you… and by my count, you owe me one from the last dead body."

The Special Agent explained, "You're not in a position to negotiate. The Federal Government of the United States of America has you dead to rights on a murder charge, solicitation and conspiracy. You will do as your told, like the mutt you are."

Without skipping a beat, Leo retorted, "You can't prove that without implicating yourself and your involvement with foreign nationals."

Bluffing further, Leo went on, "You think I don't keep track of all these meetings? You think you aren't being videotaped right now? I'll let you know when I need something from either of you. If all you came here to do was ask another favor, then you can leave. We are done. Next time, I'd appreciate if you called ahead of time and made an appointment with my office. Show a little professional courtesy."

If these guys actually work for Agent Long, that means the head of the feds is coordinating all of this. The feds know we committed that murder… but it was for them apparently. That means – the entire FBI was threatening me the other day when Agent Long came to the hospital and blackmailed me. They already knew then about the murder.

Special Agent Long whispered into Rimmy's ear, while Luka stared holes into Leo.

After a moment, the FBI Agent said, "Well, I suppose if you won't be cooperative, that will be all for now. We'll be in touch."

They quickly exited the premises. Leo could see Rimmy glancing around the room for hidden cameras, which would be impossible to find in the dim library. The simmering fire was the only source of light in the small room fighting off the shadows of night. Brushing that interaction off, Leo went right back to enjoying his evening alone.

He woke up early the next day with a lot of business to accomplish. Leo briefly met up with Seth for breakfast, where Leo handed him his official business card for the Stills Corporation. After the two agreed on a compensation package, they shook hands and Leo made a couple additional errands on his way to the office.

His last stop was to meet the real estate broker, Ms. Charlotte Smith-Jones, at the local park to discuss coming on board as an employee of the Stills Corporation. She was pleased when she received Leo's invitation to get together, though wasn't quite sure of his intentions for the date.

Charlotte was clothed quite pleasantly in a flower-print dress and it appeared as if she put a decent amount of effort into making herself presentable for her meeting with Leo.

When he approached, she greeted him warmly, "Good Morning, Mr. Stills. How are you this fine day?"

"Very well, Ms. Charlotte. I trust all is well with you?"

She nodded in agreement.

Leo went on to explain his desire, not for her personally, much to her chagrin, but instead for her to lead the newly formed Stills Brokerage company, another legitimate arm of the Stills Corporation family brand.

After talking strategies and compensation, she accepted the job, saying, "I've got to be honest, Mr. Stills. I was hoping you didn't call on me strictly for business reasons."

Thinking about the tangled web that already was his love life, he dodged the question by responding, "Well, for now certainly, that is all I can offer. I wish you the best and welcome aboard. Now I can sleep better at night knowing our fledgling brokerage company is now in good hands."

"You have no idea how good."

Whoa. Okay then.

At that, Leo smiled politely and excused himself from the park bench, while loosening his tie a little to let out some of the steam that was building up under his collar. When he got to the family office, Rome was waiting for him to discuss the further expansion of their business into San Mikel. The plan was for Rome to take down a platoon of foot soldiers and forcefully take over the Hot Cups location once and for all.

They were to immediately begin operating it and collecting the revenues themselves. Rome was set to meet up with a group of Rubenfield's crew as additional firepower and a show of unification between the two families that hoped to strike fear into the Sanchez crew and avoid retaliation altogether.

Sanchez should know better than to engage in a war against both the Stills and Rubenfield clans and would hopefully retreat to his other strongholds in the Texas region. In two days' time, Rome planned to make the long trip down to the hellish heat of Southern California.

On his way out of the office, April stopped Leo to get his signature on their latest project. The Stills Corporation was contributing to a college plan and a trust fund for every child of the family; Phil and Jane's son, as well as Eli's four children.

Even when I'm gone, I will be able to take care of my family. If I can just do enough, I can control everything that happens to them. Reality will bend to my will. What are you talking about, 'reality will bend to your will?' What is this, a movie? Who talks like that? Plus, that's craziness. Shut up in there!

Leo said to April, "Thank you. Please make sure Jane and Eli get the letters that explain what's going on and the details on how to access these accounts."

"Sure thing, boss," she replied, though didn't move from out of his way.

"Anything else?" Leo asked innocently, his head still thinking about the million different things he had to get done.

"I guess not," was all she said, as she trotted back to her desk clearly disappointed.

Leo shrugged, confused. Not thinking of it any further, he went home for the day.

A couple days later, when Leo woke up during a restless night, he texted Rome, who was scheduled to hit the Hot Cups spot down in San Mikel later that night with Rubenfield's boys. Rome texted back that all was well and that he was just meeting up with the Rubenfield crew now.

Leo replied, "Send me updates. Let me know when we are up and running at that location."

Leo had his whiskey shot and headed into the Stills Corporation office where he was bombarded by Eli as soon as he got in the front door. "Leo! Have you heard from Rome?"

"Yeah, he just texted me a few minutes ago. Why? What's wrong, Elijah?" Leo asked.

Eli shot back, "That couldn't have been him. Our crew was jumped when they arrived in San Mikel. After getting down there, Rubenfield's soldiers disappeared. A quarter of Sanchez's army showed up and got our guys bad. They were tipped off. This all happened at sunrise this morning, about four hours ago. Whoever you were talking to, it wasn't Rome."

"How do you know?" Leo said, his fury mounting.

"We just got a call from one of our guys who made it out of there alive. There was a huge skirmish, he couldn't see what happened to everyone, but he did say he saw Rome get shoved into a dark van. There were so many people and so much blood everywhere."

That dirty bastard. I'm going to kill Rubenfield with my bare hands if anything happened to Rome.

Leo replied, calm on the outside, "I'll take care of it. Get back to work."

Worriedly, Eli went on, "What are we going to do about Rome? We can't let him just…"

"Eli! I said I got it. Let me handle it."

Leo stormed out the front door and made a phone call to his favorite Special Agent at the FBI.

Agent Long picked up on the second ring, "Hello?"

"It's Leo Stills. We need to talk. Meet me at the Belmont park in twenty minutes. I'm already on my way." Leo hung up the phone.

He better come.

Leo was waiting on the park bench, constantly getting up and pacing back and forth from a mix of anxiety and rage, when FBI Agent Nathan Long arrived on scene.

"What can I do for you in such a hurry, Mr. Stills?" Agent Long asked.

Leo dove right into it, "I know you know what happened between Rubenfield and Sanchez. Tell me."

Sheepishly, the Special Agent played coy, "What do you mean? It's not like we are watching every…"

"SHUT… UP!" People at the park looked around at the commotion as Leo continued, "Shut the hell up, Nathan. I don't have time for games. They have Rome and I know you have been keeping an eye on all my business. The next time something like this happens and you *don't* tell me…"

Special Agent Long cut him off, "Let me stop you there, Mr. Stills, before you threaten a federal agent. Hmmmm, let's see. Roman Stills, you say? Yes, I may have heard a thing or two about what happened."

Silence.

Agent Long continued, "Sanchez flew into Seattle late Tuesday night and met up with Rubenfield for dinner after hearing rumors around town about a potential takeover attempt on his San Mikel coffee distribution channels. They had a two-hour meeting and left looking incredibly friendly, considering what you and Rubenfield were allegedly planning against Sanchez. Word around town is, Sanchez offered to turn his loan-sharking clients in San Mikel over to Rubenfield's 'Payday Loan' business, which would make Rubenfield a national powerhouse in the private lending industry and double his revenues fast, quick and in a hurry. Rubenfield obviously offered up information on the hit you two planned, as well as promising an infamous Stills brother for revenge because of the nefarious plot you schemed against him… to teach you a lesson. The two of them partnering together have become the talk of the town. Rubenfield is just a businessman and he used your deal to leverage an even better one. Sanchez is the crazy one, because besides avoiding you and Rubenfield teaming up against him, the only thing he negotiated was taking Rome as retribution… it's the principle of the thing for him."

"What happened to Rome?"

"He's safe, for now… badly beaten, hardly alive, but our latest intel places him safe in a prison cell owned by Sanchez on the outskirts of San Mikel. So, I hear, anyway."

Using up his favor earned from the previous dealings with the militia-requested murder of the SOPA director, Leo requested, "Get him back here tonight, alive, and we're even. I'll be at my office waiting until he gets there."

With that, Leo stormed off, calculating his next move.

Agent Long poked at him as he walked away, "What? Not even a 'goodbye'?"

Already on a short fuse, Leo paused -

No one talks to us that way. Go smack him upside the head. Don't do it. Do it! He's not worth it. But it will feel so good! We got to get Rome back. Focus. Focus.

- and then decided against turning around in response to that disrespect. He had bigger fish to fry.

As Leo arrived at the family office, his emotions got the better of him and he became incensed. Rage seem to grab hold of him, as he kicked open the front door with a loud bang. The glass window in the door threatening to shatter in response, he went on, crashing his way through the lobby. He flipped over one of the desks and threw a metal chair through the small conference room window as he screamed like a wild animal.

Everyone else who was in the office at the time kept very still, not wanting to become the focus of that anger. Leo kept on up the stairs, where instead of breaking down in tears, he punched through the glass of a picture frame hanging on the wall that showed him and Rome fishing on the town lake last year.

He stormed into his office and slammed the door behind him. This time, the old, fragile glass window shattered out of its frame, crashing all over the floor. He sat down in his desk chair, panting, while his knuckles carried shards of glass from the picture frame and dripped blood slowly into a puddle on the old wooden floorboards.

With them working together, I have no chance against Rubenfield and Sanchez. I'm losing control. I have to break them apart. I gotta regain the leverage. Ooooooh man! These guys aren't going to know what hit 'em.

Hearing the ruckus, Ms. Charlotte, who was using the previously quiet time to settle into her new office, came running in.

She asked, "Are you okay, Leo!?"

Leo sat there silently fuming. Stepping over the piles of broken glass, Charlotte walked over to him and hugged him. He didn't respond.

After a few moments of that uncomfortably awkward position standing over him, she sat down on his lap and grabbed his face in her hands, forcing eye contact, "Leo!? You're scaring me!"

Silence.

Overwhelmed with the emotional situation and combined with her previous attraction to Leo, Charlotte simply embraced him, wanting to be there for him.

Leo then said as he tried to create some distance between their two bodies, "I'm fine. I'm fine."

She was unconvinced and kissed him on the cheek. Pausing to find Leo not refusing her advances, she kissed him again on his neck, as she continued sitting on his lap. "I want you to feel better. You know, I've been meaning to tell you how much I like you."

Another kiss as her hands found their way around his trembling body, which was not shaking from the same excitement she was feeling, but instead from his bubbling anger.

She went on, "I've been waiting for you to ask me out on a date, you silly man."

Charlotte couldn't help but be somewhat intrigued by Leo's dark side. There was a true monster in there that Leo had not quite learned to control.

Just then, April rushed into Leo's office to check on the disturbance, only to see Charlotte comfortably positioned on Leo's lap. Charlotte was embracing him, while Leo sat there distractedly staring off into space. Though shocked at the scene, April then saw the blood leaking from his hand forming quite a pond on the floor.

"Leo! Your hand!" April shouted, rushing over to Leo, nonchalantly pushing Charlotte out of the way in the process… pretending she didn't even notice Charlotte sitting there caressing her boss. "Let me take care of that for you," she demanded.

Leo followed April to the bathroom so she could clean up his hand, as Charlotte spoke loudly toward them, "Let me know if you need anything else, Leo. I'll see you later."

After April silently cleaned Leo's self-inflicted wounds, she held his hand, unable to wait any longer to ask, "So, what was that all about?"

"Huh?"

"With *her*… in your office?"

"Huh? Oh… I don't know, April. I don't have time for this right now."

"You never do," she said, losing her temper. "Do you need anything else from me… *sir*?"

Silence.

Unsatisfied with his lack of commitment to her, April stormed out of his office as she said, "I guess I'll just get someone to clean up this mess. Bye."

Leo didn't say anything. After about an hour of brooding there at his desk, feeling the aches in his hand, he heard a commotion downstairs where he could clearly hear Seth yelling. Leo made his way downstairs to find Seth and Donny loudly clamoring back and forth. Seth was trying to open up a whiskey bottle, of which he clearly did not need any more. It was difficult to understand what Seth was so noisy about until Leo got up close.

Leo asked, "What's going on, boyos?"

Seth and Donny, now noticing someone else was in the room, looked at each other and laughed as if they were both reliving the same recent memory. As they were giggling to themselves, Leo began to notice their battle wounds; ripped clothes, black eyes, fat lips.

"What happened," Leo asked.

Seth finally cracked open the bottle with an exasperated sigh of sweet relief and poured three glasses. Handing one to Leo and one to Donny, he took his own and found a seat with a loud groan.

Seth explained in between hiccups, "So, me and the Don-man went out for a drink, right? As soon as we walked in the joint, this group o' guys start hassling us, ya know?"

"Why?"

"Well, Donny being Jewish… you know, people don't take kindly to religious folk no more. Funny how intolerant the people are that say they push for tolerance. Anyway, nothing new, especially for Don, being so apparent with the yarmulke… haha… we let it slide for a little bit. But then they came up to our table and started hassling us, taking Donny's head covering off and tossing it back and forth."

For the last several decades, anti-religious sentiment has taken a stronghold in American politics and the culture at large. Even though this country was founded and still relies upon a set of Judeo-Christian values, religious institutions have been beaten down as bigoted and outdated. It started with separation of church and state, and then became worse. They said religious ideals were discriminatory and thus were made illegal in the public sphere. There were more terrorist acts at churches and synagogues than ever, fueled by intolerant political rhetoric that said the religious fools were just getting what they deserved, reaping the hate-filled crop of the intolerant seeds they sewed for themselves.

"Did you explain you were part of our company?" Leo asked, as he made eye contact with April who was coming into the room.

"It devolved too quickly, Leo. You know how it gets. These guys must'a been drinking long before we got there. They come up shouting all sorts of nonsense, 'Your kind ain't welcome here,' and all that jazz. You know we can't take that type of disrespect lying down. See what I'm saying? As soon as they grabbed his yarmulke and tossed it to another guy, though… boy howdy, Donny hit that first jackal with an uppercut right under the chin. That guy dropped - out cold, son. Donny went to pick up his head covering when two of the other guy's friends tackled him. I was wrestling them off when I got tackled too. We held our ground. The other guys don't look much better than us - right, Don? Crazy! The whole bar started into a brawl after that, but it was still me and the Don versus five or six of them guys. Five, I guess, if you don't count the one Donny knocked out in the beginning… haha!"

They both started laughing, obviously unbothered by the disgraceful prejudice they just experienced. As Seth let out a breath and went to take another gulp of his whiskey, he made eye contact with Leo, who was not laughing at all.

Leo asked, "You think they're still there?"

"Well, after we had our fill, we left the bar. I think they went back to their booth and kept partying. Why? No harm, no foul, man. We got some good shots in too."

Leo turned around to Eli who had since entered the room, "Eli, take at least ten of our guys who are looking for a good tussle over to this bar. Seth will show you the way. Seth, when you get there, I want you to let those jokers, and everyone else in the bar, know what family they messed with, and then let Eli and the boys finish off the good work you started. We can't let word spread around this town… my town… that things like this go unavenged."

This is the exact situation that caused Sera to leave me long ago. My decision to be so brutal. But it's necessary. She just didn't understand the world I inhabit. The only way to make it, is to play dirtier than the next guy. I hope April understands.

"You got it," was Eli's simple and unquestioning response.

Eli promptly rounded up the troops and followed Seth back out the front door, whiskey bottle in hand.

Seeing April staring at him, Leo pulled Eli aside and quietly gave him an additional instruction, "Eli, after you boys beat the living hell out of those suckers… torch the place."

Eli looked up, surprised by the severity… but at the same time, not really surprised by the severity. Eli simply nodded and went on to carry out his mission.

Now that the excitement was over, Leo's mind returned to Rome.

He should have been here by now. Where is he?

April was making her way over to Leo in a hurry. Leo was unsure if she was going to continue the conversation from upstairs, or object to the orders he had just given his men. Either way, he wasn't looking forward to that particular dialogue.

Luckily, before she could get going, the front door opened again. In walked two federal agents pushing a wheelchair. Rome, looking like hell, drugged up from painkillers, was sleeping uncomfortably with his neck bent over sideways. Leo looked at them, thanked the agents briefly and then showed them the door.

"April, call Rome a car to take him to my house."

Wishing to have a lengthier conversation with her boss, but understanding the situation, she groaned, "Fine."

Leo went on, "And April?" She just paused for a moment, not turning around to face him. He said, "Go with him, and wait for me there?"

She didn't turn around, but Leo was sure he saw her head nod ever so slightly in agreement.

I wonder if she will be there when I arrive. She's been through a lot, but always stayed by my side. Held me down.

Story 14

The next day, Leo and April rode into work together. They arrived at the family office around 2:00 p.m., after a late breakfast at Leo's house. Leo proceeded to sit at the desk in his office and finalize a plan to recapture the Hot Cups location from Sanchez down in San Mikel.

As he sat there plotting, he received a text from one of his copper friends, "Fed Special Agent arrested your man Seth after a brawl in a bar last night. Leveraging for information. FYI."

What the hell is he thinking. What's going on here!? How could life get any more chaotic than these last few days. On top of losing the battle for San Mikel thus far and Rome being beaten half to death, Seth is in jail now for some reason… everything is turning against me! I'm struggling to maintain the support and safety of my family. We need to get leverage back on several different points within this precarious house of cards we have built. My life could not get any more complicated!

Speak of the devil. As that thought was put into Leo's head…

Wait. What do you mean put into my head? It's my thought. No one put it there. What makes you so sure it's your thought? You don't know where your thoughts come from. What? Who's saying that? Thoughts pop into your head from seemingly nowhere – from the black chaotic depths of nothingness that is your conscious mind. We don't understand consciousness at all.

… just then, Leo heard a knock on his door, interrupting the insanity brewing in his cranium.

April poked her head into his office, saying, "Leo?"

"Not now. I'm losing my mind."

"There is someone here to see you."

"I said not now, April."

"Ummmm, Eli said you would really want to make time to meet with her."

"Her?"

"I guess her name is Sera, or something? She's very pretty."

Silence.

After a few seconds, Leo wiped the shock off his face and picked his jaw up off the floor.

"Please, show her in," Leo said, scrambling to straighten up his desk and clean up a few things around his office.

Just before he heard the two female's high heels tap their way to the top of the stairs, he plopped back down into his leather chair, pretending to look busy and nonchalant.

"Hi, Leo," said a quiet, timid voice that Leo was only able to hear these days while he dreamt during those long, lonely nights.

Sera.

After closing his eyes for what felt like years, Leo tried to wake himself up. He opened his eyes and raised his head, maintaining his composure as he began to realize that this was no dream.

"Sera! Please, sit here." He rushed to lead her to a seat.

Sera nodded at April, who slowly left them alone, but only after closely studying their body language as long as possible without being overly nosy. Leo didn't even say 'thank you' to April. Instead, he was fully focused on Sera. April left the door slightly ajar and then took her seat at the desk right outside Leo's office, not necessarily closing her ears.

After Sera sat down, Leo found room on the other side of the couch, leaving an open seat in between them and giving her space.

She said, "I'm sorry we haven't talked in so long."

Silence.

She went on, "I'm sure you think I was cruel in taking away our child, but I didn't know what else to do. The unrepentant beast that I saw inside you was… horrifying. You scared me. You weren't the boy I met in school that saw only good in the world around him. The harmless boy that I grew to love, that wouldn't hurt a fly."

Silence. Leo couldn't stop staring at her.

The most beautiful woman I've ever laid eyes on.

Sera continued, "I've been meaning to come back… to reach out. But you know how it goes. Life got in the way. I got busy. I'm sure you…"

Silence.

I can't believe she's back. I hope she is here to stay. I don't care what happened in the past. I need her now more than ever. She belongs with me… my other half.

Getting unsettled at his lack of response, Sera shouted, "Say something, Leonardo! I feel just awful. I've missed you and I realize now that abandoning you was wrong for us and for our son."

At that, she lowered her eyes in submission, in defeat. She had no better excuses and simply laid herself at his mercy.

Leo finally moved, taking her hand in his and staring straight through her dark brown eyes into the very depths of her soul. They had previously been two parts of one great whole. They had given everything to each other, held nothing back – except perhaps hiding the darkness that sometimes resides next to the light within all of us and is always there waiting to break free from its eternal chains.

He spoke, "I want you now as much as ever. I can love you in a way that you deserve to be loved. All that matters, is that you're here now."

At that, she threw herself onto him, hugging him with all her strength. Instantly, it all came back – the familiar embrace of not just a lover, but of his one, true beloved. The commotion raised April's eyebrows as she strained to look over the railing through her boss' office window.

Leo asked hopefully, "Have dinner with me?"

Shocked at his mercy and lack of anger or resentment, Sera hesitated, "I can't. I have something that I need to…"

Leo stopped her, halfway smiling, "Tell me over dinner. That's not a question. I know a really fancy place right on the corner. It's so expensive, I usually don't have a good enough reason to eat there – until now."

That's one of the main reasons she loved him. He always knew what he wanted, and he was never afraid to fight for it. His confidence, his calm, his brilliance, his beautiful green eyes.

Sighing, Sera answered with a tiny smile against her better judgement, "Fine."

Leo's grin, on the other hand, went from ear to ear.

He said softly, "Great. I have some things I need to finish up this afternoon. I will send a car to pick you up at 7:00 p.m. tonight – just leave your address with April."

Though it was not at all her business in a sense, given her decision to leave Leo so long ago, Sera couldn't help herself, "Is April your assistant? She's very attractive."

Leo laughed, "Yeah, yeah. I'll see you tonight."

Unsatisfied with the response, but excited about their dinner date, Sera said, "I guess I'll be on my way then, good sir."

Both of them stood up, now in full view of April's wandering eyes, and Sera leaned in to give Leo a kiss on the cheek.

Leo blushed for the first time in a long time and quickly motioned towards the door, inviting her to precede him on her exit. He closed the door to his office after she left and went to sit back down in his chair, frozen in amazement at what just happened. That is, until he saw that April and Sera were talking much longer than necessary just to confirm an address for dinner.

What are they talking about? What's taking so long? Go break it up. Stop. It'll be fine. Just be cool.

After a few minutes of making Leo sweat, the girls smiled at one another. April gave Sera a hug and then Sera left.

Hmmm. Quite the sight to see there.

After an all-too-cordial interaction with Sera, April walked back into Leo's office on the hunt for answers. Leo looked up and saw April's face as reality set in on his previous interactions with her, and how that situation would be infinitely complicated with Sera now coming back into his life.

Not wanting to get into it right now, and not really knowing what to say, Leo blurted out, "I gotta go."

Sensing the palpable anxiety, April got on her tippy toes and went in to give Leo a kiss goodbye.

Leo pulled away, whispering, "Not now, April."

A little hurt, she tried another route, "Okay. I'm still coming over tonight, right?"

That might be a bit much.

Leo replied, "I can't, April. It's complicated. Sera and I have a serious history that I can't just ignore."

With that, he quickly left and went home to get ready for his dinner date. The first thing he did was have a glass of whiskey, or three, to calm his nerves. Then he took a long bath, shaving afterwards. He had another glass of whiskey as he waited for the moment to arrive.

When the time had come, Leo ordered a car to pick him up and take him to the pub where he was to meet Sera for dinner. As he beat Sera there, he found a table and ordered a pint.

He was absentmindedly sipping a cold lager when his eyes were drawn to a beautiful angel walking towards him.

He stood up and greeted her, "Good to see you again."

Sera found her seat on the other side of the small, square dinner table.

As the two sat there nervously, not quite sure where to start, the waitress arrived and set a drink down in front of Sera, saying, "Lemon Drop for the lady."

Sera looked up at Leo, amazed at his memory and his thoughtfulness, "My favorite drink. You remembered."

It felt just like old times when the two of them were inseparable. They ordered their food and finished the rest of the dinner mostly in silence. Some small talk here and there in between several rounds of drinks – but, for the most part, they simply enjoyed each other's quiet company.

Sera ordered such an expensive banana split after dinner, Leo couldn't help himself, "Let me have some of that. I want to know how good a $27 bowl of ice cream can really be."

With such few words said, when the end of the meal approached all too soon, Leo asked if they could continue their time together, "I don't want this to end. Come back to my house?"

Our house.

"I really don't think that's a good idea."

"Sera, come on. We have so much to talk about. You didn't stop by just for this."

"Lee, it wouldn't be right…"

"Why not? Besides, didn't you say you had something you need to tell me. We can talk about it more at home. You know, I mean, at my house."

Sera was not sure if it was the alcohol that got the better of her judgement, but she reluctantly agreed. As they were heading towards the door, Leo spotted two men entering the restaurant and they looked like nothing but trouble.

While they had their backs to Leo talking to the bartender, Leo overheard them say, "I'm sure you are familiar with Sal Rubenfield. He sent us to find Mr. Leo Stills and deliver a message. We were told Mr. Stills would be here tonight."

Hastily, he whispered to Sera before the men had a chance to pass by them, "Kiss me."

Caught off guard, Sera said, "What? Leo… I don't…"

Leo shot back, "Unless you want to die tonight, kiss me now."

With that, Leo pulled her in, pressed her up against the wall and leaned in for a kiss. Without hesitating, Sera reciprocated with a long, sweet embrace – just like the old days. The two men finished questioning the bartender and turned to go check the rest of the restaurant for Leo, barely noticing the couple that was engaging in a lengthy kiss further down the dimly lit hall.

When the men were gone from sight, the kiss didn't stop right away. After a few heartbeats, when it was definitely safe, Leo called for a car to take them straight back to Leo's house – the same house he used to share with Sera and his son, Caden.

As they were riding home, Sera asked, "So you're still getting into trouble, huh?"

Leo sighed, "Oh, come on, Sera. Let's not get into this right now."

She acquiesced and they rode the rest of the way back in silence.

When they got back, Leo poured them both another drink, started a fire and then sat down next to her on the plush leather couch.

Leo asked, "So, how's Caden?"

She responded, "He's good… with his grandmother right now."

Leo nodded.

That sparked a conversation full of reminiscing about their past. They talked for a couple hours and had several more cocktails.

As Leo noticed their empty glasses and went to pour another drink, Sera resisted, "I should probably go. I'm pretty tipsy at this point. I don't think I could handle much more drinking."

Still disappointed at the thought of her leaving, Leo said, "Oh, definitely. Uhhh, yeah, here. Let me get your coat."

Forgetting exactly where she dropped her coat earlier, he finally found it on the floor in the hallway, just outside his library. When he came back carrying her jacket, he paused in the doorway. She was standing there, the light from a roaring fire illuminating ever feature, every curve. He stood there amazed, staring at the mother of his child and, except for in recent years, one of his best friends.

She looked at him and smiled.

I wonder what she sees when she looks at me.

Sera always was able to focus on the true beauty of Leo's character; the hope which lied underneath that rough exterior. Not wanting to ruin the moment with words, he walked over behind her. She put her arms behind her back and raised them slightly, inviting him to slip her coat on.

As he did, his hand touched her silky skin and both of them swore they felt a literal spark. She sighed lightly as he continued to put the coat on, until all the sudden, he stopped. He let the coat fall off her arms, straight down to the floor. Instead, he put his hands on her waist and pulled her back gently into him. The fire roared hotter in one of those ever-elusive heaven-on-earth experiences, until they both fell asleep next to the fireplace in absolute bliss.

Hours later, when the ashes were smoldering, Sera was awakened by a loud banging on the front door. She stirred and groggily tried to open her eyes, heavily fatigued by the amount of alcohol still flowing through her veins. She shook Leo, attempting to wake him from his deep slumber.

After a few moments of that proving unsuccessful, the banging stopped. She prayed that she got lucky and whoever was there would just go away.

"OPEN UP!" was all she heard from an irate voice on the other side of the front door.

Leo sighed and rustled but slept soundly.

Sera slid her leg off Leo and unwound their bodies which were previously coiled together so peacefully by the fire. Still clearly tipsy, trying to regain her balance, she walked over to the bar and poured herself a quick double shot of whiskey.

She said to herself, "Wake up, wake up."

Only wearing Leo's large overcoat, she walked down the long hallway to go see who was at the door. As she did so, she paused and looked at the father of her child sleeping soundly next to the fire.

"Heavenly," she muttered to herself.

The knocking continued, loud enough for the neighbors to hear at this point – banging, banging, banging.

As she walked down the long hallway to the front door, she hollered back to the uninvited visitor, "All right! All right! I'm coming."

As Sera swung the door open, she was instantly hit with a barrage of yelling, "Who the hell do you think you are, huh? Some chick comes into town and you just throw me to the si…!"

Shocked, Sera was confronted by April who whirled around yelling before she also paused, quite surprised to see Sera standing there. April had apparently gone out for a night on the town herself. She was outfitted quite scantily in a tiny dress and obviously had a little bit to drink. Without being invited, she stumbled into the house making quite the commotion.

April said, "I didn't like how he treated me earlier. So, I went out to a couple bars where I met a lot of fun guys. I got so many free drinks…"

Sera conceded, "… I can tell. Wait here."

Sera walked back to the library, not quite sure where this was going to go. Unable to let Leo sleep any longer, she walked over to him and kicked him gently on the side.

Little did she know, those were the previously-broken ribs and it didn't feel like such a soft kick to Leo, who shot up in pain, saying, "What was that for?! Jeeze!"

Sera stared at him and flatly said, "Someone's here to see you."

Leo joked back, "Goodness, did you just have another drink? I don't like you when you're drunk. You get so physical."

Forgetting to be upset, Sera laughed, "Oh, I didn't hear any complaints earlier."

Leo chuckled and threw on his pants that he discovered sprawled out over the top of a chair. As he went to find out who urgently needed to see him, he was hit in the head with his shirt.

"Put some damn clothes on," Sera said. She pushed further, "After you get rid of her, maybe we can take them back off."

Her?

Leo did not pause to make any promises. Instead, he pulled the shirt over his head as he walked out into the hall, shutting the library doors behind him. As he got down the hallway, he saw April there leaning against the door. When she heard him coming, she quickly straightened herself up. It seemed like she had just passed out while she was waiting. She was clearly dressed for a night out on the town.

Or a night out on the dance pole, more like it.

April began, arms flying with emotion, "How dare… Oh!"

Leo reached her mid-sentence, grabbed her flailing arms and shoved her firmly up against the wall, ordering, "Stop."

She pretended to struggle against him, but changed her tone to a soft, sweet sound, saying, "It's good to see you. I…"

Interrupting her again, he said, "Why are you dressed like a hooker? It's not safe for you to be completely wasted and walking around town like that so late at night."

Unoffended, she replied, "What do you mean? Don't you think I look good?" As she said this, she twirled around for him, inviting him to take a look at her outfit. "I dressed like this because I thought you would like it."

Though quite intoxicated himself at this point, he said, "You're drunk. You shouldn't be here."

"It's not like we haven't had fun here before while I was drunk," she purred back.

She kept trying to move closer to him.

Leo said firmly, "Stop. I'm with Sera."

April replied, "I don't mind."

Wondering why it was taking Leo so long to simply throw her out, Sera came walking down the hall in a hurry.

Ohhhh boy. Okay. This is not good. I'm pretty drunk, they are both really drunk. This could end up really bad. Focus.

Untangling from the aggressive April, Leo turned and said to Sera, "Babe, give me a minute. I'll get her…"

Sera put her hand up to stop Leo from talking and walked right passed him.

Uh oh.

Leo tried again, "Sera!"

As Leo slowly backed away from the situation, Sera got really close to April, saying something Leo couldn't hear. Sera then put her arm around April and the two of them held hands as they walked down the long hallway passed the library to the guest bedroom.

I should leave.

<u>Story 15</u>

The sun rose on that chaotic house the next day. Leo woke up, not sure if what happened a few hours earlier was only a bad dream. He sat up straight in his library chair, which served as his bed last night. He made sure not to leave the safety of the library until the light of the new day came shining through the windows. Now with a clear head, he went to get his morning medicine.

One glass of whiskey later, he poked his head out of the library, listening for any signs of life. Hearing nothing, he walked down the hallway to his bedroom, where he found Sera and April sleeping peacefully together.

So, not a dream. Right. Okay. Great.

Unsure really what to do next, he went to the kitchen and made some bacon and eggs. The smell of bacon frying pervaded the entire house.

Sera walked in a little later while Leo was getting ready to finish cooking and said, "Good morning, Lee."

She doesn't seem mad. Ask her if she slept well.

"Good morning," he replied cautiously.

He just kept cooking and working studiously as if nothing was amiss. He went to grab plates and then he paused.

Uhhhh, should I get three plates? Is April coming to eat?

Leo grabbed two plates and served up some bacon and eggs. He placed one plate in front of Sera and sat across from her at the table.

She said, "I didn't know you cooked."

Silence.

Sera went on, "I enjoyed *our* time together last night, before the unsolicited guest showed up."

"Me too."

"Look, Leo, I can't believe we ended up where we are. This is definitely not how I pictured our lives going. I know I left you years ago, but I feel like I had no choice. You had already given up."

Leo was confused. "What are you talking about?"

She hesitated and then continued, "You gave up on the good, Leo. You gave up on doing life the right way. That's no leader. You left me alone to stand up for my values. You left me alone to teach our son honor, courage and the lessons that build noble character. You gave up, but I have been fighting against the corruption that has nested within our society and drained the lives of so many Americans. The poverty, lack of innovation in healthcare, the unemployment, among so many other things, is dragging America back to the dark ages and more people are suffering than ever. Things are the worst they've ever been and if something doesn't change soon, we will no longer have anything worth protecting. Only the people in power have any sort of comfort these days."

Leo never really thought about how bad things were, especially for so many people. He didn't like the system himself, so he simply exited it. That's why he started his underground business operations and basically went off-grid in the first place. He became his own man, created his own society so that he wouldn't have to deal with these consequences that the large majority of his fellow Americans still endured.

The problem is, he left everyone else to fend off the corruption of the state for themselves.

He said, "I hear you. That's why I'm doing my own thing. I'm happy with my life. I could make you happy too, if you came back to me. I can provide for you and Caden."

Sera interrupted, "Leo, I left this life for a reason. You aren't living! You're merely surviving… even with all your fancy things and no real worries other than getting shot. That's a shell of a life."

"But, exactly. I mean. That's why it's great. You don't have to deal with the corrupt politicians lecturing you from their ivory towers; instead, we just reap the rewards. I can show you what true freedom is."

"Does that sound right to you?"

"Right? What is right? What is wrong? I lost faith in right and wrong… ha, a long time ago."

"That I know. You think we should teach Caden to reap the rewards of something without working for it? Leo… gah! You had so much promise as a kid, but now you're useless. There are things that need to be done and you could be so much more. People are starving, eating out of trashcans and off the street. I can hardly recognize America anymore."

Leo brushed off this heavy conversation, saying, "I don't see how any of this is my problem. Look, finish up your breakfast and then why don't we take a shower… together."

She quickly trashed that idea, "No! How can you brush this off?! We are on the brink of destruction. Frankly, I'm surprised we've lasted this long as a nation. We need people like you if we are going to avoid another civil war. The only way to fend off this oppression is to have people with good character working directly against it. It is your responsibility, every person's responsibility, to repair the government when it becomes tyrannical, so it works for the people again." She sighed, "You're not the Leo I used to know."

"Jeeze, you sound like someone with morals or something," he joked, trying to lighten the mood.

"At least one of us does."

Ouch! This is not going well.

Leo shot back, "Why would I go back to being a productive and truthful member of this corrupt society. It does no good and in fact, I get punished for it! You can't change the past. One person can't make a difference in the grand scheme of things."

The conversation now heating up, she calmly replied, "That thinking right there is at the root of the very problem you are complaining about. *You* are the problem when you think and act this way."

I'm the problem? What does she mean? Just because I figure a way around the troubles that everyone else just accepts? I simply go with the flow. I'm supposed to stand up to the mob? No! Just listen.

Leo would have none of it, "Stop! You have no idea what you're talking about!"

With that, he stormed out of the kitchen and out of the house, silently passing April in the hall who was coming to check on the commotion. Not attempting to impede his exit, April continued on to find Sera crying in the kitchen. April went up and put her arm around Sera, comforting her.

The first thing April blurted out was an apology for her abhorrent behavior last night, "I'm so sorry for crashing your party. I don't ever drink that much… I'm so embar…"

Cutting her off, Sera mumbled through tears, "Oh, it's okay. I understand. I just don't get him. You know? Why won't he be the leader I know he can be? It's such a waste of the good Lord's gifts."

Meanwhile, Leo was pacing around sporadically out in the fresh morning air.

Maybe she's not wrong. You have so much potential.

"I know that," he said aloud, answering the thoughts in his head. "I am pretty great," he laughed mockingly at himself, trying not to go insane.

He has shown me some of the great things that are planned for your future. You are destined to do great things for His world – here and there.

"What do you mean? Who are you?" Leo asked his head.

I think the better question is, who are you? I know who I am. Do you know who you are?

Leo replied to himself, or to whomever was putting these thoughts in his head, "Haha! Oh, I probably don't - but I suppose you know who I am?"

I've known you since the initial thought that created you ran through His consciousness billions of years ago.

Instantly, Leo's head was filled with a vision, unlike any experience in his life before. Not just thoughts in his head, but a clear picture like one might see on a television screen.

Let me show you. Let me show you who you are. Society is not doomed already, but merely well on its way. Times have not been so dark in ages. The assault on human freedom and its counterpart, personal responsibility, has never been greater. But! We must rescue this democratic republic – the nation that once symbolized better than any other on earth the true principles of His humanity – the nation that once served the Greatest Good, none which anything greater can be conceived. This Truth, this Reality – it lives in you!

Leo succumbed to the overwhelming vision where he saw a proper democracy. Leo saw himself standing on a podium in a suit and tie, waving his hands in the air while he addressed a stadium full of supporters waiving 'Stills 2052!' signs. Leo saw himself standing there, proclaiming the truth to people in desperate need of it, when suddenly an overwhelming light engulfed him.

Leo gasped, "What's going on?"

Leonardo! My child…

"Dad?"

You've forgotten Me. I made you to be more than what you've become. It is time for you to stop running from the fight. I need you to battle the shadows of corruption and tyranny that fill your lands. Never forget who you are – a child of the Light. You… are… My… son – a true heir to the kingdom of Heaven. I created specifically for you a guardian that guides your thoughts and shields you from the manipulation of the most evil one and his minions. This renders you invulnerable, so long as you cooperate with My grace.

With that, Leo was slammed back into his own head and the vision was over.

Leo continued to argue with whoever was in there, "But that means I have to reconcile with my past – with everything I've done and the monster I've had to become in order to survive; something I've been avoiding for so long."

He did not make you to be weak, but strong instead. You can run from your past, or you can learn from it. You have learned how to be strong, but you do not use your strength for good. It is time now, for your strength to be directed according to His will, the only true and proper Way. I do my best to shield you from evil thoughts, but the more you feed them, the stronger those demons become and the louder you hear them. Your thoughts are not your own. You are not you, but instead you are the decision. I provide you with good thoughts – thoughts that align with His will. My counterpart who resides in the darkest part of chaos seeks to fill you with perversion. We, however, merely provide suggestions. The only thought in your head that is truly your own is when you use your creative capacity to make a free and conscious choice. This is your share of the divinity within you that is made in the image of the one, true Creator and Sustainer of all things. That choice… is you. The rest is noise. So, what is your decision?

Leo shouted aloud, "I will do it! But, do what?"

At that, feeling crazier than ever for the conversation he just had in his head and the vision he saw, Leo made a choice going forward to do what he knew to be right.

Quit lying to him. He can't change the world. He's just one man.

"What?" Leo shot back, "I may not be able to change the whole world in an instant, but I can change myself. Every vote counts, as they say."

With that, he made a phone call and after a few rings, a female answered, "Hi, boss."

"April," Leo said, "I need you to look into how to run for public office. Figure out what needs to be done for me to get in the next major race, and make it happen."

Not waiting for a response, he hung up. Finally feeling a little genuine excitement about something for a change, he picked up the pace and headed to Bravo Tower.

Our hero! Slow down with the hero talk.

Leo hyped himself up as he went, "It's time for me to grow up and fix the things I can; to take responsibility where I am able. Ugh! I'm going to miss this false eutopia, though."

Excuse me, ladies and gentlemen. We are making a detour, exiting the easy route and merging onto the Straight and Narrow Path.

As he walked down the streets of Belmont, his city seemed more different than ever. He noticed rows and rows of people sleeping on the sidewalk; something that seemed just normal before. He saw the poverty-stricken society created by the void that is secularism. In our rush to put emotions over rationality, and at the same time argue rationality over everything else – we were left with run-down communities bereft of hope. The stench of urine and liquor-stained streets filled Leo's nostrils and it made him sick.

He texted his whole crew, "Family meeting in fifteen minutes."

He finally arrived at the family office and everyone was there waiting for him, chatting idly while they listened to news radio.

Washington State Senator Beth Adams was answering interview questions, "Senator Adams, what do you say to your critics, that endorse the notion you are really a socialist in disguise? That argue your open borders policy combined with the welfare programs you support are crippling our state? They say our high regulation and exorbitant taxes have stifled economic productivity and innovation - and are actually turning in on themselves. The food is gone, the companies have all moved out to more business-friendly areas. There's no wealth left to redistribute."

Senator Adams smiled, having already responded to this criticism a thousand times by appealing to people's surface-level, natural response for empathy, "Thank you for that question. Great question. Plain and simple, I was elected by the people, for the people of this great state. We are in a crisis, yes – but not an economic crisis. We are in a crisis where the rich and powerful make all the rules that only everyone else has to live by. I was voted in because I promised to take all the rich people's dirty treasure and give it back to the real working people! If we need more money, we will just raise taxes on the rich! They need to pay their fair share."

The interviewer rebuffed, "We've heard that trope before, but it is quite clearly no longer just affecting the richest of us. What say you about the fact that the marginal tax rate of someone making over $25,000 per year is 68%?! That means I only get to keep $0.32 cents for every dollar I make over $25,000. We are taxed at over 94.5% on every dollar over $42,000 per year!"

Ready with her headline talking points that would certainly be supported by her already affluent base constituents, the lady senator calmly replied, "Look, naysayers are going to say nay. Bottom line: it sounds like there is another 5.5% we can raise the taxes. It's simple and in fact, this seems like the right time to let you all know. We are pleased to announce a revolutionary government program that will most certainly solve every single one of your problems. No one pays for anything directly! Everything is free! How does that sound everyone!?" she asked, turning to the crowd and getting heavy praises and applause.

She went on, "People will go to work and all the money that would usually go from your paycheck to your personal bank account will instead go directly to the government treasury… every penny. Here's the kicker, though – we will then provide people everything they need in weekly rations; clothes, food, public housing projects for all… for FREE! It really is amazing. You don't need to worry about surviving or about how to take care of your family. The government will provide everything you need. Trust in me!" she said with an unwavering smile.

That's it!

Leo startled everyone by muttering, "Why worry about your freedom, individuality and the dignity of providing for your loved ones? Just sell your soul to the government. Give absolute power over to them and see what results come. What do people really think will happen when we centralize complete power in the hands of a few, rich politicians in D.C. that are completely shielded from the ramifications of the very policies they push on the rest of us?"

When they heard him, Rome quickly turned off the radio and everyone got quiet. As Rome sat there, uncomfortably adjusting in his chair, he took a few capsules. He had lingering pain from the San Mikel beating and found that taking some of the Paradise Pills helped him stay on top of things. Given where he and Leo left this conversation last time and the fact that Leo bought the Coffee Spot in an effort to get Rome off caffeine and other drugs, Rome kept this on the down low.

Leo began, "Thank you for coming, all. Cutting to the chase, what you just heard from our state senator is a major problem and actually sums up our crisis quite nicely. I've decided I'm going to run for mayor when the spot comes up for election here in the coming months. This is our kingdom – if we don't fight for it, who will?! Our country has lost its way and the state has become corrupt, no longer serving its people, but instead catering to the few that have managed to usurp power by purchasing our votes. I don't know exactly how we are going to succeed, but we've got to try. Who's with me?"

I'm nervous. Outside my wheelhouse here. I hardly feel like the right leader for this endeavor. I have a goal, but no strategy to get us there. What am I doing? My crew will turn on us. We are showing weakness. We must always be strong. Fake it if you have to… lie! Just don't lose their confidence or you will fail.

Not quite sure if he was serious or where Leo was going with this, Rome and Eli unhesitatingly spoke out, "Stills for Mayor! Haha! That's what I'm talkin' about! Yeeeeeah boyyyyy!"

The rest of the crew clapped raucously.

April spoke out, "Boss, you've taken care of each and every one of us standing in this room today. Even if you aren't sure how you're going to get us there, no one here would bet against you making it to the top. You are our man, our chief. We would follow you to the depths of hell and back."

"I've never been prouder to call you all 'family.' April, please get a public press release in all the local media announcing my decision to challenge the sitting mayor. Everyone else, let's get back to work. More on this topic soon."

As everyone disbursed, he picked out Charlotte and pulled her aside, "Hey Charlotte, can we talk a minute?"

She nervously approached and followed him up to his office, where he closed the door.

Leo said, "Look, about the other day in my office – I fear I may not have been as straightforward as possible with you. You're a great person. It's not you. My love life is a chaotic mess, but one thing of which I am certain – I can't undertake anything romantic with you at this time."

She quickly shot back, "I don't…"

He cut her off, saying, "That said, I don't see any reason to not keep you on, heading up our real estate division. You *are* the best in the business, after all. That's why I hired you in the first place."

Charlotte simply nodded, somewhat at a loss for words and quite embarrassed.

She tried to rebuff him, "Very chivalrous of you. Though, don't act like you aren't really that type of guy. Are you saying there is no chance that you'd enjoy forgetting those other girls every now and then? It doesn't bother me, whatever else you have going on. We could be great together whenever it works."

Leo finished their one-sided conversation, "Great. Now that we have that resolved, let's get back to work."

Silently, she left his office and went back to her own.

Exhausted, Leo headed down the stairs of Bravo Tower, and grabbed Rome and Eli on his way out, saying, "Fellas, anyone else need a drink? I'm buying."

The three brothers took a trip down to their customary hangout, which Leo recently purchased as a present for Rome. The men walked down the cold, lifeless streets of Belmont. There were people milling around here and there, but there was no hope... no light. It was really quite a dreadful place if one didn't grow up here with his own understanding of Belmont's potential. To the people of Belmont these days, it was simply… home.

As they walked, Rome and Eli did most of the chatting with Leo trailing behind them engrossed in thought as always.

They heard a screeching voice come up from nowhere, "You bastard! Who the hell do you think you are!?"

The boys wheeled around, ready for a fight, when they saw a small woman racing towards them, face full of tears.

Eli, the spunky brother who was never afraid of hostility and who maybe even rather enjoyed conflict while still in his youthful naivete, took the lead in the cross-examination, "Whoa whoa whoa, lady. Who are you and what do you want? The fact that your husband chose to spend his paycheck on coffee and not you… not our problem."

The two older brothers gladly allowed Eli to take the lead, as the accusations could be the result of a wide variety of activities in which they were engaged and neither of them felt up to the verbal boxing match that was sure to ensue. It wasn't uncommon to be approached by people that were affected by their line of business.

She shouted back, looking through Eli directly at Rome, "You know *who* your problem is?! Felicity Garner. Do you remember her, Mr. Stills??"

Rome looked confused and had nothing to say to this irate woman.

She continued, "You should. You murdered her while speeding through our community intoxicated off your ass! She was my daughter, Mr. Stills. She was a mother. She was a friend! You stole her from us!"

At that, she quickly pulled a small metal wrench out of her purse and before anyone could stop her, she smacked Rome on the side of the head, immediately causing blood to gush down his face. She didn't stop there. Eli, who had previously retreated a bit so Rome could engage directly, instantly grabbed the woman's arms, causing her to groan in pain and drop her weapon.

Rome now fully understood. He was previously insulated from his crime, not feeling the full burden of his guilt. When he ran over that young lady the other day, Leo had fixed the legal consequences for him. That, obviously, was only one component of his misconduct.

Rome was just starting to forget how it felt; just beginning to forget how he hurt that young woman. Felicity was her name apparently. The emotions came rushing back to him now and he could feel the void he caused in the world; the shadow he helped bring about in an already tenuous universe.

Rome yelled, "Eli! Stop! I deserve that and whatever else I have coming. Better for me to pay for my transgressions than to have them eat me up from the inside. Let her go."

Eli only complied halfway with the orders that came from his superior in the chain of command, and forcefully walked her down the sidewalk away from his older brothers.

Rome stood there in shock, motionless, taking a few more miracle capsules to alleviate the burden of reality. Leo silently grabbed his arm and guided him along the other side of the road knowing that everything Ms. Garner said was true.

Eli caught up to them just as they were arriving at the Coffee Spot.

The three boys went straight back to their private room and Eli posed the first topic of conversation, "So, what's the deal with Seth. Why did the feds really pick him up for a simple bar fight and how are we going to get him back?"

Leo responded, "The feds don't care about some small-town saloon battle. They are using him as leverage against us. I'm not sure yet what they want exactly, but we'll get him back. I'll have a word with our FBI friend tomorrow."

They sat there throwing back whisky shots for a good while. When the bottle ran empty, Leo walked out of the back room to get some air and stretch his legs.

A while back, when Leo purchased the coffee shop from the previous owner, Thomas Pocks – it wasn't exactly 'For Sale' in the conventional sense.

Thomas stayed on as an employee though, and he greeted Leo, "Mr. Stills, the usual?"

Leo nodded.

Thomas went on, clearly unhappy with their last transaction, "I'm not really authorized to say this is on the house anymore, am I?"

Picking up on the obvious frustration, as Thomas had owned this shop going on twenty years, Leo said, "Mr. Tom, what's with the attitude? I offered you a fair market price for this shop, didn't I? I didn't have another option."

Thomas scoffed back, "Ha! Fair the price may have been, but it's not like it was an offer I had a choice to refuse, right?"

Maybe it was the first bottle of whiskey talking but, tiring of this conversation rather quickly, Leo said, "We always have a choice, Tommy."

I recall myself giving Thomas' same excuse once or twice before to rationalize some of my previous decisions: 'I don't have a choice.'

Not allowing that train of thought to continue very long either, he went back and continued relaxing with his brothers. After a long night in the backroom, the boys split up and headed home their separate ways. On the way back to his abode, Leo took a shortcut through the Belmont train station.

The station wasn't very crowded this late in the evening and as Leo was humming a jazz tune to himself, lost in the moment, he saw Sera standing on the platform a ways off, getting ready to board the train. Leo got very excited when he saw their young son with her, whom Leo hadn't seen in quite a long time.

Leo quickly began making his way over to them, but as he got halfway there, he saw a man come and hand Sera a single rose, put his arm around her and kiss her on the cheek. She smiled warmly and accepted the rose, as the three of them boarded the train together.

Her favorite flower is a daffodil...

Without much of a second thought, Leo turned back and headed for home muttering to himself, "What could I expect after so long?"

Meanwhile, across town – Michelle woke up to a knock at her front door. She went down to open up and was confronted by two federal agents. Agent Long was the first to speak, "Good evening, Ms. Stills."

"What do you want?"

The Special Agent invited himself in, saying to his two goons, "Wait out here."

Michelle gasped as he pushed his way into her home.

The FBI Agent walked over, again uninvited, and sat down on her couch, "Please… sit," he requested.

She walked over and sat down at the other end of the couch, clutching her robe around her chest.

Michelle asked, "Does Leo know you're here?"

Agent Long chuckled, "Was I supposed to coordinate with him or something? Ask his permission? Ms. Stills, I'm a federal agent… I do what I please. That being said, I'm sure you heard Seth was picked up after a crazy bar fight the other night."

Silence.

He went on, "I know you have always cared for him like a mother, since your aunt passed away so long ago."

Silence.

"It must pain you, Michelle, to think of him suffering in a cold jail cell all alone, when you are here at home, warm in bed… all alone."

"What do you want, sir?" Michelle asked again.

"Well, I was simply wondering if you wanted to help him get out of prison?" Agent Long asked, lighting up his tobacco pipe.

Michelle quickly retorted, "Leo will take care of him. Leo always takes care of our family."

Agent Long turned up the pressure, saying, "Ehhhh, Mr. Stills won't always be around to take care of you guys. Who knows… something could happen to him any day now, an accident of course. What will you do then? Don't you care about Seth? You two go way back, since you were children."

Michelle responded, "Well, if Leo can't make it happen, what could I do? I really think you should be having this conversation with him, and to be clear, I'm going to tell him you interrupted my sleep and forced your way into my house."

Agent Long ignored the threat, answering her first question, "Ahhhh, exactly. What can you do? What do *you* have to offer that Leo does not?"

As he said this, he eliminated the space between them by sliding into the middle of the couch. Michelle immediately began to feel even more uncomfortable than before when she was only scared for her safety.

She asked, trying to be brave, "What do you even want with Seth? He's not a major player, especially in any activity with which you should be concerned.

He doesn't even get briefed on those activities. He's worthless to you, unless I'm missing something."

He responded with a slimy smile, "You are 100% correct, Ms. Stills. Well, almost. He really doesn't have anything that I want in connection with Mr. Stills, but I have had my eye on you for some time. I must admit, you are one of the most attractive women I've seen, here in Belmont anyway. Such a delicate flower. Plus, I've been so far from home, from my family during my work here in your God-forsaken city. I have to say; it could make even the strongest man feel lonely."

Silence.

Feeling his pressure digging into her will and using her emotions against her, the Agent said, "Look, Seth isn't a big deal, but I can make him disappear. Simply put, however, what I want in return also isn't a big deal. I would just like for you to allow me the honor of, well… you know."

Michelle sprang up from the couch, "You monster! Straight from hell… you are pure evil!" she yelled. "You're sick and you won't get away with this!"

Calmly, he stood up and removing the space between them yet again, replied, "That may be. Bottom line is, you are Seth's only hope of ever seeing daylight again. One time is all it will take. You might even like it. Either way, Seth can be home tomorrow. That is, *if* you really care about him."

A few minutes later, eternity to Michelle, Special Agent Long left her house, taking everything with him.

Story 16

As time went on and things grew ever more complex, Leo thought it might be a good idea to draft a will. After all, he was a lawyer by trade. In his current line of work, it was not possible to be too anxious about one's impending doom and Leo's primary concern was always that of his family's well-being; especially considering his not-quite-fully-formulated and extremely dangerous plan to meet up with Rubenfield yet again. He was hoping to change Rubenfield's mind about teaming up with Sanchez and double-crossing the Stills crew.

When the will was complete, Leo shared it with Rome, who notarized it and was the only family member to know Leo created one at all. After that business was finalized, Leo left on an urgent mission, alone.

Right after he left, Michelle was unaccompanied in the Bravo Tower lobby doing some filing, when she heard the door open.

She didn't turn to see who it was, but simply heard a familiar voice joyfully exclaim, "Well, getting arrested sure was exciting. I'll try to avoid it in the future though, haha."

Michelle wheeled around, incredibly relieved to see her cousin Seth standing there. She had always empathized with Seth in a way that none of her brothers did and the two of them maintained an incredibly tight and special bond.

"Seth!" she yelled back, running over to hug him.

He hugged her back for a few moments before she broke free, saying, "I have something for you."

Making sure no one was around, she went over to the family safe in the back office and returned with a large duffle bag.

He asked, "What's all that, sis?"

She replied, "Look, this life isn't for you. You can be so much more instead of us dragging you down into the shadows."

He said, "What do you mean? I am a part of this family. I care about you guys and, more importantly, I can help. Leo has never shown me anything but kindness, and I am determined to help him succeed."

She went on, "You were almost killed!"

He said, "What are you going on about, Shelly? I just did an overnighter for a bar fight. What does that have to do with the family business?"

She shouted, "You don't know what I had to go through to get you out of there! The Stills don't just get arrested in Belmont because of a bar fight. That was the feds that swooped on you, and it wasn't because of a simple assault."

Getting more confused by the second, Seth said, "What *you* had to go through? You mean Leo? He was the one that done got me out, right?"

Michelle reluctantly confided in him about what happened only the night before with FBI Special Agent Long.

Seth was enraged, but she explained, "Look, I had to save you! He's just toying with our family at this point. He's got a personal vendetta against us. We can only stand up so much to the feds. Leo can only hold out leverage for so long. The FBI could've made you disappear last night. My heart couldn't take that, Seth. Please, just take this money. It is more than enough to get you started again. There is also a fresh passport and driver's license in there. I want you to be safe more than I want to be close with you – and unfortunately, last night proved we can't have both. I did what I had to do, but you have to go, or it was all for nothing. Agent Long could do this again anytime he wants."

Meanwhile across town, not knowing any of this was going on, Leo hopped on a plane for Seattle to visit his old friend, Sal Rubenfield, who had just double-crossed the Stills family and teamed up with Mateo Sanchez for the promise of bigger bounty and greener pastures.

Sanchez outbid me, offering Rubenfield more than me. I'll have to figure out how to get the leverage back and soon. I don't know quite what I'm going to say.

Leo left the airport and had his driver take him straight to Rubenfield's estate. He buzzed the intercom and without hearing any verbal reply, the front gates swung open.

Hmmmm, wonder if that's a good sign.

Seconds later, he was greeted by four guards from the Rubenfield payroll. They each carried an automatic rifle with them.

Those are extremely rare, automatics… wow. I want one so bad.

When they got through the front door, the four guards turned on Leo and one of them demanded, "Turn around. We are going to pat you down."

Leo pulled out his gun and was getting ready to surrender it. As might be expected though, this caused them all to quickly raise their weapons in response.

Leo instantly shouted, "Wow! Whoa. Okay. Calm down, fellas. Just saving you the trouble. Here you go."

With that, he handed over his pistol… his only defense.

At least I'm not dead yet. What next?

"I'm here to see Rubenfield," Leo ordered, hoping they would take him straight there and not make a detour to bury him out back.

"Mr. Rubenfield is expecting you."

Whew. Step one down. Don't know what's next. Focus. Focus.

They got down to Rubenfield's office and most of the guards walked back out to cover the door from the outside. They left Leo to talk with only Rubenfield and his right-hand man.

Rubenfield smiled and greeted him, saying, "Mr. Stills… I must say, you have some brass."

Silence.

Rubenfield went on, "I'm guessing you would like to discuss what happened with our last arrangement to take down Sanchez, but my question to you is - why shouldn't I feed you to my pet sharks like I've done so many others?"

Wonder if that's a figure of speech, or if he really has actual sharks here that would eat me.

Speaking quickly now while looking around for a nearby fish tank, Leo lifted up his shirt to reveal a wire with a microphone, saying, "Sally boy, you don't think I'd come in here without a plan."

Rubenfield shrieked furiously at his second-in-command, "You idiot!?" Turning back to Leo, in a red-hot rage, he shouted through gritted teeth, "You rat!"

Leo calmly said, "Look, the feds flipped me. They are listening on the other end of this line and are ready to come in any second to save their newest asset. So, take it easy unless you want them exploring your compound here. I'm working a much bigger case for them, so they wouldn't hesitate to take your operations down to save me."

Silence.

Leo finally took the breath that he was holding since he first rang the buzzer at the front gate.·

He went on before Rubenfield had the chance to seriously contemplate an unfriendly decision, "Now that another one of our meetings has officially begun: I came to get you to reconsider our deal against Sanchez."

Fuming, Rubenfield made a simple calculation in his head and replied, "Go on."

So far, so good. What next? Any ideas would help! Hello in there?

Leo continued, "Tell me what happened to our deal and how we can make sure it doesn't occur again?"

Resigned to going down this line of reasoning, Rubenfield said, "Well, you see, it's just business for me. Sanchez offered me more than you could, so I took it." Sighing a bit and seeing a little of the opportunity he once passed on, Rubenfield continued, "Lucky for you, Mr. Stills – Sanchez got greedy too. Turns out, he couldn't really offer me what he promised and I'm actually quite happy you came by, your copper friends aside. What say you, we simply revert to our original deal? Haha! And this time I won't try to kill you. You have my word."

Thank you, God. Wow. I mean, obviously can't trust him, but I don't have a choice right now.

"Deal," Leo said.

With that, Leo stood up and said into the 'microphone' on his chest, "All clear, coming out."

Ha – too bad there is no one really on the other end of this mic. I've got to figure out now how to keep Rubenfield's incentives aligned with ours, so his disloyalty doesn't happen twice.

"I can show myself out," Leo said, briskly exiting the downstairs office. As he left the premises, he heard eight shots.

Two shots for each of the four guys that let me in without a pat down. They won't make that mistake again, haha. Not funny.

Leo wasted no time getting back to the airport to head home and gather his troops. He wasn't going to trust Rubenfield's guys again, so this time the plan was for Leo to take nearly his entire crew and go down to San Mikel personally. They would, in the course of one day, physically capture all of the weakest Sanchez locations that were ripe for the taking.

The next step would be to renegotiate and take over all of Sanchez's suppliers. Leo had already begun months ago adding San Mikel Police Department coppers to his payroll. That way, just before the Stills Corporation takes over Sanchez's shops by force, the coppers will simultaneously execute long-standing warrants and arrest most of Sanchez's men.

It was quite the sight to behold, hundreds of the Stills crew members boarding a private flight to Southern California on a jumbo jet. It was nothing if not subtle.

When they arrived, Leo began to dispatch his guys to their various details. Leo, Rome and Eli were going to personally take a squad to overthrow Sanchez's main location. This location was by no means weakly secured, but instead was the most heavily fortified of all his shops; and rightfully so.

This location was the crème de la crème and whoever owned that spot maintained an iron fist on the coffee market in San Mikel. It was a beautiful spot, centrally located on the waterfront, overlooking the pier. Tourists came from all around the world and it was also a local favorite as well. It was a machine designed to churn and burn through thousands of customers all day and all night long. This location, Hot Cups, was underestimated by Leo last time.

This time, Leo was prepared with more than double the power he would need. On top of the local police support, Leo expected no casualties today, but instead, simple surrender.

This is the most ambitious and orchestrated hit I've ever done. Monumental. It will explode our revenue base and add stability to the family for years to come. Pride comes before the fall. Focus.

Leo's phone was ringing over and over when he and his men arrived at Hot Cups a short while later. When the boys were walking in the front door, Leo got his fifth phone call in a row. He wasn't going to answer, but then his phone rang again and at this point he was the only one left outside. He glanced at the Caller ID, which read 'Baby Mama.'

Sera?! One of the only people I'd answer for right now.

"Hello? Sera?" Leo answered hastily, as commotion from inside Hot Cups quickly became audible outside the shop.

"Leo! Ahh, thank God you answered. I've been trying to call you! What took you so long to pick up!" she asked angrily.

"Sera, do you need something? I'm busy," he asked losing his patience, not forgetting the last time he saw her at the train station.

"Well, fine. This couldn't wait though. I'm pregnant," she said, pausing for his response.

"I'm happy for you guys," Leo replied.

"What do you mean?" she asked puzzled, never having told Leo there was another man in her life that liked to give her sweet-smelling roses.

"Look, we can talk about how we want to deal with this afterwards. I gotta go," he said hanging up abruptly and joining his crew inside so they could plant the Stills Corporation crest on his newest flagship shop.

After the deed was done, Leo left more than one hundred of his guys in the area to continue running the show in San Mikel. That, plus the ongoing police support should be plenty.

Leo, Rome and Eli led the rest of the crew back to the airport just before 11:00 p.m. Leo was trailing the pack, watching all his guys go through the security checkpoint.

When it was his turn to get through, several TSA agents pulled him aside, "Mr. Leonardo Stills? Please come with us."

Leo nodded to let his crew know that it was okay.

The officers led him to a dark room in the basement of the airport terminal. There were no windows down here and as he followed the agents along the damp, musty tunnel, he couldn't help but say a prayer.

Here we go again. God, help me. Don't know what craziness is in store for me this time. The players I'm dealing with just keep getting bigger and bigger. I'm getting more attention than I want from people I don't even know are watching me. I gotta get back on the right path. I don't even know where I'm going. I'm losing control.

His thoughts were interrupted when they arrived at what Leo could only assume was a broom closet with a small desk in it and two chairs. Leo sat down and one of the agents cuffed him to the hard, metal seat.

The room was even more damp than the rest of the facility, with puddles of water everywhere and the creepy crawly sound of various insects was almost audible to the naked ear. Leo saw more than a couple rats down there along the way. Two men wearing dark suits walked in next and said nothing at first.

Breaking the silence, Leo asked, "How can I help you gentlemen on this fine day?"

One of them, clearly the boss, handed his watch and phone to his subordinate. He whispered something quietly into his subordinate's ear and then, without speaking, walked over to Leo and punched him in the stomach.

"Shouldn't be a smartass with the FBI. That was a warm greeting from my friend, Nate Long. I understand you two have had some trouble getting along in that hell hole you call home."

Trying to gather his breath, Leo said back in reply, "Ahhhh, good ole FBI dogs. Wish there was more of them like Nate… one of kind. Truly."

With that, the agent went on to beat Leo for a solid fifteen minutes, in between short breaks. At this point, Leo was hardly conscious.

Well, this is it. How many damn times do I have to be on my death bed before I learn? God, if you are out there, I promise I will do better if you get me out of this. Stop right there! God isn't a genie with which you can negotiate. I can be better. I have so much more to accomplish. Why does it take so much for you to finally talk to Him? Maybe that's why it keeps

*happening to me – because when things are good, I ignore Him. Help...
me... please.*

At the sound of a gun cocking, Leo closed his eyes and resigned his fate to
God, leaning back in his metal chair so his head faced the ceiling. Just then,
BANG!

A loud thump as the superior agent bounced off the metal table and hit the
ground, blood pouring out. Shocked, Leo looked around to see where God's
lightning bolt landed. Instead, he found the junior FBI agent wiping blood off
an FBI standard-issue knife.

After taking out his boss, the young agent tranquilly sat down across the
table from Leo in the other chair and said, "Mr. Stills, I want you to understand
something," as if nothing crazy as hell just happened.

Leo interrupted him, saying, "You couldn't have done that sooner? You
wait for him to beat me half to death first?"

Playing at being unphased, Leo could feel his very soul shaking from the
overwhelmingly complex and chaos-filled lifestyle he had chosen for himself.

Ignoring that, the agent went on, "Mr. Stills, I have a message for you.
Originally, Agent Long ordered us to have this... conversation. However, his
boss, Director Charles Monroe, thinks the Special Agent has run his course
and is near retirement age. Director Monroe wants to say 'You're welcome' for
saving your life here tonight and to let you know that he will be in touch when
your services are needed in the future. You will know when that time comes.
That is all for now."

At that, the FBI agent uncuffed Leo and gave him a ticket for the next flight
out of town. Though bruised and broken inside and out, Leo promptly stood
up and made a straight line for the door.

*Before this nut job changes his mind. He just killed his boss and acted like
nothing happened. This is too much... everything is too much. There's no
light at the end of this tunnel anymore. I'm just worn out. I'm done. I can't
handle this lack of control. Drowning in chaos. Ahhhhhhhh!*

Leo made his way to the plane, unable to prevent the first tear in a long
time from escaping his swollen and fatigued eyes. He fumbled around for his
cell phone before takeoff, seeing more missed calls from Sera. He mustered

enough strength to send only one text to Seth, requesting a meeting tomorrow morning to expedite the legitimate front of their business empire. Motionless, empty and shattered… he went home.

Meanwhile, back in Belmont, Michelle heard a knock on her door late in the evening for the second night in a row. The standard-issue knock was all too familiar. When she opened the door, FBI Agent Long was standing there with a smile that stretched from ear to ear.

He said, "I was happy to get your text. I see I left you wanting more."

Michelle bowed in a sort of half-curtsy and submissively invited him in, "Please, come inside."

The Special Agent silently followed her into the house after nodding to the two agents that came with him, indicating that it was okay for them to wait outside until he returned. They climbed back into their black SUV and waited with the heater on.

Michelle asked him, "You wear a wedding ring. What would your wife think, you coming over here, having your way with me? You have kids?"

He responded nonchalantly, "You would never say anything. I can have Seth picked up and disposed of any second of any day. I own you. Now, let's get to why you asked me back over here," he said, taking off his large overcoat.

"Yes. Let's."

At that moment, Seth walked out from the shadows that were cast on the curtains by the firelight. Silently, he took his wooden baseball bat and cracked Agent Long on the back of the head. A once innocent man, one of the last few unstained souls left in the Stills Corporation, Seth now literally had blood on his hands. At the same time, the whole neighborhood could hear car windows shattering and a loud commotion outside.

Moments later, when Seth walked out the front door, he took in a deep breath of the cool evening air and looked around as all the neighbors closed their window blinds. He watched two Stills crewmembers drag the lifeless bodies of Agent Long's two subordinate agents from the front seat of their SUV and put them inside their own trunk. His guys then promptly put the FBI Agent in the back seat as well and proceeded to drive the government-issued vehicle off the east side of the Belmont bridge.

<u>Story 17</u>

Leo got home to Belmont in the early morning hours. Weak and dejected, he was worn down by Sera who convinced him that this conversation could not wait. Not really feeling like he needed more bad news at this point, Leo didn't find the fact that she had a baby by another man quite so urgent. Nonetheless, as it tends to do, the feminine spirit won the day and Leo limped his way into the office to meet her.

While Sera waited in the lobby of Bravo Tower for Leo to arrive, she sat quietly on a bench reading her latest novel, a romantic comedy. Charlotte and April walked in the front door together.

Charlotte, who was not even aware that April was also ahead of her in the line for Leo's heart or that Sera once occupied the position at the front of the line before them both, paused to talk to who she thought was Leo's newest love interest. "Hi there, girly. How you doin' today?"

Sera nodded, "Fine. Thank you."

Sera didn't know much of anything about Charlotte, but Charlotte was painfully aware that Sera was taking Leo's precious attention away from her. Wanting to dig deeper, Charlotte sat down next to Sera uninvited.

"Sooooooo, what's the deal between you and Leo. He seems to like you a lot," Charlotte said throwing out a line, hoping for a bite.

Sera apathetically shook her head and stayed silent, not really enjoying where this was going or caring to engage much on this particular topic.

Charlotte kept on, "Yeah, Leo's a really great guy. All the girls love him around here. A real man's man, huh?"

Silence.

Charlotte continued, "Yeahhhh, he's so passionate, you know? Oh, I'm sure you know. What am I saying? You're probably, like, his favorite out of all of us… the way he looks at you."

Silence.

Charlotte smiled, knowing her seeds of discord had been planted, and finished by saying, "Well, congratulations. I just wanted to come and wish you luck. I, like, super am hoping that you win, but I don't mind sharing him with someone as awesome as you either. Too-da-loo!"

And off she went.

Sera sat on the bench in the lobby, trying to read her book amongst racing thoughts. A few moments later, she saw Leo approach and he winced as he sat next to her.

She asked worriedly, "What's wrong, Leonardo? Are you hurt?"

He responded curtly, "I'm fine, I'm fine. What is there that we still need to talk about?"

Offended, she asked rather defensively, "What's your problem? I tell you I'm pregnant and you act like it's not even a big deal. What's up with that; especially after our date the other night?"

She lowered her voice, looking around the lobby at the other people working the day away. Silence resounded as Leo shook his head back and forth, full of emotion and clouded by pain.

Sera made her case, "Leo, when we first met so long ago, I was just a naïve little girl attracted to a rebel. I could see something in you, though, that I'm not sure you even yet see in yourself. I saw limitless potential. You were always so confident and outright dominant in everything you did. I loved watching you win. As we matured together, I loved helping you win. I know it was my job to rein you in – to tell you when you had gone too far. So, I guess I failed – because you are far from civilized. I just found that out too late. It was so obvious in hindsight that you were more than a rebel... you were a monster. That's why I said 'yes' when Fred asked me to marry him, but I know now that he isn't right for me. He's actually downright boring."

Leo interrupted her speech, "Civilized?! You don't know the world I inhabit, Sera. The things I've had to do just to survive and protect my family. Plus, who says you want a tame partner anyway? How dull! And when things get crazy - when you're surrounded by darkness and everything hits the fan, you think some domesticated rube is going to save you? I may be a monster. Fine. I've earned that label but becoming less of a monster isn't the right answer. I've learned recently myself that we are supposed to channel that ferocious ability towards something good because we are in a war with other monsters that channel their powers towards the bad. Being a soft, harmless sheep won't be able to stop that machine."

Sera blurted out, "Lee, I see that now. I was just a girl and you scared the hell out of me. So, I ran away. Maybe I was running from reality, more than running from you specifically. I didn't civilize you then, but I came back to finish the job. Frankly, your amazing intellect can be used for far bigger aspirations than the Stills Corporation's current activities here in Belmont."

Leo finally had a glimpse into her reasons for leaving.

He responded, "Look, I enjoyed our evening the other day, but I understand if you have a new life with another guy. I didn't realize you had moved on with… *Freddie.* You never told me. I saw you and your new man getting on the train the other day… with *my* son."

Shocked and horrified somewhat about how the truth came out, she said, "Leo, I meant to tell you before. That is my fiancé. We are engaged to be married this Spring. That's why I had to come see you. I didn't expect our night to go like it did, obviously. I never got over you. I'm still not over you."

Leo scoffed, "Getting engaged to and having a baby with another guy isn't moving on? Haha, that's rich."

She scornfully replied, "It's not his baby. It's yours."

He sighed invisibly with relief, "What'd you mean? How could you know that already if you're with us both?"

Sera straightened up like a proper lady and said, "I've never been with him… like that. We haven't even kissed on the lips yet. Given how you and I turned out, I thought it would be best to wait until we got married. Him and I are no longer engaged. I ended it the other night. I know it's your baby, because you're the only person I've ever been with."

Leo smiled, but that lasted only for a moment until she cross-examined him, asking, "What about you since I left? Your assistant? That other crazy chick? Are they even the only ones?"

Leo got nervous and then confessed, "I wasn't the one who left without so much as a word of warning, Sera. I haven't heard from you in years. You could've been dead for all I knew. You didn't let me talk to my son or even let me know that he was doing okay. How long was I supposed to blindly wait before I move on with my life like I assumed you had. It was never serious and there isn't anything anymore."

I hope she understands.

Sera said nothing, but instead, leaned in and embraced Leo in the way that they should have done for so many years.

Leo waited as long as he could before pulling back and saying, "I got work to do. Come by my house tonight?"

She nodded in agreement, kissed him on the cheek and left the office.

Leo called April to him and said, "Get everybody together. Family meeting in one hour. Also, when Seth gets here, please have him come straight to my office. I want to speak with him before the family gathers."

"Yes, sir," she replied, scurrying off to follow orders.

Leo hobbled up the stairs towards his office to wait for Seth and fell into his plush, leather office chair, groaning as he did. Leo poured himself a glass of whiskey and stared up at the spinning ceiling fan.

I'm so tired. Hang in there. One day at a time.

A little while later, Seth arrived and knocked on Leo's office door.

"Come in!" Leo hollered across the room.

Seth opened the door and stuck his head in to make sure it was okay, then proceeded to take a seat across the desk from Leo. The two of them spent nearly thirty minutes talking about the next steps necessary to rapidly expand the legitimate portfolio within The Stills Corporation.

By the time they were wrapping up, April knocked on the door and said, "Lee, everyone's waiting for you downstairs."

"Okay," he replied.

After finishing up his meeting with Seth, the two of them walked down the stairs together. Leo ignored the stares he got from Rome and Eli.

Those two have struggled to embrace the company's new direction. When we first talked about going legal, it was simply to maximize our profits by adding another revenue stream and they had no problem with that. Now that we are talking about making legitimate business our main priority, Rome and Eli seem to be anxious about that fundamental change. I mean, change is hard... no one would argue. If it ain't broke, don't fix it, as they say. Not hard to understand how they feel. Whenever you make such a big change like this, it represents what change always represents; growth, yes — but also an admission of prior fault. To completely reverse course and say, 'what I was doing before was not the best way to operate,' you are admitting that you made a mistake in doing so previously. In this case, a bad, bad mistake carried out over a long, long time. When something becomes such a big part of your life, it is difficult to let that part die off for the good of the whole. However, you must let that part die off, so you can continue growing in a positive direction using the proper foundations you have built on firm, moral ground.

Seth went to sit in the back of the room in a brown, creaky wooden rocking chair.

Leo went and stood in the front as he prepared to address everyone, "Morning, all. Hope your day is going fantastic. Beautiful day out there, huh? Well, I wanted to discuss another expansion opportunity that I can't stop thinking about, and then we can open the floor and get to whatever anyone else wants to address."

Everyone was listening quietly.

Their leader went on, "How many of you know the name Malafante?"

Everyone looked around, no one speaking up, until Rome chimed in, sighing in anticipation of where this was heading, "Oh boy, bro. You mean, Fitzroy Malafante, the jungle leader of countless, soulless soldiers. The subject of the stories, no, the nightmares we heard about when we were stationed overseas in Africa?"

Leo smiled, "Ding, ding, ding! One in the same, my man."

Rome asked skeptically, "What about him? That's a bad man."

Leo responded, "Look, guys. The way the coffee game is going - the number of new competitors entering the fray every day - we are losing our previous competitive advantages. Our profit margins are shrinking, and our overall revenue is being sucked up by the competition. We are no longer the new kids on the block and we definitely aren't the only ones. We have to make a big change if we want to maintain a stronghold within the industry here on the West Coast."

Eli jumped in, less familiar with the legends, "Leo, I know I was only over there for a year and I didn't get as deep into this as you guys, but from what I hear, that guy is a psycho; plain and simple. The *least* scary thing I've ever heard about his cartel was their favorite way of killing dissidents. They preferred to feed you to one of his various exotic pets, watching while the beasts tore you apart and placing bets on how many pieces you would end up in before the animal got full or choked on your bones. They say he is without conscience. You mean that Malafante?"

Leo nodded in affirmation.

Eli paused, waiting for Leo to continue. When he did not, Eli responded, "Uhhhh, okay… yeah, just making sure."

Leo continued, "Bottom line, taking over Sanchez's product line down in San Mikel has done a huge job of keeping that sector afloat for now. That said, looking at how our profit metrics are trending, we won't last more than a few years without some sort of change. San Mikel is just giving us some breathing room and allowing a little more time for us to come up with a permanent remedy. Malafante is that solution."

Rome asked, "What exactly is the *solution* you are proposing? Please don't say war."

Leo said, "Great question. I simply want to go direct to the initial supplier. 83% of the world's coffee supply can be sourced back to Malafante's cartel."

Rome cut him off, "Leo, *IF* we could even find his base, and that's a big 'if' – the most likely scenario is we get chopped up into pieces. The chances of finding him AND negotiating a deal are slim to none. We can't ask any of our guys to go on a suicide mission like that."

Unphased, Leo went on, "You are correct, sir. I wouldn't ask anyone to go over there. I'm going to do it myself, alone. I know a guy over there who knows a guy that can guide me deep into the African rain forest where Malafante allegedly holds out. It should be fine. I leave tomorrow night on my first trip there. The only goal this time is simple: to cement plans with our local contact for me to travel to Malafante's camp at a later date. I'll be back within a few days depending on how the archaic travel goes on the other side of the ocean."

Not wanting to field any further questions or entertain additional concern on the topic, Leo stood up and said, "Does anyone else have anything to bring up?"

Rome ignored his attempt to deflect further conversation, saying, "I call for a vote on the Malafante expansion."

Leo simply said, "No."

However, Rome didn't give up so easily, barking back, "Look, besides my primary concern being your safety, going over there alone like a crazy man with nothing to lose – even if you are successful setting up this relationship, we have no idea how it's going to turn out if we get into bed with these lunatics. Do you really think we need to go that far?"

Leo replied, "Literally and metaphorically, yes. It's not that I have nothing to lose, it's just there is so much to gain. Simple calculation. If we can make this happen, we will run the coffee game not only along the entire West Coast, but nationwide soon thereafter."

With that, Leo exited the meeting as the rest of the family began murmuring frantically.

April followed him up the stairs back to his office and before she could object as well, Leo said, "Move my flight up from tomorrow night to tonight. My family will go crazy until I just get this over with."

April objected, "But…"

Leo turned and simply looked at her sternly with tired eyes. She stopped before she really began and went to go call the airline to change his flight to tonight. Leo sat at his desk and tried to rest a little bit more. He got fifteen minutes of silence with his feet up on the desk when April came back into his office.

She said, "Flight is ready for tonight. The pilots should be there on time, but they are coming from New York and will have to rush to get here."

"Fine. Thank you."

April went on, "I also got a call from Senator Adams. She heard you are joining the run for mayor and wanted to wish you luck over a lunch meeting. She is excited to see a competitive race take place here, as she has run unopposed for the Washington State senate seat the last three terms after crushing her opponents on the first senate race. I told her you were busy for the next couple weeks, but she insisted on meeting you as soon as possible. I tentatively scheduled you a 3:00 p.m. lunch with her today at the pier, but I'll call back and cancel if you don't want to go."

Leo sighed and remained silent for a few moments.

Finally, he said, "I'm hungry anyway. Call back to confirm and tell them I'll be there in thirty minutes for about one hour. If they can make it, I'm happy to meet with her."

"Consider it done, sir."

Leo shuffled his way down to the pier, enjoying the bright, but surprisingly windy afternoon unfolding around him. He relished the cool breeze that tended to drift in from the waterfront.

Man, sometimes, you just have to stop and look around. The world really is so beautifully amazing. Nature is so complex, and the inventions of man are truly remarkable. Overwhelming sometimes.

He arrived at the restaurant and told the hostess, "Reservation under Stills."

"Right this way, sir," responded the cheerful young woman as she led Leo to a corner booth near a window that overlooked the water.

Leo walked behind her until they got to his booth. He thanked the young lady and proceeded to enjoy the meditative white noise that is a restaurant on a lazy afternoon.

After a few moments, Leo checked his watch and saw that Senator Adams was already five minutes late. So, he called the waitress over and proceeded to place his order.

I'm leaving here at 1:30 p.m. regardless. For her sake, hope she doesn't have much to talk about, because time is runnin' out and it don't stop for her.

They brought out his Irish whiskey and he was nearly done with his first drink by the time the senator finally decided to show up, not that it took him long to finish a drink.

She greeted him warmly, as politicians know how to do quite proficiently, "Mr. Stills! So lovely to finally meet you. Sorry for being a couple minutes late. I've heard so many things about you."

I bet she has.

Leo stood up and, instead of accepting the hug that she was offering as a greeting, he extended his arm to invite a handshake.

Hugs are so unprofessional. In business, you shake hands… you don't hug.

As she recalibrated and accepted the handshake, Leo replied with a smile, "Can't always believe what you hear."

Silence, as the senator attempted to force a faux smile.

Leo motioned for her to sit across from him on the other side of the table. He said, "I already ordered, if you were hungry."

Senator Adams placed an order for a lunch salad and an iced tea before engaging Leo in several minutes of small talk – asking about his plans, why he decided to join the race, etc.

Then, getting down to business soon after her order came out, she said, "Mr. Stills…"

"Please, call me Leo," he invited.

She smiled, still playing the game, and affirmed, "Leo, I understand you are planning on a trip to Africa this evening."

How does she know that?

Leo said nothing.

She continued, "As I'm sure you are already aware, given your desire to run for political office, that Washington State is a leading force for the coffee industry, both good and bad. As my constituents know and given the fact that they keep voting me back into office over and over, I'm sure most agree with my position - I am not a proponent of the legalization of coffee. That said, the interplay between federal and state jurisdictions, the balance between legality versus decriminalization – well, it can be tricky."

She went further, "Washington State is also one of the nation's leaders in coffee distribution. We have a real problem with illegal coffee products entering the United States, in particular through our lovely state as one of the main import channels into the country. We are also working with the African government to squash the illegal exports originating from their shores. I was certainly wondering… why a respected businessman like you would be going over there?"

As intrigued as he was and making it up as he went along, Leo responded, "That's fascinating. Then you understand why I'm heading over there. It will be good to get firsthand experience and bring that knowledge back to inform my voters. It's going to be one of my main campaign promises."

What was that?? Don't over speak. Don't lie. But I can't tell her the truth… obviously. I have no choice.

Senator Adams confirmed, "Oh, of course; brilliant strategy. Well, the main reason I wanted to meet with you today is so I could ask for your help."

Silence.

She said, "Before you joined the race, we were going to have the current mayor take on this mission, but it seems like a great opportunity for you to get involved and help build some name recognition for you throughout the state, even if you already have a stronghold on Belmont."

What's her angle? Why would she help me? What does she know about my stronghold?

Silence.

Not needing an invitation to continue, she said, "Given your… *background*, we think you are the man for the job we ultimately require. We need you to start by simply having a meeting with the African government tomorrow afternoon to discuss our strategy. The USA is providing aid, including drone technology that will allow them to monitor the coastline for ships that are illegally exporting coffee products out of Africa, as well as canvas the interior of their country for the growth and production of said product. Relatively straightforward, we just need our local representative to be the lead for the newspapers – and we think that will be you soon enough."

Leo said without thinking, "Well, I would love to help you. In return, I'm sure you would love to endorse me for mayor in the upcoming election."

She hesitated, but reluctantly agreed, "Sure. I mean, I'd be honored, Mr. Stills. I know how to pick the winning side." Using her political charm, she added, "Though I'm sure you could triumph without it. That's why we're here. The sitting mayor has become fat and lazy, without anyone running against him the past few elections."

Kind of like you, huh, senator?

He smiled and replied, "Call me Leo, please. Well, sounds good. Seeing as how I don't really need the endorsement, like you said - I will do this for you guys in exchange for your endorsement in this race… annnnnd a small-*ish* favor to be named at a later date?"

She pushed her empty salad bowl away from herself, stood up briskly, and reached out her arm for a handshake, "It's a deal, Leo."

What just happened. I might actually win this thing.

<u>Story 18</u>

Leo arrived back at the family office after his lunch with Senator Beth Adams, where she asked him to help broker a deal with the African government. He was leaving tonight on a twenty-hour private flight where he would be greeted by local government officials. Leo called Rome and Eli into his office and told them about his lunch with the senator, the opportunity that presented itself and the slight change in plans.

He said to his brothers, "Guys, this is the real deal. If we get Senator Adam's endorsement, my notoriety will go through the roof statewide. We already have Belmont, but I've been looking for a way into the broader demographics. This is a Godsend."

Just then, April furiously swung Leo's office door open, sending it crashing into the wall with a loud thud.

She yelled at Leo, "How dare you!? Who the hell do you think you are?"

Leo motioned his head towards the door and his brothers silently turned and walked out, leaving him alone with an irate April.

I'm sure this has to do with the fact that I looked into a guy she went out with a couple times. Probably shouldn't have done that. After doing a background check on one Lorenzo Capanini, asking around about him, I confirmed this guy was a bad guy; serial criminal, some rumors of sexual assault against previous girlfriends… just all around, not a good fit for April. She deserves better. Soooooooooo, I had some of my boys in blue send him a message, a tiny message, by having him arrested and put in a holding cell for a few months. It's not like he got hurt or anything. Well, they probably didn't hurt him too badly.

Not waiting or caring if Rome and Eli had gone all the way out yet, she continued ranting, "You had Lorenzo arrested?!"

Leo shrugged, saying nothing.

She screeched, "What the hell is wrong with you?"

He finally responded, "April, he's a bad dude. You don't know everything about him. You can do much better than someone like him."

She shot back, "Ohhhh, what? You mean someone like you?! That's not an option anymore, Lee. You need to back off."

With that she stormed out of his office as loudly as she had arrived, letting out a loud shriek as she walked back down the stairs of Bravo Tower.

Hmmm. That could have gone much worse.

Leo shrugged it off again and prepared for his flight to Africa. Before he left, he put Rome and Eli in charge of the family business and asked them to simply not make too much noise while he was gone.

"Just keep things going and if anything big comes up, delay it and I will address it when I get back," he said as he walked out the door.

Lo and behold, a short while later, Rome and Eli were sitting down in the lobby of the family office, listening to the radio with some other members from the crew.

April came up to the boys and said, "Fellas, Lorenzo Capanini Senior is here. He respectfully requested an audience with Leo, but I told him you guys might be available to see him. Do you want me to invite him in?"

Now, the Capanini family was a small crime empire that paid the Stills a monthly stipend for the ability to operate within Belmont. The Stills Corporation was much larger and commanded a sort of reverence within the community that any and all smaller outfits obliged.

Eli turned off the radio and Rome said, "Bring 'em in," as the rest of the crew gathered around.

A couple heartbeats later, Lorenzo Senior walked in and greeted the boys amicably through gritted teeth, "Mr. Stills," he nodded to Rome, and then to Eli, "Mr. Stills."

Rome responded in kind, "Lorenzo! Good to see you. Hope all is well in your world."

Lorenzo Senior gave little response.

Already losing patience, Eli cut to the chase, "What can we do for you today?"

Lorenzo Senior said in his scratchy, deep voice, which sounded like his throat was covered in sandpaper, "I came here for an explanation. Rumor has it that your family ordered my boy be picked up by the *idioti in blu*."

Knowing full well the truth, Rome asked, "Who is telling you these rumors?"

Eli piled on jokingly, "Ha, yeah. What kind of business you think we engage in, eh?"

Unamused and ignoring a couple chuckles heard around the room, Lorenzo Senior said, "You deny it? It was the same coppers that are on your payroll that done it. If you wanted something from my family, there is an etiquette that should have been followed. Why did you not speak with me first so we could work it out peacefully? You didn't do right."

Lorenzo Senior never would have talked so directly or sternly to Leo.

Eli shot up out of his seat, blowing up at the lack of deference, "Look, Lorenzo boy, you should choose your words more carefully, especially in our house. Belmont is our town. We don't have to tell you nothin'. Why don't you and your boys get the hell out of our shop. Don't come back here again without calling first. If you ever show up unannounced again, you'll force blood on my hands. Are we clear, Lorenzo?"

Rome was silent, not wanting to quarrel publicly with his younger and incredibly hot-headed brother. However, Rome, who could be his own savage at times being the main enforcer for the Stills Corporation, was nonetheless a firm believer that you could catch more flies with honey than with vinegar and that confrontation was generally bad for business.

Lorenzo Senior, who ran his own crime family, wasn't used to having to swallow his pride, but knew better than to pick a fight at this moment in time, outnumbered heavily at the Stills family office.

He replied, "You little snake, this isn't the relationship I have built with your brother over the years. This type of unearned animosity can't be allowed. Capeesh? I want my boy back. I don't want there to be any trouble."

Rome sat idly by while Eli, with clench fists, said quietly, "You may leave now."

Lorenzo Senior spat on the wooden floorboards before turning around and uttering a threatening epithet in Italian, "Attento a come parli. Chi di spada ferisce di spada perisce."

After the Capanini crew left in a huff, Rome quickly stood up and as he walked out of the lobby, he gave Eli an order, "Increase the amount of security we have in the T-district. This isn't going to be good."

Somewhat confused because he wasn't used to his family fearing anybody, Eli asked his older brother, "Rome, what are you talking about? That guy knows better than to try anything. What did he say anyway?"

Without breaking stride, Rome said over his shoulder, "He said, 'He who lives by the sword, dies by the sword.' Just do what I said, and don't tell Leo about him threating us."

Off he went, but Eli wasn't convinced. Rome was older though and had lived through the territorial wars with the Capanini family before the Stills finally won out years ago, largely due to the intelligent leadership from Leo.

Eli wasn't so sure he agreed fully with his older brother and was still fuming from the confrontation. He listened to Rome's advice, but added some of his own.

He called the coppers that were on the family's payroll, the ones who had arrested Lorenzo Junior to begin with, and instructed that he be treated less than kindly, meaning beaten half to death; an order the boys in blue promptly carried out the same day. Eli wasn't one to back off from a fight. He hadn't matured that much yet and instead preferred to feed the flames.

Leo arrived home a short while later and went straight to meet with Senator Adams to brief her on how his meeting went with the African government. When he arrived at the restaurant, Ms. Adams was already there sipping on an iced tea.

"Senator," Leo greeted her as he sat down across the table.

She looked up and smiled, "Mr. Stills! How lovely to see you again."

Leo smiled back, "Leo, please."

She chuckled, "Of course… Leo. How are things? I trust your trip was productive?"

Leo said to the waitress passing by, "Whiskey, neat," before turning back to Senator Adams and saying, "It went great. The African officials picked me up from the airport and after a quick meal and some small talk, we went out to investigate firsthand."

The senator nodded along.

Leo continued, "We looked at the export situation along the Northwest coastline, though some of the exports are now being funneled from the Southern coast as the local government started cracking down on exports up north. We then went only a short distance from their offices to the front of the jungle, wherein most of the coffee is produced and transported. We didn't travel inside, they said due to the level of danger involved."

The senator nodded in approval, "Please keep me apprised of any developments, big or small." She then asked with a smirk, jeering a little, "Danger, huh? You weren't scared, were you?"

Leo simply chuckled, not dignifying that with a response. They finished their meal while discussing some plans and strategies for Leo's upcoming debate. He was scheduled to have his first debate against the current mayor in the next couple weeks.

Near the end of their meal, Senator Adams said, "That all sounds great, Leo. I think a good way to end this meeting would be to discuss the next steps with Africa. Now, I have to be honest…"

You weren't being honest before?

She went on, "… you were chosen not simply for your potential, but also for your… how should I say this… willingness to bend some rules here and there. Sometimes, this *determination* is necessary. In this case, we have a sensitive matter which requires that resolve."

Silence.

She said, "There are a couple different prongs to this strategy we have been working on with the African régime. Now, the next step to promote our goals with respect to this situation is for you to meet with a confidential informant we have on the ground. It is critical you mention this informant to no one. The scope of their work is of upmost national security and no one must ever find out about this part of our work overseas."

Silence.

She continued, "You can't even tell your buddy at the FBI, Director Monroe."

How does she know about any relationship I have with the FBI Director?

Silence.

Going further, she added, "In the coming months, when the time is right, you will be approached by my undercover contact."

Leo nodded.

"When they connect with you, they will provide you with the security clearance code written on this paper and fill you in on what they need from you," she said, sliding a folded piece of paper across the table to Leo, who picked it up and slipped it in his coat pocket. She went on to say, "Anyone touching base with you that does not give the correct clearance code must be eliminated. Are we clear on that? Our plans here must not be leaked."

What the hell! What is she trying to hide and how did this turn into a potential hit job? I should not keep going down this road. A sitting United States Senator…

Leo replied, "Understood."

"I don't mean arrested, Mr. Stills – eliminated," she said in a hushed tone, looking around the restaurant to ensure no one was listening.

Silence.

Switching emotional gears in an instant, she reverted back to the peppy, excited politician that everyone was used to seeing on television, "Great! Now that we got that worked out, hope you have a wonderful day. Remember to vote!"

With that, they shook hands and she left. Leo sat there for a while finishing his drink and contemplating all the choices he had made over the years that led him to this place and time. After a bit, he paid his bill and headed back to the office to see how things went while he was gone.

He called Rome into his office and briefed his older brother on how the dual-purpose trip to Africa went. After he had his meeting with the African official, Leo had ducked out of the hotel room and met up with his cartel contact. Leo confirmed that the ball was in motion to meet with Malafante in person soon enough and that Malafante's contact would reach out when the time had come.

After wrapping up that conversation, Rome sheepishly broached the issue, "Leo, while you were gone, something…" but he was interrupted when Michelle was heard yelling downstairs.

The brothers looked at each other and shrugged, neither having an explanation for the commotion.

As Rome was about to continue, April poked her head in Leo's office and said, "Leo, you should get down here."

Leo nodded and said back to Rome, "Can it wait?"

Rome nervously said, "I guess it can wait a few minutes. Let's go."

The two brothers got up and went downstairs to the lobby where Michelle and Eli were going at it.

"Calm down, calm down. What's going on here?" Leo asked Michelle.

She yelled back, "Ask him," motioning to Eli.

Eli avoided eye contact and paced around, saying nothing.

Michelle quickly lost patience and answered, "Rumor has it that the Capanini crew is plotting to kill Eli because he thought it would be a good idea to stoke the flames after what happened."

Leo was confused and looked to Rome for clarification.

Rome quickly said, "That's what I was trying to tell you. Lorenzo Senior came by while you were gone, asking about what happened to Lorenzo Junior getting arrested. He thought we had something to do with it and he wasn't happy to say the least. Eli… kind of went off on him."

Leo looked over at Eli for confirmation, but Eli was still silently pacing around the lobby.

That's a yes.

Leo sat down at one of the desks in the bullpen and quietly listened to his siblings argue over a plan of attack.

After a few minutes, Leo had heard enough and finally spoke, causing everyone else to go silent, "Okay. Eli was right to be tough on that jackal. We have to keep our feet on their throats, or they will revolt against us the first chance they get."

Eli sat there nodding silently, half triumphant that Leo agreed with his initial interaction with Lorenzo Senior. Eli also felt half guilty because no one else knew that the real reason for the recent price on his head was because he had taken it even a step further after that and ordered Lorenzo Junior be beaten in prison as well.

Rome interjected, "But Leo, peace is better for business. We can't fight the whole world."

Leo acknowledged that point, but went on anyway, "That caffeine is making you soft, Rome. We can't afford to be weak. If we let this disrespect go unavenged, others will do the same. Our authority in Belmont can never be questioned. We are the kings of Belmont, period. The Capanini cowards think they can threaten my family without fear of punishment? We need to crush this rebellion now. Rome, take Eli and some guys, I want you to teach Lorenzo some manners."

Rome objected, "But…"

Leo talked over him, "Take some of our boys and you guys go trash their dance club. Send a very clear message."

Rome stood up slowly, tapped Eli on the shoulder and said, "Come on, bro. We'll hit 'em tonight when they are busiest."

Leo glanced at Michelle who looked like she was going to have a heart attack at the arrogant show of male dominance, and he said to her, "Not now, sis. I gotta go."

Later that night, Rome was at home with his new girlfriend, Mary Anne. She was fully aware of Rome's past and was downright determined to get him back on the straight and narrow path towards salvation. Her southern charm was just as thick as her accent. Part of what Rome liked the most about her was how different she was compared to the rest of the people in his life, including the person he had become himself.

Lately, Rome had been having a harder time getting out of the house, especially at night, because Mary Anne said repeatedly, "The Good Lord knows, ain't nothing good happen after midnight."

So, instead of telling her he was about to go trash a heavily guarded, completely crowded club on the north side of town, taking an army of guys loaded with weapons – he tried an alternate route.

As she sat there cozied up on the couch reading a novel, Rome said, "I gotta go into the office tonight; emergency situation. We had some orders get cancelled and one of our trucks broke down. I need to reconfigure our schedule for tomorrow's deliveries."

As he did this, he nonchalantly kissed her on the cheek and then grabbed his coat off the rack.

She accepted the kiss, but asked him somewhat suspiciously, "Tomorrow's Sunday."

Silence.

She clarified, "I thought you guys didn't have deliveries on Sunday."

Racking his brain for an excuse, he said, "Normally we don't, you're right."

That being the end of anything even semi-intelligent he could think up, he simply shut his mouth and walked out the door without looking back.

<u>Story 19</u>

Another bright, sun-shining day came around in Belmont. Things had been relatively quiet for a few months and Leo was up early in the morning working on some material for his upcoming debate with the current mayor of Belmont. Leo and Sera were back on good terms, but they were taking it very slow. It was still somewhat new to them, even though they were once so close. Sera had brought over their son, Caden, a few times and it was a heavenly reunion for Leo.

I don't get to see him as much as I'd like to yet, but soon, Sera can move back in here and we can be a family again. Spending time with them makes it all worth it; the chaos, the struggle. Some days, I have to just stop running around and ask myself, 'What am I doing all of this for?' There has got to be something in life that holds you down. When I'm with my girl and my kid, that's when time stops, and everything makes sense. That's what makes all the other pain life throws at you worth it.

Leo was constantly daydreaming about his new and improved life. Sometimes, it was downright hard to focus on anything else, but he needed to really concentrate if he was going to open up his first debate with some credibility in the eyes of the voters. You know what they say about first impressions. He was loved within Belmont, but both locally and statewide, his reputation was still stained by… *rumors* of… *certain* activities related to the Stills Corporation.

Anyhow, this first debate was supposed to be pretty high-level, covering a wide array of voter concerns facing today's political climate. While Leo was at home going over notes, the rest of his crew was at the office.

April called everyone to the lobby and said, "Guys, Leo wants you all to attend his first mayoral debate tonight." April directed them, "Here are the details. Be there early. I'm sure he would like you to be front and center when he lays out his policies and the ideals for which he stands."

Everyone nodded.

She almost didn't, but would have felt remiss if she hadn't, so she did say, "And boys, be on your best behavior."

Everyone chuckled but then agreed to try.

At 6:00 p.m. sharp, Leo and the current mayor, Wilton Shaw, walked out on stage. This was the first time Leo had ever seen Mayor Shaw, who was a tall, husky fellow. The two of them were set to articulate their positions on the hottest topics contained in the modern-day, political sphere.

Leo exuded confidence, though, only externally. Inside, he was as nervous as a 6th grader giving a presentation to the whole class on a topic he was supposed to research but then decided he'd rather play video games instead. That wasn't to say Leo wasn't prepared. Quite the opposite. Leo was very good at presenting his beliefs in an easy-to-follow manner.

The mayor looks pretty shabby, wearing a cowboy hat and overalls. How in the world does he resonate with his constituents? Not saying you should usually judge a book by its cover, but maybe this time. Haha. I hear he wins debates by using the power of his office to scare off potential contenders. He hasn't had to run against anybody in quite some time. Democracy? More like dictator.

Leo was laughing to himself as he crossed the stage to the audience's loud applause. The cheers could have been for either candidate.

The moderator addressed the crowd and thanked them for coming. He then went over some ground rules on decency and what would happen if the session devolved into a yelling match or if the crowd became too raucous. After the standard spiel, he opened it up for Mayor Wilt Shaw to give an address.

After a brief opening about the dismal political climate facing their city today, the mayor went on to finish his preamble, "People! I sure do appreciate you taking the time to come on out here this beauty of an evening to hear me and Mr. Stills opine on the current state of affairs in our fine hometown."

Cheers from the crowd.

He continued, "Before I get much further into it, though, I need to address directly the quality of candidate against which I am running. On the other side of the stage here, by golly, we have Mr. Leonardo Stills."

As he was pausing for effect, the true popularity of Leo to the Belmont locals became readily apparent as the crowd erupted in an untamable session of hooting and hollering for their hometown hero.

Whoops — I haven't even given my positions yet. He should really focus on why his policies are better than mine, because if it is just going to be a popularity contest, he might not do so well.

Flustered by the now-obvious support for Leo, the mayor proceeded quickly, speaking over the loud clapping, "Well, it sounds like a lot of you are familiar with Mr. Stills, but I'm sure you wouldn't be giving him a standing ovation if you knew what line of business he was really in. This gentleman standing across the stage from me is nothing but a thug, a common criminal."

The crowd instantly started booing.

This guy doesn't give up. These are my people. Even if I am a 'rob-from-the-rich, give-to-the-poor' type of guy, these are the poor people that I feed. They love me because I take care of them when his policies as mayor obviously haven't. Let's see where this goes. No, no, no! You can't let this guy talk to you that way. He is a punk. You should take him out. Shut up! What a dumb idea. Take him out? On stage? Idiot. Focus, focus.

Leo tried to ignore the voices battling for primetime attention in his head and he decided to listen to what seemed to be the good voice telling him to 'focus.'

Trying to adjust to the jeering he received from the last attack on Leo's character, the mayor tried a slightly different approach.

He laughed rather awkwardly, "Mr. Stills, do you deny it?"

Silence from Leo, scoffing from the crowd.

The mayor continued, "Do you deny that you participate directly in the corruption of the society by engaging in less-than-legal behavior on a regular basis?"

The crowd started to boo again.

However, the mayor pressed on, "*You* are the problem, Mr. Stills! Yet, you stand up here pretending that you care about these people and that you are the solution!"

The crowd erupted furiously, some even throwing their crumpled paper pamphlets up onto the stage, obviously rejecting the current line of personal attack with which the sitting mayor chose to start this debate.

Even though the mayor had several more minutes allotted for his opening, Leo perceived his rattled expression and decided to help him out, "Now, now, everyone. Let's take it easy. Mr. Mayor, your description of our current state of affairs is rather shocking, given the fact that you were the one in charge of our fantastic city the last several years."

Cheers and laughter from the crowd.

The mayor cut in, "There is so much fault to be rested on your shoulders, in particular, Mr. Stills. Do you deny it?"

Leo answered, "No, I don't, but it's funny you would."

The mayor shot back, pleased at the successful prosecution of his opponent, "Then you're guilty! How can we trust you to do anything but make the situation worse?"

Good question, Mayor. Are you going to be setting us up for homeruns all night?

Leo said, in a display of good character that most would struggle to even dream about, "I am responsible for my part in the corruption of our society. Of that there is certainly no doubt; as are we all. I am a good person who has done some bad things."

Let him who is without sin among you be the first to throw a stone.

Leo went on, "But who here today could say with a straight face that they've never done anything of which they are currently downright ashamed? Mr. Mayor, might I suggest that we quit with the ad hominem attacks and let's just try addressing my policies on their merit."

The crowd erupted like when the seventh-grade victim of previous mistreatment finally stands up to the class bully with a 'Yo Mama' joke: "Ohhhhhhhhhhh!!"

Stifling his own laughter, Leo addressed the crowd, "No, no, I'm serious and please, we really shouldn't have the mob controlling this discussion. Wilt, continue on with your introduction, especially if there is anything substantive in there, other than more personal insults for me."

As much as Leo asked for civility, this type of leadership garnered a standing ovation again. The moderator struggled to regain control of the audience, but eventually invited Mayor Shaw to continue. Much less arrogantly this time, the mayor proceeded to open with some vague platitudes about the current crises facing the city without giving too much of anything that resembled a real solution to the problems he described.

Leo opened up his dialogue, saying, "I'm excited to be here today with you all. I feel like I know you already."

Cheers from the crowd.

He continued, "I've lived in Belmont my whole life. Until now, I've never really focused on consciously giving back even a fraction of what Belmont has given me over the years. Our city really is amazing, so I found it fitting that the topics the moderator wanted us to address tonight were two, simple yet extremely hard-to-answer questions: 'What's wrong with our society today?' and conversely 'Why is our society so great?' These two seem irreconcilable at first, but I suppose, like most things, there is a combination of light and darkness. As they say, our democratic republic is the worst form of government, except for all the others."

Chuckles from the audience.

He continued, "My opponent here claims to be associated with one of the official political parties. Though, his most recent policies seem to be copied and pasted from the SOPA website. Personally, I don't really affiliate with any party. Our society operates like a pendulum. Sometimes we swing too far left and sometimes too far right. One tends to be more emotion-based, and the other is generally more fact-based. One has a vital role in not allowing the structure of our society to become tyrannical and too top-sided. They are at their best when they are a voice for the dispossessed among us. The other side of the aisle, which tends to be viewed as cold and uncaring, is focused on maintaining the structures that provide us all with security and a proper framework in which to thrive individually. We must remember that every cooperative system will result in some amount of people being dispossessed. We can't all be trillionaires. Even though our society has done a good job reducing the number of people that suffer unnecessarily, we must still put in safeguards to care for those among us that legitimately can't survive within our chosen hierarchy. The important thing to remember is that both sides want the same thing when discussing our objectives at a high level... namely, the best for everyone. We just have a broad spectrum of temperaments and prejudices that cause us all to view the problem and create the accompanying solutions from a diverse set of perspectives. Though it causes tension, this is one of our great strengths as a nation. Neither side is immoral: not for putting empathy before practicality, nor for doing the opposite. The tension caused between the two sides battling properly within our democratic republic is what allows us to navigate the chaos of this world and form some sort of a habitable system. Some among us might say that even though we are economically the most prosperous nation in the history of the world, we are found lacking on the humanitarian front. Fair enough *perhaps*, but so does every other nation. The fact that we have the best economic system is a symptom of a well-structured society. Every society suffers from overwhelming chaos at times, as well as tyrannical rigidity at others…"

You will know them by their fruits. Are grapes gathered from thorns, or figs from thistles? So, every sound tree bears good fruit, but the bad tree bears evil fruit. A sound tree cannot bear evil fruit, nor can a bad tree bear good fruit.

Leo went on, never haven spoken more truth in his life, "The way you can tell a good tree is to look at its fruits. Miraculously, for the most part and way better than anyone else in the history of mankind, we have figured out a way to structure a society so that the *most people possible* thrive. Not all people, certainly – but the most ever per capita. This economic prosperity directly reduces the amount of poverty and suffering in the world. In theory, we could do better. In practice, this is the best most prosperous nation in the history of the world."

At that, another standing ovation for the local favorite. Leo stood back from the microphone and seemed to regain his personal consciousness.

What was that? Where did that come from?

He looked down at the notecards he prepared; none of what he just said was on there. He wasn't sure where those thoughts came from, but they weren't the remarks that he stayed up all night preparing. Suddenly, he heard a voice introduce itself, more clearly than any thought he'd ever experienced:

Leo, it's me. There is a battle going on inside your head right now, fighting to take control of you in the war that is occurring all around you. I am your guardian angel, an ambassador for His Majesty, you may call me Truth. There are other voices inside you, the darkness, that attempts to weave deceit amongst my wise counsel. These are entities old as time itself, which sew discord and steal peace. You hear my good advice, one that aligns with the will of the Father. You also hear the lying voice, that seeks to pervert Truth and all that is Good. The only voice that you hear in your head that is truly yours, is the free choice you make, and by doing so, you put on the mantle of the Image of God that is your ability to create reality. When you speak truth properly, you turn that infinite, chaotic potential into a specific reality and in doing that, you participate in the divine ability to create the world as you see it exist around you.

Leo almost fell backwards on the stage. Did he really hear what he thought he just heard?

"I must be nervous," he mumbled to himself, shaking off the public speaking jitters.

Why here? Why now? I've been lost my whole life… where were you then?

As he thought this to himself, he began to feel the voices separate in his head and could start to isolate them in his mind.

Truth: I have been with you always, as much as you've ever needed me or allowed me in. You blocked me, and Him, out of your mind for so long. Now that you are finally attempting to fight a worthy cause, the one for which you were made, you can now hear me more clearly. I am the hopeful, loving voice that seeks only to encourage you along the right and just path. You can tell the devils are speaking to you when you feel an overwhelming sense of nervousness, anxiety, shame, guilt, anger, fear. None of these are generated from the pure Love that is the Father.

While this battle raged on in Leo's mind, the moderator asked the first question to the mayor, "We thought we'd get to know you gentlemen a little bit better today by asking you two open-ended questions. First, let's start with you Mayor Shaw, what would you say are some of the biggest areas that we are struggling with that you would most want to address in your next term?"

Mayor Shaw, accustomed to rallying up crowds, eloquently began, "What's wrong with our society today? That's simple. The injustices of the past have caused certain populations to get a head start on everyone else. How can we move forward on a clean slate, without first acknowledging and repairing the sins of our past?"

The mayor went on for a while like this, railing on the current inequity found in our system.

He concluded his monologue, saying, "There is plenty of money in our society, it's just in the wrong hands. If you vote for me, I will take it from those who don't deserve it and give it to all of you hardworking Americans. It's our moral duty."

The crowd erupted in applause; free stuff is definitely a very well-received message.

The moderator turned to Leo and said, "Mr. Stills, your turn."

Leo cleared his throat, regaining his composure, and began, "Thank you, and thank you again to everyone for coming out and helping us progress this dialogue on the path towards truth. I am, perhaps, more optimistic than my opponent here today. I too understand, as do most of us, that the pages of history are bathed in blood. Slavery, genocide, oppression and war, among countless other travesties, have scourged the history of any nation or society or religion. No one would dispute that fact. I think the real question is not, who was damaged the most by whom, or how to fairly and accurately quantify past injustices, if that were even technically possible. I think the real question is, as always, what should we do now that we are here to move forward righteously. That said, and in light of the fact that by far and away, we still live in times of extraordinary prosperity, I think the problem facing our communities today stems from us forsaking our nation's unifying principle. It is human nature to regress into tribes of race, status, class – but those things cannot unite a nation as diverse as our own. Something that is able to unify a melting pot such as ours must transcend skin color or religion. I'm speaking back to the beginning of our great nation, when our founding fathers had the courage to create the greatest system ever developed. Their emphasis revolved around the sovereignty and respect of the individual as an abstract, objective truth. This does not mean protecting every individual, but instead protecting the idea of the individual's sovereignty as a principle. Even our president is not above the rule of law – not even our most sovereign is above sovereignty itself."

Silence.

Leo went on, guided by something within, "We have been handed by our ancestors a society that is far greater than we earned ourselves. As a nation, we have progressed so far that obesity now kills four times as many Americans as malnutrition. We no longer have to fight for our day-to-day existence, but instead have the luxury of sitting around our comfortable cities, which by any world metric is far richer than our global neighbors. Because we have become soft as a people, younger generations are no longer as adept at confronting the challenges that remain before us. Our parents spent all their excess energy protecting us from the suffering they endured, and as such, we didn't get to increase our problem-solving skills throughout our childhoods. Fast forward to a generation of these hapless children becoming adults, and when we are confronted by chaos, my generation chokes.

"Our ancestors traversed the world in rickety, wooden boats, sailing off into the complete unknown. We are scared just getting on an air-conditioned plane.

"Our ancestors waged war with some of the worst evils in modern history during the 20th century alone. We are scared of hearing ideas that conflict with our own.

"Though our journey to get here was imperfect and broken to say the least, we… are… here… now… and here really is an amazing place compared to the rest of the history of the world."

Leo finished and stood there for a moment in the silence of the audience, feeling drained, as if something akin to truth was just poured out of him. After what seemed like eternity, the crowd erupted into cheers and Leo was finally able to take a breath.

Despair: What nonsense was that? They didn't understand a word of the propaganda you just spouted.

Anxiety: You think things are okay right now? That there is nothing we could be doing better?

Truth: Good job. You spoke the truth the best you could and as you know it. Keep letting Him work through you.

Me: Wow. Hi, there. It was almost as if that wasn't even me speaking.

Truth: He was speaking through you, as it is meant to be. When you empty yourself, He fills the void.

Leo stepped back a bit from the podium, now realizing that his palms were sweating. The paper stuck to his hands as he was lifting them off the pedestal that was supporting his notes.

The moderator chimed in, "Well, hello, Mr. Stills! It's great to meet ya!" The crowd started another round of applause before the moderator continued, "Remember, the next debate will focus on specific policy issues. I think tonight is proving to be very effective for us to get to know these two gentlemen and for what more general principles they stand. Before we get into the Q&A portion of this evening, one last query to end on a more positive note: What is our society doing well today? Mayor Shaw, if you'd like to begin please."

The mayor, a skilled politician, jumped back in with a smile, "Well said, Mr. Stills. I couldn't agree more with most of what you said there."

Truth: Ha! Liar. Prove it.

Mayor Shaw went on, "Unlike my opponent here, who apparently believes we have nothing on which we could improve, I think there are quite a few things I'd like to see change for the better. Sure, we are doing okay on some issues, but there are so many topics on which we utterly fail."

Leo ineloquently jumped in, "Just okay on some things? Try fantastic on a lot of things. Plus, we are evolving and learning all the time. We never fail, we either succeed or we grow in our understanding. You only fail when you give up and we are a nation of fighters."

The crowd erupted in applause again.

Truth: The people of your great land have been doused with pessimism and resentment for too long. They want so much to have a message of hope and a clear path forward to a bright future. They don't want to hang onto the fading bleakness of the past.

As the mayor was about to complain, and the moderator about to object to Leo's impolite interruption, Leo pushed forward, "The people of our great land have been doused with pessimism and resentment for too long. They no longer want to buy into the notion that we should hang onto the fading bleakness that, unfortunately, is our past. Instead of fear-mongering rhetoric, I offer a message of hope and, over time, will lay out a clear path forward into a bright future that I know is possible for every, single American. We are tired of hearing what is wrong without an accompanying, rational solution for making it better. Our future is our responsibility, the duty of every individual in this room. No politician with their empty promises can absolve you of your personal responsibility as it relates, quite literally, to the fate of the world."

This time, the crowd genuinely exploded out of their seats. For so long, politics in America have been dominated by both sides using fear tactics and promising material goods in exchange for votes. Leo now offered hope emphasizing personal responsibility in pursuit of truth.

After being forced to wait a couple moments for the crowd's clapping and screaming to die down, the mayor tried again, "How about this man, right, folks? Amazing speaker indeed. Couldn't agree with you more on most of what you said there. To answer the question briefly, because I'd like to get to some of the questions our wonderful audience has, I'd say that what America is doing great right now is recognizing the injustices that still exist in our system and being determined to eradicate them completely. No one should have to suffer in today's America. If we can just get the right policies in place, the right governmental oversight, we can achieve a perfect world in which no one suffers unnecessarily."

The crowd cheered heartily this time, but it was quite clear sentiment had shifted towards the Stills' campaign.

After waiting for the diminished approval of the mayor's statement to subside, Leo tried to sincerely answer the question, addressing it at its core, "Well, as I alluded to before, America's number one accomplishment occurred back in 1787 when we signed the United States Constitution. Obvious now in hindsight, looking around today at the most free and prosperous society ever created, *that* was the most monumental discovery of mankind: how to set up a free community of people so as to give it the best chances to succeed. What that means is incredibly complex, but it boils down to creating a fair game that gets the most people to want to play for as long as possible with the least amount of unnecessary restrictions and regulations. So far, so good, but still only being less than 300 years old as a nation, we have a lot to prove as far as stability over time. That being said, we are on the right path. We are doing great, but we must remember that it is so much easier for things to go wrong than for things to go right. Thus, we should be careful not to make too many large and fast changes to our society. The world around us can best be conceptualized as a battle between good and evil, but sometimes that can be so abstract. As for us, active and free beings that decide with each choice which reality to bring into existence when facing the infinitude of potential that stands before us constantly – we strive to walk the fine line between structure and disorder. Too much structure is tyranny, yet we will drown in excess disorder – both extremes, quite literally, being slices of hell. Paradise is to be found maintaining the best we can that narrow path which lives on the border of both extremes. When balanced, structure provides us protection and stability, and the chaos of disorder allows us to constantly renew the parts of the structure that have rigidified and become obsolete.

"One thing America did great long ago, and one vital truth we must preserve, is the distinction between the individual and the state. The question is, what should be subordinate to what? The key truth upon which we predicated our entire society was that each individual had intrinsic value, made in the image of God. We created the state to serve the individual, because the individual is the thing that actively navigates the state. If the state is superordinate in relation to the individual, the state will corrupt and rigidify over time. Certainly, we must all belong to the group and work to uphold its values, but the individual must be superordinate, as the individual is what maintains the proper goals and values of the group. We all have privilege here: 21st Century American privilege. As many great, wise men of the past have said, we see so clearly now because we stand on the shoulders of giants, and not because our sight is better or because we are taller than our ancestors. Let us start the march forward from here with a feeling of gratitude for those generations that have come before us. Those that fought in wars to prevent tyranny abroad and at home. I do disagree with the mayor though, that if we just give complete power over to the government, we can fix all the pain and suffering of the world and just eat rainbows and clouds. We are all privileged, but every one of us is also a victim in one sense or another and we will always be. This is, perhaps, an unfortunate reality about our world. This isn't Heaven."

So much of the crowd roared in approval, and just as many murmured in confusion, at what they just heard.

Doubt: Heaven? I don't even believe in Heaven… do I?

Me: Well, I'm starting to act like Heaven exists, even if it's hard to believe rationally.

Rows of people exited their seat to line up behind the microphones for the question and answer session. Leo and Mayor Shaw took a brief moment to walk to the middle of the stage where there was bottles of water set up.

They spoke to each other in a tone that the audience couldn't hear, but it appeared amicable. The question and answer session was fairly uneventful. After a couple hours of being there, the two candidates shook hands and went their separate ways.

<u>Story 20</u>

A few months had gone by and Leo's girlfriend, Sera, was about to give birth to their second child. Ever since the country switched over to a single-payer health care system, there was a huge surge in the wealthiest people hiring private doctors in order to secure the best care possible.

Leo was among the few that had the ability and desire to splurge on the best medical care for his family. Thus, as the baby was nearing his birth day, Leo called on the best private doctor in Washington State to come deliver the baby at home.

It was almost noon on an exceptionally warm day in Belmont. Leo and his family were chatting and hanging out, as usual. What was infrequent, though, was having Sera's family around as well. This is the first time Sera's family had ever been in Leo's home and, like most other people these days, they were flabbergasted by his apparent wealth.

As Rome and Eli sat on a plush leather couch snacking on pine nuts, gouda cheese, Honeycrisp apples and some delightful champagne – Sera's family was moseying around the vast estate, murmuring to one another. Everywhere they turned, they found something they'd never seen in person before; priceless original paintings, a grand piano, swimming pool… you name it, Leo had two of them at a time when most working class folk couldn't afford to even go to the movie theatre anymore. It was clear her family was enjoying the dirt bikes and ATV's out in the backyard acreage, as well as the basketball and tennis courts that were swarmed by the younger teenagers enthralled in sport.

While the two families were without animus, they still blended together downstairs as well as water and oil. Leo and Sera were upstairs having another spirited conversation. Although Doctor Samantha Rosenfeller was unfortunately caught in the middle, it was not uncommon for doctors to experience this level of excitement between parents just before birth.

Sera was simply out of patience. The baby, sex left to be a surprise at birth, was already three days past its expected due date. This did not bode well. The mixed news that contractions had recently started at least signaled the beginning of the end. Unfortunately, Sera's labor was going on hour sixteen, with no real signs of the contractions getting closer together. To say the least, she was at her wits' end.

As all well-meaning fathers endeavor to do, Leo was attempting to help Sera keep her sanity.

He asked Dr. Rosenfeller, "Doc, how much longer you think this is going to take?"

The doctor barely got a word in, "Well, it's hard to…" before she was cut off by Sera's response to Leo's obviously silly question, "Lee! How is she supposed to know? The baby will come when it comes."

Leo wisely stayed silent and simply sat there holding Sera's hands. After the doctor finished up her last round of checkups, she excused herself from the master bedroom, leaving Leo and Sera alone to do breathing drills for a while.

Sera was trying desperately to help the birthing process along by doing every trick she had ever been told. She was pacing around the room, eating spicy food, doing jumping jacks… well, not really jumping jacks, but she was pacing.

Nothing was working. Leo decided to draw Sera a warm bubble bath but as he watched her get ready for it, he thought of another clever way to help things along naturally. They were both riled up from the frustrated conversations that were frequently taking place ever since Sera passed her due date. Without hesitating, Leo climbed in the tub, too.

A while later, Leo came down the stairs much more relaxed only to find his family leading the way in drinking games using the more expensive bottles of Dom Perignon. He also saw his first son, Caden, playing the newest video games with his older cousins.

Although Sera's family, apart from a few of the older relatives, really seemed to be enjoying themselves, Leo called his crew into the library and scolded them for being so obnoxious.

"Guys, this isn't a frat party. Until Sera's family leaves, I want you on your best behavior. Try acting like gentlemen, huh!"

Sammy jabbed Eli in the ribs trying to get him and Rome to stop snickering.

Leo went on, "I know it is difficult for you animals, but this is an important day for me. I want nothing crazy going on from our side! Be nice and show them all a good time, but for Heaven's sake, certainly don't be yourselves and definitely don't embarrass me."

They all laughed nervously, while at the same time knowing he was quite serious. A few hours went by and the newest member of the Stills family was finally born, a baby boy they named Timothy.

After brief introductions and without too much further humiliation, Leo said goodbye to Sera's family and invited his crew to leave as well so his new family of four could enjoy some quiet time alone.

About six months later, Sera and Leo were finally taking a long-overdue honeymoon. They eloped a few months back; just their two boys were at the ceremony. However, they wanted to wait for Sera to give birth and then recover before going on a proper honeymoon. Their destination: the tropical islands of Hawaii – or at least that's what Sera thought.

Just before they left, Leo received a text from an anonymous number that read:

DON'T TRUST THE AFRICAN GOV'T... PLAN TO DITCH YOU AFTER GET WHAT THEY WANT. STAY AWAY.

Leo had no idea what to make of that text, neither its content nor its reliability, but he kept it in the back of his mind.

The two lovebirds soon thereafter arrived at the airport. When Sera had printed off their boarding passes from the automated kiosk, she noticed the destination had changed.

She asked her new husband, "Oh, no. I think they got the tickets screwed up. It says we are going to Africa?"

Without making eye contact, Leo kept walking on toward the security checkpoint as if nothing was supposed to be suspicious, "I wanted to surprise you. You know, we've been to Hawaii before and I hear the African beaches are beautiful this time of year."

Sera snickered. She just loved surprises. "Sounds good to me, hubby," she squealed with excitement.

When they landed in Africa, a security officer came up to them and sternly requested, "Mr. Stills, please come with us."

Never really being caught off guard these days by the strange things that happened to him, Leo said, "Sera, wait for me at that bar there. I won't be long."

Confused, Sera made her way to the bar and grill across the aisle without question and promptly ordered them some food and a craft beer for Leo. Four gentlemen with guns and badges escorted Leo past a couple locked doors to a small dark room with one table and two chairs.

Leo sat in one and, afraid of becoming bored, asked, "What can I help you boys with this fine day?"

As he did this, he smiled and looked around at the guards who were not quite as amused. They plopped his duffle bag on the table and Leo immediately knew what this was about.

Me: This is what I get for flying commercial. No privacy.

Fear: Oh, no! They're gonna catch me.

Anger: I should just knock down the chubby one by the door and get the hell out of here.

Fear: These guys are scary.

Me: Shut up.

As Leo quarreled with his thoughts, the tallest officer of the bunch unzipped the brown leather bag. Inside was some clothes and a few miscellaneous items, but Leo knew that was not why they pulled his bag from the general screening. The officer dug around a bit more and then pulled out seven or eight one-gallon sized bags filled with jewelry and loose diamonds.

The officer held it up in the air, as if the obvious question was asked aloud, 'What's this?'

Deceit: Can't tell him the truth obviously. Lie to him!

Unfortunately, Leo agreed with this thought. He couldn't tell them what this was really for, but at the same time he hated to lie.

Me: Let's try deceit.

Truth: As if that's any different from lying…

Ignoring that last admonishment, Leo falsely explained, "Fellas, you can see I'm on a honeymoon with my new wife. Those are gifts."

Deceit: Not gifts for Sera, but gifts, in a way, nonetheless. Haha! Nice one.
I didn't lie.

The officers looked at him with resentment, interrogating him further, "Mr. Stills, there must be millions of U.S. dollars' worth of diamonds and gold in this bag."

They stopped there, again as if Leo would simply admit to the absurdity of his last statement.

Playing the part, Leo smirked and quickly responded, "She's worth every penny."

After another fifteen minutes of this unfruitful back and forth, the officers realized that they were getting nowhere and, not having any other evidence, decided to let Leo go free.

He got back to the main terminal with the rest of the public and found Sera sitting at the restaurant, nursing a side salad and getting a bit anxious at Leo's extended absence.

Relieved to see him come back, she kissed him on the cheek as he took his seat next to her and she asked, "What was all that about?"

Deceit: Here we go again. We gotta do it. Can't tell her the truth.

Leo replied, "You remember, I'm working with Senator Adams on the illegal coffee trade here in Africa."

Sera nodded, waiting for him to continue. He did not.

Not knowing she should be suspicious, Sera simply let it go and they finished their meal in peace.

As the two of them rode in the back seat of a taxi to their hotel, Sera couldn't help but express herself, "Leo, you're so smart. You know, you don't have to do any of the… shady stuff that you do. I just don't want to lose you. I need you. The kids need you."

This was a conversation these two once had before, long ago.

Leo looked his new bride in her dark brown eyes and swore, "I will always keep our family safe. Don't worry."

They shared a long kiss and relaxed the rest of the way.

As they were getting settled into their hotel suite, Leo told Sera the plan for the next day, "Tomorrow morning, we are going to have a lovely breakfast in bed. I had April book you a full spa day. You've earned it. I just want you to relax. You've been working so hard. You are such a great mother. You deserve it."

She smiled and jumped on him in a spectacular hug.

Leo continued, "There is a mud bath, a massage, sauna, whatever you want. The whole day is already reserved."

She giggled with excitement, and then asked, "What will you do?"

Truth: We don't need to lie. When are we going to stop with all the lies?!

Leo replied, "I'm just going to take it easy, maybe hang by the pool. I've been trying to read that novel, you know. I'll probably just have some drinks and relax."

She smiled at him. The two of them were both jet-lagged and after a brief embrace, they went to sleep.

The next morning came and Sera headed down to the lobby to catch her shuttle to the spa. After she was gone only a few minutes, Leo made his way out of the hotel's back entrance where he had a car waiting to pick him up. His contact had arranged for this car to take him to a boat, that would then transport Leo deep into the African jungle. The leader of the entire cartel, Fitzroy Malafante, would be expecting him.

Leo traveled for quite a long time on sparse, dirt roads. The guides did not speak English, so it was a lengthy, quiet ride indeed. There was not a lot of people around these parts. After a bumpy ride in a cheap jeep, Leo made his way onto a rickety, metal boat that looked like it could sink at any moment.

Truth: Count your blessings back at home. You enjoy a lot of comfortable things. Not everyone is as lucky as you. It's sometimes hard to remember to be thankful for those things that we don't have that we don't want.

Me: Amen.

Leo hesitantly climbed in, not wanting to crack the damaged boat any further. The small motor purred, and they pulled away slowly into deep vegetative growth. If you weren't familiar with this body of water, you would hardly even be able to tell that there was a path up the river at all. The boat, having made this trip on a regular basis, was equipped with an improvised metal barrier that blocked the low hanging tree branches. No one sat at the back of the boat because as the tree branches stretched across the front barrier, they quickly snapped back into place before the boat could fully pass by. If you sat in the rear, you were likely to get knocked off your keister into the water.

An indeterminable amount of time later, Leo arrived at the entrance of a less-than-glamorous work camp. Coffee products were scattered everywhere, and countless people dressed in rags hurried around the work site.

A very short man came to meet Leo at the dock and, with a smile larger than you'd expect from someone in this line of work, said in broken English, "Mr. Stills, we are expecting you. Glad you make safely."

Again tentatively, Leo stood up and hopped out of the metal deathtrap.

He shook hands with the man and said, "Thank you for having me."

The man replied, "I am Fitzroy. Please, you come this way."

Not expecting that the first person he would meet would be the leader of this cartel, and definitely surprised at Malafante's cheerful demeanor, Leo quietly followed.

Fitzroy led Leo past a wide array of divisions within their operation, from harvesting to refining to packaging to distribution. It was not meant to be a tour, but the main cabin was simply at the back of the camp.

As they walked, any of the workers who were wearing a uniform - apparently Malafante's private army - stopped what they were doing and saluted their leader. It was definitely a sight to see how such a small man demanded so much respect from even the most gigantic soldiers, some literally three times Malafante's size.

Leo and Malafante sat across from each other at a handmade wooden table that was basically two tree stumps with another tree placed on top. The top had been shaved down to something resembling flat and was marred with burns, stains and knife scrapes.

Anxiety: Are those blood stains?

Fear: I'm not sure I should be here.

As they were sitting down, two women came up and served them tea and toast. This meeting was starting to feel strangely civilized, nothing like Leo thought it would be as he rode in the metal death boat through the jungle marsh.

Malafante took a sip of his tea, a bite of his toast and then asked, "So, tell me what an American wants so bad he willing to risk life coming to see our humble operation."

Leo replied bravely, "I wouldn't call your operation humble, by any means. That is why I'm here."

Leo took a sip of his tea and attempted not to spit the awful brew all over the floor.

Forcing down his throat what Leo could only assume was good coffee brewed in dirt water, he choked out, "I run a profitable coffee distribution company in The States. These days, though, everyone and their dog wants to open up a new shop. By the time the coffee products make it through all the middlemen to my company, quality is terrible, and the price is unsustainable. I want to come direct to the initial source so I can get the best quality and the fairest price."

Leo took another sip of his tea, thinking he must have exaggerated the first time. It couldn't be that bad, he thought. He was wrong. This time, he was barely able to stifle his gag reflex while the lukewarm tea almost shot out through his nose.

Not completely surprised at Leo's comments, but perhaps taken aback, Malafante said, "I must admit, it's not every day we get visitors here, let alone Americans. It is true, we produce eight of every ten pounds of coffee consumed worldwide. Most of it does start here, yes. No argue. We already have longstanding relationships with many of our customers. None go direct into the American States. It is extremely dangerous getting too close to your government. They pitbulls, you know. How do you plan get past them?"

Setting his tea down and sliding it away discreetly in an attempt to stop smelling its fragrant perfume, Leo responded confidently, "That's not your concern. All you have to do is get it to your local airport and then I will take it back on my private plane. As soon as it boards my plane, your liability is released. For this order, my plane leaves in four days if you can get my shipment ready in that amount of time."

Malafante considered the proposition. Although he was one of the richest, most powerful men in Africa, there was still a lot of room to improve on the global scale.

Eventually his greed got the best of him, and Malafante continued, "Fair enough. How much you have in mind?"

At that, Leo pulled out his duffle bag, and dumped out the bags of jewelry he brought with him onto the table. "There is plenty more where that came from. This is just to start us off."

Malafante grinned as the gold and diamonds shimmered in front of him.

Leo negotiated further, "Going forward, as much as I liked seeing your fine country for the first time, I don't want to have to come back." Leo handed him a schedule he had prepared with Rome, with dates and amounts, saying, "We stick to this schedule. I will drop payment. You load the product onto my aircraft. Done. Easy. Do we have a deal?"

Malafante jumped up and, instead of accepting Leo's handshake, pulled Leo in for a hug. "Deal! Before go, you celebrate with me. We must."

Worried that they were going to give him more tea, Leo was about to refuse when the same two females from before brought out a bottle of Irish whiskey, properly labeled with the American company's logo.

Me: Thank God.

Leo paused and remembered he could really use a drink. Leo and Malafante drank half of the bottle, before the conversation took a very interesting turn. Though clearly not a lightweight drinker, Malafante was beginning to slur his words when he let some critical information slip about another one of his main customers, "You Americans. Always so arrogant. Your money very good. So, you lucky."

Leo had no idea what he was talking about, but asked an obvious question, "I thought you didn't work with any Americans."

Malafante continued, "I said none of my customers go *direct* to America. We work with one other group of you guys, government, and they channel their shipments through Mexico. Nothing direct. No ties."

Amazed and confused, thinking he must be drunk, Leo asked, "Government? You mean American government officials?"

Malafante rambled on, pouring himself another glass of whiskey, "Yes, yes. Your leader from Washington."

Leo asked, growing more confused by the second, "The President of the United States is involved?!"

Malafante laughed, spewing whiskey all over the floor.

He mumbled to himself, mocking Leo, "The President? El Presidente? Hahaha! No, no. Some lady. Think you all call them senators there. She does big operation here. Supposed to be stopping the coffee from leaving here. No. Instead, she take it all for herself. Why you think USA start being here so many years ago? She learns everything about the coffee trade here and she contact us and work out sweet deal. Why you think no one stop us yet? If America really cared?"

Truth: Senator Adams?!

Arrogance: Impressive.

Me: Holy hell.

Truth: No wonder Washington State has the highest rate of coffee consumption and distribution in the entire nation. So much for draining the political swamp.

Leo asked impatiently, "Is her name Adams?"

Malafante replied, "I do not keep track of her name. She give me lots of money. American dollars and technology too. We give her coffee. That's it. It's not like we have choice. When America asks, we listen."

Leo went on, "Well, what does she look like?"

Malafante exploded with laughter, "I not know! You all look same to me!"

Unamused, and needing to process this staggering revelation, Leo said, "Fitz, I must be going. It's been real. I appreciate your time."

Malafante offered, "How about some tea first, so we sober up?"

Horrified at the notion of drinking more of that concoction, Leo quickly refused as politely as he could, saying, "Wish I could stay longer, but I have plans I can't break. My people will be in touch with yours. Appreciate your time."

With that, Leo headed back to the boat and made his way to the tourist resort where Sera would surely be waiting for him. When he got back into cell phone range after he emerged from the jungle, he saw two missed calls and several text messages from Sera asking where he was. He texted her that he would return soon and then sat back in the jeep, almost falling asleep to the melodic bumps in the winding, dirt road.

He finally made it back to the hotel. Sera had no idea the adventure Leo just undertook, let alone how lucky he was just to make it back alive. The two of them spent the next several days by the pool, relaxing like they were on a proper honeymoon.

On the last day of their trip, they were getting ready to have their most extravagant dinner yet to cap off a wonderful week in paradise. Unable to contain her excitement, Sera was taking an exorbitant amount of time getting ready for their date. She wanted to make it special and she loved getting dressed up and going out for a night on the town with Leo. He always treated her like a princess.

Leo quickly grew tired of sitting around the hotel suite though. As he idly paced around from room to room within the large hotel suite, his phone vibrated.

He looked down and saw a text from a blocked number which read: "Senator. I have clearance code. Hotel bar. Five minutes. Red coat."

Anxiety: Uh oh.

Truth: This must be the contact that Senator Adams told you would reach out. What are they doing in Africa? How do they know you are here?

Leo brushed off the feeling of panic that instantly washed over him and yelled at the bathroom to Sera, "Babe, I'm going down to the bar. I'll be back in time for our reservation." Then, chuckling a little, he added, "If you're ready by then."

He didn't wait for her flippant response, which came in the form of muffled indignation yelled through the bathroom door two rooms away. He walked down the hallway, noticing the diamond pattern on the hardwood flooring which led to the elevator bank.

Deceit: Black elevators, huh? How ugly. This is supposed to be a high-end resort. I don't know what I expected necessarily, but I don't like that. The hardwood floors are nice, and the views are spectacular.

Truth: Focus! Don't let him distract you. Find this undercover contact guy.

Me: You fellas are crazy.

Leo exited the elevators on the first floor and took a sharp right to head toward the bar located on the side of the lobby. When he arrived, he smiled at the hostess and walked on by to look for the man in the red coat that had just texted him. However, when he arrived, he saw only a few lonely patrons that looked as if they had been there for quite some time already. These sad souls were mixed in with some scattered tourists.

Gluttony: Why not? It is 5 O'clock already isn't it. May as well get a drink while I wait.

Truth: Maybe we beat him here. Get a seat in the corner so you can watch for him to arrive.

Me: Okay.

Leo found a seat at the end of the long wooden bar and hung his jacket over the gold railing that went all the way around.

The bartender came up and, listening to both voices in his head, Leo said, "Whiskey, three fingers, two ice cubes."

He sipped on his drink and then glanced toward the bar entrance so he could track people coming and going. As he swung around, he noticed a stunningly bright red coat hanging over the back of a stool at the far end of the same bar. Leo was surprised to see a female sitting in said stool.

Truth: Could it be her? Why not? Let's get this over with.

Lust: Very pretty.

Me: Shut up.

Certainly not going to leave his beverage behind, Leo picked up his drink and made his way over to the other side of the bar. As he approached, the woman turned and looked at Leo, her face mostly hidden under a large, burgundy hat. Without a word, he sat down next to her.

Truth: Hopefully this is her.

After a few seconds, the woman glanced over her shoulder.

Then, she leaned close to Leo and whispered into his ear, "The code is 'Liberty has landed.'"

She turned back to take a sip from her martini and Leo mumbled in reply, "So, what do you want from me?"

He was beginning to sweat.

She replied with some generic information about the revolution and after only a few short sentences, she finished their introduction by saying, "Meet me tomorrow morning at 6:30 a.m. The back entrance to the breakfast hall in the lobby. Come alone. We will meet the next contact and go from there."

Leo nodded, finished his drink in one gulp and quickly got up to leave. As he was leaving, he swore he saw one of the other tourists in the bar watching him a little too closely.

Anxiety: That guy was definitely taking pictures of me.

Anger: I should go snatch his camera out of his hand and tell him to mind his own business.

Truth: Maybe. Might be a tourist perusing through photos from his trip. It's hard to tell for sure. Might not even be a camera. Could be nothing.

Deciding not to let his paranoia get the best of him, Leo walked straight out of the bar and headed back up to his room. As Leo exited the elevator on his floor, he made a phone call. His shoes tapped rapidly across the wooden floorboards in the hallway to his suite.

A woman answered the phone just as Leo walked back into his room, "What, miss me already? Do you have free long distance?"

Sera was sitting on the edge of the bed, enjoying a little champagne.

As soon as the door opened, she said, "It's about time. I was ready like five minutes ago. It's almost time to…" as she noticed Leo was on the phone, "… Oh! Sorry."

Unable to address Sera currently, Leo said hurriedly into the phone, "April, I need you to book Rome on the next flight out here. Find him, get him on our plane in the next thirty minutes. Have him text me when he is taking off."

With that, he hung up.

Sera grew indignant, scoffing "April?! You're calling April on *our* honeymoon?"

Leo took the glass of champagne out of Sera's hand and didn't dignify her line of questioning with a response. Instead, Leo finished the glass and said, "Ready for dinner?"

Sera asked, "What was that about?"

Leo replied, "Get your coat. We don't want to be late."

Sera didn't appreciate how the conversation was going, but this wasn't the first time she'd had a similar tête-à-tête with Leo. Knowing who the victor would be in the end, she reluctantly grabbed her coat and put on a smile.

He said, "That's my girl," as he helped her put it on.

The two of them went on to enjoy a spectacularly luxurious dinner, followed by a delectable dessert, both of which were eclipsed in joy by the hours that followed. Worn out and exhausted from the recent tussle, Sera laid resting in bed. Wearing only the million-dollar diamond necklace Leo had given her earlier during dinner, she was enjoying how the silky sheets felt against her skin.

Leo sat up by the fire in the other room, drinking his whiskey and smoking his cigar. He was switching back and forth between deep contemplation and the newspaper that was meant to distract him from the web of thoughts in his head.

Several hours later, when both were sleeping, Leo woke up to his phone vibrating. Rome was calling from the lobby of the hotel. Leo put on his robe and glanced over to see Sera sleeping peacefully on the bed. He left to meet Rome at their newly-booked suite down the hall.

Leo knocked on Rome's room and the door swung open to a not quite hysterical but still very worried Rome, "Bro! Everything okay?! April didn't tell me why, but she got me down here in a hurry. What's the deal? Hell of a long flight if it was for nothing. What's up with the robe?"

Leo spoke, "Calm down, Roman. We have a situation."

Leo filled Rome in on the background with Senator Adams and the undercover informant that he met earlier in the bar.

Leo went on, "She gave the wrong damn code."

Rome was not quite as shocked or worried about it as Leo, "So what? Maybe she got flustered or confused? Maybe the plans changed since you spoke with Senator Adams?"

Leo shook his head, "No. Doesn't matter why. I was told – and remember Rome, this is the United States government telling me – that if the wrong clearance code was given, we were to tie up any loose ends. The government, bro."

Deceit: It's not like I have a choice.

Leo sighed, "It's not like we have a choice."

Truth: You always have a choice.

Rome very much did not want to be involved in any murders here. The Stills Corporation already had plenty of blood on its metaphorical hands, with Rome topping the charts. That being said, as Rome grew older and finally found a good, strong woman to help him stay on the straight and narrow path, he thought that part of his life was behind him.

Rome retorted, "Bro, is that really necessary? Can't we just have her arrested."

Leo paused, and then replied, "I need you to take care of this and stay here with me for backup. We aren't in Belmont. If we don't do this, they *will* kill me. Over and done with. Quick and easy, then meet me at the airport."

Truth: This isn't right.

Rome pleaded again, "Lee, for real man. I can't take it. My soul can't take it."

Silence.

Rome looked into Leo's eyes and Leo looked back. After only a moment, Leo simply slid a note containing a time and place in Rome's front pocket, patted him on the shoulder and walked out the door back to his own suite. Over the course of the next couple hours, Rome would execute their business plan, drop it off in the ocean to feed the fish, say a quick prayer for the forgiveness he knew he didn't deserve, down half of a bottle of Paradise Pills for numbness, and finally meet up with Leo and Sera at the local airport to head back home on a private flight that was loaded up with more coffee than you could count.

<u>Story 21</u>

After a long, quiet flight back to the states, Leo dropped Sera off at home and went to meet up with Senator Adams at her local office.

When he arrived, her secretary asked, "May I help you?"

Leo kept on walking and went straight to the senator's office.

Swinging the door open, Leo saw Senator Adams in quite the compromising position with a young man, who was clearly not her husband.

As the senator scrambled to regain her composure, her secretary came storming in after Leo, apologizing, "I'm sorry, ma'am. He just went right past me." Obviously unsurprised by what was going on behind the closed doors, the secretary continued, "Shall I have security remove him from the building?"

Senator Adams straightened her outfit, whispered something to the young man and responded to her secretary, "No, thank you. Mr. Stills, please sit," she said, motioning for Leo to sit down.

The young man departed, and the secretary closed the doors again as Leo found his seat.

The senator asked, "You don't know how to make an appointment or, for that matter, how to knock?"

Leo took a dig at her, "How's your husband doing?"

She instantly lost her politician's façade and crossly asked, "What do you want?"

Leo stood up and told her about the woman who texted him, pretending to be the undercover informant sent by the senator, "… but she gave the wrong code."

Silence.

Leo went on, "I disposed of the situation."

Silence.

Leo continued, "… as we discussed."

Leo would not stop staring into her eyes, while the senator constantly broke eye contact. Without speaking, the senator went to the corner of her office and opened a painting which clung to a hinge, revealing a wall safe behind it.

The senator glanced back at Leo, as if to say, 'Don't look at the combination,' and Leo obliged, swiveling around in his chair to face the other direction. He heard the safe open and then close again a few moments later.

She came back and placed a small duffle bag on the table. Leo opened the bag and found stacks of $100 bills, banded together in sets of $10,000. There were too many to count.

Greed: Good. I should get compensated for my trouble.

Truth: Give it back. Forget her. She thinks she can buy my soul?

Deceit: What's done is done. It's not like they had to ask or had to give me anything. They could force me to do these things.

Greed: Exactly. I may as well get paid for it.

Deceit: It's not like I have a choice.

Greed: At this point, who's going to get hurt by me taking this money.

Truth: What good is it for one to gain the world…

Without saying a word, Leo zipped the bag closed, picked it up, and set it down next to his chair. She smiled at the cheap price she just paid for the ending of one human life and the gradual corruption of another human soul.

She moved the conversation forward, "With the unpleasantries out of the way, time for your next, *official* assignment. We need you to meet the Africans at the pier to broker, secure and inspect a shipment of drones and other technology bound for Africa." She spent another few minutes describing in detail what would take place and the important publicity this would bring to her campaign, "… and by consequence, the good publicity would be extended to your campaign through my endorsement for your mayoral bid."

Me: Eli will be perfect for this job.

Leo stood up, grabbed the bag full of cash, shook the senator's hand and headed back to the office. He was looking for Eli so he could fill him in on his next project. He found Eli and Justine arguing in the office lobby, loud enough for the whole place to hear.

Ever since Justine became Eli's nanny and had taken over the domestic responsibilities of cleaning the house and essentially mothering his kids – the two of them had grown close. So close, in fact, they got hitched themselves shortly after Leo and Sera's wedding.

Now, Eli and Justine were both young and emotional. It was not uncommon to find the two of them in the middle of some spirited conversation. The passion that drove them apart, also brought them back together with just as much force.

Leo shouted, "Hey, hey, hey! Enough of that. Jeeze. Get a room."

Eli protested Leo's infringement on their conversation, "Back off, bro."

Leo would have none of it, "Look around. You're not at home. You're at the office." Sighing, Leo continued, "Come with me."

Eli reluctantly agreed.

When they had gotten upstairs to Leo's office, Eli began to explain, "You know that was nothing serious. Just trying to communicate…"

Leo didn't want to hear it, "It is neither appropriate nor wise to tear your partner down in public. Besides being rude, when you do that, you undermine and diminish the relationship that you voluntarily joined and continue to pursue. When you guys fight like that in public, ripping on each other, you may as well be holding a sign that reads, 'I'm with stupid and I'm an idiot for choosing this idiot.' If you love someone, you work to help them reflect themselves in a way that is most beneficial to you both over the long run."

Eli merely nodded, knowing it to be the truth.

Leo switched subjects right away and went on to explain Eli's newest assignment as it related to the African drones before wrapping up that conversation and heading home.

A few months went by and Leo was at the Coffee Spot with Eli, carousing around dinner time on a Friday night. Rome, now the owner of the joint, was behind the bar, working hard serving a packed crowd. The music was loud, small fights were constantly starting and promptly being broken up. Business was good. Things were running smoothly and there had not been a lot of serious drama recently.

After quite a while in their private back room, Leo stumbled out into the main bar area to see Rome using an Espresso shot to down another Paradise Pill, just to keep up with the crowd. Leo kept walking outside to get some fresh air.

As he walked around aimlessly, staring up at the clear night sky, he was suddenly grabbed and pulled into the back of a van. Leo struggled violently against his attackers as the van screeched away down the dark road.

Truth: Who is dangerous enough, or foolish enough to snatch me up in Belmont?

Pride: These jackals are going to pay for this.

The van lurched to a stop and Leo's resistance ceased. He sat up and saw that they were in the middle of a dark alley.

One of the men addressed him with a heavy African accent, "Message from your government. They say no more SOPA, or else. If you ever see Jane lady again, just maybe no one will ever see your pretty wife or darling sons ever again. You think you are safe at home. We can get you and your family anywhere, anytime. SOPA bad for your government, they say. Now that you run for mayor, no more, no more."

Truth: Feds? Senator? Mayor?!

Leo spit at them through his bloody teeth, saying, "Go to hell!"

After delivering the instructed message, the men proceeded to beat Leo for a couple minutes and then they dropped him outside the van into the alley on the wet pavement. Leo was gasping for air as he scrambled for his phone. He immediately called Sera.

She distractedly answered, "Hi, baby. I been missing you!"

Leo yelled back, "Sera! Where are you? Are you okay? Where are the kids?"

Now having her full attention, Sera replied, "I'm getting my new necklace cleaned with Michelle and then we were going to grab a late dinner. It was so dirty when you gave it to me. What's going on?"

Leo continued, "Where are the kids?!"

Sera was getting worried, "They are at home with the nanny. Leo, what's wrong?"

Unfortunately, she didn't get an answer but simply heard the other line click, ending the call. Leo hung up and raced back to his house.

When he got there, he sprinted inside to find the entire house trashed, turned upside down. The damage was clearly meant to send a message.

Leo ran through the entire mansion, yelling out for his kids, "Caden! Timmy!"

He raced from floor to floor, jumping over debris and slamming open doors. There was broken glass everywhere.

He was about to give up hope when he heard them.

"Daddy!"

"Mr. Stills?"

"Dad!"

Sprinting to the front door, he saw his two sons and the nanny hovering there, scared to enter the chaos.

Leo ran to them and hugged them like never before, "I'm so glad your safe. I thought I lost you. I love you, boyos."

He kissed them over and over, delighting in their embrace and checking them for any signs of harm.

Me: I'm going to have security here full time from now on. My family goes nowhere alone. It's too dangerous.

The victory was short-lived, however, when Sera came storming in from the garage screaming at the top of her lungs.

Leo ran over to the washroom, where the garage connected to the house, to find a hysterical Sera. At first, he thought she was scared about the state of the house, until he saw her charging directly for him in a fit of rage as soon as he turned the corner.

She yelled, "What the hell is this?!"

He was confused at this point. She was holding her cell phone, thrusting it up into Leo's face.

He tried to calm her down about the fact that their house was broken into and trashed, but she shrieked louder this time, "Who the hell is this, Leonardo?"

She was smacking Leo over and over. He grabbed the phone and shielded himself from her blows as he tried to see what was on her screen. He was finally able to catch a glimpse of himself sitting at the bar in Africa with the woman in the red coat leaning in far too close for his wife's comfort. Now, Leo knew there was no intimacy involved and this was simply her leaning in to covertly give him the clearance code, but he had to admit the picture looked different. Just looking at the photo on the screen, the two of them did look cozy.

Leo chuckled slightly at her confusion, but that merely enraged Sera further who really began to wail on him, now using her purse.

"On our honeymoon?!" she yelled as she threw the diamond necklace that he gave her, hitting him square on the side of his head even as he ducked to escape its path.

Not allowing her to continue beating him upside the head, Leo grabbed her arms, pulled her in tight and yelled, "Babe. Babe! It's not what it looks like."

Anxiety: Oh, that's going to work. Like that line hasn't been said a million times throughout history.

Sera struggled with all her might, but without success.

Leo continued after only a heartbeat, "Sera, that was a business meeting, plain and simple. There was nothing crazy. That was my first and only meeting with that woman. It lasted all of ten minutes, maybe. That picture is misleading to say the least. How did you even get it?"

He let go of her and backed away slowly.

Sera calmed down slightly, but still worked up, she shot back, "Some random number texted it to me and said you would know what this was about."

She smacked him again on the shoulder.

Leo grew excited, "Look around. Look at our house! This is what it's about. These are some bad people."

The reality of the situation finally sank in, as Sera looked around her destroyed house in a daze. All the feminine touches she added since she moved back in were thrown around and dismantled. Nothing even close to resembling peace was left standing. Somewhat penitent now, Sera saw her diamond necklace lying amidst the disordered rubble. She stooped down and picked it up, dusting it off.

Truth: Fruit of the poisonous tree. Get rid of the necklace. We need to go 100% legit. Let go of our dark ways.

Deceit: Who cares if I got that necklace and most of the rest of my riches through what our corrupt government would call 'illegal means?'

Greed: It's mine. I'm keeping it.

Leo saw the necklace and conflated it with the growing resentment he was feeling for this illicit lifestyle that introduced nothing but increasing turmoil to his life lately. With his family back in his life now, his priorities were changing.

He said to her, "I should take that back. It seems like it has brought nothing but bad luck."

As he said this, he reached out for it, but she pulled back, saying, "No! It's mine. You gave it to me, and I love it." Leo was about to continue his protest when she spoke over him, "I want to wear it tomorrow to the completion party for our newest community housing project."

Leo shook his head and let sleeping dogs lie.

He said, "I will call April and have her get this stuff scheduled for cleanup today."

Sera offered, "I will take care of that."

Leo paused and then nodded in agreement.

That night, Leo was thrown into another world within his dreams. Now, at this point, he hadn't had a dream, or better yet, a nightmare, in many months. Unfortunately, this one picked up where his past ones left off.

Leo found himself running again, clearly sprinting through his hometown of Belmont. Leo was very familiar with the area, so he was ducking quickly into back alleys and taking every shortcut he could utilize in an effort to get away. He glanced back over his shoulder to see a frightening specimen hot on his trail. For someone so large, it was unnatural that his pursuer would run so fast and, at the same time, plow straight through anything that got in his way. The man, if he was even human at all, was bloody and dirty, scratched up and scarred all over. It's as if his face was a leather mask. He was shirtless so you could see his clammy, overweight body bulging from his blue, jean overalls and he was well over seven-feet tall; ugly, ugly, sweaty thing. Leo was humble enough to recognize that he could not physically overpower this guy, so Leo sprinted away. As Leo ran and ran, he would knock over a bookcase or throw a chair at the man – without adding so much as a scratch to the already mutilated face of his pursuer. No matter where Leo went, though, whenever he turned around, he saw this monster right behind him. Leo ran through door after door, slamming them shut behind him only to hear them burst open seconds later. Not making any ground after what had to be hours of running,

Leo finally decided to make a stand. Leo thought to himself, 'Well, I can't beat him, but I'm tired of running. So, kill me, or leave the hell alone.' Leo quickly jumped through an entryway, slammed the door shut and stood silently behind a filing cabinet. Terrified, though unsurprised, Leo flinched when the entire door frame splintered, and the animal-of-a-man ran through. For a split second, Leo had the advantage and he jumped on the savage's back. Leo yelled and punched, and the giant just laughed menacingly. Leo knew he couldn't hurt this demon, but one can only run for so long.

Just as the monster was finally about to get his paws on him, Leo shot up in bed. Waking up a clammy mess, he proceeded to toss and turn the rest of the night.

<u>Story 22</u>

Morning came none too soon and Leo sat up in his bed covered in sweat. The sun was not quite peeking out over the mountains, leaving a red-orange light just glowing through the curtains. Nonetheless, Leo had no desire to stay in bed any longer and he was more than ready to start his day.

Later that evening, The Stills Corporation was hosting a party for a recent community housing development. It was part charity, part celebration, part sales; but more of a party than anything, and it was certainly by invitation only.

That didn't mean, however, that it was an intimate gathering of a few friends. There were hundreds of people gathered in the future lobby of the first ever residential apartment tower in Belmont. Construction wouldn't be completed for a few months now, but things were proceeding nicely on the 32-story high-rise.

It was the single, biggest project here in over three decades, located directly between the center of the city and the waterfront. A beautiful building on a marvelous location boasting a 360-degree, unobstructed view for miles.

Over the last few years especially, the Stills Corporation had provided quite generously to the community. They offered affordable housing without accepting the government's tax breaks like most other real estate investors in the area. In fact, the company was auctioning off five luxury condominium units that would be given away to five needy families for free, with the sale proceeds going to the local food bank.

This party was also a very important part of Leo's campaign for mayor. The publicity would be amazing and his optics in the community could use some polishing, even though most of the local citizens already loved him for one reason or another.

The drinks were endless, and the food was free. Everyone had been eating and drinking and schmoozing for about an hour before Leo and his pretty, young wife, Sera, arrived causing quite the stir. People took pictures and tried anything to shake hands. Plenty of guests just wanted a few minutes with Mr. Stills to pitch an idea or ask for business help. Sera loved and admired Leo for his newfound dedication to the good these days, even though she thought he often carried out that mission in a crude and brutish manner. She watched him talk with would-be voters and genuinely care about their perspective on various topics.

Only the most rich and powerful people attended this event, investors, local representatives etc. Even Senator Beth Adams was in attendance, pursuant to her promise to endorse Leo's campaign. Leo invited only a select number of these guests into a walled-off section of the lobby where they would be adding their handprints to wet cement as a memorial to the building. Leo took Sera, some of his closest men, including Rome and Eli, as well as several other prominent guests to the private room.

There were murmurs from the small crowd, cheerfully requesting a speech from Leo, the man who made it all happen.

Leo looked into Sera's eyes, saying a thousand words with one glance and she responded lovingly, "Go, go. I'll be fine. Go change the world. I'll be here waiting for you when you get done."

With that, she gave him a quick peck on the cheek, and he trotted up to the stage. After giving a thirty-second spiel, thanking the lenders and investors on the deal and recognizing his local support with the community, he ended by taking some pictures and cutting the ribbon.

Leo didn't much care for all the spotlight and took his first opportunity to get off stage. As he did so, a man came up to him and whispered something into Leo's ear.

Leo paused, tapped Rome on the shoulder and said, "Rome, this guy is the undercover operative the senator said would make contact. He gave the right security clearance code and wants to meet next at the Statterman Suites building. Can you get him set up and figure out what exactly he wants to do next?"

Rome replied quietly, "You got it."

Relieved to have that part over with, Leo searched the crowd for Sera. He finally found her smiling at him from across the room. The two lovebirds made eye contact and it was as if the whole world had suddenly stopped. The two of them felt completely alone in the middle of a crowd.

Leo was walking toward her, inadvertently bumping into bystanders and potential constituents. In these tight quarters, it felt even busier than when they were with the other hundreds of guests outside in the main lobby.

He finally got to her and as they went in for a quick hug, Sera said, "I thought you'd…"

Just then, as the two began to relish the moment together, Leo heard yelling. Someone was angry and Leo could tell they were getting closer because now the bellowing seemed like it was right next to him.

Truth: He's got a gun. Watch out!

Leo wheeled around to find Lorenzo Capanini Senior pushing his way through the door, screaming at the top of his lungs, "Per la mia famiglia!"

Gunshots rang out of Lorenzo's primitive, but effective 22-caliber pistol.

Before Lorenzo's henchmen could make it through the door into the private backroom, the security staff took them down. The whole world was now moving in slow motion as two bullets hit Leo, one in the stomach and one in the shoulder. Rome and Eli moved quickly, smashing a chair over Lorenzo's back, knocking him to the ground. Without hesitating, they dragged him out and dropped him in the rotating mixer filled with wet cement as all the bystanders looked the other way. Leo staggered, attempting to maintain his balance. Eli ran over to him and grabbed him before he fell, helping him lay down gently on the ground. Blood was leaking everywhere.

Barely half-conscious, Leo coughed up blood and mumbled to Eli, "Get Sera out of here."

Eli didn't respond, but Leo could hear him shouting to the onlookers, "Call 9-1-1! We have people shot here! Someone… call 9-1-1!"

Leo was getting frustrated now and he repeated himself, this time mustering all the strength he had left to speak louder, "Elijah! Forget about me. Get Sera out of here now!"

Eli looked at Leo and said, "I got it. You just stay with me, bro!"

At that, Leo began fading in and out of consciousness, but before he passed out, Leo swore he could faintly hear, "… no, no. That's not his."

The last thing Leo remembered was looking over and hazily seeing that expensive diamond necklace covered in blood.

<u>Story 23</u>

A few months went by and, although Leo's physical wounds were healing, he was still left emotionally broken from the loss of his wife, who ended up being collateral damage as a result of Leo's poor career choice.

Every waking moment of every day, Leo reminded himself that it was his fault she was killed, even if someone else pulled the trigger. Two bullets meant for him, indeed found their target, but one missed Leo altogether, finally lodging in Sera's heart. Her soul had left her body before she hit the ground.

Leo had gathered his strength and called a family meeting. Everyone was waiting in the lobby of Bravo Tower when Leo hobbled his way through the front door on crutches. April took his coat from him and helped him lean back on a desk in front of everyone.

For a long time, Leo said nothing. No one else dared to break the silence either. Those gathered there, looking at Leo deep in thought, assumed he was looking for the right words amidst an ocean of grief. This was not the case. Leo was shallowly looking around the office, disgusted with the kingdom he had built.

He gazed at his family office; once so humble. He now saw the extravagant wealth wasting away. The riches for which he had paid with Sera's blood, as well as with his soul and those of his whole crew. In hindsight, it was all meaningless in comparison. For once, a light shined upon Leo's mind. Although he didn't know exactly where he was headed, every time he saw Sera's lifeless body in his memory, Leo was reminded from what exactly he was running away.

Truth: Give it all away. Start over building on a proper foundation. Give it all away.

Guilt: It's all my fault. I don't deserve to live. God must be ashamed of me. God can't love me. I am ashamed of me. I don't love me.

Greed: I may as well wallow in my riches. Giving my TV away won't bring Sera back.

Gluttony: I need a drink. A drink would help. A drink sounds good.

Finally, able to speak, Leo addressed his crew, "Thank you for coming, all. I'm not sure where to start. The way we have been doing business is officially no more. We cling to this life of careless fun and unearned extravagance when we need to let that go in order to become the people we truly want to be."

Greed: We can just keep living this life. What's done is done. I can't get her back, so no sense in suffering now. Think about what I'd be giving up! It won't bring her back.

Truth: It's all worthless. It's nothing, and worse, it distracts me from my true and proper purpose.

Leo went on, "I don't quite have a clear picture of what our operations should look like, but I know it doesn't look like how we have been carrying on. Michelle, Seth and Charlotte – if you accept, I want you three to move over to our newest office in the central division of the Mars civilization, where we will have our universal real estate headquarters. Here is a list of priorities."

Without skipping a beat, all three of them nodded in agreement, never hesitating to follow Leo wherever his direction led them.

Leo continued, "Our illicit business, if any remains, is to cease at once. Immediately. Unwind and shut down. Take a loss on any contracts if you have to. Rome, I need you to lead up this effort. Legitimate business is now our one and only priority."

Rome nodded silently. Leo went on for a few more minutes about their going-forward strategy. He concluded the meeting and was headed to the Coffee Spot to have a beverage. He drank a lot these days since Sera went to Heaven and every now and then, when the pain was just too much – Leo leaned on the Paradise Pills to make it all go away.

Before he could escape the crowd, Michelle beckoned.

Leo turned around, asking, "What's up, sis? Mars sounds exciting, right? Thought you'd like to get as far away as possible from this craziness and the opportunity there is out of this world."

Despair: Haha.

Not smiling, she said, "Yeah, that's all fine, Lee. Something else I've got to tell you. I have it on good authority that Senator Adams is actually taking bribes from the African cartel, so they get a free pass to smuggle coffee into the country. She's the friggin' ringleader."

Knowing this already, Leo said, "I really got to go. Can we discuss this later?"

Michelle went on, "Not terribly crazy, considering how corrupt politicians have become these days. Here's the twist. My contact shared that Senator Adams knows her time is running out and so she is looking to cut ties with the cartel now that she has already made a fortune that could last several lifetimes. She's been burning any and all evidence connecting them with her, and she is planning to hand over Fitzory Malafante to the African government in the very near future. I can get you whatever evidence remains - my contact has been keeping records on all of these dealings… paper copies, originals."

Arrogance: How can we use this to our advantage?

Truth: Focus! We have to get out of this back and forth situation while we can.

Me: That's what I'm trying to do. It's not like you can just walk away from this life whenever you want. Need to get the proper leverage to ensure our safety.

Leo patted Michelle on the shoulder and said, "Good. Let's start with that."

At that, he walked out into a sunny afternoon, mumbling to himself, "I need a drink."

Several hours and a couple bottles later, he stumbled home. On his way up the stairs to take a nap, he passed by the nanny who was making lunch for his two sons, Caden and Timothy.

Timothy excitedly yelled out, "Hi, Daddy!" before Tim's nanny shushed him, telling the young boy to be quiet and to leave his dad alone.

At this point, Caden knew to give Leo his space and hardly acknowledged his father at all. Leo paused for a moment, but drowning in grief and chaos, he continued on upstairs to enter the less sorrow-laden world of dreams.

The next morning, Leo sat up in bed, disgusted with his actions the day before.

Truth: I have to do better for my kids. They deserve my best.

Guilt: I'm such a failure.

Gluttony: I may as well drink until I pass out.

Despair: I'm not good for anything these days anyhow.

He looked at the bottle of whiskey sitting on his end table and pushed it away.

Truth: My kids need me to be strong. I have got to do better.

Anger: But they need their mother.

Despair: I need their mother.

Then, again, as it has done so often since that dreadful day when his life got turned upside down, his heartache hit him like a ton of bricks as he remembered Sera. He looked over and saw her empty side of the bed. He placed his hand where she used to sleep, and he swore he could still feel her warmth. He grabbed the bottle of whiskey, unscrewed the cap and took a large gulp with his Paradise Pill… just to get the day started.

He got dressed, though still looking quite shabby, and made his way downstairs. Before heading out the door, he accepted a glass of orange juice from his motherly nanny and patted his two sons on the head. He made his way to Statterman Suites. He was uninvited but figured the information he had couldn't wait. Back at the party to celebrate the community housing project, he was approached by Senator Adam's undercover contact who gave him this address. As Leo was going to knock, the door swung open as two gentlemen were about to leave at the same time. Before they could cover it up, Leo saw several other men stacking what must have been hundreds of gold bricks into a wall safe the size of a small bathroom. To say the least, the next thing Leo saw was the end of a pistol pointed at his face and an angry man yelling at him to come in.

Leo loudly said, "Calm down, princess. Your boss, Sergi, gave me this address. I have information for him that he needs as soon as possible."

Mentioning the boss' name quickly deescalated the situation, but that didn't stop them from smacking Leo on the head and forcing him into a seat while they waited for their leader to come in.

A short while later, the man who approached Leo at the community housing party walked in and half-heartedly said, "Oh, I apologize for my men's rudeness. That being said, you weren't supposed to show up today."

Leo wiped some blood off his eyebrow and calmly replied, "I have it on good authority that the lady senator has plans to double cross you. She is conspiring to turn over your boss once and for all, now that she is fat and rich off exploiting your cartel."

"When?"

Leo went on, "Any day now. I can tell you the exact date when I get back and procure the evidence."

"You have evidence of this grave accusation?"

Leo answered, "You think I'd come in here if I didn't? Also, the senator has to die."

Sergi replied, "That's American business. Get me the evidence for this betrayal and whatever happens to her is of no consequence to the Malafante Cartel. Although you came here uninvited, now is as good of a time as any to give you your instructions. We need you to intercept a shipment of drones and technology that your government is sending to Africa specifically in an effort to crack down on our coffee trade. We will pay you handsomely for your services. Here are the reports detailing the location of the shipment and when it is set to dock in your local ports for only two days. You will have to hit it then before it is shipped out to Africa."

Truth: They will never pay me. This is the end game. People are put in early graves at this point. Everyone is cutting ties and deleting evidence.

Leo stood up and the two of them shook hands in agreement. Leo left the Statterman Suites building, somewhat surprised he actually made it out alive. He had meetings back to back and was now headed to see an old friend, FBI Director Monroe, who was the only person more powerful than Senator Adams in Leo's rolodex.

For this one, Leo had April call ahead and make an appointment for the director to travel down to Belmont. Leo walked down the brick alley road towards a dingy bar and grill on the edge of town.

He was familiar with this neighborhood, every building and most of the people in each of them. Everyone knew him. Leo walked slowly, attempting to enjoy every second he was given. He walked down the three steps leading to the front door of the bar, not daring to rely on the flimsy metal handrail that clung to the decomposing sidewalk for dear life. Leo was pleased to find the director already there, poking at some soggy French fries.

The two of them shook hands and then Leo jumped right into it, "Appreciate the time, Charles. It couldn't wait. You know as part of my campaign for mayor, I've been working with Senator Adams on a key issue for local voters, namely the problem of African coffee flooding our markets."

Monroe chimed in, "I think I know where this is headed."

Leo went on, "To get down to the brass tacks, the senator is playing both sides. Publicly, she is working to eliminate the coffee distribution channel out of Africa. However, she is also accepting bribes from the cartel to let it through her inspection check points. She's probably made tens of millions of dollars at this point."

Monroe looked genuinely upset, "Are you sure about this?"

Leo nodded as he replied, "100%. I have evide…"

Monroe lost control of his temper, shouting, "That much?!"

Now it was Leo's turn to be confused, "What do you mean? You already knew about this?"

Monroe shook his head, as if to dislodge an unruly thought, and came back to reality, saying, "You think the senator would pull a scam like that without my knowledge? I'm just disappointed on the scale of things. It seems as if she wasn't being completely truthful, if you are correct about how much she has made these last few years. She's only been giving me one million per year. I'm going to have to renegotiate."

Truth: He's saying this completely unashamed, so calmly. This guy has no fear of getting caught.

Leo sat there silently for a moment. This isn't how he expected the meeting to go. He thought he was calling in the cavalry who would ride in and save the day. Instead, he finds out Director Chuck is a co-conspirator in the coffee trafficking scandal.

Me: What to do, what to do?

After a few sips of his drink, Leo continued, "Well, I hate to ruin a good thing, but the senator's time has come. I'm getting proof of her misdeeds and plan to turn her in."

As he said this, his phone vibrated with a text from Michelle, saying she would bring the last of the evidence over to the family office in a few hours.

Leo texted back, 'Take to my house. Library. Bravo Tower not safe.'

Monroe wised up a bit, setting his drink down on the table, realizing he had probably had enough to drink now that the meeting was taking this turn, "You have proof?"

Leo replied, "I will have it in hand tonight and will distribute several duplicate copies to various parties in order to ensure my safety. To be clear, I want you on my side. I want you to help me take her out… quietly."

Monroe asked, "What's in it for you to take her out? We could just cut you in. Hasn't she been vital to your current campaign? This is a dangerous mission. You could get hurt."

Leo said, "She's getting too out of control. I don't like where things are headed with her. Plus, Senator Stills has a nice ring to it, don't you think? There are only one hundred senators in a nation of five hundred million people. That's power."

Monroe retorted, "And there is only *one* Director of the Federal Bureau of Investigation in this country. Don't get too big for your britches now. That said, I can see that Senator Adam's time may be coming close to an end, especially if word is getting around about her nefarious schemes… so sloppy. She also has her sights set on bigger things and she is probably not a liability I need on my books anymore."

Leo stood up, finished his drink and slammed it on the table rather loudly, asking, "So, we have a deal then?"

Monroe stood up and threw his wrinkled napkin on top of his untouched fries. He shook Leo's hand, cementing their accord.

Leo made his way back to the family office, mumbling to himself, "Two down… how many to go?"

Truth: The cartel can't be trusted to keep their word.

Me: Agreed.

Anger: Agreed. So, let's go on the offensive.

The thoughts were swirling around Leo's never-sleeping brain until he arrived at Bravo Tower. He called Rome and Eli into his office upstairs. The two of them trailed in and plopped down into a couple seats across the desk. They were a bit sluggish, as they shared a late evening last night, drinking and singing karaoke over at the Coffee Spot. Their lack of attention was annoying.

Leo addressed the two, "Boyos, the wheels are turning. I need you focused. This is huge. We have several schemes at play right now. Rome, I need you and Eli to head up the sabotage of a government shipment of technological weapons. We have indirect approval from the senator to carry this out, so shouldn't be too complicated. They wanted us to steal the weapons and hand them over, but I told them we would permanently dismantle them instead. I don't want any more innocent blood on my hands by turning over that technology to those psychos. The cartel has hired us for this job, and they say they plan to compensate us quite richly. That is, if you have faith in them to keep their word. Bottom line, this web of lies our government has built is unraveling and soon all will be revealed. I don't trust those guys to do anything but kill us in an attempt to tie up any loose ends. It's not like we are dealing with a bunch of Mother Theresa's."

Silence.

"So, while we do this job for the cartel, we will also rob the cartel. I found out they have a stash house at the Statterman – more gold than I've ever seen in real life before. I will handle this portion. Their vault is on the first floor. I'm going to hijack the underground train that runs through the center of town. We will have a flatbed cart in the middle of the train. We will stop under the Statterman, blow a hole in the Statterman's floor causing the safe to fall through. We then release the back half of the train containing all the passengers, and we simply drive the train to the first fire escape hatch and use a crane to load the entire haul onto one of our semi-trucks. Easy."

The two brothers responded simultaneously, "Done."

Now, unbeknownst to the three fellas upstairs, the females on the crew had formed a bit of a gossip party. They were down in the lobby, drinking a few bottles of some fine Sauvignon Blanc. Jane had come by, along with Mary Anne, to visit Michelle for a quick drink before heading out to a night on the town. April joined in the lively conversation as well. After the third empty bottle joined the first two in the center of the round, wooden table, Michelle opened up and shared some of the juicy news regarding Leo's plan to turn on the senator.

Although Jane should have known better perhaps, she unwittingly brought with her a tail from the senator's office. Jane was unaware of the threats that Senator Adams had levied on the Stills clan if they chose to keep associating with her and, by extension, her SOPA comrades. The senator's private investigative team was recording this conversation from a van outside the family office. They listened as Michelle described the large manila envelope which contained the damning evidence that she had dropped off at Leo's house on the way here for safekeeping - and how it was the last bit of evidence that remained. Mary Anne, who was pregnant with her and Rome's first child and hoping to get out of the criminal lifestyle sooner than later, didn't like the idea of such a dangerous arrangement. The rest of the women generally agreed, although Jane, a radical herself, didn't feel as strongly. April simply supported whatever Leo thought was best.

The three guys came down from upstairs and Leo jokingly said to the congregation of ladies, "Whoa, whoa, whoa. Disperse! This can't be good. Too many high-quality opinions in one place."

April stood up, obviously tipsy, and softly punched him on the arm. The two of them had remained close friends, and only friends. April had been a critical line of support for Leo since Sera passed away. Leo smiled at her and put his arm around April in an effort to stabilize her and prevent her from tripping over the various chairs scattered throughout the lobby that she clearly didn't see.

Me: Some nights, when I was completely lost, she has kept me from literally going insane and giving up on life.

The boys helped the females finish the rest of the wine and then sent them on their way for a fun night out. The guys stayed back at the office and polished off a bottle of Irish whiskey themselves. Although there were actually quite a few crazy plans in the works, tonight felt like a pretty normal night. That fun lasted until Leo got home a few hours later, just passed midnight at this point. When he got to his house, the front door was open, and the wood was splintered as if someone had forced their way in.

These days, Leo had a four-person, rotating security team made up of off-duty cops that constantly watched his house. He drew his pistol, opened the door quietly and stepped in to find his home ransacked. It looked like a run-of-the-mill robbery, the way all of his belongings were turned upside down and thrown around.

Leo knew better, especially when he saw two of his security officers left unconscious; their feet and hands bound with zip ties. Unfortunately, these two were luckier than the other two officers he found on the deck in the backyard – at least the first two were still breathing. Leo's heart was pounding. He had to find his nanny and his two sons.

He had searched his entire house and found the library equally raided. The safe into which Leo had Michelle put the evidence implicating the corrupt senator was shattered into pieces, nothing was left. This confirmed his suspicion and his worst fear. Leo's heart sank into his stomach as he fell to the floor, broken in pieces like the rest of his castle.

Truth: They must have my kids. We have to get them back.

Fear: How are we going to get at her now?! They took the only evidence left that incriminated Senator Adams. We're losing our leverage… our power. We've got nothing!

Unfortunately, after Leo left Rome and Eli earlier that night, those two headed straight out to coordinate their assignment. This left Leo with little options. He quickly called Seth, who was set to go to Mars next week for an exciting business opportunity and to escape this unlawful lifestyle. He asked Seth to meet him at the Coffee Spot immediately.

Leo walked quickly towards the Coffee Spot, not able to discuss such a sensitive matter over the phone. As he went, he worked out what he thought must be the senator's plan. As far as Leo could tell, he came up with a hypothesis on how Senator Adams was planning to tie up all of her loose ends.

He figured that once he completed sabotaging the shipment of drones bound for the African government, she was going to arrest whoever was involved in that scandal. Regrettably, this now also involved Leo's crew, including Rome and Eli who were not dispensable to him. Once they were arrested, she could blame the past corruption on this group of ne'er-do-wells. She would easily flip the lower-level African cartel members and eventually get Fitzroy Malafante in handcuffs, silencing him forever as well. Malafante would likely get an expedited, private trial that would most certainly result in his swift execution.

Now that Leo didn't have proof anymore, his leverage was also gone regarding his deal with FBI Director Monroe, who would most definitely hear about this from Senator Adams. With Senator Adams having the leverage again, he wasn't so sure the cartel would stand by his side either. Enemies were stacking up on all sides.

On his way, he picked up the phone and called Senator Adams.

She answered, feigning ignorance, "Mr. Stills… I mean, Leo… how lovely to hear from you. It's a bit late, isn't it? What are you doing up?"

Leo's fury raged within; the tentacles of this anger seemed to be planted firmly in the bowels of hell. He did everything he could to keep his voice steady. "I want my children back now."

The senator acted surprised, "Whatsoever do you mean? Your children aren't home? A fit parent should really know where his children are at all times - especially young, innocent, fragile creatures such as these. Maybe they ran away?"

Leo responded forcefully, "Where are they?"

She seemed to deflect, but unintentionally showed her hand ever so slightly, "How could I know that? They certainly aren't with me. With them in mind, though, I'm sure they'd come back from wherever they ran off to if you were to cooperate with our efforts here. We know you are planning to break into the Statterman Suites building."

Silence.

Pleased with holding all the cards, she went on, "Also, my good name will need to be restored with our mutual contact from the cartel. I can't have my relations with Malafante disrupted before the right time. You will go straight over there and apologize for the misinformation you previously provided them about me, won't you?"

"Done."

The senator pushed further, "I will also need the money the cartel is set to pay you for the sabotage, as well as the gold you plan to steal when backstabbing Malafante's crew. All of it."

"Done. Just give me back my boys."

She continued with her list of demands, "We also know you were originally preparing to simply dismantle our shipment of drones headed for Africa. Change of plans there. We actually need the ship blown up. No one can be left alive."

Knowing that would mean killing dozens of people, including innocent crew members and some of the cartel alike, Leo responded without thinking twice, "Done."

She said back quietly, "Good boy. That wasn't so hard was it. If we run into any hiccups, or you try to double-cross me, I don't see why your children would want to come back to you ever. Do we understand each other?"

"Yes, ma'am," Leo said, having no leverage greater than the lives of his two sons.

She chippered up, "Great. You know, you really should be more careful who you get in bed with – mobster loan sharks aren't known for their loyalty."

Pleased with the discord she had sewn, she hung up and that was the end of the conversation.

Leo finally got to the Coffee Spot, where he found Seth waiting frantically for him. Leo explained that he needed Seth to track down his sons. They were just an insurance policy for the senator. Her real goal was untangling herself from the Malafante Cartel without being implicated.

Leo said, "They have my kids. They couldn't take them to a public place, and they wouldn't go far. I met with her a couple months back at a warehouse down by the pier. There is a string of buildings there that have the same shell company listed as the legal owner. She must be holding my boys in one of those shops. I need you to take some of our guys and retrieve my kids in case I can't pull this deal off in time. If anyone is there, take them out. No witnesses."

Still one of the purest members of the Stills family, Seth was worried, "Leo, you're talking about eliminating government agents. I don't think…"

Leo shouted him down, "THEY HAVE MY KIDS, SETH! They took Caden and Timmy… my blood! Now, they owe me theirs."

Seth quickly changed his tone, "Okay, okay. You got it, boss."

Story 24

The following day, Leo went to Statterman Suites and struggled out an apology to the African cartel on the part of Senator Adams. As humiliating as that was, it was the easy part. Next, his crew had to blow up a government shipment on behalf of the cartel, while simultaneously double-crossing the same gang by breaking into their vault and relieving them of all their gold bricks. As soon as Leo got to the office, April handed him a telegram.

Leo asked, "Good morning. What does it say?"

April responded as she scrolled through their calendar for the day, "I don't know. I didn't open it. It's from Director Monroe."

Leo paused mid-step for only a second before picking back up again, heading to his office.

Anxiety: Holy hell. It's going to be bad news. He's going to kill us or worse. I'm never going to get my kids back. They are as good as dead.

Leo pushed his anxious thoughts aside and sat down to open up the small envelope, which read: 'No evidence, no deal.'

Leo threw the paper on the floor and screamed at the top of his lungs, "AHHHHHHI II II II II I!!!!!"

Anxiety: My kids are dead.

April came rushing in, "Is everything okay?"

Leo handed out orders, "Send Rome and Eli in straight away."

She walked out and pulled the two brothers into Leo's office.

Rome asked, "What's the deal, bro?"

Leo went straight into it, "Seth is going to find my sons. Roman, regarding the shipment of government technology..."

Rome interrupted, "No problem there. We are already set up. We got EMP charges for the tech and we got the specs on their weapons, so we know exactly how to disarm them permanently. It will cost more to fix them than to start over. Eli handled that part," he said, punching Eli on the shoulder with a big smile. "In and out, thirty minutes. No one will even know we were there."

Leo sighed heavily, though Rome expected at least a nod of approval.

Leo said, "Change of plans. They want us to blow up the ship instead, so get some explosives from Mackey's joint on 5th Avenue. Just enough to take an entire boat to the bottom of the ocean."

Confused for only a second, Rome said, "Leo. No. How can you ask me to do that again? I've killed enough in my life… too much. I told myself that the last time would be the last time and it's the only way I got through it at all. I made my peace with God and I moved on. My soul can't take it again. It ain't right."

Leo continued, "I know, Rome. Screw 'em. We ain't doing that, but we have to make it sound like we did to the Senator until we can regain leverage. Just stick to the plan, but have the bomb blow up our family boat in the middle of the open water. Eli, you're with me. We're going to take out the African cartel's vault and then I need you to bring back the gold to our southern warehouse. We need to make a pitstop first. Let's go. I don't need to remind you what is at stake here."

The brothers went out, with Eli and Leo going to visit their old friend, Rubenfield. As Rome left, he tapped his suit pocket to make sure he had his good friends, the Paradise Pills.

The Stills didn't interact much with Rubenfield directly ever since they straightened out their dealings in San Mikel. In fact, business was booming and the two of them were making more money working together than they could count. Because this relationship was going so well, Leo trusted Rubenfield to help with some key components of his recent plans involving the cartel.

Truth: It was most certainly Rubenfield that tipped off Senator Adams. She must have put pressure on him, being a businessman connected to me. I'm sure he sold me out to the highest bidder.

Anger: No doubt about it. This guy has to go. Do I have my pistol?

Leo needed a backup plan for handling the evidence that implicated the senator in her nefarious dealings with the Malafante cartel. So, he filled Rubenfield in on the details and told him that he'd have ample evidence to take out the senator. Once the public finally figured out that she was corrupt and Leo won the senate seat, Rubenfield and Leo could do some serious business together, safely.

Leo got to the front gate of Rubenfield's estate and asked to see the boss. Rubenfield's men showed Leo and Eli in through the front door and they were taken down to the cellar. As normal, this mad man was behind his desk, counting money. Leo and Eli sat across from him, surrounded by two armed guards with plenty more soldiers stationed behind the closed office doors. Rubenfield finished counting a stack of $100 bills and, after banding the $10,000 bundle together, he poured three glasses of whiskey.

As he handed a drink to each of his business partners, Rubenfield asked, "Well, what can I do for you fine gentlemen on this even finer day?"

Although Leo was quite certain, he thought it prudent for Rubenfield to confirm his alleged betrayal one way or the other.

Leo asked, "Well, Sal, ole friend, just have a pretty simple question for you actually."

"Shoot."

Anger: Funny choice of words.

Leo asked, "Are you the dirty, damned rat that snitched to Senator Adams about my plans?"

Rubenfield was clearly caught off guard. However, perhaps due to his pathological nature, he didn't act like there was much to discuss. "Sure did. Had no choice. You understand, I'm sure. It's just business."

Now, Leo had already given Eli instruction, were Rubenfield to give this very answer confirming his betrayal yet again. As soon as Rubenfield admitted that he was the one to betray the Stills by giving Senator Adams the information she needed, Eli shot up out of his seat. He caught the two, armed men off guard, stabbing both of them dead before they could even get the safety switched off of their new rifles, which were most certainly gifts from the senator in exchange for their boss' cooperation.

After Eli attacked the two guards, he picked up one of their rifles, took the safety off and pointed it at Sal, saying, "Shhhhhhh."

As the bodies hit the floor, Sal Rubenfield jumped up out of his seat like a cat from water, now rightfully shocked, though psychotically unafraid; even chuckling a bit at the amusing twist this meeting had taken.

Leo still sat in his chair, unmoved, cool as a cucumber; never taking his eyes off Sal's anxious face.

Anger: Not such a tough mobster now. Let's kill him.

Deceit: He deserves it. It's his fault my kid is gone. There's no redemption for that. He doesn't deserve my forgiveness.

Leo waited a moment, trying to control his rage against the man who was, in part, responsible for the kidnapping of his sons.

Breathing heavily, Eli said to Leo, "Let's kill this asshole and shoot our way out. He doesn't deserve to live."

Leo ignored that tempting invocation, for now, and he asked Rubenfield, "Sal, what the hell were you thinking? We had a good business arrangement. Things were working out for both of our crews and our plans were limitless."

Leo was getting worked up as he pictured his kids and he stood up while grabbing his pistol.

Rubenfield scoffed, "Don't be such a girl scout, Leo. It's just business. When the American government is hounding me, what do you expect? That's *bad* for business. People like us don't have a chance against someone like Senator Adams."

Leo raged, "Not if we turn on each other, you're right!"

Rubenfield continued, "What's the big deal? So, it cost you a seat on the senate. You think you really deserve that anyway?! You're more crooked than I am," he giggled at the thought, "I don't know what you…"

Leo interrupted him with extreme intensity, keeping quiet enough not to alert the rest of Rubenfield's guards, "Sal, they took my sons!"

Silence.

Leo went on as he gripped his pistol even tighter, preparing for the worst answer, "They took my boys, Sal. Did she tell you that she was going to take them away from me?"

Rubenfield merely shrugged. It wasn't a 'yes' or a 'no' answer, but more like 'what do you expect from me?'

Leo lost it. Screaming, he moved briskly into Rubenfield's face and jammed the end of his pistol directly into Rubenfield's left eye. At this point, Sal's guards outside heard the ruckus and came blazing in, guns drawn.

Rubenfield called them off, "Whoa, whoa. Everything's fine. Everyone, calm down."

Leo went on, "You crossed the line, Sal. They have my sons! They…"

This time, it was Sal's turn to put an end to Leo's unwarranted, righteous indignation, "Crossed what line?! We're so far from the line we can't even see it anymore. How many sons and daughters, fathers and mothers have you and your crew killed or imprisoned? There are no lines in the world we inhabit, *Mr. Stills*. We live in chaos."

Anger: Kill this guy. Enough of this. He doesn't deserve to breathe.

Leo stood there, shaking, unable to make the choice between pulling the trigger or not.

Finally, Eli made the decision for him, yelling, "I'm going to blast him!" though, he still waited for Leo's orders.

Leo finally and quietly said, "No." He lowered his pistol, saying, "He's right, E."

As Eli began to object, Leo gave him a look that told him it was time to go. Eli stepped over the two bodies on the ground as he and Leo left the premises without any resistance from Sal Rubenfield or his crew.

After they left, Eli and Leo made their way to take care of the cartel heist. Rome was set to sink the Stills' family boat at exactly 2:00 p.m. According to plan, Rome met up with a large faction of the local African cartel to set up the job.

Knowing this, Leo and Eli took advantage of the decreased security at Statterman Suites. Leo was getting his guys into position. As Eli crawled down into the underground railway, Leo checked his phone, hoping for a message from Seth saying he had completed his mission already and safely recovered Caden and Tim. Unfortunately, nothing.

The two brothers climbed down the rickety, corroded ladder into the musty tunnel below. Following the blueprints that they obtained from a couple desperate city officials for a small fee, they made their way to the spot directly underneath the Statterman.

Eli began to wire up the explosives that would result in the floor of the African cartel's suite dropping into the tunnel, bringing the vault with it. Leo sat idly by, nervously smoking a cigar. They had twenty guys from their crew lined up to get there in the next hour to handle the transportation of the bricks. The plan was to blow the explosives at exactly 2:00 p.m., the same time that Rome was going to detonate his own.

Fear: If my kids are not recovered safely…

Truth: We'll cross that bridge when we come to it. Focus.

2:00 p.m. was steadily approaching as Leo's gold transportation team began quickly climbing down the tunnel shaft. Leo checked his phone for news about his sons… nothing.

At 2:00 p.m. on the dot, an explosion was heard throughout all of Belmont, shaking every building to its foundation. Unfortunately, Rome was not an expert on explosives, so the blast was larger than planned and resulted in the death of several recreational kayakers enjoying the previously calm waters nearby.

This horrific news was offset ever so slightly by the completely successful gold heist. The gold made its way safely back to the Stills most heavily protected warehouse on the southside of town. The Stills Corporation's biggest score to date – more than a normal, middle-class family could spend in a lifetime. The Stills family, however, was anything but normal.

Leo climbed out of the tunnel and walked aimlessly down the bustling sidewalk contemplating the safety of his sons, as Eli escorted the loot to their shop. Now, Rome executed his part of the plan very quickly, getting out of there as soon as he had pressed the bloody button. The gold heist didn't take much longer, as Eli was an expert in tactical planning and real-time coordination; one of the few fortunate side effects of his time in the army.

It was just past 2:25 p.m. when Leo was walking around in the clear and his phone vibrated.

Leo had been holding the phone in his hands every chance he got, waiting for this very message, which read: 'Caden and Timmy are safe. Bringing them to your house. Adams not present.'

Anger: Ahhh, I wanted that animal dead.

Fear: She needs to go. She has proof of multiple crimes committed by each one of us, more than enough to lock me and my family away for the rest of our days… clearly, though, it's not like she needs any of that to make us disappear.

Leo sighed with relief as the mounting pressure of his sons' potential deaths was lifted off his shoulders.

He couldn't help himself from shouting aloud in the busy town center, "Thank you, Lord!"

Leo couldn't control it. When he thought about his two boys being safe, he simply smiled. That euphoria, regrettably, was short lived. The heavenly thought was pushed aside by the ever-pressing understanding of the deep, deep hole that he dug for himself and in which he still stood.

Truth: Next priority now is to prevent this from ever happening again. Unfortunately, the senator stole the remaining evidence when she kidnapped my boyos, so we are in the same spot we were before. Without some kind of leverage, there is nothing stopping her from trying this again. Plus, now she has proof of us carrying out even more crimes. This web is getting too tangled and something has to change.

As he walked along, with the final destination being Bravo Tower, he came up with several different strategies that they could possibly employ to regain the upper hand. None of them were particularly pleasant, though. Before he could go see his sons for the first time since they were taken, he had to make sure this couldn't simply transpire again at the drop of a hat. As such, he made a quick detour to visit his lovely friend, Senator Beth Adams. He wanted to face the beast head on and lay out some ground rules.

The senator had made plans to be in town today, knowing some of what Leo's crew had in store. She was held up at a nearby, posh hotel. As he walked into the lobby, he got nauseous. The thought of seeing this villain again face to face made him physically sick.

After Leo made his presence known and agreed to a pat down from the senator's security detail, he sat in one of the oversized, leather armchairs in the lobby and waited. Soon thereafter, Senator Adams came out, slightly disheveled but elegant, nonetheless.

She greeted Leo, "Mr. Stills, how lovely to see you again! Looking at the news, seems like everything went according to plan today. I'm sure my payment will be delivered promptly. Is there something that we should be discussing? My secretary didn't see you on my calendar for the day."

Leo didn't really have much of a Plan A, so he blurted out, "I have my sons back."

Without skipping a beat, though it was unlikely she had already received this information, she replied, "Well, congratulations. Did they go on a trip or something?"

Leo said, "That behavior is unacceptable, and my crew won't be doing any of your bidding again. We are done. You're nothing but a white-collar thug and you're not even good at it."

She sneered, "You dirty, little miscreant. We are done when *I* say so. You understand me, boy? You think this won't happen again tomorrow if I feel like it?"

Being a boss himself, Leo was not used to being talked to in such a demeaning manner.

He cut her off abruptly, "I realize you're a big fish in your own pond, but around these here parts, I'm the man. If you want my cooperation, you'll have to earn it. I will not be a party to a one-sided agreement. If you want to do business with me, you will play fair. There is nothing left to say."

She replied, "Hmmph. Okay. We'll see."

Leo stood up without shaking her hand as he had done ceremoniously in times past. He quickly departed from the lobby while the soles of his shoes clicked loudly against the white marble floor.

Truth: That wasn't enough. She won't be stopped. There is no reasoning with her. My family isn't safe. I've got to do more.

<u>Story 25</u>

Leo made his way back to Bravo Tower. When he arrived, he called Rome and Eli to discuss how their endeavors faired today. As the three senior members of the crew were having a relatively heated conversation, the front door of the family office busted open. State troopers and county sheriffs poured into the Stills Corporation lobby, none of which were local coppers on the Stills' payroll.

This was still an unexpected occurrence, even though the family had long been involved in… less-than-savory activities that could have resulted in this a while ago. That was the exact reason they hired the local police. Unfortunately, they hadn't yet expanded this relationship statewide. April came running into Leo's office, where he and his two brothers were getting up to inquire about all the racket downstairs.

Leo asked, "What's going on?"

April hastily shot back, "Police. They're putting handcuffs on everyone, including Sammy. Michelle and Seth are not here, but I heard the coppers saying they had a warrant out for their arrest as well and are in route to pick 'em up."

Leo wasn't necessarily astonished. In fact, every day they stayed out of jail was the surprising part, considering all the dark deeds they had done.

Deceit: Let's go down shooting. We can't let them take us alive. Wonder which crime they picked out of a hat to show up for today… could be anything.

Truth: Wonder who is ordering this.

Leo nodded and proceeded in front of Rome and Eli. He knew it was never smart to mess with the police. As he walked slowly down the stairs, Leo saw the inevitable scene that he previously conjured up in his imagination on a fairly regular basis; the family office being ransacked, and his crew led away in handcuffs.

Leo shouted to everyone in his employ, "Don't resist. Go quietly. We will deal with this in the courts. Don't struggle. Officers, we will go peacefully."

When the four of them got to the bottom of the stairs, they were met by a mob of state troopers, who clearly didn't know who the Stills family was… or perhaps they did.

Although Leo was in front of the other three, holding out his wrists so the police could place handcuffs on him, the troopers walked right passed Leo without even looking at him. Instead, they grabbed Rome and Eli, savagely throwing them to the ground. One of the officers put his hands forcibly on April, shoving her up against a wall.

Anger: Knock some gentlemanly sense into that guy!

Truth: Easy now.

Leo was tempted to knock some gentlemanly sense into that guy, but fortunately for both of them, his self-restraint got the better of him. That is, until the officer went to pat April down, clearly enjoying his search of her more sensitive areas.

Me: Nope. Not happening.

April yelped when the officer groped her, and Leo could not resist. Enjoying the freedom that comes with not wearing handcuffs yet, he lunged at the officer, pushing him off April and up against the same wall, saying, "You better learn some manners, boyo. You got a lot of friends with you here today, but I have friends too…"

Leo couldn't finish his sentence before two more policemen came over and detained him, but Leo got out one last promise, "… and my friends are a lot more dangerous than you clowns."

At that, they pushed Leo back further - though again, handling him with a surprising lack of ferocity. Most suspects would have been beaten to a pulp for such an aggressive move against a cop.

Leo watched as his family was dragged out of Bravo Tower one-by-one, but kept shouting reassurance over and over, "I will fix this! Don't say anything until our lawyers get there. I'll get you out!"

One of the state troopers jeered back, "Doubt it, rat. We got every one of your family members on capital offenses. They will be promptly executed for their crimes against the state. We already filed for an expedited hearing due to the overwhelming evidence and complete lack of any reasonable doubt as to your guilt. Once our boss gets done putting pressure on them, they will plead guilty and waive the right to appeal, facing death row in a matter of months."

Leo's heart sank, but he said nothing.

He was the last one in the room with a handful of cops tossing most of his possessions around the room and onto the floor. He waited for his turn to be handcuffed and marched out, but that moment never came. Shockingly, after a few more moments of time passing by in slow motion, Leo was left there all by himself. They even took April. There were windows broken, desks overturned, and papers strewn everywhere. Leo stood there, alone, which was fitting, as this is how he felt every day of his life.

Guilt: I know why my family hates me, while at the same time depend on me to lead them. All I can give them is money. In return, though, they give me everything; their hearts and souls. Hardly a fair trade.

Leo had no time to waste feeling sorry for himself or his crew. The walls were caving in around him. His business relationship with Rubenfield was breaking down again. He had one of the most powerful and corrupt people in the world gunning for him, the lovely Senator Beth Adams. Not to mention, it wouldn't be long before the African cartel figured out who double-crossed them and stole their gold.

Leo made a phone call to an old friend, saying, "I will be at your office in four hours."

Without waiting for a response, he hung up and ordered a car to take him to the airport. He made one stop at his house along the way. He needed to grab a few things, as well as see his sons for the first time since they had been abducted. Having his entire crew arrested and threatened with the death penalty for crimes he knew they committed had really turned his life upside down. He didn't know where he would be tomorrow, so he had to take advantage of what time he had remaining with his two sons… the main sources of light still left in his life since Sera's untimely demise.

After a heart-wrenching reunion with Caden and Timothy, Leo said to them, "I love you, boyos, to the moon and back, twice. Daddy's got to go and take care of some things. I'm not sure exactly when I'll be back. Caden, take care of your brother."

With that, he patted them on the head and walked out, even though all he wanted to do was hold them in his arms forever.

After a short flight, Leo arrived at FBI Director Monroe's offices. He made his way up and was quickly escorted inside. Not because he was a friend per say, but more because the director didn't want to be seen with the likes of Leo after what just went down.

Leo said, "Thank you for meeting me. I…"

Director Monroe cut him off, "Look, son, I know what happened. It had nothing to do with my people, but obviously I was briefed. I don't really know what you expect from me at this point. I already made my position clear. If you don't have evidence incriminating her explicitly, I won't help you. It's in my best interest to simply maintain the status quo and let your family fade into the pages of history."

Leo regained control of the meeting, "Bottom line, she has become a loose cannon and a liability for you, as I'm sure you wouldn't deny."

Leo paused, as Monroe nodded ever so slightly in what Leo chose to take as agreement.

He continued, "Frankly, I expected more cooperation from you. That said, you've made your position clear. So, now, I must make mine equally transparent."

Monroe leaned back in his black office chair, clearly uncomfortable with Leo's obvious determination and evident lack of desperation. The only sound in the room was the old government furniture squeaking from its ancient age.

Leo adjusted his $12,000 tie before he went on, "I hoped not to go this route, in an effort to maintain a more cordial perspective on our arrangement. Unfortunately, I have no choice."

Meanwhile, he had pulled out a voice recorder and placed it on the table.

Monroe scoffed, "You were recording us just now? I haven't said anything incriminating. I'm afraid you're still on your own, sonny."

Attempting to take the high road by not rubbing in that mistake, Leo explained, "You're right, I had nothing to record today, but when we met in the park the other day, you were quite candid on your relationship with the lady senator as well as explicitly stating your knowledge of her illicit activities."

Monroe looked puzzled, "How? We gave you a pat down. My guys wouldn't miss…"

Leo stopped him short, filling him in, "You should really be more careful when you meet someone in public. Your men didn't miss anything on the pat down, but they did miss the recorder that was taped to the park bench before you arrived."

Silence.

The recorder began to play, and Monroe could hear his own voice loud and clear from the park where he met Leo that now fateful day. Suddenly, the director shot up out of his seat, grabbed the recorder and threw it against the wall, smashing it to pieces.

Leo paused for effect, letting the realization sink in that he was not going to be another anonymous piece of trash Monroe could throw away when he no longer had any use.

Never leaving his seat, Leo calmly chuckled, "Of course, that was a copy of the original tape, Chuck. The original is safe... don't you worry."

Silence.

Leo took the soundless invitation to go further, not looking to waste any more time, saying, "She took all the evidence I had, but I know you would have kept records of your dealings with Senator Adams. It's going to be you, or her."

Leo then explained in detail the situation that occurred with his family just hours earlier.

After a full briefing and a list of demands, Monroe sighed, "I'm not sure you understand the impact of what you're asking me to do; the effect it will have on the intelligence community as well as the entire country. Senator Adams is no small fish. In fact, she's on a short list, just a few spots under me, of some of the most powerful and, frankly, dangerous people in the entire world."

Leo's turn to remain silent.

Monroe continued, "Let me see what I can do that won't create too much of a ripple. You better believe, I'm not going down for any of this."

Leo then said, "I was told my family's execution would be expedited. We need this to get resolved sooner than later."

Monroe responded, "I *might* be able to get the death penalty waived, but even that will take some serious time. This is not..."

Leo interrupted, "We don't have any time! They're trying to kill my family, Director - and if that happens, a lot of you government bureaucrats are going down with me in a real blaze of glory. Trust... it won't be pretty for anyone."

Monroe responded to this aggression with fierce anger, muttered through clamped teeth, "I will see… what I can do. It will take as long as it takes."

Leo stood up, "I'm glad we understand each other."

With that, he walked out of the FBI building and headed home, for once in quite a while maintaining a glimmer of hope.

Fear: They're never getting out… definitely not alive.

Truth: Focus. I have two boys at home that need me. I've done what I can for now. We'll have to see what path Director Monroe chooses for himself.

Me: I just want all my family to come back home.

Days passed, as Leo's family members rotted away in solitary confinement and rumors began cropping up in local newspapers about their arrests. The family had not made many friends amongst the criminal network in the area because the Stills either beat them outright at their illicit activities or had some of their crewmembers imprisoned.

Leo received an anonymous note on his front door, which read: 'You think your family is safe in prison with all the people you got locked up?'

This threat was later confirmed, when he got a report from one of his informants at the jail stating that Rome and Eli were currently in the hospital ward, doped up on large amounts of the Paradise Pills and various other drugs. They were jumped late one night, when the cell doors were supposed to be locked.

Leo paid for the best lawyers in the country, but nonetheless, the evidence was overwhelming and incredibly damning. Government officials had always had ample evidence of crimes committed by the Stills family at their disposal. The only thing protecting the Stills was ensuring the appropriate leverage, which they no longer maintained. There was not a lot even the most skilled legal advocate could due to the reduce the chances of the death penalty being ordered. It would be considered a success in his attorneys' minds, just getting Leo's family members a life sentence, alive, in a maximum-security prison.

Story 26

One windy night, going on 11:00 p.m., Leo was sitting in his library, listening to the evening news and opening his second bottle of whiskey for the day. He was thinking back on the main campaign slogan he used in his first mayoral debate. He had promised to battle the corruption that currently filled a large swath of government employees who far too often abused their powers.

Leo knew he shouldn't publicly declare his desire for a senate seat yet, so as far as the public was concerned, he was still in-it-to-win-it on the mayoral trail.

As he brooded alone in his big house, the radio broadcaster announced the latest polls for the state races: "Mayor Shaw is maintaining a stronghold on his race against Mr. Leo Stills, a local businessman from Belmont, even though Mr. Stills seems to garner a lot of favor during the debate sessions. At this point, it looks like it would take a miracle for the sitting mayor not to get re-elected to yet another term."

Leo sighed as he took another gulp from his glass and tamped the ashes off his cigar.

After a few rambling sentences, Leo clued back in when the broadcaster continued, "For the open senate seat, Senator Adams is still running unopposed and is the sure favorite to win re-election hands down."

At the mention of her name, Leo smacked the power button on the radio and now the room was filled with a heavy silence.

Breaking the quiet, Leo heard a soft knocking on his front door; so soft he might not have heard it if he was on the other side of the house. He set his cigar in the ash tray and gulped his drink. It was far too late at night for proper company, so he picked up his pistol and walked to the front door. He quickly swung the door open and raised his gun, always ready to go out in a blaze of glory.

His heart was racing, and his breathing was quick. As his gun sprung up into the air, he paused. To his surprise, what was waiting for him outside his front door was… nothing. He felt a little silly at this point. He lowered his weapon and stepped out of his doorway to look around at who might've knocked. After all, it only took him a few seconds to get to the door after he heard the tapping. As he walked out onto the porch, he stumbled over something on the ground, almost causing him to trip off his front stoop. The whiskey was not helping his balance, but he managed to keep his composure and avoid an epic faceplant.

Looking down at the obstacle that almost caused him a fair amount of pain, he saw a copy of the local Belmont Inquirer, a small newspaper company, of which Leo was *not* a regular subscriber.

"What the hell?" he mumbled, as he checked around again to see if anyone was out there.

The streets were silent and still. He quickly snatched up the paper and brought it inside. Wondering if there was some sort of explosive, as soon as his front door was shut, he rapidly searched through the pages.

Nothing.

"Hmmm," he said.

Truth: There has to be something to this newspaper. I am not a subscriber. I have never received it before and it's darn near midnight.

Leo continued checking and then it clicked. He saw the date at the top of the paper, checked his watch and let out a silent gasp. It was *tomorrow's* edition, which wouldn't be delivered to normal customers for another several hours at least.

Gluttony: I need a drink for this.

Leo went back to the library, poured himself another drink and sat down to read through the paper as he pulled on his cigar, reviving the previously dying flame. He was beginning to tire after spending quite a long time searching, when he was near the end of the paper.

He started flipping through the pages faster, mumbling, "If someone had something to say that was worthwhile, they should've made it easier to find. I don't got the time or the patience for this."

However, this undeserved apathy was short lived. Just before he was about to put the paper down, he flipped through the obituaries where he found his name. Not only was his name there, but the names of his entire family. Under their names, the note read: 'If only they minded their own business. Running out of time. RIP.'

"Damn it!" Leo yelled, as he threw the paper into the fire, hoping the threat would burn up and go away along with the pages.

Despair: Lovely. More threats.

Leo sat there brooding on his unfortunate circumstances until the weight of sleep overtook him.

The next morning, the sun was shining irritably bright through the curtains, peaking through any open cracks. Leo groaned as he adjusted himself in the plush armchair, trying not to wake up. After losing that battle, he felt his way to the kitchen for a drink of water, not wanting to let his eyes open all the way. Ever since his entire crew was imprisoned, he didn't bother going into Bravo Tower. So, he chugged a bottle of water and headed back down the hall to his home library to create a game plan for the day.

Step one, of course, would be to pour himself a drink. As he did so, he saw the partially burnt front-page article of the paper from last night and it just now got his thoughts racing.

The paper read:
‘Socialism's Official Party of America (SOPA) Gaining Momentum. Workers around the country striking. Looks like Socialism might win over capitalism in the battle of the century.’

Leo stopped reading, recalling recently that his workers were striking at a lot of the businesses the Stills family operated throughout Belmont.

Deceit: Socialism isn't so bad.

Truth: The infection is spreading everywhere. Appears to come back every few generations.

It seemed to be worse in the big cities, where a large portion of the vastly rich class of Americans gathered in their ivory towers to decide how the entire state of the world should run. They spread nonsense about the power of the worker taking back what was rightfully theirs. However, companies were fleeing these high-tax, anti-business states faster than a blue-ribbon pig at the fair.

Me: That doesn't make any sense.

Several of Leo's shops were closed altogether due to these strikes and he was starting to lose a lot of money. He was going to be forced to permanently close some of them down soon.

Wealth redistribution was gaining traction, as the gap between the 'haves' and the 'have-nots' grew increasingly larger. The dispossessed in the country were growing in number. In their desperation, they swallowed the story that the rich essentially stole the money from them. That's why they didn't have as much as the next guy… because they were robbed. Leo was now faced with a tough decision. Should he jump on the socialism bandwagon or fight the current?

Though wildly successful and disgustingly wealthy at this point, Leo was a perfect picture of the American dream, apart from the illegality of his endeavors. He started from nothing, in a poor town surrounded by no opportunities and turned himself into a success story. This is the dream on which America sold the whole of humanity.

Thereby, he inhabited two worlds. However, if he didn't join the SOPA movement, he would likely be branded a traitor and thrown in the fire with the rest of the greedy, heartless capitalists that dared to make a profit off their hard work and ingenuity. He had to pick a lane quickly.

Joining SOPA was obviously the easy way out, because the funny thing about joining SOPA was, there was no potential harm. The current system didn't punish people for being socialists. In fact, it was incredibly tolerant. SOPA, on the other hand, damned to hell anyone who wasn't a member as an immoral, non-human entity that deserved any suffering that crossed their path. In this way, the politically oblivious and largely apathetic masses were incentivized to join SOPA.

Ignoring previous warnings to leave SOPA alone, Leo reached out to Jane, his late brother's wife, to ask for a major contact within SOPA. Leo was intent on striking up a relationship and getting to know more about SOPA's objectives, plans and current standing within various communities around the country. Jane delivered on the request, providing Leo with the contact information for SOPA's leading authority on the West coast who was stationed in the upscale area of Norfast. She was a short little firecracker of a lady, with blonde hair down to her waist and a smile that would get a mouse to walk into an alligator's belly.

Leo met up with her for dinner at the most popular Italian restaurant in Belmont, an off-the-track spot known only to locals where reservations took months to obtain, if you were lucky enough to get them at all. Fortunately, Leo knew the owner and he was able to get in later that same night for a beautiful dinner setting.

Leo arrived early and waited while he sipped his whiskey and puffed on his cigar. She was running a few minutes late, but Leo didn't mind being able to just sit their quietly and enjoy some peace and quiet. He usually had so much to do that he rarely stopped working or thinking. For now, he sat there quietly, listening to the murmur of so many conversations filling the air around him.

As he was coming back from the restroom, his attention was snagged by the low sound of the radio playing from the kitchen area, "… and with that, I must bid you adieu. I'm Julianne Moore, the head of the SOPA's west coast activities, leaving you with our mission statement: We are socialists, fighting against today's supposedly free market where the rich only get richer; with its exploitation of the worker and the theft of profit that is rightfully the result of the common man's labor. We are determined to destroy this corrupt system at all costs…"

The sound trailed off as he got further away and finally made it back to his table, out of earshot, where he continued to wait for his date.

When she arrived, she was just as described, but Jane might have done her a disservice by portraying her as merely 'freaking beautiful.' Leo sat there with his cigar as he watched the scene unfold. She walked in elegantly, whispered in appreciation when the server took her long trench coat revealing a stunning green dress wrapped around a striking canvas. The gentleman he was, Leo stood up briefly as she was being seated and the two of them sat down together at the same time.

Leo poked at her, "Glad you decided to finally join me," he said with a slight smirk.

She replied innocently in kind, "Oh, I hope I didn't keep you waiting."

Leo replied, "No longer than from the time we both said we would be here, but I guess that may be on account of me living around these parts."

She scoffed, "Oh, dreadful. You actually live here, Mr. Stills?"

Leo nodded.

She skeptically continued, "Belmont. Hmph. How *civilized.*"

Leo responded, "Not really." He went on, "You can call me Leo, nice to finally meet you. I've heard many good things."

She replied, "They are all true, I promise you. I am Julianne Moore. It is my pleasure. I sure do promise, sweetie, if Jane had told me you were so handsome, I might not have been late."

A short back and forth ensued, where some common niceties were wrapped up in lovely banter. The two were genuinely having a good time for a short while.

Leo cut that nonsense off, saying, "Well, not that this hasn't been wonderful, but there is a reason we both came here tonight."

Just then, the waitress came by, asking, "Would either of you like anything? Mr. Stills, another whiskey, perhaps?" she asked, smiling a little bit too nicely.

Julianne turned her away, saying, "No, thank you. We are fine."

"Yes, probably better for me to stay sharp around this one," Leo said, pointing at his date for the evening.

Julianne mockingly laughed, "Ha-Ha," along with the young waitress who really did find the comment amusing.

After the waitress left, the two then proceeded to get down to business.

Leo began, "Seems you have made every one of my workers in Belmont go on strike; to bite the hand that feeds them, so to speak. If you weren't so nice, I might be offended."

She brushed off the attack and with the cocktail in hand causing her to enjoy herself, she tried to keep the conversation fun, "Oh, it's just business. Most business owners aren't as good as you. They deserve what they get for taking advantage of their employees."

The two of them went back and forth like this for a while. With very different objectives for the meal, they didn't get very far in their dialogue. After a while, Leo had gotten what he came for: a little information and a connection to the SOPA movement.

At that, he began to prepare for his exit, "Well, Ms. Julianne, I have thoroughly enjoyed our time together this evening. I do have an early morning tomorrow, so, unless you are planning on making me breakfast, I must bid you adieu."

To the clear attempt at humor, she responded, "Now, Mr. Stills, how could you get it into your head that I would go home with you after just one cocktail?"

Truth: Whoa.

Not looking to engage in that line of conversation much further, for fear of where they might end up, Leo replied jokingly, "Originally, my plan was for three drinks; maybe some dessert."

She gasped, just as proper ladies do, a mix of embarrassment, resentment, disgust and intrigue.

Leo continued excusing himself from the date, sliding several $100 bills into the checkbook, when Julianne inquired, "Leo, though I am not naïve to you being the animal you are, I must admit, it is even a bit exciting. On top of me…" she slipped, "… Haha, whoopsie…" she giggled, trying to get her mind out of the gutter, "… I mean, on top of *that*… on top of that, I am also not naïve to the influence you have around these parts." She slid her chair closer to his, "Mr. Stills, I must ask you, is there anything I can do to persuade you to join our righteous cause? It would go a long way in turning the tide in our favor."

As she said this, she let her arm fall casually, brushing his leg under the table.

Truth: Man, the devil is working overtime to get you distracted.

Keeping his eyes on the prize, he finally stood up. He took her hand in his, briefly kissed it ever so softly and, while holding on, he said, "At this point, I am just shopping. I love what you are doing, Julianne. Certainly, a pleasure to behold. I'll be in touch."

With that, he let her hand go, though, she was in no hurry to get it back.

The waitress helped him with his overcoat and Julianne whispered over her shoulder as she stayed behind to finish her drink, "Maybe next time we can have that dessert."

Leo paused, only for a moment, and then walked on along his way. He was headed out of the restaurant as the waitress walked to their table, where his date was still seated, bringing Julianne the chocolate souffle that Leo ordered when he first arrived.

Story 27

Leo woke up early the next morning to a phone call.

He answered, "Hello?"

Still half asleep, Leo heard his lead attorney on the other end of the line, "Mr. Stills. We have urgent news."

His lawyer proceeded to fill him in on the dire situation. Leo hung up and immediately called Director Monroe, unsure of what exactly he planned to say.

Monroe was barely able to answer before Leo yelled, "Charles! What's going on with my family's release?"

Taken aback, Director Monroe said, "I've actually got good news, Leo. I was able to get it worked out. Their release is almost approved. We just need a couple weeks for the paperwork to make its way through the courts. Until then, no change and they are still in solitary confinement. Sorry it took so long, but it was the best I could do given the circumstances. At least we got them out in the end, eh?"

The news was a huge relief to Leo, especially after his lawyers told him their original goal was to get his crew's punishment reduced to life sentences instead of the death penalty.

However, Leo did not respond with the joyful glee that Monroe expected.

Leo pressed further, "My attorney just informed me there was official notice granting the expedition of their capital punishment. They are set to be killed two days from now. What the hell?"

Silence.

After too long, Monroe responded, "That's not enough time for me to do anything. I'll have to investigate it. If any laws were broken, I might be able to head it off."

Me: Who would be trying to tie up these loose ends? We have to get smarter here, adapt or die time.

Truth: Someone very powerful is trying to outmaneuver me.

Arrogance: And I'm not usually outdone. Whoever is able to do this must have a lot of juice — and for what reason does someone with that much pull care about us?

Anger: I'll definitely return the favor when I get the chance.

Truth: I need to get my family back to Belmont as soon as possible. It's the only place I can ensure their safety. The people in my hometown would never turn on their local hero.

"And if there wasn't anything illegal in the expedition request?" Leo asked skeptically.

"There is a possibility that this was done in accordance with all regulations… in which case, I could do nothing. It's too high profile."

Leo frantically yelled, "We are out of time. Make it happen! I hope you are properly motivated. If they die, we all go down in flames, Chuck. That's a promise."

Monroe tried to reply, "Now, let's…" but all he heard was the clicking sound of Leo's line going dead.

Leo was fuming. His head went into a tailspin, with chaotic thoughts bombarding him from every side.

Truth: Someone this powerful has got to have us under constant surveillance.

Anxiety: I've got to get eyes and ears inside the prison and start throwing some money at this problem.

With not much Leo could do at this point, his family felt a million miles away behind those maximum-security prison walls. Leo brooded for hours, waiting to hear on the fate of his family. He spent two sleepless nights, tossing and turning in his bed.

Truth: I must be patient. It's not like I can go storming into the prison, guns blazing and break them free.

Deceit: Can I?

Me: No. Shut up.

His family was set for execution in less than 24 hours at this point. Leo rolled out of his bed bright and early on that fateful day. He looked at his phone as he sat in his library drinking – nothing came through. He was hoping to hear back from Director Monroe before now, as his family's execution was scheduled for 11:30 a.m., only a couple hours away.

Just after noon, Leo's phone began to ring, the caller ID read: 'Good Ole Chuck' and Leo had never felt sicker to his stomach.

He realized that his whole life was encapsulated in this phone call, as he stood there shaking with anticipation. It was not merely the physical phone he held that caused him to tremble, but what information it will eventually transmit. When he answers, his life will shoot in one direction and the path that leads any other direction will die off and be closed forever. *Did I save them or not? Does that potential way of life spring into a real existence, or die off along with the other, infinite possible futures that we all continuously confront?* He saw all of that, when he simply saw the phone in his grasp. The information exchanged on the next call would change his world forever.

Leo answered, "Hello?"

Monroe responded, "Leo."

"Hi, Charles. What's the word?"

Monroe continued, "I've got good news and bad news. I was able to get your family pardoned. They will be home before dinner."

Leo sighed, "Great. Great. That's amazing news. What's the bad news?"

Silence.

Monroe paused, probably hoping the situation would pass him by, because once he delivered this painful message, he had no idea how the crime boss, Mr. Leo Stills from Belmont, would react.

He half whispered, "Well, Leo, I wasn't able to save all of them in time. BUT! That doesn't mean we need to do anything crazy."

Silence.

Monroe sighed, "By the time we got down to the execution chamber, the injections had already started."

Silence.

"The coroner just confirmed time of death. Your brother, Rome, didn't make it. But he was the only one! Everyone else..." and the line went dead.

Truth: Oh, no.

Anger: That senator is going to die.

Me: She went too far this time.

A couple days went by in a slow blur. The family had all separated and the siblings weren't talking to each other. Leo and his remaining siblings, along with the rest of their crew, came back together only to attend the funeral of their eldest brother.

Though Leo was the official leader of the family business, Rome was, in many ways, a rock on which the whole family leaned. The family came together today though and prayed for the repose of Roman's soul. Roman had left a lot behind, including numerous loved ones that were praying day and night for him to rest in peace. Life just wasn't the same without him.

Guilt: Imagine the pain he felt, watching the poison drip into the IV. The burning. The tingling. The regret. The remorse. The guilt. The blame.

Me: Our Father, Who art in Heaven, Hallowed be Thy Name…

Leo dove further into prayer, to drown out the horrific images rolling through the movie theatre in his brain.

As Leo was entranced in grief and sorrow, Michelle, feeling the same, pulled Seth aside and pleaded with him, "Seth, we've always been close… tighter even than any relationship I have with my other siblings. I've always watched over you. Seeing how broken Leo is from losing Rome, I know exactly how I'd feel to lose you. I couldn't take it. Let's leave this chaos as soon as we can."

Silence.

Michelle begged, "We don't need this. We have enough for a simple life on an island far away, someplace no one would ever find us. If not, let's just head out to Mars early. Leo, well, the truth is, he will never leave this life and so many of the crew would stand by him through anything."

Seth let her speak on this sentiment for a few minutes, and he had to admit it was convincing. As he sat there and watched a hollow Leo mouth the words to a God he probably now doubted even exists, Seth could see the appeal of running as far away as possible from this life.

He finally spoke, "Mi-mi, you know I can't do that."

Frustrated, she shot back, "Why not?"

He replied calmly, "First off, this family took me in when I had nothing… no hope. I am loyal to this family and to Leo. I want to help him set his ship straight before I leave, get him back on the right path. He has so much potential. I see greatness in him. He just gets lost sometimes. Boy howdy, don't we all. But I just can't abandon him, especially now in his hour of greatest need. You're not being selfish in your motivations to protect me from this life, but I would be selfish to go along with it. On top of that, you think whoever was able to make this happen, whoever had enough pull to legally expedite an execution on American citizens, couldn't find us on some island in the Atlantic Ocean or even on another planet? These guys are everywhere. If we run, if we separate, we become weak, and they will find us and pick us off, one by one."

Michelle was torn. She knew he was right, but she was scared. She was determined to make a change though.

She finally conceded, "Fine, but as soon as all of this is over, we go away. Deal?"

"Deal."

<u>Story 28</u>

The next day, Leo did his best to enjoy being back at Bravo Tower with most of his family for the first time in a long while, ever since they were all arrested. The crew was game planning when the bell chimed over their front door and in walked a team of government agents.

The lead agent stood, shabbily dressed by any objective standard, in the front of his team and identified himself while holding up a weathered badge, "Chief Mathenson. Is Leonardo Stills here?"

The Stills crew parted ways like the Red Sea, with Leo popping his head up from the back of the room where he was working with his new righthand man, Eli.

Leo spoke up without leaving his seat, "Right back here, my man. What can I do you for?"

Chief Mathenson simply replied, "Everyone, please stand up and consent to a pat down. Inform us of any weapons."

Everyone looked at Leo, who nodded, indicating it was okay for them to comply. Slowly but surely, each and every member of Leo's crew allowed the agents to search their persons as well as the nearby vicinity. After an exhaustive examination, a secret service agent in the back whispered something into his headpiece and, a few moments later, in walked the President of the United States of America.

Truth: What are the chances this is a good thing?

Leo's smile fell from his face as he said, "April, please show President Curry upstairs to my office and bring two sparkling waters."

The President said, "Oh, nothing for me. Thank you."

Leo hid his smirk, saying, "Great. Just the two waters then, April. Appreciate it."

After a couple minutes of pretending to be too busy to drop what he was doing, Leo made his way up the creaky stairs to his humble office where the leader of the free world was waiting patiently. Leo sat down at his desk with President Jamaal Curry sitting across from him.

Leo popped open a sparkling water and began the dialogue, "I suppose it's not quite as pretty as the Oval Office, eh?"

The President smiled, "We can't all be the most powerful man in the world, can we?"

Leo scoffed silently at the unabashed arrogance and asked, "Well, what is the reason for you to grace my humble abode with your stately presence?"

Never losing his politician's smile, the President seemed to look genuinely perplexed as he asked, "You didn't hear the news?"

Anger: He better not be talking about my dead brother.

As President Curry inquired, he slapped this morning's edition of the local newspaper bearing a headline:

'WA State Senator Adams Corrupt. Mayoral Candidate, Leo Stills, Vital in Discovery. Forget Mayor. Senate Run for Stills Instead?'

Me: Wow.

Leo was caught off guard and admitted, "I hadn't seen this yet. How about a drink to celebrate? We can't all say we had a drink with the most powerful man in the world, can we?" he jeered, as he stood up and poured President Curry a glass of his best Irish whiskey and got President Curry one of his finest cigars.

Anger: The prezzy is obviously just here to jump on this good-publicity bandwagon.

Leo handed the President the drink and the stogey, saying, "I'm sure you've had better," as Leo began to silently read the article in the paper.

Truth: This must have been Director Monroe's handiwork, as there is no mention of him whatsoever in this article and he'd like to stay unidentified, I'm sure. It says an anonymous tip leaked the story, providing ample evidence, which was turned over to the local authorities.

Guilt: The article calls me a hero? That's a bit much, don't you think? A worthless criminal from a small town in the Pacific Northwest.

Truth: I am given all the credit. Corrupt Senator? My political goodwill is going to skyrocket. The media is already calling for me to run for the open senate seat instead and to abandon my petty mayoral ambitions. Just a no-name gangster from a small town… underdog the whole time.

Me: People love an underdog. I promised to get rid of corruption and voters respond when you deliver on your campaign promises.

Greed: I should get a book deal for this before the publicity dies down.

After Leo had finished reading the story, the President set down his barely used cigar in the ashtray and said, "The media folk were starting to congregate outside. Not sure who called them."

Truth: Yeah, right.

President Curry continued, "Let's go say a few words to them. I'm sure they are thirsty for an update and I'd love to stand by your side as a show of confidence and support."

Anger: I bet you would, schmuck.

April had come into the office to refill the pitcher of ice water and she overheard the President saying to Leo, "Given some of my other business associates and the fact that I'm on the other side of the aisle from you politically, I can't officially endorse your campaign. You understand. Still, what do you say to a photo?"

Leo silently nodded, still processing everything. April quickly finished up and went back out to her desk. The two men stood up and proceeded downstairs to go address the media outlets swarming around outside Bravo Tower. When they got to the lobby, the noise was deafening. With the clamor of the secret service inside and the news outlets shoving each other for prime space outside, Leo could barely hear himself think.

As they were just about to open the front door of the office, President Curry put his arm around Leo, pulled him in and leaned close, whispering, "Oh, and by the way, so sorry to hear about your brother's tragic death. That shouldn't happen again…" he said, causing Leo's heart to drop into his stomach before continuing, "… just make sure to leave SOPA alone."

Leo turned and looked into the President's eyes – his cold, dark eyes. The smile on his face was gone now.

Truth: SOPA?!

Caught off guard for the second time today, Leo mumbled, "Certainly. We want nothing to do with them."

"Glad we understand each other," the President said with the politician's smile popping right back onto his face. He went on, "When you get to where I am, you step over a few bodies to get there. I run a different, more sophisticated organization than your podunk, hillbilly, drug-dealing self. I'm watching each and every person you know, 24/7… that is, except your dead brother obviously."

Silence.

Leo stood there in shock, as President Curry hissed, "I could've had you disappeared in the middle of the night, without anyone ever knowing why, including yourself. No. I want you to know your place. This is my world, I simply let you rent space here as long as it suits me."

Leo was flabbergasted. This meeting took several wild turns. The President, feeling that his point got across, did not wait for Leo to regain his composure. Instead, he motioned for his agents to open the French doors leading out onto the wooden wrap-around deck that circumscribed The Stills' family office.

The President immediately addressed the crowd, as only a veteran politician could, "Thank you for coming out today, everyone. How are ya'll doing on this beautiful day!?"

There was quite a bit of cheering, as local supporters of Leo's mayoral campaign were also gathering along with a handful of news reporters. The event was turning into a real rally.

The President continued speaking about some general issues and then, addressing the matter at hand, he said, "Leo, come over here if you would be so kind! Everyone, I'm sure you know who this is by now. I am privileged to introduce everyone's favorite hometown hero; a shoo-in to win the upcoming race, Mr. Leo Stills!"

The crowd began to yell and cheer excitedly. Leo came over and shook the President's hand, posing for pictures.

President Curry continued, "I'm sure you read all about Mr. Still's extreme bravery in uncovering one of the most heinous and despicable abuses of power in the last several decades. He put himself in danger and, in the end, exposed a fraud that has, perhaps irreparably, damaged our great democratic republic."

The crowd continued cheering for Leo, as some also simultaneously murmured about the corrupt ex-Senator Adams.

He went on, "There has been some unfounded speculation bordering on slander about Mr. Still's involvement in some potentially illicit activities. I want to put that conjecture to rest, ending those terrible rumors. Any alleged crimes Leo may have possibly committed, if any at all, would have been done on behalf of the good old US of A, in the service of his beloved country, and I am happy to preemptively pardon him and his employees of any wrongdoing in this matter as it relates to his heroic efforts in taking down that tyrant."

The crowd roared with approval as the President again took a moment and posed with Leo for pictures.

He said quietly to Leo, "Making headlines, Mr. Stills. Stay on my good side and I will help you ride the wave all the way to the top."

Anger: Smack this guy in the face. Who in the heavens does he think he is?

Me: I will. Watch this.

Truth: Temper your hubris.

The President motioned for Leo to address the crowd, whispering to him, "I got them warmed up for ya."

Leo took center stage and spoke to the crowd, "Good day, my people!"

Loud cheering.

Leo continued, "Given recent events, I have to admit, I was taken by storm. Hard to explain how these things unfolded to the point where I'd be standing here next to the President of the United States. Thank you again, sir."

More cheering.

Leo went on, "First and foremost, I promised you all as I prepared for the mayor's office, that I would do my best to rid American politics of exactly this type of corruption."

Clapping ensued.

Leo continued speaking over the crowd, "I was just told before coming out here that the crooked Senator Adams was arrested this morning on several counts of bribery, extortion and tax fraud. That is just the beginning of justice in this matter!"

More cheering rang out.

Leo didn't stop there, "This type of corruption has no place in American politics and no place in America… period!"

The onlookers spent the next thirty seconds cheering and hooting in support.

After this brief pause, Leo said, "Next, I want to start by getting this out of the way. I am officially withdrawing from the mayoral race and formally conceding victory to Mayor Shaw."

At this, the crowd became a bit gloomy, unhappy with the news that their rising star was giving up on becoming the mayor of Belmont.

Leo got in front of the unpleasantness before it got out of control, "I know. I know. I would have worked really hard to be a great mayor, but I just feel…" he said, pausing for a brief moment.

He waited so long before continuing, the crowd was getting excited and nervous at the same time. They didn't know what to expect.

"… I just feel that I could better serve our amazing Washington State by working really hard to be a great senator instead!"

The crowd absolutely erupted into a wild cheering session. The President wasted no time in joining the spotlight by adding to the applause.

Me: That went well…

Leo was very aware of the President's overt support in front of the cameras, so Leo decided to flip the script a bit on him before the crowd could really die down, adding, "… and, Mr. President, I want to extend my utmost appreciation for you being here today…," Leo slowly spelled out, as the President feigned humility but clearly enjoyed the compliment. That is, until Leo finished his sentence, "… for you being here today, and showing the public just how much faith you have in me by giving the Stills Campaign your official endorsement for the open senate seat here in the upcoming election…"

The crowd went wild. The President had never looked so startled, but quickly regained his composure and silently affirmed Leo's statement.

Leo added some humor, saying, "… even though I voted for his opponent in the last election!"

The crowd continued chuckling amidst the applause.

After a few pictures, the impromptu press conference began to die down. Leo and the President were going around, shaking the hands of their constituents. When they got back towards the front, the President was shaking hands with the remaining Stills' employees when he got to April. She recalled the fact the President explicitly stated he would not officially endorse Leo. She trusted Leo completely, so she knew that there was good business sense in Leo blindsiding the President like he did.

As her pride got the best of her, she put on a faux smile and said, "Appreciate the endorsement, Mr. President." Leaning in and whispering now, letting her emotions take over, she added a piece of advice, "Stupid to cross Leo Stills."

Leo was nearby shaking hands and didn't hear exactly what was said, but the harsh tone leaving April's lips definitely captured his attention. Leo moved in between April and the President, both of whom were still smiling for the cameras. Without knowing what exactly she said, or how exactly the President would respond, Leo ushered the world's most powerful man back to center stage for one last photo-op.

<u>Story 29</u>

Later that evening, while Leo was still running on a high from his press conference with the President, he took a break from his late-night carousing to pay a visit to an old friend.

Truth: Ugh, I'm drunk.

Gluttony: Ugh, you're right. I need another drink to make me feel better.

Leo stumbled down the sidewalk on his way to see the ravishing Ms. Julianne Moore.

Me: Ravishing? Calm down now, son.

Truth: Focus. We have to figure out the connection between the President and SOPA. Why would he tell us to disassociate from SOPA? The more I think about it, I doubt the Senator has the pull to expedite an execution on the down low.

Leo was on a mission. As soon as the President finished his visit earlier that day, Leo contacted Julianne requesting a meeting over drinks at a local watering hole. He sent a car to pick her up.

Me: This way she won't be late.

Or so Leo thought. Ms. Moore kept Leo's driver waiting for over half an hour. She certainly acted like she knew she was a high-class member of the elite.

Me: That's a nice way of putting it.

It was no skin off Leo's back. He actually lost track of time, sipping his whiskey, nursing his cigar and listening to the news play on the radio whenever the clamoring patrons' conversations calmed down enough for it to be heard. He was in the middle of ordering another drink when a glittering angel caught his eye.

Lust: If you're going to be late, at least have the decency to show up looking like that.

Julianne made her entrance as if she was walking down the red carpet. Picture perfect, though such an uptown lady looked quite out of place tiptoeing into this dive bar; her high heels tapping on the rugged, old brick floor. She didn't mind slumming it every now and then before coming back to the comfort of her aristocracy for air.

Me: Great. Last thing I need.

Truth: Focus.

When she got to the area where Leo was sitting at the bar, he stood up and took her coat. He handed it to a nearby hostess who went to search for a coat rack, though she was not even sure if they had one. Leo pulled out her bar stool and let his eyes linger on her creamy complexion as she gracefully took her seat.

She spoke softly to him, "I see you decided to skip dinner and go straight to drinks this time, huh? By the looks of it, though, they don't serve souffle here. Did you bring dessert with you?"

Leo leaned in slightly and said, "I don't think I could handle any more sweetness."

As she hid her blushing cheeks, pretending to turn around and examine her surroundings in the dim bar, Leo got ahold of the bartender and ordered her a glass of their finest white wine.

When it arrived, she giggled, "Such a gentleman."

As they clinked their glasses, silently saying 'cheers,' she playfully asked, "Just wine, hmmm. Nothing stronger for me? You have a whiskey after all. Is that a man's drink or something?"

Leo didn't turn his head, but looking straight ahead and smiling, he replied, "Just looking out for you. Dangerous part of town you find yourself in tonight, Ms. Julianne. Wouldn't want you to make any bad decisions."

"Hmmph," she said, taking a sip of her wine, not accustomed to being the submissive party in conversations – though, not unhappy about it in this instance. "I like it," she added.

Truth: She better be talking about the wine.

Knowing she wasn't talking about the wine, Leo still pretended she was, "I knew you would. It's the finest selection in the joint."

Not quitting with the banter, she replied, "I wouldn't be so sure about that."

The two went back and forth for a little while, enjoying the evening together.

After a few rounds of drinks, however, Leo brought up the reason for his invitation, "I have been enjoying you tonight…"

"Uh huh," she interrupted with a small grin, liking where this was going so far.

Ignoring the smirk, he continued, "… but there is one thing I'd like to address before we have another drink."

"Oh?" she asked, inviting him to go on.

"Yes, I want to discuss more about joining your cause."

She didn't realize how heavily she was leaning into him before.

When he brought up work, she tried to straighten herself up a little in her seat as he continued, "SOPA has convinced a large part of the country to revolt against the free market, capitalistic system, which you claim, and rightfully so, has dispossessed them and only made the rich richer while the poor get poorer."

Truth: Am I being serious right now? Am I really going to join SOPA, or am I playing her?

Sloth: It would be better for me, simpler, to just take the easy way out and join the winning side. Who cares if some people say socialism is immoral?

Fear: If I'm on the losing side, I will end up broke, dead or in prison. I have no choice.

Truth: He must be tricking her. Wait and see what he actually chooses. There is a reason we were not given omniscience and divine foreknowledge of that which is yet undecided and still in the domain of man's free will.

Me: Quiet down, guys.

Leo went further, "It actually looks like our push for Socialism might win the civil war in American politics. As you know, this wouldn't be good for my company. We would go bankrupt for sure, and that would be just the beginning. I need to get out ahead of this."

She noticed his wording and asked, "You said '*our*' push for Socialism, Mr. Stills. Will you help our righteous cause?"

Truth: Here's your chance at redemption. You can take the easy way out. Save your own skin and join the damned if you'd like, but this isn't right. Better to take my medicine for all the petty crimes I have committed over the years...

Sloth: ... or I could slide by...

Truth: ... yeah, by diving headfirst into sin itself.

He replied, "It's just good business. May as well be on the winning side. Can't fight the current, right? I don't have a choice."

Truth: What am I doing? Nothing in life is free.

She smiled back at him, "I will have to see what you can do for me, then." She leaned heavily on the bar, braced herself for extra support and stood up, saying, "Why don't you take me back to your place and we can work out the details."

"Yes, ma'am," came his reply, as the two of them made their way out onto the sidewalk, realizing how delicious that cool, crisp air tasted after being in the dingy bar for so long.

Leo had a car waiting and while they were on the way, the two of them got cozy in the backseat. When they arrived, Leo led her to his library where he poured two whiskeys and started a fire. They laughed together and talked about how various circumstances interacted with the political climate in their communities, at times getting very loud and passionate in their disagreements. A short while into the evening, the two of them were standing together in front of the fire.

She volunteered her congratulations and appreciation, saying, "I am glad you decided to join our cause. You are so fun. I look forward to spending more time with you. Of course, given your status and influence within the area, you will immediately be inaugurated as a senior member in the SOPA cabinet, with all its privileges and security clearances."

Julianne proceeded to lie down flat on the couch. She continued rambling in a manner that seemed rather aimless in tone and rhythm, but the words themselves were quite specific, "We *will* win this war. We have the most powerful man in the world on our side."

Truth: There's that phrase again…

She went on, "The free market is the greatest existential threat this country has ever faced and it is our duty to make sure we speak on behalf those that have been dispossessed by this rigged system and don't have the power to speak for themselves. We will take back that power and give it to the people as we see fit."

Her mind wandered, her gaze grew blank, and then she popped back, giggling, "We lie to voters; do whatever we need to do. Our politicians say one thing to their constituents publicly and then actually support a completely different approach when implementing policy. Most voters don't pay attention to how their representatives vote in Congress."

Again, she became silent and her eyes closed all the way this time.

After a minute or two, she shot up with no shortage of vivaciousness and flipped the script, "Hey! Come over here and lay with me," she said with her arms flailing about.

Lust: Don't mind if I do.

As Leo remained by the fire, she continued requesting his company on the oversized leather couch that directly faced the blazing flame, "Why are you so far away? Ugh."

She tried to sit up and, with a slight chuckle, felt her head get dizzy and she decided correctly that it would be best if she remained where she was.

Lust: I should go over there.

Me: Idiot.

Leo walked over to her and looked down at the flickering light caressing off her youthful silhouette. He grabbed a blanket, sat down in front of her and removed the whiskey glass from her almost-limp hand. Even though the couch was large and the cushions wide, they were still relatively close. He covered her with the blanket and brushed the hair out of her face. She looked up at him and smiled.

She mumbled, "He is our silent leader… in the shadows… implementing our policies and not pushing back like he should… allows us momentum."

Truth: I should press her for more information.

Leo perked up a bit, "The President?" he asked.

"Yesssss," she slurred as she continued dozing off. "The puppeteer. Heh, heh"

"The Vice President, too?" he asked, horrified of the potential answer.

Julianne didn't answer at first and Leo thought she might not at all.

Then, she began to scowl, and she mumbled under her breath, "Nooooo. Not yet anyway. She has not been very…" she trailed off. "Bad boy," she continued, "You can be our little double agent."

Pride: What do you mean little?

Truth: Focus.

Julianne went on reciting her fairytale that she had pronounced countless times before, "We will overthrow the current individual-centric regime of capitalism and turn it into the paradise of a completely government-controlled economic system. We will run the world, and we will turn it into heaven on earth. I know we can do that. Suffering isn't right and if we just centralize enough power, we can end everyone's suffering."

Truth: How arrogant – she truly believes that. Humanity has struggled with Mother Nature since the beginning, but this lady here has the answer for all of life's ills? I'm sold. Let's just give her the reins of power. Why not?

At this, she had to make a decision to either pass out or to jump on Leo. She chose pouncing.

It wasn't difficult for Leo to fend off her attempts at canoodling and he was quickly able to tuck her back in under the plush blanket. He let her sleep on the chaise lounge as he went to the other side of the room to light a cigar in his armchair by the fire and ponder the mysteries of life.

Story 30

Early the next morning, Julianne woke up on Leo's couch with quite the headache. She looked around and saw a note on the table in front of her, which said Leo had to run for an early meeting and that his cook would make her something for breakfast if she liked.

She muttered aloud to herself, "I swear… he tries not to be, but he's such a thoughtful gentleman."

She quickly gathered her things and promptly went home.

Meanwhile, across town at the Stills family office, Michelle was working the day away when she received a phone call from a private number.

"Hello, this is Michelle," she answered mechanically.

A deep, masculine voice responded, one she could swear she had heard before, "Ms. Stills. How are you doing on such a beautiful day?"

"Good. Who is this?" she asked, racking her brain for a connection to the familiar voice.

He responded, "Well, I certainly am happy to hear that you are doing so splendid. This is Jamaal Curry. Do you have a couple minutes?"

Flabbergasted, and skeptical, she followed up, "President… Jamaal Curry?"

"The one and only," he responded cheerfully.

"I can certainly make time," she said.

To which, he gleefully replied, "Great! Would you please meet me at the Belmont Park in about four hours? I am traveling to Belmont as we speak. I trust you are familiar with the park, correct? My guys are telling me right now that, based on your coordinates, you are currently only a short five-minute walk away, so I assume the answer is yes."

"Yes, I know the place. I will be there."

"Phenomenal! See you then!"

As soon as the shock and confusion wore off, Michelle went straight to her most trusted family member, Seth, and filled him in on what just transpired.

She then went into her plan, "This could be our one chance to get leverage on the President of the United States. I'm not exactly sure what he's going to talk to me about. I need you to come with me. One, to keep an eye on me, keep me safe and if something does happen to me, come back and tell Leo."

Seth nodded in agreement.

She went on, "Also, as a backup plan, this could be our chance to make a break for it."

Seth was unclear, "What do you mean?"

She hesitated, and then explained, "Look, we already talked about this. My main goal is to protect you, like I've always done. If Plan A doesn't work and we can't get leverage on him, I'm assuming he's going to offer us a deal."

Seth started to get the picture, "If Plan A doesn't work, we should come back and tell Leo. Regroup. In fact, we should be telling Leo this right now. What are you thinking?"

Getting excited, she replied, "I'm thinking about you! Seth, we have to be realistic. We are running out of options. Our ship is headed towards the iceberg and it looks like we are going to hit it head-on. We might all make it out alive, but maybe it's time to start thinking about getting the most of us out that we can."

Seth did not like where this conversation was going. Leo, and the rest of the family, had always been fair to him; always had his back since the first day he showed up. They *were* family. He originally agreed to leave this life behind and go away with Michelle after all these loose ends were tied up. He never agreed to tying them up himself.

He declined, "No, Mi-Mi… we aren't even going to talk about that. There is no acceptable number of casualties in this war. Once they divide us, we've lost."

She yelled back, "Don't worry about it! I will do everything. You won't even know either way. Forget I said anything. You come, and you record from the other side of the courtyard. I will handle Plan A, getting him to slip up in his speech - and if necessary, Plan B. We leave in a few hours. Agree? I need you with me."

Seth reluctantly and half-heartedly agreed.

A few hours later, as the two of them were walking out the door, Leo came running down the stairs and shouted out, "Seth! Oh, great. Glad I caught you. I need to run a couple things by you related to your underwriting of those two real estate investments over in Brooklyn."

Seth glanced at Michelle, who kept walking out the door and returned a silent look. The full weight of Michelle's plan to throw Leo under the bus in order to save themselves came down on Seth as he looked Leo face to face.

Seth's face flushed red, as he agitatedly asked, "Can it wait, bro?"

"No, I need to understand these figures and get back to our client," Leo ordered, as he and Seth began to work out a couple issues hanging up a very large real estate transaction.

When they were done, Leo smiled, "You are the man!"

As he patted Seth on the shoulder, he looked up from the reports and saw Seth's worried expression.

Leo asked, "Everything okay, Seth?"

Seth opened his mouth to speak, then paused as the internal battle raged on between loyalty to Leo and his allegiance to Michelle.

Leo asked again, "Something you need to tell me? Anything we should talk about?"

Seth looked down at his shoes and shook his head.

Truth: I know he has something more he'd like to say.

Me: I don't like to play games. People should say what they mean and mean what they say. He says it's nothing, so I'm going to leave it at that.

Leo punched him again on the shoulder, saying, "All right. Enjoy the sun out there on this rare rain-free day! Where are you two going for lunch?"

Seth feigned a smile and said, "Probably get a hot dog."

Leo chuckled, "Those things will get you killed. There has been a new gourmet cart out there lately. You should definitely try the Chopped Salad instead."

Seth nodded, "I'll check it out," as he walked out the front door to meet back up with Michelle.

Seth and Michelle then made their way to the park, wanting to get there a little early so Seth would have time to get set up in one of the hotel rooms overlooking the park. This hotel was one of countless buildings the Stills family owned throughout Belmont and the surrounding area, so getting the perfect room, even on such drastically short notice, was no problem at all. He got his microphone and camera equipment in place.

He mumbled to himself, lovingly thinking about Michelle, "She better not do anything stupid."

Across the park at the same time, Michelle had found the perfect bench for Seth to do his surveillance. It had a direct shot from his room with the hopes of optimizing the quality of audio and video they captured. Unfortunately, right off the bat, their plans needed adjustment. This obviously wasn't the President's first rodeo. When the secret service agents arrived to clear the park, making sure it was safe for the President, they came over to Michelle and patted her down.

After confirming she had no weapons and that she wasn't wearing a wire, they said, "Follow us."

Worried about her plan, she asked, "Where are we going? This is a relatively quiet, private spot here."

They didn't respond, but their body language was a clear demand to comply.

"Okay, okay," she said, glancing up at Seth.

She couldn't see him from that far away, but he could see the worried look on her face.

Seth whispered, as if she could hear him, "Don't worry. I got you."

Michelle walked about fifty feet away to another nearby bench where the President was waiting with a warm smile. Seth quickly repositioned his gear and was largely able to maintain most of his surveillance integrity – though, it wasn't perfect. The audio cut out a bit and the video feed was partially blocked by a tree. Still, with all that secret service around and other cameras nearby, proving it was the president should be pretty easy. The audio was the most important thing at this point.

Now, there were crowds of tourists and cart vendors hustling and bustling all over the town park. There was a nearby corner spot, under the break in the trees, where food vendors would regularly set up around mealtimes and this meeting was taking place right in the middle of the lunch rush.

The President greeted her, "Michelle! Can I call you Michelle? I apologize for my agents having to search you – so embarrassing – but can never be too careful, right? How are you doing?!"

"I completely understand. I'm doing great, sir. Thank you," she said, as she sat down on the other side of the bench. She cut to the chase, "What can I do for you?"

The President paused, inhaling a big breath of the park's fresh air before saying, "Well, Michelle, to be honest, I could really use your help. You see, I am hoping my information is incorrect or incomplete – though, it rarely is. I have been told, unfortunately, that your dear brother, Leo, had yet another meeting with Socialism's Official Party of America leader Julianne Moore."

Michelle was unaware of Leo's latest rendezvous, so she merely shrugged, silently inviting the President to continue.

President Curry said, "Well, you may or may not be aware, but I've specifically forbidden him to do this once before and…"

Michelle cut him off midsentence with a loud chortle. She couldn't help herself from exploding in laughter at the idea. After several seconds of uncontrollable howling, she struggled to breathe.

She finally got the words out, "You *forbid* him?" before the laughing picked back up. "Sorry," she said regaining some of her composure, "I have never heard someone talk about Leo that way. He's not one to be forbidden of anything, even on account of the likes of someone such as yourself."

President Curry found no humor here, "I assure you, Michelle, neither you nor your charming kid brother has ever met someone like me. As I was saying, however, any political figure's association with a radical group like SOPA is not in line with American interests."

Michelle prodded, "Is that what happened to my brother, Roman? Was he an example of what happens when someone crosses your line?"

Not letting her get very far on this dialogue at all, the President simply said, "Let's cut to the chase. Are you looking for me to say something that your cousin Seth can record from up in room 5A of the Ashford Suites? Little girl, we watch everything you do and everyone you know, 24/7."

Just then, Seth was being led passed their park bench in handcuffs for her to see firsthand. Michelle tried to maintain her composure.

She said, "He didn't commit any crime."

The President smiled and leaned in, whispering, "Doesn't mean he won't disappear – and yes, that is exactly what I did to your brother."

With arrogant smile in tow, he then leaned back and just sat there waiting… enjoying the moment.

Too impatient for this game, Michelle asked, "So, what do you really want?"

He carefully responded, "What do you have on offer?"

She sighed. She had nothing left. The family had nothing left. She mumbled something that the President couldn't hear over the busy noise of the park.

"What was that?" he asked.

She spoke up, "I can deliver Leo to you, if you let the rest of my family go unharmed."

"That should work."

She went on, "I don't even care if you secretly promote SOPA agendas and run this nation into the ground with your collectivist ideology; being twofaced the whole way down. I just want as much of my family to be safe as I can manage. I just want out. What you are doing here, Mr. President, is the death of democracy. You're a tyrant, but I have no choice."

He replied again, "Hmmph. You *are* a smart girl, Ms. Stills."

"What will you do to Leo?" she asked.

The President responded, "Well, given his recent rise to fame, it won't be easy to give him the Roman Stills treatment, but that's exactly what needs to happen." Whispering again, he chuckled, saying, "Wouldn't be the first time I got rid of one of the rats in your cancerous family."

Michelle almost broke down in tears, but she kept calm, stood up and, before leaving, said, "You have a deal. Good day."

As she walked away, she met up with Seth who was being released from his handcuffs, and thought to herself, 'It's not often, if ever, that Leo gets outsmarted.'

<u>Story 31</u>

Later that night, the Stills were having another family meeting in the same lobby of Bravo Tower. The same family office that they had always occupied. The sound of friendly chattering could be heard throughout the lobby as everyone waited for the meeting's leader to arrive. Just as Eli and Sammy were about to start the tie-breaker round on their arm-wrestling competition, Leo walked down the stairs and the two of them straightened up – though, they didn't cease the trash talking about who was going to win the next match.

Leo smiled at the childlike enjoyment they were getting out of such simple comradery.

Nonetheless, he chided them, "All right, shut up, you two; bickering like an old married couple."

Eli said, "Well, I'd be the husband, cuz I just made him…"

Just then, Sammy smacked Eli upside the head.

Eli knew better than to take it further at this time, so he whispered at his little brother, Sammy, "Uh huh. I'll see you soon."

Leo started in on the action, "Okay. Business at hand. Most of you don't know everything about everything. So, let me start by reminding everyone that our backs are truly up against a wall at this point. We are at a fork in the road and things are about to either go very good for us, or very bad. We've had several different lines in the water, trying to make the connection between some serious heavy hitters and their illegal goings-on."

Everyone listened intently.

He continued, "We were able to take down a United States Senator and, rightly so, for corruption. The question before us now is, should we try for the President next?"

Some of the senior members were already aware of the issues with the President, but most of his crew was completely taken aback.

He continued, confirming their worst fears, "It's likely going to end up with us in the bottom of some secret prison, never seeing the light of day again. That said, what's the right thing to do?"

Truth: I have no choice.

Leo continued, "Like I've far too often said in the past, we have no choice. However, this time, we have no choice but to do the right thing. No longer will this crew be pressured into the morally cowardice position of running away. Until this business is complete, I want everyone to stay in Belmont. That's the only place we can for sure be safe. Stick to your local joints and keep around you only the company that you know well and trust with your life. If we leave, the President will pick us off one at a time like a pack of lionesses hunting gazelle. We are safe here, amongst our peoples and especially because we own every building in a ten-block radius around this office."

Eli had enough, "Leo, that's all well and good, but are you seriously talking about taking down the President of the United States? The Commander in Chief of the largest military power in the history of the world? What in the hell are you thinking?"

Anticipating this concern, Leo simply replied, "April, play clip #6. Guys, this is just a taste. We have the whole interaction on tape."

"You got it, boss," she complied.

She pressed the button and a video began to play on the projector. Everyone watched, but Seth, who was there in person earlier, knew that the angle they were watching now was not the angle of the video he started to take at the park before getting caught by the Secret Service.

He asked Leo, "Lee, what is this?"

Seth was perplexed that anyone else besides Michelle knew about that meeting.

Leo said, "Just watch for now."

He played them a highlight of the President talking to Michelle in the park a little earlier, where President Curry was narcissistically bragging, "The people don't know. The people don't even want to know. I tell them what they want to hear, and then I do what needs to be done. They are so stupid, and I mean that technically and literally. They are just like sheep. They can't think for themselves. So, I think for them. I know what they need better than they do. Sometimes, the ugly truth doesn't always appeal to voters, so I lie. One thing I do know for sure, I... can... fix... this. I can fix this country. I can fix everything. I can give the people everything they need, if they just bow down and vote for me."

April stopped the tape.

Again, Seth inquired rather nervously, "Dude, how did you get that video?!"

"Not a bad angle, huh? Is the picture quality good enough?" came a familiar voice from the back of the room.

At first, no one dared to move. 'It couldn't be,' most everyone in the room thought at the same time.

After only seconds, but what felt like eternity, everyone whipped around. Lo and behold, there stood their eldest brother – safe and sound, but extremely dirty. Despite the grunge, everyone ran over and hugged him, except Leo, April and Michelle.

"What!?"

"Rome!"

"We thought you were dead!"

"Are you okay?"

"Where did you come from, dude?"

Rome finally had enough. Laughing, he said, "Guys, guys, okay. I've been missing you too."

The crowd turned back around and, seeing Leo unsurprised, Sammy asked, "Lee, you knew about this? How could you keep it from us?"

Understanding their emotions, Leo spelled it out for them, "Family, we had to keep this as close to the vest as possible. You know the President's reach. What we just played you – which we made 1,000 copies of and mailed to just as many different P.O. boxes around the world – is the smoking gun that will take the President of the United States down for good. His career will be over after this. Impeachment for sure, jail time maybe."

The hugs continued for Rome, along with the occasional knuckle-bump with the homies.

Leo continued, "We had to stage Rome's death to get at least one person who was not constantly on the President's surveillance radar. We knew that bastard was watching us. When Michelle told me that the President contacted her, I knew his hubris would overtake him and once he concentrated on Seth's obvious surveillance attempts, he would underestimate us and miss Rome altogether.

Truth: Pride comes before the fall, as they say.

Leo went on, "That's why, if you were wondering, Rome looks homeless. He went undercover from the day he 'died.' He hasn't showered or shaved since, and his hot dog stand blended right in with the other food cart owners in the park. I didn't know exactly how it would play out, but I knew this ruse would be a vital weapon we could unveil at the opportune moment. Turned out, God bless, I was right."

His family was digesting it all. It was a lot to take in.

Eventually, Seth asked, "Wait, but the state's coroner independently verified Rome's death and issued a coroner's report."

Leo smiled, "That's nothing a little incentive won't cure; only took a little persuading. Fortunately, you can purchase that type of acting by simply creating three scholarships for his children's college fund. So, as of today, no coffee shops, no illegal activity of any kind, no trouble, no nothing. Everything and everyone is to be on the up and up. We are going to Washington DC, fam!"

The entire crew started to hoot and holler. It was going to be a long road ahead, but the goal was clear and it's never more exciting than when the stakes are highest.

"That's all for now, everyone. Thank you," Leo finished up the family meeting and dismissed the rest of his crew.

People slowly began to disburse, many of them taking Rome up to his old office and pouring rounds of drinks with their long-lost brother – and it didn't miss Leo's attention to see Seth trying to slink his way unnoticed out the back door.

"Hey, Seth! Let me holler at you for a minute," Leo shouted across the room to his cousin.

Seth stopped in his tracks, afraid to turn around. Eventually, Seth made his way awkwardly back to the front of the lobby where Leo was pouring a couple whiskeys.

He handed Seth a glass, they clanked them together and as Seth buried his face into the cup, Leo began, "I know what happened."

Silence.

With no visible response from Seth, Leo continued, "You know, Michelle brought her plan to me after Curry contacted her. I knew we had to keep everything under wraps. I told her about Rome. Besides April, Michelle was the only other person that knew Rome faked his death – and we couldn't tell anyone else, even you. That being said, I spoke to you minutes before you went to potentially stab me in the back."

Silence.

Leo stared at Seth until Seth got the courage to respond.

Seth finally spoke, "I wanted to tell you, man. Michelle's not just my cousin… she's damn-near my mother!"

"And what am I?!" Leo roared back.

Seth said, "Look, bro, you all are my family. I love you with everything I have. You know how close Michelle and I have become since we were kids together, with her practically raising me. You've been amazingly good to me and I want to help you on your mission – but, frankly, if it comes down to it, and it is Michelle versus… well, anybody else in this world… I'm going to choose Michelle every time."

Leo was getting agitated and said, "I took you into this crew, and you would just throw me to the wolves the first time it suited you?!"

Seth shouted backed, unable to control himself, "She has been like a mother to me, Leo!"

"And that mother of yours answers to me!" he yelled back. Leo took a deep breath and, more calmly, he finished, "… and so do you."

Seth was shaking his head in disagreement and said, "I would sooner die than betray Michelle's trust."

The fact that Seth did not realize how close that statement came to becoming reality made Leo laugh out loud.

Leo chuckled with a straight face, "If you ever betray me again, I will make that happen."

Seth started, "Lee…"

Leo talked over him, "Boyo, you do what you gotta do, always. I'm telling you right now, though, if you weren't my blood, I'd rip that pretty face of yours right off your body in the middle of Main Street with the afternoon sun shining down for everyone to see."

Seth let out a nervous chuckle, until he saw Leo's emotionless appearance and realized that Leo was 100% serious.

This tension was short lived, as screams rang out from the second floor. Leo immediately sprinted up the stairs to find Rome collapsed to the ground, shaking wildly. Rome had long been struggling to stay away from the deadly combination of alcohol and Paradise Pills. Almost dying in prison only exacerbated the addiction. These drugs are the only thing that helped him overcome the trauma from his past and made him able to just get out of bed in the morning. Now, Rome constantly yearned for more and had apparently just overdosed.

Rome was hardly conscious as he spoke, "I could feel the burn running up my arm," he said, recalling the death penalty's poison actually starting to enter his veins before the capital punishment was cancelled at the last minute.

He collapsed into Leo's chest and Leo held him until the ambulance arrived.

<u>Story 32</u>

Later that night, Leo made his way to meet up with Vice President Jillian McEnroe, having the recording of President Curry in hand. The meeting was actually very short – just long enough to play the clip and a quick discussion on next steps. The tape was so incriminating, it pretty much spoke for itself. They didn't need any other evidence.

On top of his ability to also uncover the President's corruption, Leo volunteered, "I was just inducted as a senior member into SOPA. Over time, if the President's scandal doesn't wipe out their supporters anyway, I will be on the inside, able to help our great country take them down and stop them from spreading the socialist virus."

After a few short clarifying questions, Vice President McEnroe approved.

Leo ended the meeting by saying, "I knew you were an honorable woman that this country can trust and at this moment in time, needs more than ever. I am sure, now that I helped you become President, when the time comes for you to do something nice for someone, you will keep me in mind."

Vice President Jillian McEnroe, now acting-President for the last year of her final term in office, said, "Understood. I couldn't think of anyone more deserving."

The two of them stood up, shook hands and Leo departed.

The next day, Rome was feeling much better and was just outside the Stills family office, walking down the sidewalk on an exceptionally warm day in Belmont when three black SUV's pulled up along the curb beside him. He was *invited* to get into the middle car by three men in dark suits. When he got into the back seat, he found himself face to face with President Jamaal Curry, who skipped the pleasantries, "Roman Stills, so glad to see that you aren't, in fact, dead. You really had us all worried there for a minute."

Silence.

President Curry continued, "Hoping you can help me out with something today, my friend. I have been hearing some nasty rumors that someone obtained damning evidence on me that I wouldn't want to get out into the public sphere, and they are planning to reveal these lies and damage my legacy."

Silence.

President Curry looked straight into Rome's eyes and said, "I just want to know who is behind it. A high-ranking member of SOPA must be involved. Your family is very well informed on these activities, is it not?"

Silence.

The President handed Rome a large duffle bag, saying, "I want you to have this."

Rome opened the bag and saw what had to be over a million dollars in cash.

Rome asked, "Is this supposed to be my thirty pieces of silver?"

The President chuckled slightly, "You are a smart man, Mr. Stills. I'm sure you will pick the right side of this."

Rome replied, "My soul can't be bought."

President Curry said, "Maybe not with money, but I hear you're quite the fiend for this," as he slid Rome a large, manila envelope.

Inside, Rome saw the label of the highest grade, most potent package of Paradise Pills in the world. Money can't buy this ecstasy, only power can. Rome had never seen this in person before. In fact, he actually questioned whether the brand was just a myth that poor addicts only talked about when they traded old, war stories. Rome scoffed, however, and knocked both the money and the drug concentrates onto the floor of the SUV and opened the car door.

He got out and just as he was about to leave, he turned around, poked his head back into the car and indignantly said, "I'm taking this with me," as he grabbed the envelope and slid it into his jacket pocket.

Leo came out of Bravo Tower at the same time and noticed Rome leaving the small parade of SUV's.

He walked over to Rome and asked, "Everything okay, bro?"

Rome straightened up his suit and nodded.

Leo skeptically said, "Cool. Let's hit the Coffee Spot. I need a drink."

"Not so fast," the President hollered from inside the car, causing Leo to pause and turn around at the familiar voice. "Leo, if you would be so kind as to join me for a couple minutes."

The secret service agents standing there made it clear that the President was not asking a question.

Leo nodded to Rome, "I'll meet you there in ten," he said in order to let Rome know how long before Rome should order the local coppers to come find him.

Rome nodded and Leo climbed into the backseat. President Curry questioned Leo on the same topic and Leo quickly grew tired of the fishing expedition.

Arrogance: For someone so 'powerful,' it really is sad how badly informed he is on this issue.

Truth: I should be careful. This man is a viper in dragon's clothing.

Me: No lawyer worth his salt would ask a question to which he didn't already know the answer. He's got nothing.

The President was getting irritated at Leo's flippant responses and started threatening Leo in an attempt to get him to spill the beans.

After understanding that Leo had no intention of helping him, the President suddenly yelled out, "He's got a gun!" knowing one of his trusty secret service agents would eliminate the threat.

Instantly, the front and back SUV's emptied of their agents, who immediately ran up and drew their weapons, training them on Leo's torso. The four agents that were already inside the car had their pistols aimed directly at Leo's head and chest before you could say 'God bless the USA.' Leo threw his hands up in the air, worried about his sudden movement, but hoping they would see he had no weapon in time before they shot him dead.

All of this happening within seconds, the President shouted again, "Someone shoot him! What are you waiting for?!"

Leo slowly put his hands down onto his lap and smiled. The President grew furious.

Leo said, "The rumors are true, Mr. President. You're not only asking the last guy in the world who would tell you, you're asking the guy who did it to you. I just had a very nice conversation with *President* Jillian McEnroe."

The soon-to-be-ex-President's face slowly dropped as he came to the realization that the end was near.

He tried again, "Shoot this mongrel!"

Leo looked around at the agents and then, turning back to the ex-President, he said, "Oh, you didn't hear the news? Jillian just became the acting President of our great nation, now that clear evidence of your corruption has been officially received by the proper authorities. She commanded these fine agents to keep you safe until you could be brought in later today. You will be impeached immediately and likely face jail time. These agents don't work for you anymore. Now, they work for President McEnroe… and the President is my homie."

Ex-President Curry reached for his own gun that was strapped to his waist, yelling, "I'll do it myself!"

Before he could even get the pistol raised halfway towards Leo, the closest secret service agent jumped on Curry and wrestled the gun away from him. At the same time another nearby agent proceeded to handcuff the ex-president to his seat.

Mr. Curry began to grovel, "Please, Leo, have mercy. Just join me and we can forget this ever happened. What do you want? I'll give you anything! Together, we can run this world."

Greed: He's right. To have the President of America hostage… that's power.

Truth: You know what's right.

Without skipping a beat, Leo replied, "No. I'm not like you." Turning to the agents, Leo, a young gangster turned empathetic entrepreneur, ordered the president's secret service detail, "Get this guy out of my face," and Leo calmly exited the administrative SUV of his own volition, with only one quick glance back at the man who was sitting in the grave that he dug for himself.

Leo walked on, a free man with a relatively clear conscience, headed to go celebrate the good news with his family. Eli was already at the Coffee Spot when Rome arrived and Leo joined up with those bash brothers when he got there a few minutes later, unscathed. Rome was half-working behind the bar and half-partying with Eli whenever there were no customers waiting for service. Leo kicked open the front door with a loud bang and a smile on his face. Everyone flinched at the abrupt noise for just a moment before seeing it was simply their local hero, who was a regular at this establishment.

Leo made his entrance like a rock star would at his last show after a long tour.

"Whiskey, Rome! Three glasses!" he yelled, as he proceeded to walk back to their private suite.

Just then, a customer came up and asked Rome for a beer, but Rome told the patron that he'd have to wait, because Rome was busy serving his best customer.

Rome grabbed a bottle of his finest whiskey and pulled Eli out of a poker game, causing him to lose with a full house, "… but I had Kings over Jacks!" Eli half-heartedly complained.

The three brothers congregated in the back room. Eli poured a large glass for each of them and it was just like old times – except, now, something felt different. There was a surprisingly long journey between the beginning of this story and now, even though both scenes took place at the same physical location.

Leo raised his glass, "To saving the greatest country with which God ever blessed this earth!"

"Here, here!"

"I'll drink to that!"

They all swigged their large drinks in one gulp and quickly poured another.

Leo cheered, "Hell of a run boys and we ain't there yet."

Rome hiccupped and then, laughing too hard, he said, "What do you even mean, Leo?! You're a freak of nature. You never stop working!"

Leo smiled, "Someone's got to take care of you guys, right?"

Eli nodded as he took another drink, "Yes, yes, but it's time for you to take a long-overdue vacation. You've earned it, Lee!"

Although it was very out of character for Leo, he finally listened to someone and decided to fly to the lovely islands of Hawaii. With everything going on, he thought it would be good for him and his two boys to take a break and enjoy the fruits for which they'd labored so long and sacrificed so much. Plus, it reminded Leo of Sera, who remained forever in his heart.

The paradise didn't last very long. As it turns out, man is a beast of burden at the end of the day and we need to be engaged in something meaningful and challenging.

Me: Relaxation and downtime are good things. Don't get me wrong – but, in moderation.

After weeks of nothing but fishing and golf, mountain climbing and hang-gliding, scuba diving and watching beach volleyball… Leo needed to get back to work. He was going insane from boredom. He decided to pack it up and head back to Belmont, head back home. The night before they were scheduled to fly back, the nightmares he hadn't had for so long came back with a vengeance.

Leo woke up in an open prairie, surrounded by a grove of trees. It felt strangely like a colosseum, with evergreens evenly spaced around the perimeter, very much resembling a gate or a wall. Once inside the trees, the tall grass sloped downward on all sides, leaving the field feeling very much like a bowl. The only way out was up the steep sides and it was difficult to see beyond the trees. Over the top of the trees, where one might expect the sun to shine forth, there was only a dark gray fog. Leo couldn't see through the mist and it was difficult to even just see the trees on the other side of the ravine. There was no sun. It was hard to discern where the light was coming from that made anything visible at all. There was no light source of any kind that Leo could see. He heard countless voices swirling about the air, but he couldn't tell which one he was supposed to follow. Not having much else to do, Leo began making his way up one of the sides of the steep hill. He made it all the way to the edge of the tree line, turned around and was surprised at how far away the center of the valley had gotten. Time seemed to stand still here, and his hair definitely stood on end. This place was completely foreign to him, but at the same time, strangely familiar. Just as Leo went to poke his head through the line of trees, a tiny little, blue goblin-type monster jumped from a branch halfway up one of the tall trees, scaring Leo half to death. The previously tranquil field was now filled with the noisy screams from this minion rebounding off the tall trees which amplified their tenacity. Leo jumped away as the troll lurched forward, barely missing Leo's head with its six-inch claws. Leo hopped back up and ran as fast as he could away from the chaos towards the safety of the plain's center. As Leo ran away, the tiny little critter pursued, and Leo saw it get bigger and bigger as they went. By the time Leo made it back to the middle of the field, the monster was bulging with muscles, stood eight feet tall and was shooting pointy spines out of its hide in random directions. As Leo dodged another spike, he longed for something he could hide behind - a stone bunker, anything. Instantly, as Leo wheeled around, he saw that there was now a small, spherical shelter made of rocks sitting in the middle of the prairie. Leo quickly dove inside the barricade, which barely had enough space for Leo's size. Leo sat there, gasping for air as the now-giant monster outside kept attacking the stone igloo from all sides. Finally, the goblin stopped, and it was completely silent. Leo dared not open the wooden door but had to take the chance of peeking out the tiny window-like opening in the side wall. As he did this, the floor began to fall out from beneath him as the troll had tunneled underground. Defenseless, Leo ran out from the protective bunker just before it collapsed, and he sprinted up the closest hillside with the troll hot on his heels. Finally, the troll caught up to Leo and was able to get its slimy, greasy tentacles around him, cutting Leo's arm with its talons. Leo screamed in agony and it was just enough motivation to get Leo to turn around and confront his attacker. Leo looked into its soulless eyes; its remorseless and mechanical desire to devour. With all of his will, Leo literally stared a hole into its head. The monstrous grip was released with a loud shudder. Leo had no idea what just occurred. The monster fell at Leo's feet, prostrate and lifeless. Leo let out a huge sigh of relief, as his mind grappled with what happened over the last few seconds. This downtime was fleeting, however, as he was greeted by yet another foe. This time, hundreds of what looked like bats came flying into the arena from the other side of the tree line. "Not again," Leo mumbled to himself as he ran away, "I need a sword." With that, Leo looked down and found himself holding a gold katana, replete with leather protective garb. He went on the offensive, wiping out dozens of them at a time as they took turns biting and pecking at him. However, every time he killed one, more and more flew out of the tree line. No matter the effort, he couldn't defeat them faster than they arrived, and his stamina was waning. Getting the hang of this, Leo thought to himself, "Bunker." Just then, on the other side of the field, Leo saw the trusty stone shelter pop back into existence. He swiped at a few more monsters, and then made a mad dash for the bunker. Diving inside, the door slammed behind him. "That won't hold for long," he thought, as he heard countless thuds from the animals dive-bombing into the structure. Game planning as fast as he could, he said, "I have to see beyond the edge here and find out where these monsters are coming from." At that, Leo willed into existence a large butterfly net, hundreds of feet tall. He ran from the door of his shelter towards the edge of the grove. He peered over his shoulder at the oversized, blood-thirsty mosquitos, and breathed a metaphorical sigh of relief to find the animals being swooped up by this huge net. Unfortunately, as he neared the trees, the net began to rip from the near-infinite magnitude of the flying attackers. Still trying to get his mind around what was going on, he dove through the front line of the trees. To his surprise, and dismay, he found… nothing. Instead, he saw endless shadows; a darkness that engulfed everything and seemed to encapsulate all. Completely unknown and, in fact, unknowable. He was worn out, about to give up. Then, he saw it! A flowing shadow that continuously changed shapes like mist in the air, made of pure potential, was currently spitting out an enormous, hideous beast covered with spikes and scales the size of small cars. "That must be what is producing all these creatures," Leo thought. Whatever it was, if it created anything good, it didn't create it here. Only death and destruction came from this shadow. No life was produced, only absorbed. As Leo stood mesmerized by the ugliness coming forth from the darkness, he didn't realize that the flying monsters behind him had broken through the net and Leo was suddenly pulled back into the grove, flying high in the air as one of the pests gnawed on his ear. Having a better perspective on his surroundings now, he could see the enormous beast from before emerging from the ebbing shadow. It plowed through the trees towards the open plain where Leo was currently being flown around haphazardly by his shirt. The flying monsters dropped him in the middle of the field. Leo felt the ground trembling underneath the giant's hooves, as he stood to face his foe head-on. The ghastly creature bounded toward Leo while the petulant bats swooped down from above. Leo's goal was clear, confront the shadow, tame it, and get it under his own control. First, he would have to get rid of the current obstacles hurdling towards him at top speeds. He waited. After only a few seconds, the time was upon him to act, with the monster now galloping across the battlefield. Without another thought, he imagined riding in a tank, and instantly found himself surrounded by 12-inch-thick steel walls, rolling on tracks and carrying a large tank gun. He immediately felt the flying monsters attempt to bombard the metal shell of the tank, but he thought, "I should have just enough time." As the walls began to crack under the continuous suicide bombings, Leo took aim at his main offensive target: the gigantic, hooved beast running towards him on all-fours. This was the strangest game of chicken Leo had ever played, as he was merely seconds away from a head-on collision with his opponent. He only had two shots without having to reload, so he had to make them count. The monster's chest was square in his sights, when Leo pulled down on the joystick, pointing the tank gun down, fifty feet ahead of himself. BANG! He let one round go, creating a huge crater in the ground, but missing his foe. "Come on!" Leo yelled. The monster chuckled as he could almost taste Leo's flesh between his poisonous fangs. It wouldn't be the first casualty this monstrosity had caused. Leo's determination beaded off him as the sweat poured down his face, the saltiness stinging his eyes that refused to blink. "One shot left, here we go," Leo chanted, as he counted the steps. The saying, 'Don't fire until you see whites of their eyes,' kept sounding in his head, but this creature had no white – his eyes were void of any light, if those were even its eyes. The time was fast approaching, as Leo was now only a few yards from the crater he just created. Leo actually drove into the crater, dove down into the hole, and fired his last shot. The pressure from the blast blew his tank to pieces and shot Leo hurdling through the air, completely unprotected. He looked down to see that he had blown off one the beast's legs, and the monster tumbled onto the ground as the flying creatures' momentum caused them to inadvertently continue to dive-bomb the bigger monster by accident. With Leo so high in the air, he looked all around and there was nothing outside of this valley, just darkness as far as the eye could see. "Here goes nothing," he shouted to himself, as he catapulted into the edge of the tall trees. "I've got to get to the opening of the shadow where it was spitting out the creatures and close it." He wasn't sure how, but the mission seemed obvious enough. Leo imagined a zip-line, and found himself harnessed in and heading down, straight towards the entrance of the shadow. He landed with a hard thud and found himself face to face with the morphing entity, who seemed to be smiling back at him as it prepared its next attack. "Enough!" Leo yelled. Committed to giving this his all or go down trying, he closed his eyes and remembered an overwhelming sense of love for his family, and he simply relaxed. All the sudden, a bright light shot forth from within him, the same light that was keeping the shadow at bay from the beginning. The brightest, most pure light emanated from the center of his very being.

"Ahhhh!" Leo shouted as he shot up in bed.

Gasping for air, heart racing, he thought back on his dream. He could swear, when that final light burst forth, torturing that ever-engulfing darkness, that he saw his own face within the shadow and, unmistakably, his face was smiling.

Story 33

The next morning could not come soon enough. Leo was growing quite weary of these nightly movies, even though they seemed to be getting more sporadic and less frequent. He was also excited to leave the psychopathy that ensued from being on his vacation and was ready to hurl himself back into the swirling chaos that was his everyday life before. When he arrived home, the first thing he did after dropping off his boys with their nanny was to head into the family office for a surprise visit.

When he got there, everyone did a double-take before greeting him with smiles and hugs. After two hugs, which was one too many, he had had enough and quietly made his way upstairs to his old office. He found Eli in there, working the day furiously away. As he passed by Rome's office across the hall, Rome looked out through the window-wall and couldn't hide the grin on his face, excited to see his little brother.

Leo motioned to Rome about Eli working at his desk, as if to say, 'I leave for a couple weeks and someone already claimed my office?'

Rome quickly finished the paperwork on his desk that he was processing, stood up and came out to greet him as Leo playfully berated his younger brother, "Elijah! What's going on in here!?"

Eli stood up, laughing as his face turned ever so slightly pink, and the two brothers embraced with Rome not far behind, jumping on the dog pile.

"Good to have you back, bro."

"Good to be back," Leo agreed.

The three brothers jaw-boned for a bit, then made plans to go out for some drinks later that evening. After a quick catchup with Seth on how their day-to-day operations were fairing, Leo was ready to get back to work on ridding his great country of the collectivist movement springing up all over. The socialistic policies that had been slowly implemented over the last few decades, one inch at a time, had almost completely bankrupted the country.

April, who was just informed of Leo's presence, came running up and jumped onto Leo, giddy with excitement for several reasons.

Struggling to find air amidst her strong, full-bodied embrace, Leo was barely able to say hello, "Good to see you, too, May."

"Ha… ha. You forgot my name already, did you?" she asked playfully. "Good to see you, Lee. Congratulations!"

"For what?"

Astonished, April asked, "You didn't hear the news? Seriously? Ugh. You are too much some times. The senate race. We won, Mr. Senator!"

At that, unable to help herself, she mounted him again for another overwhelming hug.

She added, "You have a victory speech scheduled Friday."

"This Friday?" Leo asked, tired already.

"Yes, silly. Goodness! The election finished almost a week ago. They've been contacting us everyday trying to get a response from you. Friday was the best I could do," she said, a little hurt that he wasn't more appreciative.

As he saw her begin to sulk, he added the formality, "I mean, thank you, of course. I don't know how I could live without you."

"I don't think you could," April said, as she ceased her pouting, kissed him quickly on the cheek and walked out of his office, smiling at him over her shoulder as she went.

A couple days went by with Leo getting back into the swing of things. Friday arrived and he showed up to the local Belmont park for his senate victory speech, surrounded by his new security detail. Leo was standing behind the podium, waiting for his turn to speak. He watched President Jillian McEnroe, who would serve another several months completing the last year of her term through January 20th, 2053. The November 2052 presidential election was practically right around the corner. Leo was zoning in and out, somewhat caught off guard by the amount of attention and spotlight he seemed to garner these days. He much preferred the anonymity of the shadows in which he previously immersed himself.

Me: Now look at me…

Truth: … on national television!…

Fear: … with a big target on my back!

Me: Shut up.

Between making sure his family was still there near him and scanning the crowd for any potential crazy people, old enemies, anything – he caught a little of the President's introduction, "I am proud to stand by such a bright, young senator. He makes me hopeful for this country's tomorrow, and with the press he's been getting lately, by now, needs no formal introduction."

The crowd cheered lovingly before she went on, "Now, on a more serious note, we haven't released this to the public yet, but many of you know that ex-President Jamaal Curry was implicated in a string of crimes that is certainly going to end in impeachment. In fact, the House of Representatives unanimously approved the impeachment inquiry the other day in a closed hearing. That's why they introduced me as President McEnroe today. What you didn't know was, that on top of stopping the crooked ex-Senator Beth

Adams, Senator Stills also shined a light on the corrupt ex-President Curry! Now, Leo wasn't intending to be a hero. He simply saw a problem that was local to him, within his control, and he did what any upstanding American would do - take responsibilty for what he can do to make things better. He tried to solve one problem, which opened a can of worms unlike anything he could have imagined at the outset of his intial endeavors, I'm sure. Let's give it up for a true hero, Washington State Senator… Leo Stills!"

Again, the crowd went crazy, hooting and hollering for him as if he was a movie star.

After a solid minute of stand up ovations, President McEnroe continued, "I don't believe it is hyperbole to say that Senator Stills single-handedly saved the integrity of our democratic republic and proved that at the heart of most every individual in this great country, lies a true and good soul, made in the image of God and destined for greatness. He saved us from the corruption of Beth Adams and the dictatorial tyranny of Jamaal Curry. He would be a shoo-in for President in 2052, if only he were 35 years of age already!"

The crowd began to cheer, as she spoke over them, "Ladies and gentlemen, as I approach my final term in office, I stand with Senator Stills now, and gladly endorse him in all of his future endeavors that will likely go far beyond Washington *the state*, perhaps as soon as 2056!"

The crowd erupted into another bout of applause as President McEnroe spun around, shook hands with Leo while posing for the cameras, and then turned the stage over to the newly elected senator for his acceptance speech.

He started off somewhat shaky, rather new to this whole public announcement gig, "Thank you, Madam President. Everyone, appreciate ya'll coming out today! I wanted to start, before really getting into the heart of my message and what I hope to accomplish here in my public service, by practicing what I preach, so to speak. I have witnessed, firsthand, the inevitable corruption that is certain when power is consolidated into only a few hands, especially when those hands are paid by the government and enforced with all the power of our fantastic military. When the government says something, it isn't asking. If you don't pay your taxes, men with guns will come and arrest you. Just because these politicians can buy our votes with promises of free things, so long as we elect them into power – doesn't mean that it isn't still theft."

He continued, "Without being too long-winded, I just want to remind all of you upon what principles this amazing country was founded - the home of the free, land of the brave. We left tyranny overseas, centuries ago, but let us not be so hasty to forget. We are on the brink once again; a turning point. Do we vote in a tyrant? Not now, maybe not today, but do we make it possible in the future by consolidating power in Washington D.C. where the interests of those in power may not line up with all of ours? The greatest tragedies of the 20th century were not simply executed by a rich corporation, or even a religious group – but by governments that had centralized the power that properly belongs with each individual. They promised free things for the masses, and all they asked for in return was complete governmental control over everything.

"I believe we are all made in the image of God, with the innate dignity and rights that come along with it. This image is not a physical one, but instead we share in the divine ability to embody the truth in order to affect positive change in the world. To confront the infinite possibilities of the future and battle in the eternal-present to bring about the greatest conceivable reality. This dignity, this grace, this worth – is grounded with the individual, not the collective.

"Our founding fathers believed this with their whole hearts. That's why they sought to create a system of government that didn't promote its own agenda, but instead sought to raise up the individuals within the society. They knew that any system would create a class of dispossessed, the needy and the unfortunate. They also believed in the goodness of the human heart to reach out and give our fellow neighbor that has fallen behind a *hand-up*, and not the government stealing from your paycheck to give me a subsidized *hand-out*. I suppose that is a long-winded introduction to my first attempt at getting us going in the right direction, and my push to privatize every non-essential government function."

He went further, saying, "The government middleman does nothing as efficiently as all of us working together directly, aided by the free market and guided by our shared morality. Whenever the government enacts a program, they must pay employees to implement, research, oversee, regulate, and impose and collect taxes, among countless other activities that take money away from its true and originally-intended purpose. Collectively, we can do all things better, faster, cheaper by giving less to government bureaucrats and more directly to those who truly need it.

"The rich will and do give so much to the poor, but there will always be a class of people who are the poorest. That is a harsh reality, but let us not drink the fruit punch of these politicians who have made themselves into gods by promising they can eradicate all of your suffering and simultaneously provide you with enough purpose and meaning to drag yourself out of bed each morning. Money will not solve all your problems.

"That being said, I'm happy to announce my plan to give back a little to the country that has given me so much. We are happy to say, The Stills Corporation is officially donating 100% of our real estate portfolio to help end homelessness."

Boisterous cheers from the crowd.

"We are proud to use our private funds to help our fellow man; not government tax dollars that we extracted from all of your paychecks. This dream sponsored by: capitalism. Capitalism, especially when bounded in the West's framework of morality, has lifted more people out of poverty worldwide than any other system in the history of mankind. The only reason I have so much to give away now is because of all the voluntary interactions my company engaged in over the years, creating a win-win for both sides all along the way.

"Our portfolio consists of over 300,000 homes in all fifty states, which will be a great place for many Americans to find refuge. It's not going to solve the homeless problem we have, but it's a start in the right direction. These people will get subsidized housing based specifically on their situation and the program will be focused on getting them back on their own two feet as soon as possible. This is not a hand-out. It is a system that provides maximal meaning for those that need a hand-up, because we all need purpose. We encourage all the less fortunate to find one of our sponsor coordinators in cities near them. This is the great social experiment of our time; anti-socialism. Restoring dignity to those who have fallen… the right way."

Silence.

"This is how we fix our nation and reunite what has been divided by talks focusing on immutable characteristics. This is what privatizing government looks like. Some among us want you to believe there is no good anymore. They want you to believe that, unless the government is made all powerful and controls all wealth and takes care of those that are dispossessed and those that are left behind, none of us will do anything to help the less fortunate. I don't know about you, but I find that demeaning and insulting. I am here. Stand with me in taking our country back."

The crowd erupted in approval.

Leo went on, "Someone most of you might know once said, 'The Kingdom of Heaven is like a grain of mustard seed which a man took and sowed in his field; it is the smallest of all seeds, but when it has grown it is the greatest of shrubs and becomes a tree, so that the birds of the air come and make nests in its branches.' Ladies and gentlemen, I would propose that each and every single one of us is that mustard seed. The responsibility and the fate of the world rests on all our shoulders individually. When we have matured enough, we can work together to create a world that is as good as the human mind can conceive.

"'One of the greatest human failings is to prefer to be right over being effective.' So true. 'I don't care, I'm right,' you may have heard someone say before. 'Yes, yes – you're right, but it's only hurting you.'

"Truth is giving up on the idea of having to tell other people that you're right, because meekness is not weakness. No – instead, to be meek is the ability to destroy, but the character to withhold.

"We must humble ourselves to let go of what is counterproductive. That's a tall order, no doubt. Where should we even start? I think a good goal to have is to focus on becoming the same you, but a version of you that contains fewer of the faults that you already know you have. Courageously use truth in order to love, which breeds life - because the alternative is to, in despair, let bitterness result in vengeance, breeding death. If someone can tell you why you're wrong, then they have actually given you a priceless gift. Because maybe then, you can stop being wrong.

"That is one of the main reasons we have long excelled as a nation… our emphasis on the freedom of speech. Speech, truthful speech, is a necessary ingredient of civil discussion that is the only alternative to war and death. If we don't resolve our conflicts with words, we will devolve into anarchy and violence.

"So, in any situation, for every decision, find the opportunity to love. My favorite definition of love is to will the good of the other, as the other. If the government provided for our every need, and all we had to do was eat, drink and be merry - we would go crazy. That is because we are adventurers by nature. No one will be on their deathbed wishing they had watched more movies or slept longer each day. Curiosity may have killed the cat, but it fuels human ingenuity and creativity. We are all made to be heroes – that is our calling. Nothing less will please our restless souls, and, in fact, it is in that pursuit that we find the deepest meaning in our lives. What easy thing have you ever accomplished that gave your life any semblance of meaning or purpose? No. Not simple things, but things like landing on Mars, climbing Mount Everest or taming the open waters of the endless seas. These challenges are what provide meaning enough to drive us forward into the unknown each and every day.

"Life is a journey, not a destination, as they say – and they were right to say it. The past is always gone, and the future never comes. We live, simply, in the eternal present and finding meaning is better than wanting utopia.

"Life is full of inescapable tragedy and unthinkable evil – both of which cause us to suffer immensely. The burden is heavy, but as our ancestors have taught us throughout all the great trials of the past, we are resilient. We can overcome any obstacle, if only given the proper positive motivation.

"The only way to prevent the chaotic communism and the authoritarian fascism of the past from ever happening again like it did so brutally in the 20th century, is to emphasize the importance of responsibility at the level of each individual soul. This can be intimidating, understanding that the fate of the world, quite literally and metaphysically, rests on your shoulders alone, as well as every one of your fellow man. Though, it is quite a fantastical message at the same time, because it also means that you could be a part of the very process that stops that type of evil from ever creeping up its ugly head into our history books once more.

"First, we must very clearly define our aim. Our goal, as humans, should be the highest ideal that we can imagine – namely, to bring out the best possible reality by using love to enact the truth as best we know it.

"Whatever your highest ideal is, whatever you value above all else, that is God to you. That is what believers mean when they say God. I think the best way to define God, is Proper Being. Now that may be 100% accurate, but it is also 100% vague. It is our mission, as humans, to define that specifically; to turn that abstraction into a concrete example. In Christianity, this hero is characterized in the person of Christ. Still, there is no rulebook which tells us how to morally behave in every circumstance throughout all of time. That would be boring anyway. Instead, the human story is to go out every day and confront the monstrous, chaotic potentiality of the world, and do our darndest to freely choose to transform that potential into the best reality. That is the same as expressing your faith in the highest possible good – to expressing your faith in God. For one to say, 'I believe in a transcendent God,' is not enough, because words are hollow, and actions invariably speak louder than words.

"It is funny how much wisdom and insight are captured in these age-old sayings, stories and traditions. We would be foolish to dispense of them too hastily. If the balance of Proper Being is violated, then all hell quite literally breaks loose. Another funny saying that is not merely surface-deep. We must find the right balance between liberals and conservatives. It is the straight and narrow path where we find Peace. Right on the border between adventure and protection.

"Mankind is limited and finite, yet we yearn for the unlimited and the infinite. This has always caused us to be restless in ourselves and pushed us to go out and pursue Truth. We are all amazing creations, but should we simply accept ourselves for who we currently are? I say, 'No way'! You are great, but you could be so much more. You should love yourself; there is no doubt that we all were born with a great dignity. However, that does not mean we shouldn't strive to be better tomorrow than we are today. It's almost obvious on its face, but it clearly contradicts how far our society has come in its efforts for equality in everything.

"I don't believe there is equality in Heaven like we try to establish on earth. There is equality in dignity and worth – the same principle we value here in the rights guaranteed by our constitution - but there is no equality in outcome. That great founding document, our constitution – nowhere in that whole thing, and believe me, I've checked, does it guarantee us happiness. No. What it does afford us is the right to the *pursuit* of happiness and, by golly, that is an amazing right for which we should all be thankful because people in the rest of the world aren't so free to do the same.

"My children would never accept a participation trophy, because it invalidates the efforts of those that put in more effort and were better-skilled at the task. At the same time, it would disincentivize my children from practicing and working harder to become better.

"A major problem with our society today is our effort to avoid qualitative distinctions, or put another way, discriminations. We don't want to say one way is better than another way because it is downright awful to be outcasted by society. Certainly true. However, it is better to be fixed by society through love and generations of wisdom than to be cast off on judgement day. We should hesitate before we seek to end this discriminative process from the public sphere because, in doing so, we eliminate the possibility of being saved. The only path towards redemption is the struggle of moving yourself further from the bad and closer to the good, as we have qualitatively differentiated the two. It is unwise to destroy goodness in an effort to promote equality.

"It is a play straight from the devil's handbook to obsess over things we can't control, like certain forms of inequality, which are inevitable in any collective, productive endeavor. Be wary of the politician that stands up on stage and promises they will cure all your suffering - solving world hunger or curing cancer - *if* you simply vote for them. Sounds to me like they would prefer to turn themselves into God. Too many of these politicians sit in their ivory towers, promising grandiose things because it's easier to shout slogans on a street corner than it is to actually solve even the tiniest problem the right way.

"They consider themselves to be too good to pick up the piece of trash on the ground and they don't even have time to do it because they need to go save the entire world. That's one way of doing things, I suppose. Just maybe, though, the best way for everyone to relieve the most suffering for everyone, is if we all relieved the suffering we see daily in our own lives. If we all pick up a piece of that burden, many hands make light work. I don't believe our goal, as humans in this life, is to defeat satan, but instead to show him why he is wrong… to win with love.

"We have to quit spending all of our time trying to fight evil, and instead, focus more on doing good.

"We have to quit telling lies, and instead, speak the truth. What is the ultimate act of bravery, then? To recognize that you are finite and limited, that the world is full of suffering and evil, and to live in the spirit of love and truth regardless. These scoundrel politicians want you to accept their offer - to get rid of your individual responsibility for making things right as payment for pretending you are a victim and asking them to take care of you.

"From time to time, I'm sure we all, myself included, have let this petty evil fool us into thinking we are victims – to take the easy way out, the path of resentment and rationalization of sin. This does nothing but help those trying to gain power by purchasing your voice from you.

"In the Old Testament, mankind tried and failed to create the perfect, utopian state, which inevitably became rigid and corrupt, soon falling into chaos. The New Testament shines a different light on humanity. If the utopian state isn't our salvation, because of its inherent corruptibility, then what is? The truthful individual is, in fact, the source of salvation.

"We cannot create our own values. Think about your new year's resolution to lose weight. After only a few days or maybe even hours, you give up, because you are not a slave to yourself. We can't force values onto ourselves that don't align with our innermost being. The New Testament makes it clear; our goal is to embody the heroic pattern of Christ in our own lives… to make His story our own. What does that even mean? Christ takes the pain and mortality of the human condition onto himself, voluntarily. We have to do that too, or we become bitter. The only way to transcend death is to voluntarily accept it as a fundamental truth and, in spite of that gory fact of life, choose to live forthrightly anyway. That is a true hero in my mind.

"We all have problems, but our problem is not that you have a specific problem. That would be easy. The real, underlying problem that humans face during this lifetime on Earth is the fact that we are not in Heaven already. The overarching problem that we all face is that life is full of problems. The overarching solution then, is not to solve any, single problem, but to build ourselves up; strengthen ourselves, so as to learn how to deal with any problem when it arises.

"So, America, we must ask ourselves, 'What unites us here in the West?' We place a great deal of emphasis on the individual… but every individual is unique. What unites us, brothers and sisters, is the sovereignty of the individual as our highest ideal. The belief that each and every human is made in the image of God.

"I am already working with other members of congress on a bill that would unify both parties - liberals and conservatives - into a force to be reckoned with throughout the world. That is my goal; not power, wealth, honor or pleasure, but to be a force for good in the world and a leader by example.

"So, I would ask all of you today, don't shirk your responsibilities. Instead, pick up your cross, pick up the heaviest burden you can find and carry out that mission with honor. Even the smallest things, when done right, bring glory to God. We have been fed a constant diet of rights over the last few decades, without the requisite servings of the responsibilities that go along with those rights. Every right to one, is a responsibility to another and when we seek to make rights for the marginalized, however noble in their intention, we create a corresponding responsibility for the majority. We have digested too much of these rights, and our souls are crying out for the counter to those… individual responsibility. What we need is a healthy dose of meaning in our lives, because without meaning, all we are left with is the immutable sufferings born from the misfortune inherent to our world as well as the freely-chosen wickedness perpetrated by those humans who have chosen darkness.

"Wake up, friends. Bring back the community, shrink the government. We can hardly recognize our country anymore. Thirty years ago, we had a fantastic society. Because our system of governance is so complex and sophisticated, it is dangerous to make sudden, substantial changes to that system, but that is exactly what we did throughout the recent past. We made radical changes based off fear, pity and empathy that had ripple effects, the magnitude of which we never dreamed. Let's get out from behind our screens and rebuild the human connection that binds us all together."

The crowd began to clap, and Leo paused here for a moment before ending his speech.

The people started to ask for his impossible presidential candidacy, chanting, "Stills 2052" over and over, and several people shouted, "Lower the voting age!"

To which Leo replied, "Haha, no, no. Just because we don't understand why something from long ago was put in place, doesn't mean we should throw it away. We should reflexively respect tradition and before we actually understand why our ancestors did it this way to begin with, we should humble ourselves a little bit and not assume we know better now."

The mob sighed in disappointment, because they loved their new white knight and shining star, Senator Stills from the great state of Washington.

Leo put on a wry smile, "But… Stills 2056 does have a nice ring to it, doesn't it?"

An explosion of cheers rang out, a deafening chorus of approval. It was so loud, a subsequent blast went unnoticed for several heartbeats.

Suddenly, confusion engulfed some of the crowd and people began to scream and run away from the stage area, as the police and other government agents all swarmed a lone shooter who was brandishing a malitia-style rifle.

The shooter was charging toward the stage, letting rounds fly all over the place, yelling, "Long live socialism and long live the one, true President Curry!"

The whole ordeal took only seconds for the armed guards to take him down, but that is all the time it took for too many casualties to accrue. As soon as the shooter was detained and the gunfire ceased, everyone began looking around to make sure their loved ones were still alive and to find out if there were any unfortunate souls that didn't make it. Rome quickly looked around for his brothers and instantly found Eli and Sammy safe nearby. All of them searched for Leo, but couldn't see him. Finally, they found him, prostrate on the ground, heaving and moaning.

They ran to him, "Leo! Bro! Are you okay!?"

The agents around him kept watch, as the medical detail went to work on him.

The paramedic responded, "Don't talk to him. He needs to save his energy. He took three shots to the abdomen and grows more unlikely by the second."

"We are here, dude!"

"Leo! We are here. You will be all right!"

"Stay strong, bro! You're gonna make it. You're a fighter."

"We'll follow you to the hospital!"

As Leo was being worked on, life was moving in slow motion all around him. Blurs of people were coming in and out of focus. He couldn't hear anything, but everything was so loud. There was a ringing in his ears and his legs were numb. He could feel the blood pooling below him, his clothes now soaking wet. Strangely, he was at peace, but only for a moment.

Then the realization of his present circumstance hit him, and he mumbled to himself, "How can I still believe in God? How can I believe life is worth living when stuff like this happens? I thought that if I did what is right, that I would be okay. I guess I was wrong."

At that, Leo passed out unconscious and the rest is history.

"To hell with you!" Leo heard in the distance, as he looked around at his new yet strangely familiar surroundings. He saw glass walls that reached to the heavens and heard a voice so powerful that the foggy ground shook underneath his feet. Everyone around him was frozen in amazement.

As Leo looked at the nearby souls who were fully focused on the stage at the center of the circular room, he was still trying to come to terms with where he was.

Nice to meet you in person finally.

When Leo perceived that thought, he almost jumped out of his skin before he realized he didn't have any! He had no body at all. Still, he whirled around to locate the friendly voice.

"Who said that?" Leo asked, confused but not scared.

"It's me, old friend. Previously, you knew me as Truth; the voice in your head that always guided you… well, here I suppose! Haha! Welcome to life after death."

9 780578 675411